Nate, his mind utterly clear and ___ utterly detached, carefully emptied his pistol, his shots ringing out across the water and echoing back from the rocky wall of the canyon. He was bruised, battered, and numb with cold. His wounded left shoulder ran a dull trickle of fire down to his wrist—but nothing mattered now, nothing. Working quickly, he reloaded both the rifle and the pistol and set the caps carefully in place.

Gunfire came his way as the soliders pulled back to the cover of the undergrowth.

Nate drew down, fired the rifle, and cursed as he missed the scrambling blue target. He laid the rifle aside and once again emptied his pistol, pulling off shot after shot. One soldier dropped to his hands and knees, called out to his fellows for help, and then very slowly turned to his side and rolled over, like a child preparing to sleep.

In the eddy, two dead horses spun slowly about.

"Paquita? Klamat!"

SPIRIT MOUNTAIN

Bill Hotchkiss

BANTAM BOOKS
TORONTO · NEW YORK · LONDON · SYDNEY

SPIRIT MOUNTAIN
A Bantam Book / April 1984

ISBN 0-553-24047-1

Published simultaneously in the United States and Canada

PRINTED IN THE UNITED STATES OF AMERICA

H   0 9 8 7 6 5 4 3 2 1

Spirit Mountain, freely adapted from Joaquin Miller's classic, *Unwritten History*, is dedicated to William Everson—major poet, master printer, nurturing spirit of the literature of the American West.

PROLOGUE

▲

The Spirit Mountain

Lonely as God and white as a winter moon, Mount Shasta starts up sudden and solitary from the heart of the great black forests of Northern California. . . .

These italicized words are Joaquin Miller's, and *Spirit Mountain* is his story. He wrote his own book more than a century ago, a volume in which he recalled a life that had fallen away behind him and a world that had vanished—had been vanishing even as he lived it. By the time *Unwritten History* was written, Miller had become a famous poet. He had defended the notorious California outlaw Joaquin Murieta and had taken his name. Miller had voyaged to England and had visited the burial site of Robert Burns. He had placed a wreath upon Lord Byron's grave and had walked the 125 miles to London, had published his own book of poems, and had met Browning and the Rossettis and Morris and the others.

Joaquin Miller's impact on the genteel Britishers was significant and immediate. With shoulder-length hair and a sombrero, a wide red sash, Bowie knives and pistols, the man was gaudy and brash and American—not merely an American, but a westerner, one of a new breed, a man who had lived among the untamed Indians and who had fought both beside them and against them, a man who had taken an Indian wife and who had had a daughter by that wife.

Miller might not have written the book about his life among the Indians at all, except for the fact that for a brief time in the early 1870s the world's attention was drawn to a small band of Modoc Indians and a leader named Kintpuash, Captain Jack, who had defied the government of the United States and hidden his warriors away in a maze of lava beds that lie to the east of Mount Shasta. The federal troops seemed helpless to root them out. It was a death struggle and would ultimately result in the near annihilation of an Indian nation.

It is not important that we no longer read the poetry of Joaquin Miller, nor is it important that the man learned the evasions of Victorian lingo and used them, wrought out an art that died with his age. He knew his hour of fame, and then the hour had passed. In part, Miller has been the victim of his own book, the greatest he ever wrote—for in *Unwritten History*, in one way or another, Miller told the truth. If it was not the whole truth, it was at least more truth than civilized, city-dwelling Californians cared to hear. The critics were nearly universal in their damnation. Miller became infamous, Indian sympathizer and Indian lover, and on the wave of that infamy his poetry went under.

What remains are the man himself and the great white mountain he made his own.

The immigrant coming from the east beholds the snowy, solitary pillar from afar out in the arid sagebrush plains, and lifts his hands in silence as in answer to a sign.

Other men, of course, have known the mountain. One thinks of John Muir, high on the peak and only a few hundred feet from the summit, caught in a blizzard, saving his life by huddling close to a boiling sulphur spring. One thinks of Norman Clyde, climbing the peak again and again. These men loved the mountain, but not as Miller loved it—for it filled his vision and changed the brain within his skull. It defined the center of his world, the only world and the only life that were ever to be real to him.

The mountain was called Ieka.

It is two mountains, actually, one shouldered against the other, the Great Bear and the Bear's Woman. Such, at least, is one story of many.

The snows gather, compact, radiate out in glacial tongues, and gouge back into the grayrock of lava and mudflow and cinder.

Mount Shasta is a volcano, and it is still active—though people do not like to think so. Earthquake swarms hum through its mass. It is the dominant feature in an incredibly complex world of volcanic debris, broken peaks, and lava flows that stretch away to the north and south and east of the great mountain.

The earth tremors, and things shift about deep under the two fused, snow-clad peaks. The fires are restless. Shasta and Shastina—they have blown before, and they will blow again. Red hair will trail down from the peaks, huge clouds of dust and rock will vault upward, and the sky will come down to touch the earth. When that happens, Old Man Coyote will have to build the world over again.

Last time, the god used pine trees to push the sky back into its proper place.

ONE

▲

When Childhood Ends

For a long while the land dreamed, but who could say what the dream was about? Lands of the Shastas, the Modocs, the Chimarikos, the Yanas, the Wintuns, and the Maidus—and no one is certain how long these people had lived here.

In 1828 Jed Smith and his men and a herd of horses passed through, Prayin' 'Diah on his way north into Hudson's Bay Country and a rendezvous with massacre by the Kiliwas, a bad day on the Umpqua. Later the Hudson's Bay men came south in search of beaver and perhaps with British territorial claims in mind.

Peter Lassen establishing a rancho along the upper Sacramento River. And Major Reading, learning the particulars of Marshall's discovery of gold at Sutter's Mill and being a gentleman given to speculation, concluded that there might well be gold on his own lands where the big hills rise from the extremity of the Great Valley—and he found it.

In came the forty-niners, the Argonauts, and tent cities began to spring up. Structures of wood and brick and stone emerged: Shasta City, French Gulch, Manton, Whitmore, Yreka, Weed, The Forks.

Mountainsides laced with shafts and pits, the rivers running muddy and foul, the salmon dying.

A new kind of dream came over the land, a dream of frenzy.

The boy urged his spotted Cayuse pony onward, up the well-worn, ten-mile trail that would take him from the upper end of the Rogue River Valley, its patches of scrub oak and undulating meadows both uniformly yellow-brown this late in the year. A thin rain had been falling for the previous two days, and the fifty-or-so-mile ride from Grant's Pass, along the swirling Rogue River and into the big valley, past the table rocks, then up Bear Creek to the foot of the Siskiyous at the shabby little village of Ashland, had been extremely slow. From time to time it had actually been necessary to dismount in order to scrape away the heavy black clay that stuck to the pony's hooves and accumulated.

It had been a lonely ride for the eighteen-year-old—down from the valley of the Willamette River and the Oregon settlements. But, as he reflected, he was no stranger to overland travel. Two and a half years earlier, only fifteen then, he had ridden with his parents on their long, long trek across half a continent, the plains and South Pass and Bridger's Fort and the Oregon Trail.

He was a far piece now from his birthplace in Indiana.

Memories—memories of the seemingly endless journey. A herd of buffalo, thousands upon thousands of the big animals, buffalo medicine skulls, grizzly bears, moose and elk and antelope, a band of curious but friendly Crow Indians, the Utes, who stole several horses, then basin and range country, near desert, and on into the big valley of the Snake River, the "accursed mad river" as the old-timers had called it—then the great canyon of the Snake and the Wallowas beyond, the Grande Ronde and the high Oregon country, and finally first sight of the magnificent white form of Mount Hood. After that, the entry into the fertile Willamette Valley—good, rich soil and fir forests so thick in places that a man on a horse could not ride through them.

Long, gray, wet winters...

The Cayuse moved along easily. The young man was up out of the Rogue River Valley now, and the clouds were dispersing. Ragged patches of blue appeared beyond the brown ridges to the east, and patterns of sunlight played across the crests of the Siskiyous.

"Nate Miller's on his way to the California goldfields," he said aloud, and then he began to whistle.

The pony snorted and whipped its tail.

Weather permitting, his friend Mountain Joe had told him, he'd be able to see Mount Shasta from the summit of the Siskiyous, and now the weather was apparently about to oblige him. Nate had also been told that Shasta was a far greater mountain even than Hood, but that was hard to believe. He recalled again his first vision of the high snow peak of the Oregon country, unreal and white, far to the west of where the wagon train had stopped on a low rise in the rolling prairies to the south of the broad, relentless surge of the Columbia River. He remembered their approach to the mountain and how he had kneeled down, uncertain why he did so, but filled with a sense of absolute wonder at the prospect of the solitary giant.

There were other big mountains as well, as he had learned, and by now he had seen many of them—Rainier and Adams and Saint Helens to the north of the Columbia, Hood and Jefferson and the Three Sisters to the south. Mountain Joe had winked and puffed at his pipe, opining that Mount Pitt would be visible from the Rogue River Valley, but low rainclouds and fog had restricted his vision at times to no more than a hundred yards.

"Them Klamat Injuns," Joe had said, "they call 'er Yaina—the hill's sacred to 'em. Clumb up thar once, clear to the top. Ain't sure why I done it. Then I set down an' drunk a whole fifth of whiskey—best stuff this child ever tasted, it was."

Soon Nate would be at the summit of the range. Only a few more miles now and he would see this prodigy called Shasta—if indeed the stories had not been simply the exaggerated ramblings of old trappers and miners, eager to impress a boy who was hungry to know things.

As he neared the top of the mountain trail, the clouds suddenly darkened and hail pelted down from the sky. Nate hunched forward and tipped the brim of his felt hat. The Cayuse snorted and complained. Cascades of hail, the pellets bounding everywhere and making the boughs of the firs shiver with countless impacts.

Lightning flashed repeatedly off to the east, and torrents of thunder poured over the mountains.

He was on the top now, and the world was dropping away toward the south. Nate reined in his pony, stopped, and saw the clouds fracture into huge masses of blue, endless fields of blue reaching out over California.

And he stared, wonder-struck. He dismounted and held his hat in his hand.

Flights of wild swans passed by, their wings churning the air and driving them eastward, toward the Klamath lakes—and their wild cries seemed to echo across the bluffs and scattered groves of forest that marked the southern face of the Siskiyous. The clouds blazed red and gold from the descending sun, and far off in the distance, as if some fragment of dream, the huge, solitary mountain of Shasta.

Nate threw a kiss southward and then mounted once more and moved on toward the Klamath River far below.

Hood is a magnificent idol, he would write years later, *is sufficient, if you do not see Shasta.*

But now the moment of reverie was past, and the more pressing needs for hot food and warmth and shelter asserted themselves. The river lay an unknown distance ahead, and within an hour, as he surmised, darkness would cloak the seemingly endless jumble of mountains that lay between him and Shasta. He noted the broad meadows far below and the irregular band of willow and aspen: grass and a stream and such shelter as the trees might provide.

The long day's ride was nearly over, and tomorrow he would certainly cross the Klamath.

A new world, and with a little luck I'm going to make my fortune. You did it, Joe—you were younger than I am when you took off for the Rocky Mountains. And I'm as tough as you or anybody else....

Eastward from Shasta rises a long, low mountain whose crown is hollow, a vast caldera with a lake at its center— Medicine Mountain and Medicine Lake, a special place to the Shasta Indians. And rising near the lake's northern edge, a cluster of perhaps a hundred lodges, some of them carefully constructed in the traditional fashion of hewn plank dwellings and some of them makeshift abodes of stretched hides and piled brush.

Chief Warrottetot of the Achomawi Shastas, a leader known to the Whites simply as Blackbeard, stood in the shadow cast by his lodge and gazed across to the great blaze at the center of the little village. In the open area around the fire, a dance was going on, and the participants were gyrating with great enthusiasm—a war dance, as specified by the Old Ways, even though the Achomawis were for the time being at peace with all who lived near them, the Whites included. But custom demanded this dance in particular, for this was the tenth night of a *waphi*, the conclusion of the *woman* ceremonies for two girls who would now take their places among the adults of the community.

"My daughters," Warrottetot said softly, nodding as he did so. "Little Grouse and Funny Raccoon. Now I will not be able to call you by those names anymore. Now you are Poonkina and White Dawn, and I must find husbands for you both—if you don't take the matter into your own hands while I'm not looking."

Warrottetot thought of the young man called Klamat, a Modoc by birth but taken as a slave by the Klamat Indians to the north—found starving by the Shastas and taken in among them; raised as a sort of common project by various old women of the tribe. The youth was now, for all intents and purposes, one of them—and a fine, strong boy he was, respected by his age mates and the adult warriors as well, but a man without prospects. Lacking any actual family, Klamat was fated in all probability to a life of poverty. And yet it was to Klamat that Little Grouse—no, Poonkina—seemed fatally attracted, just as he was to her.

"I almost wish I could accept him as a son-in-law," Warrottetot said, speaking to the shadows. "But such a one cannot hope to wed the daughter of a chief. Even though I must break my pretty one's heart, I cannot allow this thing. It has been very hard for me to raise my daughters in a lodge where there was no mother, and yet I have done well. I should have married again, perhaps, but my own heart would not allow it. Now my daughters are women, and they must both have husbands who have wealth and who will treat them kindly. It is not an easy thing to be a woman, but my girls do not understand that yet."

The chief watched his two daughters as they moved through the carefully practiced steps of the dance. And there, he noted, at the edge of the circle stood the young man—Klamat—his eyes fixed on the woman who was now and henceforth to be called Poonkina, a name that was not even Achomawi. The old medicine woman, Mountain Smoke, had presided at the naming that concluded the *waphi* ceremonies. And when the child called Little Grouse had been asked if any spirit had spoken to her in dream during the ten days of fasting and seclusion, Little Grouse, heedless of the consequences because she did not know of them, related a fearful dream in which Whitemen poured into the lands of the Achomawis, causing all the wild animals to run away. Then the forests burst into flame and the skies were filled with terrible noise. The Great Mountain itself exploded and rained boulders upon the earth. The mountain became a great hole in the earth, and there were no more people after that. There were only wolves and coyotes that danced for a short time and then ran away toward the rising sun.

Normally a *waphi* girl would confess her dreams to her own mother, who would choose to forget them if they contained any kind of disaster—but since Little Grouse and Funny Raccoon had no mother, the medicine woman received the dreams.

Long ago, as Warrottetot had heard first when he himself was but a young man, when a girl dreamed of disaster, she was ordered to dress up in her finest clothing and was ceremonially burned alive—so that her dream might be consumed with her body. But never, in fact, was such a thing ever done.

Still, Little Grouse's dream seemed to foretell of the kinds of disasters that had never happened, as far as anyone knew, except in the Ancient Days, when the tribal myths were born. And so, under the circumstances, the medicine woman had to do something. And the result was the giving of a Yuki name, Poonkina, "wormwood."

After one season the girl would be told the significance of her new name.

A mother would have told her daughter that there had been no such dream—that it was never to be mentioned. . . .

The significance of the dream had quickly been put away, and the headband of bluejay feathers had been removed and the naming had taken place. Little Grouse, the chief's eldest daughter, was Poonkina. And Funny Raccoon, her younger sister, was White Dawn. The bands of feathers had been duly cast toward the east, and now the dancing and celebrating were in full progress.

Warrottetot noted a band of old men, off to one side of the dancing area, engaged in gambling with the grass game, the twenty slender rods, half in the possession of each of the two contestants, each trying to outguess the other. And the stakes might be horses or bows or lances or nets or even prized guns. A game might go on for days, and losers had occasionally, in times past, even resorted to suicide as the only means of restoring honor to their names.

Warrottetot noted first one couple and then another slipping away from the fire circle—married people, but not in the company of their mates. And because the dance signified the completion of the *waphi* rituals, everyone pretended not to notice.

Sunrise would bring the official restoration of tribal order and renewed fidelity.

Warrottetot remained back away from the firelit dancers this night, partly because he knew that a particular young wife had given every indication that she planned to seek him out. Two days earlier, and knowing that he stood close behind her, she had spoken softly of bearing the child of the chief and of raising it in her husband's lodge.

"It would be a good thing, and yet it would not be a good thing," Warrottetot mused. "The woman brings pleasure to my eyes, but afterward it would not be pleasure. I will stay here in the shadows. . . ."

When he looked back at the dancers, he realized that Poonkina was no longer among them.

The one who had formerly been known as Little Grouse had felt Klamat's eyes upon her as she danced, and she had also felt the blood inexplicably burning in her cheeks. Indeed, he was her favorite, and the two of them had been in many ways almost like brother and sister for several years. Unlike her sister, Poonkina had often chosen to spend her time among the boys, engaging in their war games and their fishing and squirrel-hunting expeditions. Klamat had already assumed a position of leadership among the boys, and when her presence was questioned, Klamat would simply grin and say he had asked the chief's daughter to come along for good luck. Heron and the others had never seen fit to challenge Klamat's word. The young man was not a Shasta by birth, perhaps, but he had quickly gained the respect and loyalty of those his own age. And so Poonkina, who had shown him kindness when he had first been found, half-dead of starvation— and who had taken happiness in teaching him the language of

the Achomawi Shastas—had gained a devoted protector. And
she had been accepted, if not wholeheartedly, as an occasional member of the boys' band.

On several occasions, when the two of them were alone
together, they had pretended to be man and wife. Once they
had even constructed a crude brush lodge in a hollow at the
foot of some crags high up on a ridge face near the base of the
Great Mountain. And they had dreamed, idly, in the fashion
of children who are approaching adulthood, that one day they
might indeed be married to each other.

But now, with the *waphi* ceremonies behind her, she was
Poonkina, a woman, one who would be expected to take a
husband within the space of one winter or two or three at the
most. And Warrottetot, several days before the ten-day initiation to womanhood, had told her that she must not think of
Klamat, close friends though they had been.

"I do not think of marriage yet, father," she had said.

The chief had nodded, had gazed into the sputtering coals
of the lodge fire, and then had turned abruptly from her.

Now she was a woman—was this the reason she responded
so strongly to Klamat's stare? As she gyrated with the others
around the big fire pit, she felt almost naked—vulnerable, as
though she would have no will to resist him if he were to
urge her to lie down with him as he had sometimes done,
jokingly, while the two of them were netting salmon or
hunting for deer.

She concentrated on the practiced movements of the dance,
remembered her dream, and recalled the concerned and
almost disapproving expression on old Mountain Smoke's face
at the telling of the vision. And the medicine woman had
warned her that she must never relate the details of the
dream to anyone else—for it was a dream of ill omen, and its
power could be contained only if the dreamer resolved never
to speak of it again and to request Grizzly Bear's assistance in
forgetting it entirely.

As the dancers moved once more around the circle, Poonkina
realized that Klamat was no longer there—where he had
been standing—watching her.

Did she feel disappointment or relief?

No time to ponder the matter. She slipped out of the dance

and began to walk very quickly back toward the *waphi* lodge,
an old structure that stood near the edge of the village.

*Why am I going this way? I cannot enter the lodge again. I
must turn and go to my father's house. . . .*

Instead she moved past the ceremonial lodge and continued along the well-worn path that led up over the rim of lava
rock and down to the lake on the far side.

The big gray owl was calling from across the water of the
lake, and a full moon was riding among curtains of heavy
cloud, sometimes appearing and lending a silver shimmer to
the boughs of the firs and pines and sometimes vanishing so
that the trees became no more than vague, dark forms in the
night.

She could hear rumblings of distant thunder, and the forest
seemed to her as though it were waiting for something to
happen—a burst of rainfall, rain that had been threatening off
and on for several days as she and her sister kept to themselves inside the initiation lodge.

"Tonight it will come," she said, the words sounding strange
to her even as she spoke them. "Yes, I think it will rain soon."

But the moonlight burst through once more, and the forest
about her shone almost brightly enough to reveal the colors
of things. And the girl stared up at the tips of a grove of firs
and tried to convince herself that she could actually see their
silver-green.

She began to run, easily at first and then faster, faster,
feeling the pulverized cinders beneath her moccasins. She
stared up at the moon as she moved along the familiar pathway
and moved her head from side to side, feeling the expectant
air moving about her cheeks and her ears and through her
long hair.

At some distance from the village, at a point where the
glow from the celebration fire was only faintly discernible,
she stopped suddenly, breathed deeply, and began to laugh.

Why are you laughing, Little Grouse?

"No," she said. "That girl is no longer here. I am a woman
now. My name is Poonkina, even though I do not know what
the word means. Perhaps it doesn't mean anything at all."

She laughed again and then was very still. She listened to
the faint lappings of the lake water against the shore, concen-
trating on the sound until it seemed almost a roaring in her

ears. She stared out at the long band of white that lay across the lake, the moonpath according to one story, the way that led into the Darkness Beyond.

"It is only moonlight on the water," she said.

She walked slowly then to the lake's edge and continued to gaze at the white smear of light until it suddenly vanished as the moon chose to hide itself behind a wall of clouds.

"I am a woman now," she said. "I am not afraid of the stories the old people tell. I do not even believe them."

She undressed, felt the cool air flow about her naked flesh, rejoiced in the sensation, and laid her clothing, carefully folded, on a broad, flat shelf of stone. She stepped to the lake's edge, felt the gritty pebbles beneath her feet, felt the cold water bite at her ankles, and stood still for a moment. Then she took a deep breath, plunged forward, and began to swim out into the darkness. The hard chill flamed about her, stinging her breasts and legs and face. She rose gasping to the surface, breathed in once more, and began to swim.

Within a moment or two the cold no longer bothered her, and she stroked forward, blinking and again feeling the urge to laugh.

"Come back, moon!" she cried out, struggling to keep the water out of her mouth and nose. "Give Poonkina light so that she can see!"

The light came, but it was not the moon. A momentary flash of such brightness that for an instant the colors of things were revealed—and then it vanished. A moment's silence, and then the great ripping sound of thunder.

Poonkina laughed and swam about in circles, her legs held tightly together as she whipped them against the water so that she turned around and around. She pretended she was a fish, and dived suddenly down beneath the lake's surface, wriggling her way through what she realized was actually her native element.

She returned to the surface, trod water, and shook the wet hair away from her eyes.

"Good-bye, Little Grouse!" she called out, and then began to swim toward the shore.

Still undressed, she stood shivering beside the flat-topped rock and stared across the dark lake. She crossed her arms over her breasts and bit down on her teeth to keep them from chattering. After a moment she grasped her hair and twisted it into a single long roll, feeling the water dripping down over her clenched fists.

"Poonkina—Little Grouse?"

Klamat's voice . . .

"Don't come any closer!" she called out. "I'm not dressed. I've been—swimming. Is that you, Klamat?"

"I've seen your body many times—but now it's different?" he asked.

"Yes. Yes, now it's different. I'm a woman now, Klamat. You must not look at me."

"That's foolishness. It is too dark to see anyway. Why did you leave the dance, Little Grouse?"

"Stay back, Klamat! I'll throw rocks at you. You wait until I've got my clothes back on."

The young man started forward but then stopped, as he was bid.

She dressed quickly, slipping into her deerskin dress and cinching the woven belt and pulling her moccasins back on. She drew her damp hair back and fastened the band around her forehead.

"All right," she said softly. "I'm ready."

Klamat emerged from the heavy shadows and stood beside her.

"I've missed you. Ten days," he said.

"Yes. But now it's different, Klamat. Have you truly missed me? Probably you and Heron and Crippled Deer have been hunting for swans over at the small lake. That's what you've been doing, isn't it?"

"No," he answered. "I have not wished to hunt, Little Grouse."

"You must call me by my new name, Klamat."

"I know. And soon I will have to laugh and be happy at the feast that will mark your wedding. Your father will sell you to one of the men who has horses and guns to give as a bride price."

"Why will that be? Will you not marry me, Klamat? We have talked of this thing ever since we were children together."

"Poonkina . . ." he managed, his voice breaking off.

Then they were in each other's arms, embracing fiercely, clinging to each other, her chin tucked up against his shoulder.

At length he pushed her from him, held her at arm's length.

"We spoke empty words," he said, "the way children often do. Your father will not allow it. What presents could I give him? I have nothing, Poonkina. It will be years before I am wealthy enough."

"Then I will wait, Klamat. Warrottetot will never force me to marry against my will. He will have to name a bride price, and I will look at no one else until you have earned it. Then we will live in the same lodge together, just as we have always said. That is the way it will be, no matter what my father wants."

But Klamat shook his head.

"It can never be," he said. "Warrottetot loves you, and he believes that I could only bring you disgrace. I have not been treated like a slave, but that is what I am."

"Then we must leave our people," Poonkina said. "I am not afraid. Oh, I am afraid of how it will be when we lie down together, but I know you will not mean to hurt me. Young girls are always afraid of that. But I will run away with you, Klamat. We can sneak away together and go to live among the Wintuns. They will take us in, and it will not matter if we are very poor. You will become a great warrior, Klamat. The others always follow you, always do what you tell them to. It is because you have great power, great medicine. Otherwise it could not be. I will go with you, and I will be your first wife. After a few years you may even take other wives if you wish—I will not mind."

"Do you mean this?"

The girl broke out laughing and rubbed her hands over her hair.

"Poonkina always means what she says. When can we leave this place? I am tired of living so close to the Big White Mountain that has fire down inside. It does not even snow where the Wintuns live."

"But Whitemen live there. They are very violent—they are evil. Sometimes they kill Indians and have no reason for doing it."

"Will you come with me, Klamat? I will go by myself if you will not go with me."

He took her in his arms once more.

"We will go tonight, then," he answered.

They did not return to the village.

Instead, they circled the Medicine Lake and moved away southward, on foot and with no food other than a small quantity of elk jerky that Klamat had brought with him when, realizing that Poonkina was no longer at the dance, he had set out to find her. The trails were familiar to both of them, and despite the periods of utter darkness that interspersed intervals of brilliant moonlight, they were able to move quickly up through the pine woods to the low saddle in the huge volcanic crater and begin their descent of the Medicine Mountain itself.

Whether they were boy and girl or man and woman, it made no difference to them—for what they felt toward each other, they supposed, outweighed even the terrible fear of leaving their tribe and of setting off toward a new and undefined and frightening world. They had no horses and no means of trading for any animals. Klamat was already a skilled hunter, respected by his peers and the older warriors alike, but he had only his bow and a dozen arrows and his prized skinning knife. In one pocket he carried a few dentalium shells and half-a-dozen scarlet woodpecker scalps—currency that would be honored among the Wintuns but insufficient to acquire more than a few bare essentials.

But they would not starve; Poonkina was confident of their ability to secure sufficient food. It was the moon of leaves-falling, and in the rugged canyon country to the south of them were a multitude of oaks, the trees laden with acorns at this time of year. And Klamat's skill with the bow would provide meat—deer or elk or possibly even an antelope.

Other young couples, as they both knew from hearing the stories that the old men and women were fond of telling, had run away from their own people under the power of love's spell. And though it was true that the lovers in these tales usually came to a bad end, Klamat and Poonkina were confident that the stories were made to end in that fashion so as to discourage others from attempting similar flights into the wilderness.

After all, Poonkina conjectured, there was almost nothing in the forest that one needed to fear. The wolves were shy creatures, much less bold than the relatively brazen coyotes, and except when rabid had never been known to attack people. The mountain lion might startle a person with its mournful shrieking and screaming at night, but these creatures likewise were harmless. A lion might follow one for an entire day, staying always at a discreet distance, but the creature's motivation was nothing more than curiosity. Warrottetot himself had insisted that this was true. And black bears? Big burly clowns that would usually turn and scuttle off if one charged at them and yelled loudly.

Only the grizzly posed a real danger, and even these giants preferred to avoid humans, knowing well, apparently, that a man with a bow was himself extremely dangerous. There was great medicine in the fur of a grizzly, and a hunter who managed to slay one of the beasts was accorded high honors.

But the grizzly sow with her cubs close by was to be avoided at all costs. Such bears occasionally killed humans, and the burial sites were marked and superstitiously revered.

Does the Great Bear truly live inside the Spirit Mountain? The rumblings through the earth are his growlings....

Klamat and Poonkina reached the rolling forests of densely grown pine and fir at the base of the Medicine Mountain and continued south toward the river that the Whitemen called the McCloud, one of the three main branches that fed together to form the big river, the Sacramento, a full two days' journey on foot down-canyon from where they would encounter the stream. And there, where the McCloud and the Pit River joined, they would find the nearest of the Wintun villages. There lay both safety and the possibility of a life together as man and wife.

At times lightning ripped the sky, and as dawn approached, rain began suddenly to pour from the heavens.

"We must take cover, Poonkina," Klamat said. "Perhaps the storm will pass over us quickly, and then we can move on."

She followed behind him, and at length they discovered a giant, fire-scarred cedar, its base eaten back by the flames of years past and providing a hollow large enough for the two of them to take shelter in.

They huddled against the old fire-scar and held each other tightly as the rain continued to pound down, its force broken by the dense growth of pine and cedar about them.

"How good it smells," Poonkina whispered. "It is always this way when the rain first comes. I am tired, Klamat. I am very tired and very sleepy. The medicine woman would not allow White Dawn and I to sleep at all last night. I am not as strong as you are—I don't know if I can go any farther right now. Can't we sleep for a while—just a little while?"

Klamat held her tightly and stared out into the darkness that was beginning to turn to grayness.

"Your father will realize that we are both gone and come looking for us," he said. "Perhaps he will suppose that we have gone to seek refuge among our cousins, the Atsugewi Shastas. Or he will think we have returned to the winter village to build a lodge as man and wife. Not even Heron and I could track two people on foot who have come the way we have come. I suppose it is all right to sleep for a while. I am very tired also, Poonkina. Have you changed your mind about what we are doing?"

"No," she said, resting her head against his shoulder. "You are the man I wish to marry, Klamat. I have not changed my mind."

He dug into his side pocket, produced a few scraps of jerky, and offered the food to the girl. She took a piece, bit off a portion, and chewed it slowly, savoring the taste.

"I will sleep now, in that case," she said.

Klamat kissed her damp hair and, as he did so, felt her body relax, begin to go limp.

"Sleep, beautiful one," he murmured and continued to stare out into the dimness of falling rain. But at length he too closed his eyes—meaning only to rest them—and fell into a profound slumber.

A sensation of brightness and the whinnying of horses.

Klamat and Poonkina were startled awake, and Klamat rose immediately, shielding the girl with his own body.

Two riders approached, and behind them trailed two other

ponies. One of these, Klamat realized after a moment, was his own horse.

"Who is it—can you tell?" Poonkina asked. "Is it someone we know?"

"Yes," Klamat answered, his voice tinged with resignation. "We know these people. It's Warrottetot and your sister, White Dawn."

"How could they have found us? You said . . ."

"I was wrong. I underestimated the chief of the Achomawis. I could not have followed our trail, but he has done it."

The heavily muscled Warrottetot glanced at the big cedar and drew his horse toward it.

"My daughter has wandered far this past night," the chief said slowly as he brought his pony to a stand. "White Dawn and I were afraid you might have gotten lost, so we came to find you. This is a bad thing you have done, Poonkina. And Klamat—I have been almost a father to you. I have made you one of my own people and have watched you grow nearly to manhood. Have I ever done you a wrong—that you would urge my daughter to run away with you? Where would you have gone, and how would you have survived? See? You did not even bother to take your pony, and so I have brought him to you."

Poonkina stood beside Klamat, her eyes blazing with defiance.

"Father, Klamat is the one I wish to marry. And that is why I have run away with him. It was not his idea at all. It was mine. I talked him into this thing."

Warrottetot shook his head and suppressed a smile.

"Young people are very foolish at times," he said. "Little Grouse, who is now the woman Poonkina, have I not been a good father to you?"

"You have been a good father," the girl answered, "and I love you. It is only that . . ."

"And have I tried to force you to marry against your will, Poonkina? No, I have not done that. But you are still young, and often the young are not capable of seeing things clearly.

"Listen now. Klamat, I bear you no ill will. You love my daughter, I can see that. But how will you provide for her? How many horses do you have to pay a bride price? How many elk robes? How many grizzly skins? Do you have a pouch full of woodpecker scalps and beads and clam discs and

dentalia? No, you have none of these things. Can you not see
that it would be a disgrace to Poonkina to marry a man who
has no wealth and no family? These things are not your fault,
and it may be that one day you will be the wealthiest man
among us. Who can foretell the future? But for now this
marriage is impossible.

"Poonkina, I will not force you to marry anyone against
your will—for then you would prove to be an ill-natured wife,
and I would have to buy you back again. Time must settle
this matter. Do you both understand what I am saying?"

Poonkina and Klamat nodded and stared at the earth.

"White Dawn," Warrottetot said, "open the saddlebag that
contains meat and nuts and camas cake left over from the
feast. I think your sister and Klamat must be very hungry.
They have walked a long way to find this old hollow tree."

With this the chief dismounted, and the younger sister
spread out a deerskin mat and quickly arranged the food
upon it.

"We will eat now," Warrottetot said. "When we have
finished, I will take my two daughters with me, and we will
ride back to the village at Medicine Lake. Klamat, you must
spend three more days on your hunting venture. Your friend
Heron will tell the others that you decided to go hunting. In
three days you may return to the village, for in this way the
reputation of my daughter will be protected. We do not wish
the old women to have anything more to gossip about, for
their tongues wag constantly. Mountain Smoke has let it be
known that Warrottetot and his two daughters rode away from
the village early this morning so that the father might speak
with the two who are now women, to counsel them. In this
way, no harm has been done. Do you understand what I have
said, Klamat? Later I will make you a gift of one of my
horses, for I have more than I need."

TWO

▲

Charley's Vaquero

When Captain Jack was but a boy, the Modocs were at war with the Whites, who were then scouring the country in search of gold. A company took the field under the command of a brave and reckless ruffian named Ben Wright.... Wright proposed to meet the chiefs in council, for the purpose of making a lasting and permanent treaty. The Indians consented, and the leaders came in. "Go back," said Wright, "and bring in all your people; we will have council, and celebrate our peace with a feast."

The Indians came in in great numbers, laid down their arms, and then at a sign Wright and his men fell upon them, and murdered them without mercy. Captain Wright boasted on his return that he had made a PERMANENT treaty with at least a thousand Indians.

In Yreka, Nate Miller tethered his Cayuse pony to a hitching post and walked across the wide, muddy main street to the only eating house in the small mining town. He was voraciously hungry, but goldfield prices, he immediately discovered, were three to four times higher than those in the Oregon towns. The few dollars in his pockets would not sustain him for long. If he was not immediately successful in finding work of some kind, he realized, he would be forced to rely on his good eye and his father's old cap-and-ball Kentucky long rifle.

He sat down at a corner table and ordered a cup of hot coffee.

The waitress, a middle-aged woman with henna-red hair, squinted at him and asked, "Somethin' to eat, honey?"

"No, ma'am," Nate mumbled, shaking his head. "Just coffee is all."

"You don't look old enough to be out on your own," she said. "An' you're skinny as a fence post. Huntin' for work, are you?"

"Yes, ma'am, I sure am."

"Well, you see that white-haired fella sitting at the bar? I heard him say he was lookin' for another vaquero. You know anything about horses, honey?"

Nate glanced toward the bar and nodded.

"I sure do, ma'am."

"Tell you what," the red-haired woman said. "Maybe I can put in a good word for you. I know the gentleman—in a *professional* way. You sure could stand something to eat, honey. I never could *take* skinny men."

She walked away, her hips moving back and forth in a practiced saunter, stopped at the bar, spoke to the man she had indicated, and then went about her business.

The short, squat, white-haired man turned and glanced in Nate's direction, then went on talking with the two Mexicans sitting at either side of him.

Nate Miller sipped at the strong coffee, leaned back in his chair, and crossed his long legs.

The smell of food was nearly more than he could bear, and he almost broke down and ordered a meal. But the eleven dollars in his pocket would not go far—not far enough. Nate ignored the food smells, or tried to ignore them, and considered his possibilities. His father had attempted to warn him of the folly of setting off on his own, and old Mountain Joe had echoed the same message.

Dammit, he thought, *it was Mountain Joe and his crazy stories that got me all wound up in the first place. Maybe I ought to just turn around and head on back to Oregon....*

But that would be admitting failure. That would be admitting, after all, that he wasn't really a man yet.

Nate stared at the people in the eating house. There was only one woman in the group—the red-haired waitress.

"A thousand men in Yreka, only thirty, forty females, Nate me boy, and damned near every soul of 'em's a whore. Your gold miner, he works all day up to his ass in ice-cold crick water for a couple of nuggets an' some dust. If he's lucky, that is. An' by the next sunrise, he's hung over, half-asleep, busted, an' back in up to his ass in cold crick water. An' the

whore, she's got his gold. That's the way they live, I'm tellin'
ye lad. . . ."

The words were Mountain Joe's. But the old man had only
started talking that way when he'd realized his listener actually had it in his head to strike out on his own. By then it had
been too late. Nate Miller was determined to head for the
goldfields.

A goddamned fool, that's what I've been, Nate concluded.

He drained the last of his coffee and was about to leave.
Perhaps they'd let him sleep in the stable for the night, along
with his horse. The livery fee would be another seventy-five
cents, though. . . .

The stocky, white-haired man turned on his barstool, stood
up, and crossed the eating house to where Nate was sitting.

"Name's Whitmore Charley," he said, extending his hand.

An index finger, Nate observed, was missing at the knuckle.

The boy stood up, managed his own name, and shook
hands—and was surprised at the hard strength of the older
man's grip.

"Elly says ye're lookin' for work, young fella."

"That's right, sir," Nate answered, the lights of hope spring-
ing up in his eyes.

"Well now. An' you know summat about horses, do you?"

"Worked with them all my life," Nate assured him.

"Well now. How long would that be? You're lookin' about
fifteen to this hombre, mebbe sixteen at most."

"I'm eighteen."

"Well now. Just haven't started fillin' out yet, I guess.
Look, lad, what I'm needin' is an honest-to-gawd vaquero.
Got a herd of beasties to move down to Pueblo Los Angeles.
Tell you what. Let me stake you to a good meal. Help's real
hard to come by. All these niggers want to do is dig gold and
get drunk and. . . . Guess you're too young to be worried
about that sort of thing, though. Well now, Natty lad, you've
got a job if you want 'er. Order whatever you like—eat up
good. Get some meat on them scrawny bones of yours. Meet
me here first thing in the mornin'—I mean early, now—and
we'll be headin' south. You want work, you got 'er. Time we get
to Los Angeles, you'll be so strong you'll have muscles in your
shit. I mean it, lad—long days pushin' horses ain't a kid's game."

"Thank you, Mr. Whitmore," Nate said, hardly believing

that he'd actually found work already—not mining work, maybe, but something to give him a grubstake.

"Name ain't Whitmore. You got to listen good, 'cause I don't never repeat myself. It's Whitmore *Charley*. I never yet met a nigger that had any real need for a last name, an' that goes for you, too. You got to learn to listen, boy."

"Whitmore Charley," Nate repeated. He could feel his face going red.

Whitmore Charley grinned.

"Ain't you goin' to ask what I'm payin' for wages?"

"I trust you, sir."

"Call me Charley. An' don't never trust no one. Well now, I've got some business with Elly. You get older, mebbe you'll have some too—if you ever get back this way. I said *early*, now."

Whitmore Charley walked back to the bar, sat down, and resumed talking to his two Mexican friends.

Nate stared into his empty coffee cup, wondering what he should do next. Was Whitmore Charley going to pay for his meal? Or should he just go ahead and order something and pay for it himself? After all, he reflected, he could afford it now.

As he was considering the matter, the waitress named Elly returned to his table, a speckled blue coffeepot in hand. She refilled his mug and said, "You hungry now, honey? Charley says he's paying."

The following morning Nate Miller was on his way to Los Angeles, one of a group of nondescript-looking employees of Whitmore Charley—some Mexicans, including the two with whom Charley had been talking the previous night, some Indians, and some half-breeds.

Despite what Charley had said, the work was easy. The men and horses moved south, passing by the foot of the great white mountain of Shasta—a Russian word, Charley assured him, that meant "white" or "chaste."

"So she's either 'Snowy Mountain' or 'No-Screwin' Mountain,' whichever you want," Charley said, laughing.

"I thought it was an Indian name," Nate said.

"Well now, mebbe it is. There's several bunches we call the Shastas or the Sastees. Different tribes, I guess, but they all talk the same lingo. They's Achomawi and Atsugewi, Iruaitus and Ahotireitsu and Kahosadi and some others. Anyhow, they're all Shasta. A man would be a fool to try and keep all the Injun groups straight. Now your Takelma up in Oregon country, they just call 'em *Wulh*."

"What's that mean, Charley?"

"Well now, it means 'enemy,' son. And that's a good thing to remember about the whole pack of 'em, Sastees, Modocs, Pit Rivers, Wintuns. You can't trust a one of 'em. Steal your shirt while you're pissin', they will. Here we are jabberin', and that sorrel mare is wandering off. Fetch 'er in, Nate."

The group moved on to the south, down the winding canyon of the Sacramento River. The thick, black fir forest changed as the river trail led ever downward. Mixed forest, oaks and manzanita blended in with pine and fir—until the pines vanished, and the river, taking on tributary streams, emerged into the upper end of the Great Valley of California, a land dotted with clusters of oaks and stretching away endlessly to the south.

The days drifted by as Whitmore Charley's little remuda passed through Peter Lassen's old rancho and on downriver, keeping to the eastern bank, crossing the Rio de las Plumas and later the American River at Sacramento and what had once been Sutter's inland empire of New Helvetia, now a thriving and boisterous town—the jumpoff place for the Mother Lode mines and towns that lay hidden among the long blue ridges to the east.

This was strange, new country for Nate Miller. He rode along and gazed toward the Sierra, imagining the tent cities of men from all over the world, drawn temporarily together in their search for California gold. Without even knowing why, he desperately wanted to be one of those men. It wasn't the prospect of riches, for he had sense enough to realize the slimness of his chances. What was it, then?

Maybe it was the gold after all—not the wealth it vaguely promised, but the substance itself. The precious yellow metal hidden away in gravel bars and quartz veins. The most promising new strikes, he knew, were in the hard rock. Companies were forming and mills were being erected. But it was the placer gold that fascinated Nate, the kind a man could dig for with his own hands—stake his own claim, have faith in it, work it out.

Then they were south of the mining areas, and Nate felt a terrible sense of having left his mission behind. It was a *mission*. That was it. Some force inside him, one that he did not really understand at all, had brought him to California to work as a miner, an independent miner, his own claim, everything. And instead he was riding with Whitmore Charley and his motley band of drovers, crossing the Tehachapi Mountains, passing on south into yet more desert lands, dry mountains, bare ridges, greasewood, scrub oak, sand.

The food was terrible. Charley may have been generous that first night, but once out on the trail, the rations turned to beans and unleavened bread, and little more than that. On occasion Nate had been able to bring down a tule elk after the men had camped for the evening, and the Umatilla Indians in the group made much of his marksmanship. And yet neither they nor the Mexicans seemed at all interested in doing any hunting themselves.

The weather was pleasant enough, however, with only one interval of rain interrupting a series of days that seemed more like springtime, despite the dry grass of the Great Valley, than early winter. A far different climate from the Oregon country he was used to.

At Pueblo Los Angeles, Charley quarreled with his men in what, it appeared to Nate Miller, was an obvious ploy to avoid paying them. When the Mexicans threatened his life, Charley swore out warrants against them. Whatever the nature of the contract he had arranged with the band of vaqueros, it was apparent that Charley meant to settle with them as cheaply as possible. When the men grew furious, Charley had them clapped in jail—it was as simple as that. Nate observed the goings-on, stayed out of the matter, and waited for Whitmore Charley to conclude his business and head northward once more, this time driving a herd of Spanish cattle—beef animals for a ready market in Yreka.

"Well now, boy—you've used your head. A man ends up in the jailhouse, he don't get paid. Remember—I told you. Don't trust no one."

"I remember." Nate laughed. "I'm also wondering if you intend to pay me when we get back to Yreka."

"Aw, lad! Just stick with me, Nate. You know you can trust old Charley. You're like my own son."

"You told me not to trust anyone."

"Wasn't talking about myself, of course."

"Hell no, of course not," Nate said, patting the long rifle in its scabbard on the Cayuse pony's side.

Charley roared with laughter.

"Figger you're going to do all right for yourself, Natty. You learn fast. Don't worry, lad, I'll do right by you. I like your spunk. That's good in a young fella. A man don't watch out for hisself, it's sure no one else is goin' to. Get back to Yreka, I figure you'll make your fortune in gold. The stars are with you, an' that's a fact."

Once back across the Tehachapi Mountains and into the San Joaquin Valley, Whitmore Charley acquired a large herd of half-wild horses as well as a band of totally wild men, the dregs of the earth as Nate imagined it, to move the animals along. And he wondered whether these men, in their turn, would end up in jail in Shasta City or Yreka. If Charley stayed in this business long enough, Nate mused, he'd have an army of enemies waiting to murder him at either end of his trade route.

On they moved, pushing their herd of ill-tempered long-horns and worse-tempered mesteños ahead of them. Nate counted the rivers he'd catalogued on the way south, each crossing taking him closer to the northern mines—Kings, Merced, Tuolumne, Stanislaus, Mokelumne, Cosumnes, American, Bear, Yuba.

Once across the latter stream, however, its waters running silt-laden from dredging and hydraulicking operations upstream, Charley made early camp, cursed roundly at his miscreant drovers, and invited Nate to accompany him into the town of Marysville, a few miles west, at the confluence of the Yuba and the Rio de las Plumas.

"Going to try some magic," Charley confided as they rode into the little city, a few burnt-out buildings still standing as mute evidence of the great conflagration of three years earlier. "Yep," Charley continued, "goin' to turn a hundred dollars into three, four times that many. You ever heard of monte, lad?"

"Cards?" Nate asked.

"Well now, you might say so. But that'd be like callin' Saint Paul's Cathedral a down-home church, if you get my drift. Six-card monte's a kind of an art, you might say. And they's some that thinks old Whitmore Charley's an artist of sorts. Oh, there's some better'n I am, but not many. I tell you, son, it's like pluckin' chickens, that's what it is."

They tethered their horses and Nate followed Charley into a saloon called Jumpoff Joe's Place. Charley ordered two whiskeys, gulped his, and left Nate to sip his drink and to admire the plump-breasted young woman in the frilly, low-cut dress. The girl's elaborately arranged hair, he thought, looked almost like it was glued in place. But she was lovely—and at that moment Nate decided she was the prettiest woman he'd ever seen in his life. Only when she took the arm of an inebriated fellow who appeared to be a rancher did Nate realize what the vision of loveliness was doing in Jumpoff Joe's.

Charley had taken his place at one of the card tables, the one that seemed to be presided over by a large man of most singular appearance—dark skin, Eastern jacket, bow tie, a huge Bowie knife strapped to his chest, and a long queue of black hair. Whitmore Charley shook hands with the man, seemed to know him. And then the cards were dealt.

Nate sipped at the whiskey, decided he didn't like the taste, and spent his time observing one person or another.

The beautiful one returned to the barroom after a time, glanced about, and then posed provocatively against one of the carved oak posts that served, as Nate imagined, to hold up the ceiling.

For an instant, no longer than that, their eyes met.

Didn't take her long to size you up. Nothing but a kid—and no money in your pockets. . . .

An hour passed, maybe more. Nate found his way to an empty chair in one corner, sat down, closed his eyes, and listened to the rhythmed babble of the voices of the men. The long day's ride had begun to take its effect on him, and he drifted off into an uneasy sleep.

Then Charley was tugging at his coat.

"Come on, Nate old vaquero. Let's get on back to our

animals. Your dumb-ass employer's just run into a better artist than he is."

Nate struggled to his feet, yawning and shaking his head. "What happened—did you lose?"

"Lose!" Charley snorted as they passed through the swinging doors and back out onto the street. "I got cleaned, that's what. You know who that big bastard is, lad? The greatest horse thief and liar that ever lived, that's who. The Crow hisself. Old Jimmy Beckwith. This child did some minin' with him and Chapineau over at Murderer's Bar about four years back, just when the Rush was first on. Them two an' Caleb Greenwood an' his kid as well. We didn't dig much gold, Nate, but for about a week there we were powerful drunk most of the time. Never played cards with 'im before, though, and Whitmore Charley don't have to be beat over the head to learn a lesson. Now if Beckwith had just told me he didn't know how to play the game, then I'd of been warned. Everything the man says is either pure bullshit or monstrous underexaggeration. Truth just ain't in 'im. Claims he used to be an Injun chief, among other things. Well, a dollar poorer an' a dollar smarter. I'll make up for it on wages I don't pay."

"How much did you lose, Charley?" Nate asked as they mounted their horses.

Once north of Marysville, Whitmore Charley resumed his practice of staying away from the frequented roads so as to find sufficient grass for the stock. On the journey up the long valley, they had already come across numerous bands of Indians—Yokuts, Miwoks, and Maidus. Now, shortly after crossing the Rio de las Plumas a few miles from Sutter's northern spread, the Hoch Farm, a band of Yana Indians came in, a group that pretended friendliness and then attempted to steal some of Charley's cattle.

When the skirmish was over, four Indians lay dead, while the remainder, some of them dropping their weapons in the urgency of their flight, had taken to their heels and were running zigzag like so many rabbits toward the scant cover of brush on the long, low ridge half a mile distant.

Nate was stunned by the suddenness of what had happened. He had pulled his rifle from its sheath and then had stared

about as the weapons of the vaqueros were puffing blue-gray
smoke into the still air. He hadn't fired a shot.

"What's the matter with you, lad?" Charley demanded. "It
ain't like they're human, after all. Shiftless, lazy cowards they
are—all these valley Injuns. They'd rather steal than hunt for
themselves. Be a good day when they're dead, all of 'em.
Shee-it, boy, you've got to keep your mind hard—or you're
never goin' to amount to nothing at all. Let 'em steal so much
as a single horse turd, they'll wipe you out. You listen to what
I'm sayin' now."

"Dammit, Charley, we didn't have to shoot them. They had
no guns—no way to protect themselves. And they looked
half-starved to death. . . ."

"Just Injuns, lad. You're still green. Another year or so an' you'll
begin to figure things out. A man's got to watch out for hisself."

"I know," Nate cut in. "No one else is going to do it."

"Damned right," Charley snorted. "Damned right, lad."

As they broke camp, Nate trailed behind. He was angry
now. Charley, he'd concluded, was not a good man—not good
at all. The old cow runner was basically dishonest and not at
all loyal to anyone but himself.

"Wonder if he's going to try to cheat me out of my wages,"
Nate mumbled. "I'm not going to let him do it. I'll shoot the
white-haired son of a bitch first."

The following morning three of the Mexican drovers had
vanished, and with them a group of the best-looking of the
wild horses.

Charley raged, cursed at everyone, and swore he'd have
them all thrown in jail as horse thieves.

"These men didn't take anything," Nate protested. "What
the hell are you shouting at them for?"

"They will yet, they will yet. Nate, you sound like a kid
that's still suckin' at his mama's tit. If we don't keep a handle
on this thing, you an' me'll end up riding shank's mare back
to Yreka—and won't neither one of us get paid. Well now,
you just keep an eye peeled and a fist on that rifle of yours.
We could lose the whole thing, all that we've worked for, in
the next couple of days. Listen to me, now. . . ."

They reached the northern end of the Sacramento Valley,
avoided the settlements of Horsetown and Shasta City, crossed

a wide, dry ridge, and came down to the Sacramento River
beyond it. They were in Wintun territory now, and here and
there along the river were small clusters of wigwams, with
smoke rising from them. With the streams running full from
recent rain and snowfall higher in the mountains, Whitmore
Charley elected to follow up the Pit River to its valley and
from there northward, to the east of Mount Shasta. The great
volcano was clearly visible now, high and white and utterly
dominating its landscape—like a lonely god, as Nate Miller
supposed.

The group crossed the pass at Hatchet Mountain, en-
countering a few inches of snow near the summit, and moved
on toward the Pit River Valley, through a narrow gorge and
then out onto the broad, level plain that lay between rimrock
formations and old lava flows. The valley was green even at
this time of year, and Nate glanced from Lassen's Peak
southward to Shasta far northward.

They came upon a great encampment of Indians—the
various bands having come in to rendezvous for the purpose
of fishing. Nate was uncertain what to expect. He felt utterly
intimidated, like a trespasser. His own father, having spent
much of his life in Indian territory and having crossed the
Great Plains with wife and family, had often ventured off
among the Redmen without a thought for his weapon—and
had never been harmed in the slightest.

But so many of them!

"Atsugewis," Whitmore Charley said. "A regular gatherin'
of the clan. A branch of the Sastees, they be. A whole
different breed from what we been dealin' with, Nate."

Astoundingly, Charley knew several of the chiefs and was
on good terms with them. While Nate and the vaqueros
nervously sat their ponies beside the herd of mustangs and
Spanish cattle, Charley talked at length with one of the
leaders of the Indians, disappeared into one of the lodges to
smoke, and emerged after a time, grinning.

"Let's head on north, boys!" the old man sang out.

The Atsugewis, displaying no sign of ill will, actually
assisted for an hour or two in herding Charley's animals
along, helping to drive the creatures across each of the two
branches of the Pit River. Then, shouting, yelling, and laughing, the Redmen turned back toward their encampment.

"All a matter of knowin' how to deal with 'em," Charley insisted. "A man's got to know who his friends are."

"Thought you said they weren't *human*," Nate growled.

"Well now, there's Injuns an' then there's Injuns. Difference between the valley kind an' the mountain kind is like night and day."

"For instance?"

"Don't get uppity, lad. Keep your ears open an' listen. I'll tell you the difference. First off, a man can reason with the Pit River boys and the other Sastees; same with the Modocs—at least most of the time. Second, when these fellas do get riled, they're holy terrors. Meaner than shee-it. Wouldn't back down from grizzly bears and the U.S. Cavalry together. I was with Fremont and old Kit Carson years ago, an' we got into a scrape with the Klamats. They damn near done us in, I'll tell you. We was lucky, no two ways about 'er. And Kit hisself said them Klamats was tougher than Blackfeet or Crows or Bannocks. I don't know about that myself, but if Carson said 'er, she's probably true.

"Anyhow, if a man wants to be moving back and forth through this country, he's got to stay friendly with the boys. You heard about that dumb-ass Ben Wright? Think I talked about him once or twice. Pulled off a massacre against the Modocs, an' they haven't forgot it. It was a mistake, I'll tell you that much. Well now, Whitmore Charley for one is going to be careful as hell when he's wanderin' about in *their* country. Like I said, they're reasonable enough, but they do hold grudges for an ungawdly long time. A man never knows when they're likely to take it into their skulls to pick up a few chips. And the Sastees know about it, of course, an' they're getting more suspicious of the Whites all the time.

"Your gold miners are the problem, lad. Them coons kill all the game and fill the cricks with mud from their placering. But there's no gold to speak of to the east of the big mountain, so the Injuns haven't got riled up yet. Someone finds gold, though, an' it'll happen, sure as hogshit. And if that happens, there's going to be blood in these hills."

Nate stared at the white-haired man, attempting to digest Charley's words and realizing that possibly, just possibly, he had misjudged his employer.

"Well now, what are you staring at me for, Nate Miller?"

Nate laughed.

"You're a strange man, Charley," he said.

Whitmore Charley frowned and arched one bushy eyebrow.

"That for sure, is it? Okay, so I said them Yanas wasn't *human*. What I didn't say was that maybe we ain't either. You ever think about that? Mebbe it's only the coyotes and the bears that's *human*. Get that cowdog look off your puss now. A bad sign, a real bad sign. You go lookin' at me that way, an' I might even be shamed into paying you your wages."

The men drove the herd of beef animals and horses on toward the north and set up camp some twenty-five miles east of Yreka, not far from the base of the massive, snow- and ice-draped peak of Shasta, in against a high spur of rock and close to thick timber. A small stream ran through the rich meadows, and Charley called it Horsethief Creek. The stream was clear, willow-edged as it flowed through its long, narrow valley. It was, as Nate observed, filled with trout. Close by the creek, the coarse, lush grass was green even this late in the year.

"Rest the varmints a week before headin' down," Charley said. "Give 'em a chance to get some meat back on their bones. You move a herd of cattle or horses, either one, any distance, Natty, you want to let 'em graze awhile before you sell 'em. Chances are it won't cost you nothing extra for your vaqueros—not if they want to get paid at all—and you'll get better prices for your livestock. Keep listenin' to old Charley, my boy, and you'll learn something yet."

The vaqueros, in fact, complained a bit—but Charley had his way, as always.

There had been no sign of either the Pit River Indians or the less friendly Modocs, but the presence of the drovers and their herd of animals had not gone unnoticed. Late one afternoon, an hour or so before the sun blazed its deep winter red across the western sky, three young Shastas rode in, boys about Nate's age, laughing and calling out from a safe distance and performing all manner of tricks on their horses.

Charley, Nate, and the others stood watching, their weapons ready just in case.

"Fine horsemen," Charley said, laughing. "You ever see anything like it, Natty?"

At length, having grown more confident that the Whitemen were not going to shoot at them and drive them off, the Shastas approached, identified themselves as members of Chief Blackbeard's band, and asked for work. The apparent leader of the group of three knew some English. His name was Klamat, he told them, for he had been born a Modoc and captured by the Klamats, the warrior nation whose lands lay to the north, at the foot of the mountain called Yaina. He had been a slave to these people but had escaped and had wandered on foot until, utterly exhausted and without food for nearly a week, he had been discovered by Chief Warrottetot's Achomawis. They had taken him in, and now he was one of them—his previous identity evident only in the name they had given him.

His companions, both somewhat shorter than he, were named Crippled Deer and Heron.

"What do you think, Natty?" Charley asked. "Suppose they'll make good help—or you figure they'll thieve all our critters?"

"If they're working for you, at least the Sastees won't be stealing the animals."

"Well now. That's not true, of course. But you're learning. You're learning, my boy."

Charley agreed and sent Nate with the Indian boys to draw the herd in for the night. Klamat was somewhat skeptical about working with the cattle, and he said so. But ultimately the three Indian youths made quick business of moving the band of horses into the makeshift corral that Charley's men had set up.

"All right, now," Nate explained. "Cattle are just like horses—but not as smart. So we have to guide them a bit more. Once we get the big spotted cow to moving, the rest of the herd will follow. That's their way."

Klamat arched one eyebrow and shook his head.

"They are not like horses," he replied. "I have never seen anyone ride a cow."

"Guess you're right." Nate grinned.

"You need a dog," Klamat insisted. "I have seen the White settlers near Pit River use dogs to move their cattle."

"You and I and your friends are Charley's dogs," Nate replied. "Come on, let's get them going."

That night, Nate, Klamat, Crippled Deer, and Heron sat around their own separate campfire, and the Indians sampled Charley's cooking—beans and sour-tasting flour cakes—but without enthusiasm.

"This is what he makes you eat?" Klamat asked. "I think it would be better to starve." Then he gestured to his Shasta companions, spoke a few words in their own language, and elicited shrugs from them.

"Sometimes I hunt for the vaqueros, who are very lazy," Nate explained. "But today I did not have time."

"I see your rifle," Klamat said. "It is a beautiful gun. One day I will have one like it."

"My father gave it to me. It's an old piece, but a good one."

"Look gun?" Heron asked.

Nate thought he understood the question, but he turned to Klamat, as if unsure what was meant.

"My friend wishes to see your rifle. I would like to look at it also, and so would Crippled Deer. We will not steal it from you—you do not have to worry about that."

Nate Miller nodded, rose, removed the weapon from its sheath, and handed the rifle to Heron.

"Be careful—tell him to be careful," he said to Klamat. "It's loaded, ready to fire."

The Indians examined the long-barreled Kentucky, running their fingertips over the ornate brass inlay work on the stock, nodding and grunting their approval.

"Are you a good shot with this gun?" Klamat asked.

Nate hesitated before answering, decided against being modest, and said, "Very good. My father taught me to shoot when I was just a young boy. Anything that's within range, I'll hit it."

Klamat repeated what Nate had said, using the Shasta language for the benefit of his two companions. They, in turn, studied the White boy, as if to determine whether they should believe his words.

"Have you killed a grizzly, Nate Miller?" Klamat asked.

"No. A black bear once, but never a grizzly."

"Are you afraid to shoot such an animal?"

Nate took another mouthful of Charley's beans and shrugged.

"Why should I be afraid? Just never had reason to shoot one. Truth to say, I've never been close enough to one to shoot it."

The response seemed to satisfy Klamat, and he translated the exchange for Crippled Deer and Heron, both of whom nodded.

At length Klamat handed the rifle back to Nate, who returned the weapon to its sheath.

Nate and Klamat talked for some time, with Klamat translating now and again for his companions—a continuing exchange of questions and answers. What was life like among the Whites? What was it like among the Indians? Why were so many of the Whitemen digging holes in the earth—why did they wish to find the yellow metal? Why did they muddy the streams and cause the salmon and trout to die?

Nate asked if it was not lonely, living always in the forest.

Klamat laughed at this and repeated the question to Crippled Deer and Heron, both of whom shook their heads at what they apparently considered a very foolish inquiry.

And by the time one of Charley's Mexicans shouted at them to be quiet and go to sleep, Nate knew that he and Klamat, and probably Crippled Deer and Heron as well, had become friends.

The following day three of the vaqueros, cursing in Spanish and English all at once, mounted their horses and rode away. The Indian boys looked at Nate for some explanation of what had happened, then at Charley, then back at Nate.

"Well now, I guess they was impatient," Whitmore Charley said, chuckling, the blowup apparently of little concern to him.

"Three you won't have to pay?" Nate suggested.

"Guess not, guess not. Meskins always did have bad tempers. Well, Klamat—that your name for sure?—I reckon you and your tribesmen have got a few more days of work ahead of you, if you want 'er."

"Does this man not pay wages to the ones who do his work for him?" Klamat asked Nate.

"He'll pay me, and he'll pay you, too," Miller said. "Those others he can cheat, but he can't cheat me—or my friends, either."

"How you carry on, Natty!" Whitmore Charley laughed. "Have I ever done you wrong, even once? Didn't I feed you when you was damn near starved to death? You're like my own son, Nat, if I had one. You boys just get that livestock on out into tall grass. A few more days and we'll have our mesteños and longhorns fatter'n hogs in clover. Bring us good money over to Yreka. Beef's a premium in the gold camps. The damned fools will pay almost any price for it. A man can bust his back diggin' for fool's dust, or he can use his noodle and get the dust that way. Me, I prefer to use my head as much as possible. I'm like old Jimmy Beckwith, only not as good at monte, I guess. Well, there'll be another day for that. Now look. You, Nate, you'll take your pay and grubstake yourself and probably end up losing everything. Then you'll come lookin' for poor old Whitmore Charley. You're a mite slow, lad, but you do learn after a time."

Nate shook his head, gestured to Klamat and his companions, and walked slowly toward his Cayuse pony.

"I shouldn't even like that old thief, but I do," he said to Klamat.

"Then why do you call him a thief?"

"Can't think of a better word, is all," he answered. But as he spoke, he realized that he was even beginning to sound like Charley. God help him, perhaps he was on his way to becoming a man just like the old white-haired rascal.

You need a big Bowie knife like Beckwith had—maybe two of them, and a couple of pistols besides. . . .

The rising sun was streaming up the narrow valley of Horsethief Creek by this time, and mists were rising from the heavy boughs of fir and cedar. The sun, just emerging above the shoulder of the ragged butte to the east, made the snow and ice high up on Shasta glitter and shimmer, the huge mountain seeming almost alive.

Nate and the Indian boys drove the herd of horses a short way down the creek and were just returning. They could see Charley and his companion sitting with their backs to a large, twisted cedar, an odor of fried bacon distinct in the still, cold air. Crippled Deer and Heron led the saddle horses across the creek to put them on tether ropes so they might graze on the thick grass, and Nate and Klamat sauntered toward the camp. Charley was celebrating the loss of his three vaqueros with a hearty breakfast, and he would, Nate knew, be in a mood to share his small supply of bacon for a change.

The hiss and crack of rifle fire was so sudden that it took Nate a long moment to realize what was happening—but Klamat had already dived for cover and was gone, out of sight.

Charley and the other man were hit with the first volley. Their tin plates piled with food leaped from their hands, and the men fell forward on their faces without uttering a word.

Indians were swarming down the lava-strewn ridgeside—Modocs, Nate realized, armed with bows and rifles as well.

Gunsmoke erupted from behind trees. Quick movements of tawny bodies.

Horses screaming. Cattle bellowing.

Nate stood still, horror-struck, his mind utterly blank, his limbs seemingly frozen. He was unable to move.

Run, you damned fool. . . .

He turned, moved. He heard the explosion of a rifle shot, close by, but he kept going, his legs working now with a will of their own, motivated by a terrible fear and the intense, overwhelming desire to live. His mind shouted *Coward*! but his body paid no attention. He gasped for breath, and broke through a tangle of fir, the branches lashing at his face.

His rifle! It was with the pony. But he had his pistol, the weapon loaded, ready. He pulled it from his belt and plunged on. Pistol in hand and heedless of where he might be going, he broke out into a clearing. Then three mounted Indians were directly before him, and he changed direction immediately, driving himself upslope toward the possible safety of the forest.

It's happening too fast, it isn't supposed to happen this way. . . .

An Indian on horseback had drawn alongside him as he strained on up the hill. He fell, rose, and attempted to continue. The pistol was in his hand—why didn't he use it?

Nate could see the hatchet coming down, but his mind could not deal with the utter absurdity and horror of what was happening. The big Modoc was holding his ax by the wrong end. . . .

The handle of the weapon struck Nate across the forehead,

and he sprawled on the wet-smelling duff, the thick odor of decaying pine needles. . . .

When Nate recovered his senses, the Modoc warrior was rolling him over—was pulling at the crimson Mexican sash he wore around his middle. The Indian seemed huge, ghostly, naked from the waist up and painted with curving lines of red pigment.

Miller grasped for the savage's leg and was kicked away. The Indian's face: disdainful, a mask of red and white grease, like some terrible vision in a nightmare.

Smell of bear, bear grease. . . .

Powerful arms, the muscles corded and hard.

Nate closed his eyes, awaited the blow of the tomahawk—he could feel it descending. In his mind's eye he saw the blade strike his skull, crushing the bony case, spilling the pink brains inside.

But the Modoc was laughing—was that what it was, laughter?

"The Whiteman is not old enough for me to kill," the Indian said, his words English but not really sounding like English—and the communication hung in the air, Nate's mind hearing but not registering what had been said.

The Indian leaned over, spun Nate about, and unwound the crimson sash. Then he rose, glanced down at the boy, and said, "Later."

Nate Miller watched the man walk over to his pony, mount, and ride slowly off in the direction of Whitmore Charley's camp.

For long moments he lay there, struggling for breath and dimly aware that the pistol was no longer in his grasp. He turned, got to his knees, and looked about him for the weapon.

The .31 Colt lay in front of him, partially covered by pine needles. Why hadn't the Indian taken the gun? Hadn't he seen it? Was his own mind simply playing tricks on him?

Nate reached out for the weapon, half-convinced that it was not really there at all. But then the pistol was in his hand, and he hugged the gun to his chest, covering the short-barreled Colt with both hands.

No more rifle fire now—only the absolute silence of the forest, only the dreamlike white form of Mount Shasta, lonely and massive off to the south, a fringe of cloud forming above the summit of the great peak.

Stunned, mindless, Nate Miller moved off upslope. A jumble of lava, some hole to crawl into, the hard, black protection of stone around him...

From the base of the rimrock, he looked back down to where Charley had been eating breakfast only a few minutes earlier. But that was another world, he realized, another time. A bluejay screamed, and a squirrel chattered angrily. Then the forest was quiet once more. The horses were gone, his father's Kentucky rifle was gone, Whitmore Charley was dead....

But the Modocs were also gone, and the world they left behind them was terribly changed.

The sun was well up over the dry, brown butte that rose to the east.

THREE

▲

Among the Shastas

A few miles from Millville, near what once had been called Reading's Springs but which had been renamed Shasta City, a young Yana girl called Eliza lived—an attractive girl, friendly and outgoing. She was working for a farmer and his wife at the time.

Three men stopped at the half-finished house and shouted, "Eliza, come out. We're going to kill you."

The girl begged for her life, pleaded with the farmer and his wife to protect her, but to no avail. The three men took the girl and also her aunt and uncle—took them a short distance from the house, raped the two women, and shot all three. The farmer later counted eleven bullets in Eliza's breast. One of the men took a drink and said, "I don't think that goddamned little squaw's dead yet." Then he turned back and smashed her skull with his musket.

Afterward, no one could seem to remember her Yana name.

Nate Miller wandered on aimlessly for an hour or more, then he came upon the tracks of four horses, one of them shod. Nate studied the tracks, convinced that one of the animals was his own Cayuse pony.

What to do?

Anger came over him, a red wave of hatred and a need for revenge. He would trail the animals—would force the Modocs to return his pony and his Kentucky rifle. What had his father said to him? "Son, don't lose that gun in a card game. Your pappy might be needing it sometime."

The gun was his. No one had a right to it but himself.

The blow to the head. Was he thinking clearly? But suddenly that didn't matter either. Nothing at all mattered—nothing but the need to regain his horse and rifle. He had the pistol, and this time he would use it. He could follow a trail, he imagined, as well as the best of them. And beyond that, he would have the element of surprise on his side this time around. The idea of a White boy, one who was *too young to kill*, following them, taking them when they least expected it . . .

Nate's mind was clear enough to comprehend the odds against success. One chance in a thousand, perhaps a million. But he had the pistol, and he was determined. If it came to that, he would die with his weapon in his hand, the weapon empty because he had taken some of them with him.

He followed the trail, but after only a few yards he heard voices, barely more than whispers, but he heard them, and took cover—and waited, the gun in his hand and the hand steady.

Three riders—and one horse trailing behind, his Cayuse.

Nate leveled his gun, took aim at the lead rider—and was nearly ready to fire when he realized his mistake.

It was Klamat—Klamat and Crippled Deer and Heron. They had escaped unharmed, and had found their own scattered mounts and his as well.

The Kentucky rifle his father had given him was there, in its sheath.

The Indian boys were searching for him—scouring the forest in the hope that he might still be alive.

Nate mounted his Cayuse and followed where Klamat led, toward the Achomawi village apparently, the village of Chief Warrottetot. The White boy trailed along, barely clinging to his horse. The fierce energy and need for revenge had both vanished now, and he was beset by an overpowering urge to sleep.

They reached the Shasta encampment. It was a long ride, but beyond that Nate had no idea of how far they had traveled. He remembered Klamat and Heron examining the wound on the left side of his head, remembered them cleansing it and applying some sort of poultice made of leaves. But he had slept as he rode, awakening fitfully, sometimes at the very moment when to have done otherwise would have been to fall from his pony.

He remembered Klamat asking several times, "What is

your name? Do you remember your name?" But Nate could not recall what he had answered.

Then the village. Groups of Indians standing near him, talking about him in words that he could not comprehend. He was taken to a lodge, placed on a pallet, and covered with elkskin robes.

He knew that days were passing, for sometimes he would awaken from his dreaming to find the lodge dark, and could sense the presence of other people asleep in the room. And sometimes it was light, the lodge empty except for himself. Klamat was often there, and when he was, Nate acknowledged his friend, spoke his name, and slept once more.

Once a girl was there beside him, a fine-featured, perhaps even beautiful dark-skinned young woman—one who was possibly his own age, maybe a bit younger.

"Will you come back to us soon?" she asked, speaking a hesitant English. "I am Poonkina, daughter to Warrottetot. I have left food for you, but you do not eat—and I must take it away again."

"Thank you," Nate managed, and then fell back into the dark oblivion of unconsciousness.

But she came other times as he dreamed. She was thin, almost but not quite a woman; or perhaps she was still a child, he could not be certain. But she did not speak to him in English anymore, not as he dreamed, and the sound of her voice was music that exploded into tiny bursts of color, like butterflies or small, brilliantly hued birds. She wore an elaborately braided front apron and an unsleeved shirt of deerskin. The clothing clung to her thin body, and her hips, as she walked away from him, were almost boyish. He attempted to rise, to follow her, but he was unable—something restrained him, something held him down, and there was no energy in his limbs at all. He attempted to cry out to her, but no words would come. And the girl looked back over her shoulder once, her hair full and loose and trailing to her waist. Then she stepped into drifting mists and was gone.

"My name is Poonkina . . ." he thought he heard her say.

Time became utterly meaningless, a current, a river that flowed on endlessly, punctuated only by occasional moments of clarity. At such times, starting awake, Nate thought about Whitmore Charley, knew the old man was dead, remembered details of the Modoc raid, and remembered the huge warrior who had declined to kill him and who had taken his red sash. Nate relived the fear, relived the crack of the rifles and the screams of the horses. But sometimes he simply lay still and studied the lodge, the lower portion dug out of the earth, a fire burning always in its little hearth of hand-fitted stones, the smoke rising up to exit through the smoke hole in the roof between the twin ridge beams at the crest. The sides and roof of the lodge were constructed of planks, hand-hewn, the work of long hours and fitted together with astounding craftsmanship, the walls lined with slabs of cedar bark. The side timbers were vertical, and the doorway consisted of the omission of a single board, the opening covered by a hanging mat of woven cedar-bark strands and tules.

The whole thing reminded Nate of a hut he had built out in the woods when he was a young boy in Indiana. He, too, had dug down into the earth and had raised the sides with sections of plank from the pile of boards that had once been a cattle barn before his father had torn it down and rebuilt the structure with new material. And he had arched up a roof, also of planks, and had overlaid it with sod, leaving a small hole at one end so that he could build a fire inside, should he choose to do so.

Nate stared at the ceiling and wondered if, indeed, the top of the lodge was covered with sod—wondered where sod might be found here in the mountains of California.

"One day I will make a lodge like this one," he said aloud—and then closed his eyes and slept again.

When he awoke next, he realized he was terribly hungry. He turned over to the benchlike projection next to his bed, to the place where he dimly remembered having seen a basket of food on several earlier occasions.

Pine nuts and a cake of what seemed to be dried fish. A small mound of black, roasted acorn kernels—live oak, apparently, from their shape.

"The whole goddamned valley and all the hills where oaks grow—one big orchard, far as the Injuns are concerned."

Whitmore Charley's words.

Nate reached for the side of his head and felt the newly formed scar tissue. A small lump, not much more.

The bandage is gone, he thought.

But neither Charley nor the Modoc attack or anything besides the need for food occupied his immediate concern. He ate, slowly at first, then more quickly. First, the fishcake, then the mound of bad-looking acorn kernels—but which, he admitted, didn't taste bad at all. Last, the pine nuts. At first he attempted to shell each one but finally gave in to his hunger and chewed several at a time, swallowing fragments of shell and all.

He was up and around now, though how much time had passed since the Modoc raid on Charley's camp he had no idea. Time in its usual sense, he realized, was not important to the Shastas, though changes in weather, storms, freezings, subtle signs of the turning season—all these things were of the utmost significance.

He was accepted by the people, some of whom, to his pleased surprise, knew a smattering of English—as did Klamat.

His friend was with him every day now, and they talked at great length about a wide variety of things. Klamat, in fact, was a natural-born teacher—as Nate realized—and explained a host of things about these, his adopted people, at tedious length.

"The Shastas have accepted us both," Klamat said. "They saved my life and took me in when I was a small child, and now they have saved your life and taken you in also. Perhaps you will wish to live with us now, Nate Miller."

"Perhaps so." Nate grinned, and then requested Klamat to continue with his lesson in the Shasta tongue.

"To speak our language will be of no use to you if you do not stay and live with us," Klamat said.

"If I come back to visit, and you are not here, then I will need to be able to speak with the others."

"You do not need to be able to speak to the women," Klamat said, his eyes shining with amusement. "They read your face, they read what is in your blue-colored eyes, and what they see is a man-child, one who needs to be cared for. Look. They have all made you new clothing, and now you have more clothing than anyone. I think they would all like to adopt you."

"What does *Ki-yi-mem* mean?"

"You do not wish to speak of how the women baby you, Nate?"

"No. What does the name of the creek mean in your language?"

"Oh, well. *Ki-yi-mem* is 'white water.' We call it that because it is different from most streams. It flows down from high up on Ieka. Often it is very full, and sometimes it is almost dry. And sometimes it brings down ashes and fine sand from the fire mountain and becomes like the color of a mother's milk. Once I remember that it was hot enough to burn a child's hand, but most always it is very cold. That is because it comes from the melted ice."

The language lessons continued, often at great length, until sometimes Klamat would grow bored and urge Nate to accompany him on a hunting venture. Nate learned rapidly and was soon able to converse, though in a hesitant manner, with the women who fed and clothed him, with the older men, the hunters and warriors, and those his own age, like Crippled Deer and Heron.

The winter wore on and began to turn to spring, but Nate's health returned slowly. Much of the time he sat by the lodges or under the trees, watching the Shastas go about the daily routines of their lives. On clear days he stared up, never tiring of the spectacle, at the great white mountain that loomed above the Shasta encampment. Sometimes, even on clear days, the entire summit of the mountain was wreathed in rapidly shifting cloud forms, and at other times the mountain gleamed brilliantly in the light of morning or turned soft shades of pink or purple in the waning hours of afternoon.

The village was half-deserted now, for Warrottetot and many of the men had left, perhaps to hunt, perhaps simply to wander. But the women and children remained, as did Klamat and Heron. Crippled Deer, however, had gone with the men—and so, as Klamat said, was himself fully a man now.

With the snow gone from the dark forest at the foot of the mountain, the women gathered and dried mountain camas roots, found in abundance around the marshy areas—and they prepared these onion-shaped bulbs for eating by roasting them beneath their drying fires.

Nate concluded that he could not have been better treated even if he were back at his own home in the Willamette

Valley. The Indian diet, however, left much to be desired, and he sometimes daydreamed of scrambled eggs, flapjacks, beefsteak, milk, and fried potatoes.

Klamat, Heron, and some of the other youths were now often gone for several days at a time, and though Nate was repeatedly urged to accompany them, he declined. If it was rest that he needed, he got his fill of it—and his life there in the deep forest was close to one of nothingness.

To the south of the village, the woods opened out into parklike meadows, and there the children and some of the young women played or simply lay stretched out in the spring sunlight. At times he walked among them, always half-hoping that he might again see the lovely girl who had brought him food when he was sick and who had wandered as well through his dreams. But now, he supposed, she was certainly with her father, the chief. For, from the time he had been able to be up and about, he had never seen her again.

Perhaps he had merely imagined her existence. She was a dream, an angel who had come to him in his sickness-induced dreamings.

He had never asked Klamat who Poonkina was, or even if there was such a person as Poonkina. If she was real, he assured himself, then he would see her again. If not, then the vision was his own, and therefore private. Perhaps one day he would indeed meet such a young woman. As he remembered the girl, he realized that his pulse actually began to quicken. He laughed, shook his head, and resolved to question Klamat when his friend returned from hunting.

But Nate—Cincinnatus Hiner Miller—was content among the Shastas, more at ease and at peace with himself, he realized, than he had ever been before in his life. No one, other than Klamat, had thought to question either his staying or his leaving. The Indians made no demands on him and, indeed, seemed to take pleasure in tending to his needs— particularly the women, who seemed to view him as something between a full-grown child and a pet bear. For a time Nate had been permitted to forget his own existence, his civilized, White existence, and to live a waking dream. His strength returned, he grew taller, and his mind became ever more active and restless.

He went on hunting forays with Heron and Klamat and

four or five of the other young men. When he brought down a deer at a dead run, some two hundred yards off, Klamat acknowledged him a finer shot than any of the Shastas, and Nate experienced an intense surge of pride in his marksmanship.

"I believe you now, Nate Miller," Klamat had said. "When I first asked you if you were a good shot, I wasn't sure, even though you said so."

Before the hunting expedition was over, Nate had taken three more deer and an elk, severing the latter's spine at the base of the neck as the big ungulate careered off downslope. By this time the young Indian warriors were in positive awe of the tall White boy with the long-barreled rifle.

Their successful return to the village, the pack animals laden with meat, was reason enough for a celebration and a feast. And when the stories of the hunt were told, Nate was accorded a new respect. Before, he had been one whose life was to be saved, a curiosity to them, an ungainly young man who was innocent to their ways and so was in need of instruction. But now the young man was seen to be both an excellent horseman among a people to whom horsemanship was an admired skill and a crack shot as well, with skills clearly superior to their own—and with a weapon more beautifully made even than the rifle owned by Warrottetot himself.

Young women who had previously been friendly enough but from a distance now drew closer. The old medicine woman, Mountain Smoke, approached Nate as well. Of all the Shastas, she had been the most distant and formal toward him until now.

"Your rifle has great power," she said. "I would like to look at this rifle."

Nate brought it to her, and she held it in both hands, studying it.

"It is heavy," she said. "That is because it contains its own *aheki*. You must keep it with you always. If you should lose it while gambling in the stick game, your power will be gone."

With these words Mountain Smoke gave back the rifle, turned, and walked quickly away, not stopping until she had reached her own lodge.

"You have conquered the shaman," Klamat said. "I have never seen her do such a thing before. All the other old women you conquered without even trying, and now you have the medicine woman as well."

"I don't understand at all," Nate protested. "And what the hell's an *aheki*?"

"You do not know this thing? And yet Mountain Smoke says there is one in your rifle! This is a spirit or a devil, Nate. Those are the words in your language. *Aheki* are strong and may bring either good or evil. To us they are the *pains*. When we come across things that belonged to the People Who Lived Here Before Us, we know that these objects contain *aheki*. Such things are prized by the shamans, but the rest of us avoid touching them. Young men go on quests to find their own *aheki*. If the *pains* are good, then the man will be strong and others will listen to his words."

"Do you believe that, Klamat?"

Klamat looked puzzled, glanced in the direction Mountain Smoke had gone, and said in a quiet voice, "No."

"Then you don't think there's one in my Kentucky rifle?"

"No, Nate. I just think that you are a better shot than I am. I have taught you about our people. Now perhaps you will teach me how to shoot better."

Nate nodded and clasped his friend by both shoulders.

The people were in a joyous mood, and four whole deer were roasting on spits above the great cooking fires. When the meat was ready, along with quantities of camas and fish and acorn meal made into small cakes, containers of manzanita cider were brought out.

Nate and Klamat gorged themselves but were hardly more voracious in their appetites than the other Shastas. Later the two friends sat together near one of the fires and observed the ritual dancing of the young men and the young women, but neither chose to participate—Nate because he did not fully understand what was happening. Several young women danced toward them, then retreated when neither of the two showed the proper inclincation.

"You have taught me how to speak your language," Nate said.

"That is true," Klamat agreed.

"I would like to know the meaning of another word."

"Soon I will run out of words to tell you."

"*Poonkina*," Nate said, pronouncing the word carefully.

A look of surprise passed momentarily across Klamat's face.

"It is not a word of the Shasta language," he replied. "It is from the language of the Yuki and means 'wormwood.'"

"Do you know their language, too?"

"No, my friend. I just know that one word. It is the name that Little Grouse was given when she became a woman. Mountain Smoke gave her the name after Little Grouse had told her about a dream. Poonkina cared for you when you were sick, Nate. I did not realize you had talked to her."

"I wasn't sure that I had. I thought she might have been a vision from one of my dreams. But I remember that she told me her name. Is she the daughter of Chief Warrottetot? I think she said that, too."

Klamat nodded.

"Yes, she is the chief's dauther, one of his daughters. Blackbeard has two children, both girls. Poonkina is a year older. Do you remember her well? I think she is very beautiful, one who grows more beautiful with each season. One day I hope to marry her, if she is willing. Blackbeard has not yet promised her to anyone, but I was not born a Shasta. I will have to earn a marriage price that is larger than someone else would. She is the chief's daughter, and so the marriage price will be very high."

Though Warrottetot had not returned from what, as Nate Miller had learned, was in fact a trading venture among the Modocs to the north, the encampment was moved nonetheless some miles to the east, to the shore of a good-sized lake in what Nate realized was the vast, blown-out crater of a presumably extinct volcano—a great, swelling mound of a mountain the Shastas called Medicine. The days were warm now, interspersed with occasional intervals of rain, and the deer, elk, and antelope that grazed in the high meadows near the Medicine Lake were plentiful. Nate rode often with his friends and learned to appreciate fully Klamat's uncanny ability to follow the tracks of any creature, human or animal— learned to appreciate as well his friend's detailed and exact knowledge of the lay of the land. Nate's own system involved making mental calibrations with regard to relative distance and direction from the high, white crown of Shasta—but along canyon bottoms or on enclosed plains, with the resident god not visible, his sense of direction was flawed, at best.

Klamat, on the other hand, did not have to be able to *see* the mountain to know where he was. It was as though he carried a detailed map, in relief, inside his skull.

They hunted elk, bear, and deer, and on one occasion were absent from the village for more than a week.

"If you daub red clay onto your face and arms, you will become one of us forever, Nate." Klamat grinned. "You do not look a Whiteman at all anymore—only your pale skin and brown hair and blue eyes. But I have read your thoughts, my friend. I believe that you will wish to leave us soon. You will wish to rejoin the Whites and dig holes in the ground, just as they do. But I think perhaps you should stay here. If you did that, you would find a young woman with whom you wished to live. You would have children, and all would call you the blue-eyed one who is almost human. . . ."

Nate doubled up his fist and gestured in mock anger.

But Klamat was right. He had begun to think once again of some way of getting a mining claim and of making his fortune. As delightful as these months had been, Nate knew—or thought he did—that he would not wish to spend the remainder of his life here. He envisioned a triumphant return to Oregon, himself a rich man. He thought of the prospects of furthering his formal education at the newly founded university in Eugene, and he dreamed idly as well of someday becoming a famous writer—of traveling to the cities of the American East and perhaps even to Europe.

When he communicated some of his thoughts to Klamat, his friend merely appeared puzzled.

"I have been told also that there are other lands and other people far across the Great Water. But that is not to the east—it lies where the sun goes down."

"You speak of what we call the Pacific Ocean," Nate said. "Far across the land, in the other direction, there's another Great Water. And beyond that, also, are other lands and other peoples. Those are the lands that the Whitemen came from."

"But you did not come from there," Klamat said, his voice trailing off.

"No. My family came from the east, though, far beyond the last of the mountains. I was born there, and we crossed the land in a wagon."

"I have seen those wagons a number of times." Klamat nodded. "Their tops are made of heavy white canvas, and the wagons themselves are drawn by fat cows, not like the thin ones that Charley had. They come here to the Center of the World from across the desert lands. Is that why the Whites come here—because where they live it is all desert, like the lands of the Paiutes and Washoes?"

"Beyond the deserts there are other great mountains, and beyond that the land is flat or rolling and covered with grass and takes months to cross. It loks like an ocean of grass, and a great river runs through it. Beyond that are the cities—the big villages—of the Whitemen. There are more Whitemen than you can believe, Klamat."

"And they live in villages like Yreka and Reading's Springs?"

"Some do. Others live in villages that are many times larger, many, many times."

"And they dig holes all about them, looking for the yellow metal, gold?"

"There is no gold. They raise cattle and grow crops."

"Why do they need to grow things? Everything grows by itself. Are there not salmon in the rivers and camas roots and acorns to gather?"

The conversations went on and on, with Klamat absorbing what Nate had to tell him about the strange world of the Whites, both eagerly and, Nate thought, perhaps naïvely. Yet he could see, granted Klamat's perspective and limited knowledge of what lay beyond the lands of the Shastas, that many of the accounts of White civilization must seem almost incredible. Nate gathered that Klamat's habit of waiting a time and then asking again about things he had already been told, of picking up on any slight variations in the accounts, was a way of making certain both that the information was not contradictory and also that he, Nate, was not simply filling his listener's ears with idle whimsy.

Though Klamat, of course, could neither read nor write and had been without any sort of schooling as a Whiteman would construe it, Nate realized that his friend was extremely intelligent. When it came to a knowledge of his own land and his own people, their customs and habits and ways of doing things, Klamat's understanding was detailed and precise. How many Whites, Nate wondered, could claim an equivalent fund of information about the places where they lived and the society in which they, as members, spent their lives?

Nate thought of the years ahead, thought of what must surely happen in this land of forest and mountain now inhabited by the Shastas, the Pit River people, the Modocs, the Wintuns, and the Yanas. At present, the Indians were not at war with the Whites, but their separate realms of interest with regard to the land itself would inevitably bring about conflict, a conflict the Indians were ill suited to win. And if at present they were not at war, perhaps that was simply because the Whiteman's terms of *war* and *peace* were essentially alien to them. From all that Klamat had told him, Nate deduced that raids and other minor conflicts, often with terrible results, were simply a way of life among the Indians. One might do battle with one band of Modocs and a week later join in a feast with another band. If the Whites had horses, and the Indians wanted them, they would simply take them—not out of malice or with a mind to sell the animals and so profit from them, but out of whim or expediency or simply from a desire to own a particular horse that happened to be grazing in a particular meadow next to a particular rancho or village.

But if Whitemen killed Indians, as the miners and ranchers sometimes did as if they were hunting bears, then the Indians were certain to attempt to take revenge—and as often as not the vengeance would be exacted against persons totally innocent of the original Whites' outrage.

And so other Whites would set out, afire with anger, to exterminate Indians. And the Indians, in turn, would strike back.

And so it would go, Nate knew, until all the Indians were safely in the Spirit World—simply because the Whites would eventually have far the greater numbers, even as they already had far superior weapons.

Spring flowed into summer and summer into autumn. Warrottetot had returned to his people, but his eldest daughter, Poonkina, was not with him. Nate experienced an unaccountable wave of disappointment, and Klamat grew despondent and then angry by turns.

"The chief does not wish me to marry his daughter, Nate.

He knows that there is a bond of friendship between us already, even though we are both still too young to think of being man and wife. So he has left her with his relatives among the Scott River Shastas."

"Are you certain of this, Klamat?"

"No, I am not certain. But see, he has brought White Dawn, his younger daughter, with him. He did not leave her among the Scott River Shastas."

"He will listen to you when you have accumulated a large enough marriage price."

"Perhaps that is true," Klamat said, rubbing his temples. "But that may take a very long while. By then an older man, a warrior who is wealthy, will pay the bride price, and then Poonkina will have to be his wife. I should never have looked upon the chief's daughter, my friend. The Shastas have been my people ever since they saved my life, but now I feel like an outcast among them. I have no family, no wealth, and I have not yet had the vision that will make my medicine strong."

The emotion was insane, and Nate knew it, but he felt a distinct twinge of jealousy—for what else could it be? And toward his friend? Because of what was, for him, little more than a hallucination, the image of a dream-child becoming a woman, a phantom that had come to him while he was sick and his mind was not whole. She had been kind to him, merely one of many who had taken an interest in the White boy who lay, half-conscious, in the lodge. And Klamat loved her, had loved her since they were both children together.

It was only right that Klamat should have her, if that was possible.

"Blackbeard has done a wrong thing," Nate said. "But if Poonkina should one day wish to be your wife, is that not more important than a bride price?"

Klamat shook his head, a gesture that indicated that he was unable to answer the question.

FOUR

▲

Partners with the Prince

Numerous settlers had found their way to the Pit River Valley, and some of these Whitemen had taken Indian women for their wives. The Pit River men, for their part, were friendly toward the Whites and often spent time about the settlements, sometimes even made donations of game they had killed.

One day a Pit River brave and his young wife went out among some Whites who were mowing the thick wild grass for hay. Two Whites from an adjacent part of the valley rode up and shot the Indian down, explaining to those in the hayfield that the dead man was "a damned bad Injun."

The two Whites hid the body under a haycock, and carried his young and terrified wife to their camp.

Nate left the Shastas that fall, for the idea of striking it rich in the goldfields had reasserted itself more powerfully than ever. He would make a quick fortune and return to Oregon as a rich man.

The months he had spent among the Shastas seemed ever more dreamlike the farther he rode from their village. What was he leaving behind? He was forced to consider the matter at some length.

Perhaps the best friend he had ever known—Klamat.

A good and kind people—who had taken him in, cared for him, saved his life, and accepted him.

The indelibly etched image of a wraithlike girl—one whom, while in his right senses, he had never even spoken to.

Poonkina.

And what was she? A symbol, perhaps, of the entire appeal of the Indian way of life—its freedom, its wildness, the allure of it all.

The Shastas were human beings, just like all other human beings, and crippled by unquestioned traditions, capable of change only by slow degrees, and blind to the future that, like a great, dark storm running in from the Pacific and overtopping the lesser mountains and even Shasta itself, was soon to bring destruction upon them, forever changing their existence and finally expunging them from the face of the earth.

With some sadness Nate reflected upon the tawny people who took their identity from the towering volcano about which they lived and which figured so heavily in their stories of creation and in their concept of an afterlife.

"Old Coyote Man and his red-haired daughter live inside the mountain..." he had heard.

Though at that moment Nate Miller had no intention whatsoever of returning to the Shastas, his debt to them was very great—a debt, he assured himself, that he would never forget. They had given him his life—and kindness and hospitality that no Whites would ever be fully able to understand. The very clothing that he now wore had come as gifts, the soft brown leathers sewn together by Indian women whose names, in some cases, he did not even know.

As the Cayuse pony moved on toward Cottonwood and Yreka, Nate recalled conversations with Klamat, recalled faces, actions, meals, fires burning within the lodges during snowstorms. The Shasta men had seemed to him tall, lean, and graceful. And the women, wild and natural, possessed a savage beauty. And the old women, many of them fat, round-faced, teeth missing or worn down from years of dressing hides and chewing the leather to make it pliable. The old men, their eyes haunted, as though they alone, having seen so much change in their lifetimes, could intuit at least something of what was to come.

He had been one with these people in a way that he had never been among the Whites—for he had been a lonely boy, given to introversion and daydreams, *the weaving of fairy dust*, for which his father and his teachers had constantly found reason to correct him.

"Cattle and horses I understand completely, but I've never much cottoned to my fellow man...."

Whitmore Charley's words.

A wise old man, Nate thought, *however untrustworthy.* "Well, now..."

Charley was gone, and the Indians who had killed him would, within the span of a few years, also be gone.

But why could not the government of the United States, perceiving not only its own best interest but also the best interest of the Indians, its subject peoples, set aside the entire area about Mount Shasta as a great national park or wild domain? To the east of Shasta, Nate thought, there was no gold, and only the Pit River Valley and a few other, smaller valleys were capable of any kind of sustained agricultural production. The terrible winters, with temperatures plunging far below zero at times, the ridge upon ridge of volcanic debris, the accumulated outpourings of Mount Shasta and the great crater at the Medicine Lake, these and a hundred smaller cones and domes, the arid rimrock, and even the soil along the smaller streams shallow and poor. Land for grazing cattle, perhaps, and eventually, no doubt, there would be railroads for shipping both livestock and timber—but what was the need of this? The land stretched open and empty eastward to the dim reaches of Utah Territory.

Why could not a great wild park be established, a final refuge for the Redmen of America, on lands that were sacred to them but worthless to the Whites?

He pulled the Cayuse to a halt.

Across the undulating valley floor below him lay the little settlement of Cottonwood—and beyond that yet another twenty miles was Yreka.

Nate thought the matter over and concluded that he was not yet ready to enter into the bustle of the larger town. Perhaps the smaller village would provide him with a period of adjustment.

He turned his pony downslope.

He spent three days in an attempt to find an opening, some kind of work that would take him to the goldfields—but without any success whatsoever.

He rode on along the Klamath River—its name, his good friend had assured him, mispronounced by the Whites. He passed numerous Indian lodges, the dwellings of perhaps a thousand Redmen in all, Shastas and Modocs, apparently at peace with one another and with the world as well.

Evidence of prospecting—test holes, piles of rock heaped up, the hills seemingly barren of gold as the river dropped down into its canyon. And yet a few Whites were at work, not satisfied that their labors would be to no avail. In one hole, three Whitemen worked, twenty feet down and up to their waists in oozing mud. On the bluff above was a small group of Indians, gazing down, their expressions curious and puzzled.

But the river itself was running high from early rains, and perhaps even snows in the mountains of Oregon, whence it flowed. The water gleamed crystal clear under the blue autumn sky, and along its banks the willows and cottonwoods produced their own kind of gold—while in side ravines, along springs, the quaking aspens shimmered an autumn brilliance ranging from deep yellow to red-amber.

The Klamat, Nate thought. *The word means "generous." The river that is generous to the Indians, presenting them with an abundance of salmon.* From this the Klamat Indians had taken their name, these people, the warrior kings, hardly generous to their neighbors at all—and sometimes capturing children and women and selling them to tribes farther north. But Klamat, his friend—surely the word was properly applied in that case.

Nate rode on along the river, his buckskins discarded and now in Whiteman's dress. Perhaps the Indian clothing, he had concluded, was itself the reason he could not find work. He still had seven of the dollars he'd had in his pocket a year earlier—for, while with Charley, where could he have spent the money, even if he had wanted to? He had lost several of the coins during his stay with the Indians, and he had given a silver fifty-cent piece to Klamat as a token. But the money hadn't gone far: a pair of used boots that, by a stroke of good fortune, were just his size. The previous owner, he'd been advised, had been shot during a poker game, and at the funeral the boots had been missing, the work of someone who apparently bore the man ill will; red flannel underwear, a cambray shirt, some used trousers (previous owner not identified), and a hat that someone had found along the roadside and had sold to the storekeeper for twenty-five cents and that the storekeeper, in turn, had sold to Nate for thirty-five cents. The hat was too large, but he'd stuffed some scraps of rag behind the liner.

A final expense: ammunition for his pistol and rifle.

The coins he'd carried with him for the past year had been worn nearly smooth in his pockets. And now there were just two left—a half-dollar and a twenty-five-cent piece.

As Nate approached the river, he saw a tall, powerfully built man who wore top boots and had a red sash around his middle. The man's voice rang out, hailing the ferryman on the opposite bank of the Klamath, and the words carried a tone of certain confidence and authority. His hat was a black Oregon felt, and his hair, full and shoulder-length, was worn in Mexican fashion. His clothing as well was black, the shirt decorated with silver thread, and a pistol and holster swung at the man's side.

Nate was filled with admiration at the aspect and over-all appearance of the fellow, an obvious dandy, a refined and civilized gentleman, one whose demeanor and clothing spelled just one thing: *professional gambler.*

The clothing was expensive, and yet the gambler was afoot.

Nate drew up his pony and waited close by as the boatman poled his little flat across the river. He too was worth observing: bald, his face a mask of suspicion, a man in gum boots, duck breeches, and a faded blue shirt that was open at the front, revealing a powerful, hairy chest, and around his middle a belt made of rope.

Miller, of course, had intended to ride on toward Yreka, but now, on the spur of the moment, he decided to cross the river—to discover where the gambler might be heading. The man in black stepped aboard, and Nate led his pony onto the craft and stood, holding the reins as the riverman poled them across.

When the boat nudged sand, the gambler stepped ashore and said, "Chalk that."

The ferryman's face grew red as he tied up his craft. Then he turned to the gambler, who stood watching him.

"*Chalk,* hell! You figger me for a Chink? Gimme my two bits and be off."

"No tin, no dust," the gambler said. "Pay twice next time."

The tall man tapped the sand with his boot.

"I'll take the pistol until next time, then," the boatman said.

"See here, my man. When I crossed yesterday, I gave you twenty dollars—told you to use it for fare for anyone who hadn't the money. Now that I've lost my horse, you don't know me at all—is that it?"

"That's the way she be, all right."

"Then give me my change from yesterday—nineteen dollars and seventy-five cents, I believe. You do calculations, don't you?"

"It'll rain shit before that happens," the boatman said, scowling, and turning half-away.

At this point the gambler grasped hold of the ferryman, swung him around, thrust one hand into the man's side pocket, took out a handful of coins, counted out the specified amount, and returned the others—to the vehement protests of the boatman.

"And here's a quarter for the lad's fare, as long as we're at it!" The gambler laughed, tossing the coin onto the ground.

"Thank you, sir," Nate managed, totally surprised not only by what had happened but by the quickness of it.

"Goddamn thief! Bastard of a syphillitic whore!" the boatman called out—but he was already out on the water, away from harm's reach.

"You're welcome, my boy. I'm called The Prince, though the Prince is a bit short of capital just now."

He extended his hand.

"How do you do," Nate answered. "I'm Nate Miller— Cincinnatus Miller, actually."

The Prince grinned and nodded.

"So you've come to the goldfields to make your fortune, I take it?"

"Thought I'd give it a try, sir."

"No *sir* around here. You make me feel like an old man, Nate, and I'm not even thirty yet. When I hit thirty, then you can call me sir. How old are you, lad?"

"Nineteen."

"Well, I was younger than that when I struck out on my own. Where you from?"

The Prince rolled his jacket and tied it on behind the

Cayuse's saddle. The two walked along, Nate leading the horse.

After their initial exchange, Nate could think of nothing further to say, and The Prince seemed equally disinclined to talk. Instead he hummed a tune as they walked. They had proceeded perhaps half a mile when he asked, "Where you from, Nate?"

"Willamette Valley, originally. Been living with the Indians for a time."

"The Indians? What in hell were you doing that for?"

"Just worked out that way, is all."

"Here along the river?"

"No. With the Shastas, south of here. Was with them maybe ten months."

"And you expect me to believe that? You start lying, always be certain you've got a reason for doing it."

"God's truth," Miller said, his face burning. The man was toying with him, not listening at all.

Nate's earlier admiration for the tall, powerful man in the fancy clothing began to fade.

At this point they reached a fork in the trail, and saw coming down the uphill branch another man, riding a mule, his costume different and yet similar in kind to The Prince's. From his waist swung a pair of Colt's new-patent pistols, and around his neck was a gold chain composed of strung nuggets. The newcomer ignored Nate's presence but hailed The Prince as an old friend.

"By the great blue Jesus, it's Prince Hal hisself! Where's your mule, Prince? You haven't been afoot since the glaciers melted. Figger to steal this kid's horse or take it from him at cards?"

"Whiskey John," The Prince said, nodding. "Out of tin, out of dust. Been riding a bad string."

"So Prince Hal went over to Cottonwood and got cleaned out—should have stayed in Yreka. We were glad you went, though—you're too damned much competition. Son," he continued, speaking to Nate for the first time, "never play cards with this man. Give him a shell game, and he'll take the devil's own pocket watch. So The Prince's luck run out? How'd she happen? That little hole full of card thieves?"

"Luck just went sour," The Prince said, not seeming particularly concerned by it.

"You're really busted?"

"Flat."

The Prince tapped the dust with the toe of his boot.

"Tell me what happened, Prince. I'm on my way to Cottonwood. If they's something to watch out for, tell me about 'er. No sense both of us gettin' skinned."

"It's a sad story," The Prince said. "Sure you want to hear it?"

"What'd you go through on?"

"Four aces."

"Truth, now, truth. If you've got four devils, what's the other coon got?"

"A pair."

"Truth, truth. How'd you get cinched? You really had four aces?"

"Best I could bring out of my sleeve at the moment."

"And he had a pair? Pair of what?"

"Colts, just like the ones you're wearing."

"They play that way in Cottonwood, eh?"

"More to it than that," The Prince said. "Seems like my sixth card showed under. Arthritis and old age, I guess. So I got caught cheating, just like a greenhorn kid, and the boys had the idea that I should leave them my horse and gear if I didn't want to swing. Hell, Whiskey John, none of us ever cared much for swinging. So The Prince is not only flat busted, but on foot as well."

Whiskey John laughed, got back on his mule, put his feet solidly in the stirrups, reached for his bottle of whiskey, took a pull, and handed the container to The Prince, who also drank—then offered it to Nate.

"No, thanks. Manzanita cider, maybe, but nothing else."

"What the hell's *manzanita cider?*" Whiskey John snorted.

"My friend's been living among the Indians," The Prince said.

"Great gamblers, the Injuns. No good at cards, but don't play the stick game with 'em. Look here, Prince, you really bust?"

"Not quite. The boatman gave me some change."

"Enough for a stake?"

"Thinking about going straight. Honest work will do me good, John."

Whiskey John pulled out a handful of twenties and, without bothering to count them, thrust them toward The Prince.

"Take 'em. A friend's loan, if nothing else. We may be in it head to head some night, and I'll need you to bail my ass out."

The Prince nodded, John nodded, and the mule, as if deciding that the idle talk had lasted long enough, set off down the trail to where the Eternal Boatman waited for his next customer.

The Prince had indeed decided to go straight, and he and Nate resolved to become partners. They would stake out a likely-looking claim, put up a small cabin, and settle in for the winter.

"As a card man," The Prince said, "I've made fortunes, yes, but I've never hung on to a thing—and you can see what a pass I've come to now. My string's run out, and I'm on dole to Whiskey John Boston. Guess it's time I tried a new line of work. Now you're down on your luck too, as I take it. I figure we'd make a likely pair, if you're willing to throw in with me."

Nate didn't wish to seem too eager, but nevertheless he said *yes* quickly enough. His unqualified admiration for the man had returned, and now he began to see that The Prince was, in fact, a more complicated individual than he had earlier supposed.

The two of them, with Nate leading the pony, continued on toward The Forks, a newly opened mining area downstream on the Klamath River, and arrived just at sunset.

As they gazed down on the mining camp from a crest in the trail, The Prince said, "That's the place for us, Nate. These towns spring up overnight and often vanish as quickly. A hundred or so years from now, some professor from Yale or Harvard will be digging around and find the rusted remains of that fancy rifle of yours—and start trying to piece the story together for the entertainment of proper easterners. And maybe our bones will be down there too, mixed in with a lot of others. But the town won't last—they never do. It's just eight years since Sutter's man discovered gold, and already a hundred towns have sprung up and vanished."

"Some will last," Nate said.

"Yreka, maybe, and Shasta City—and the valley towns, where there's water to grow things with. But that doesn't concern us, either. When it's all said and done, who the hell will ever remember either one of us? A gambler down on his luck and a fella who's been off living with the Injuns and is dead already, as far as anyone knows. Just two guys that starved to death while working a useless claim."

"Prince, we're going to strike it rich, I tell you. If a man just watches and listens carefully, he'll be all right. A man named Whitmore Charley told me that."

"Charley, eh? The old thief that runs cows? I haven't seen him about in a year or so. Where'd you run into him?"

"I worked for him last year—went down to the Los Angeles Pueblo with him."

"You been a cow runner, too? Where is old Charles?"

"Dead. The Modocs attacked our camp, and I was lucky enough to get off into the forest. That's how I ended up with the Shastas."

"Dead, eh? *Requiscat in pace*. So maybe Whitmore Charley didn't look and listen close enough himself. What's his advice worth now?"

"The advice was good," Nate insisted. "Just that his luck ran out, like yours did."

"So that's the goddess we have to court, then? Lady Luck. Well, she's found someone new to bed 'er, and she's left The Prince high and dry. Guess maybe I should have sent flowers more often. . . ."

Nate laughed.

"I guess a man has to make his own luck, Prince. And we've got good luck coming."

"Keep saying that, Nate. Like any kind of gambling, a man's got to believe in himself. If we want the gold bad enough, maybe we'll find it. Right now there's a town down below, and it's time for us to attack. Think of it, Nate. Maybe three thousand people down there, and not a woman or child, likely as not. Oh, an Indian squaw or two, perhaps, that have hitched up with miners."

"Not much chance for a love affair, then," Nate concluded.

"Afraid not. He who consents to descend with me into this deep, dark gorge in the mountains, and live the weary winter through, will see neither the light of the sun nor the smiles of women. A sort of Hades. A savage Eden, with many Adams walking up and down, and plucking of every tree—nothing forbidden here, for there are neither the laws of God nor the laws of man. But, damn it, no women!"

Nate grinned.

"Beautiful, the way you said that. You're not only a gambler and a prince, but a poet as well."

"One of my many talents, Nate. Shall we amble on down?"

The Forks consisted of a carelessly laid-out assemblage of framed tents and rough-hewn, half-finished shanties strewn along a high shelf of land above the river. In addition, there were a general store, two butcher shops (each, in fact, sending out two mules each day, laden with meat, and leaving as much at each claim as had been ordered—an essential matter, for meat was the one provision that the miners could depend on, the one thing that could be procured locally, by men employed as hunters), and three taverns, the principal of which was called Howlin' Wilderness—a huge cabin built of pine logs, its walls higher than the roofs of most of the cabins, an earth floor, and a great stone fireplace, where a fire roared night and day.

It was to this latter that The Prince and Nate Miller made their way.

The Howlin' Wilderness was a sort of community center for The Forks. It gathered a larger crowd than the other taverns and always had a bigger fire inside. Further, all the important fights took place here—and here the news of the outside world was passed on. The proprietors, standing behind the bar, had piled up bags of sand so as to construct a bulletproof wall within the counter. Should shooting start, a not altogether uncommon occurrence, with the customers fleeing through the door, turning the monte tables and benches on their sides for protection against the flying lead, the owners had only to crouch behind the sandbags, pistols in hand, and wait for the fun to cease.

The Prince, in his capacity as cardsharp, had been here on several previous occasions—and, as a result, was well known both by the owners of the Howlin' Wilderness and by many of the patrons as well.

Nate and The Prince went directly to the bar, and The

Prince ordered two shot glasses of whiskey. Nate was about to object—but it was necessary, he realized, to seem like *one of the boys*.

The Prince raised his glass in a toast, and Nate did likewise.

"Here's to the partnership!" The Prince laughed, draining his glass in a swallow.

"Here's to good luck," Nate echoed, and attempted to do as The Prince had done. The whiskey took him by surprise, burning its way down his throat. He struggled to suppress a spasm of coughing, gritted his teeth, and closed his eyes.

"Take it easy if you aren't used to the brew, Nate," The Prince said in a low voice. "Don't go showing off. Just sip the stuff. Try another?"

"Don't mind if I do," Nate answered, squinting through watery eyes.

"Come to steal a little money, Prince?" one of the owners asked, refilling their glasses.

"An honest game of cards, perhaps," The Prince replied. "But tonight's my last. The Prince and Nate Miller here have entered into a grand partnership. By this time tomorrow we'll be staking our claim. After that I'm just one of your basic, hard-working miners. Give us a year, and we'll be owners and operators of Consolidated Mining, Incorporated, chief owners of the city called The Forks, and mortgage holders for the Howlin' Wilderness. You're looking at your future landlords, my friend."

"Damned right," Nate added, lifting his second drink.

"In a pig's ass," the bartender said, wiping half-consciously at the waxed surface of the stained-oak counter.

"You really going to play cards tonight?" Nate asked The Prince.

"We need a grubstake, and Whiskey John's money won't last very long; dried apples, salt, flour, bacon—everything here costs twice the prices in Yreka, and that's already two or three times what things cost in civilization. A man's got to do what he knows how to do best, even if he is starting up a new kind of life. Tonight's the last time, Nate, I give you my word on it. And an honest game it'll be, too. As I have reason to believe, the other kind doesn't always pay off. If the bitch goddess of luck is with me, come closing time we'll be set to go."

"Thought you said the Howlin' Wilderness never closed?"

"Speaking metaphorically, Nate, speaking metaphorically. You just watch, now. This card thief feels a strong run coming."

The night wore on, and The Prince found customers willing enough. For a time Nate watched closely, deeply impressed by the obvious skill and certain assurance with which his new partner operated. The Prince kept up a running monologue of casual pleasantries and stories of this and that, all the while that his sharp, brown eyes were intently studying his opponents' faces, fixing on the discards, and occasionally sipping at his drink, but no more. For a time things seemed even enough, The Prince's stack of coins now diminishing, now increasing in height. The other cardplayers, intent upon "taking" this man whose reputation they apparently knew well, drank heavily.

And the game continued, seven-card draw with no joker.

As the result of one long and studied hand, The Prince's hoard increased threefold. He now had numerous nuggets and a quantity of gold dust.

Nate saw clearly enough, or supposed that he did, what the eventual outcome would be—and ceased to pay close attention.

Perhaps, after all, the newly formed partnership would die a-borning, now that The Prince had persuaded Lady Luck to return to his bed. If so, Nate thought, he would go back to his original plan—find some sort of work, get together a grubstake of his own, and stake a claim. Perhaps he could hire on as a hunter for one of the butcher shops. In any case, with an adequate supply of lead and powder, he wasn't going to starve to death—not if there was game available. Beyond that he'd need—what? Pick, shovel, pan, a hammer, and some canvas and nails to frame together a tent for shelter. He could dig out a hole and log up the sides, like a lodge of the Shastas. He'd need an ax—yes—and a new skinning knife, one with a heavy enough blade so that he could use it as a draw knife for squaring the edges of his logs. . . .

He listened to the ebb and flow of conversation and argument among the patrons of the Howlin' Wilderness. He stood before the big stone fireplace, warmed himself, and tried to take it all in.

A Chinaman, wearing a strange little hat, and a red-faced

old miner, a greasy man with a green patch over his left eye, his checked shirt yellow with mud stains and one of his suspender bands missing—the two of them in heated discussion.

"Ought to run ye slant-eyed leetle bastards out of the mountains, that's what. Cheatin', thievin' leetle pigs is what ye be," the miner said.

For a moment Nate supposed that one or the other would go for a knife or a pistol, but within moments the two men were clapping each other on the back, laughing, and drinking once more.

The big room was decorated with cheap prints in bright colors—bulldogs, race horses, prizefighters. At one end of the room was apparently the work of a local artist, judging from the amateur nature of the rendering. It was painted on a wide piece of planking, half the size of the door. The picture was of a bull, a huge, black beast with enormous yellow eyes, staring straight ahead toward the customers. A bullfighting scene, decorated with plumed lances and strings of large-petaled blossoms. Irregularly printed below the painting were the words THE MEXICAN BULL.

The real showpiece of the Howlin' Wilderness, however, occupied the wall behind the counter, a painting of a grizzly bear and a hunter—the very hunter who had also painted the picture, as Nate learned. The picture showed the hunter in the huge bear's embrace, the man thrusting an enormous knife into the creature's heart. The blade, as broad as a handsaw, was dripping blood. The grizzly's forelegs were disproportionately long and large, so that the total impression was that of a creature of immense power, emphasis on that portion of the bear's anatomy with which the hunter himself and the viewer of the painting as well would be most concerned. Nate thought over this matter of artistic proportion and concluded that the rendering was, indeed, a work of genius.

The bear's jaws were open wide, the fangs poised, timeless, motionless, close to the hunter's head.

Another instant and . . .

Nate stared at the painting for a long while, but the bear's head never moved, the jaws never closed. The hunter, as well, remained strangely motionless, as if frozen in death. Nate realized that the painting could not be very old, and yet its full impression was that of some heroic time long since past, an age already vanished.

From one corner of the painting hung a brace of Indian scalps, the long, matted hair trailing over the ears of the bear and the red, open mouth with its massive white fangs.

Some sheaves of arrows in ornate quivers were affixed to the wall on the right side of the painting, and to the left were a tomahawk, a scalping knife, a boomerang, and a war club.

In front of the painting and other artifacts, the two proprietors, as if unaware of the frozen drama being played out behind them, continued to fill tumblers and shot glasses and to wipe white cloths over the dark surface of the bar.

Nate finally fell asleep in the chair he had taken. But when he heard The Prince's voice close by, he woke with a start.

The Prince was grinning from ear to ear.

"Come on, Nate old partner," he said. "It's closing time, and we've got our damned grubstake. Let's get some sleep, and tomorrow we'll find us that gold."

▲

FIVE

In Search of Poonkina

Mountain Smoke, the Achomawi medicine woman, told this story, and this is what she said:

It was the time of the first people, and they wished to build a path to the Spirit World so that when they grew old and blind, they could go there and become young again and then return to the lands near Spirit Mountain. Vulture was helping them to build.

Old Man Coyote came along and told them it was too hot to work, but they told him to go away. "Too hot! Too hot!" he sang over and over, so finally the people sat down in the shade.

Then Old Man said, "I like having people get old and die. Then the others can go to buryings and cry. It is good."

But the people did not agree.

Coyote said, "You probably wish the snow could be salmon flour and the acorns could have no shells. But boys and girls like to shell them and throw the husks at one another. And snow must be cold so that when people go hunting in it they will die. It is better as it is."

Vulture said, "Old Man Coyote only loves death. He is no friend to the people."

"That is wrong," Old Man replied. "It is I who save the people. And it is because I love life that I honor death. Death is what gives life its meaning, but Vulture does not see that."

The people looked at one another. Then Old Man Coyote disappeared, and the people covered over the path they had begun.

After Nate's departure from the village, Klamat grew ever more moody and distant. No longer did he wish to join Heron and Crippled Deer on hunting ventures. And though

he was aware that several of the girls who would soon become
women appeared interested in him and at times followed him
about in an open and almost shameful manner, he was not
interested in any of them. One woman alone possessed his
thoughts, and that was Warrottetot's eldest daughter, Poonkina,
whom the chief had apparently left to live permanently with
the Scott River Shastas, Chief Slippery Salmon's group.

Klamat had asked Warrottetot about Poonkina and had
been led to believe that she had wished to visit her relatives
in Slippery Salmon's village. And Warrottetot, reading the
concern in Klamat's face, repeated what he had said earlier,
at the time when Klamat and Poonkina had attempted to flee
the village after the ritual of her becoming a woman.

"I will not order my daughter to marry anyone she does
not wish to marry, Klamat. But she is the daughter of a
powerful chief, and her bride price will be very high, as
befits her station. Have you now accumulated many ponies
and weapons and dentalia and woodpecker scalps so that you
may ask for her hand in the proper way? If that is true, then I
will discuss the matter with you. I bear you no ill will,
Klamat. I wish you to understand that."

And Klamat had turned away without speaking, his eyes
cast down, and had ridden off by himself for several days.

Surely Poonkina would soon grow tired of visiting her
relatives, Klamat had thought. Surely she would soon return
home.

But the days and weeks and months had passed, and no
one in the village seemed to have any idea when the chief's
daughter might return.

The loneliness Klamat felt was eased by the company of his
White friend, Nate Miller. But then Nate too had left, had
gone away to join the men who dug holes in the earth in the
attempt to find the yellow metal—the soft, worthless metal
that could be found easily enough in the sands of Numken
Creek, should anyone wish to do so. Klamat had considered
telling Nate about this gold, thereby enticing him to stay
among the Shastas. But two winters earlier Warrottetot had
warned his people of the trouble that was almost certain to
come if the Whitemen discovered what lay hidden in the
sands of the Numken. And so Klamat, tempted though he
was, had told his friend nothing.

But if the Whites deemed the worthless metal valuable and dug and fought and even killed one another to get it, then obviously it wasn't worthless at all. What real value, after all, had beads or woodpecker scalps or clam shells? In themselves, no value—and yet they might be used to purchase things that did have value, like horses and weapons, for instance.

Klamat even considered gathering as much of the gold along the Numken as he could find and riding away to the villages of the Whites.

Perhaps I could buy a rifle like Nate's, he thought. *And men like the white-haired one the Modocs killed, Charley— such men have horses for sale. Others have pistols and rifles....*

But would the Whites sell any of these things to an Indian? And since he had no idea how much the gold was worth to the Whites, he would have no idea how to go about trading for those things he wished to buy.

When all was considered, it was better to leave the gold alone, just as Warrottetot had said. If an Achomawi had gold, then the Whitemen would certainly come looking for it—they would find their way into the lands of the Shastas, and after that everything would be different.

As it was, the gold seekers did not come into the lands to the south and east and north of the Great Mountain, for it was believed that no gold could be found among the beds of lava.

But the rocks along Numken were different—beds of sand and gravel along the stream, and in that place only.

Nate had been gone for nearly a month now, and the season was approaching *Kapchelam*, the moon of the first snows. Still Klamat felt listless and melancholy.

Heron was concerned about his friend—concerned that he might take it into his head simply to wander away into a snowstorm when the winter came on or climb up the taboo slopes of the Great Mountain and lie exposed on the ice until life had left his body and his soul had begun its journey across the wide band of stars to the Spirit World.

It was not merely the departure of the White boy, Nate, that caused Klamat to wander about like one of the living dead people—so Heron surmised. No, the much more probable cause was what had happened earlier—when the chief had taken his daughter Poonkina to the Scott River village.

Heron sought out White Dawn and was able, with repeated vows of absolute secrecy, to get her to confide in him about what had happened on the night of the conclusion of the *waphi*.

"I would climb to the top of the mountain and jump down into the hole where the fires are before I would speak a word to anyone," Heron insisted.

"Oh, you would tell Klamat, and then he would demand to know how you found out. In a little while the rumor would be on everyone's tongue. Poonkina would be dishonored, and my father would be very angry with me."

"I will never help you dig camas again if you will not tell me, White Dawn. And I will tell all the young men that you said lying down with a man is disgusting."

White Dawn, normally the subdued one, broke suddenly into a fit of hysterical laughing. She wiped at her eyes and attempted to regain her composure.

"You would never do that," she said at last, "because you know it is not true. Do you believe the other women like lying with a lover more than I do? Tell me the truth, Heron. Did I disappoint you the time when we... ?"

He touched her face with his fingertips before answering.

"No," he said. "Of course not. But listen to me, White Dawn. My friend Klamat is in trouble, and I think it is because of your sister. Warrottetot took her away and left her with Slippery Salmon's people so that she would not be near Klamat. Am I right?"

"That is what some of the women are saying," White Dawn answered.

"It is true, then?"

White Dawn looked into Heron's eyes but made no gesture.

"Klamat has said nothing, not even to you?" she asked.

"He has said nothing. Whatever happened, he has held his tongue ever since. They tried to run away that night, didn't they?"

White Dawn did not answer the question directly but said only, "My father has told Klamat that he must not think of

marrying Poonkina because he is poor. He could never raise
the kind of bride price my father will ask. But he will not ask
so much for me, Heron, because I am the younger sister."

"Tell me what has happened between them, White Dawn,
so that I may help my friend."

"Will you swear before the Earth Spirits to hold your
tongue once I have told you what I know? Will you do this,
Heron?"

"I swear to Old Man Coyote and to Grizzly Bear and to
Bluejay and to Raven. I do not wish to tell stories like a
gossiping old woman. I wish only to help my friend."

"Do you love Klamat?" White Dawn asked.

"Of course. He is as a brother to me."

"Then I will tell you. But first you must know that if it is
the love sickness he suffers from, then there is no help for it.
My father will never give Poonkina to him. Besides, perhaps
she has already chosen a mate from among Slippery Salmon's
warriors. That is why Warrottetot sent her there. Now I will
tell you all that I know of what happened on the *waphi* night,
even though you have already figured it all out...."

Heron listened with great interest, embraced White Dawn,
and proceeded directly to Klamat's makeshift elkhide lodge.

"No longer will you act badly toward your friend!" Heron
exclaimed. "Do you think you can continue to pretend to
hate me when that is not how you feel? I think you are
lovesick for the chief's daughter and are halfway to the Spirit
World because you think you cannot have her. Tell me if this
is true or not. Klamat, there are many women in the world,
for Old Man Coyote brings in a new crop of them every year,
just as he does the acorns and the camas and the grass itself.
Now listen. Do you remember my cousin who lives with the
Atsugewis? He has told me of two sisters, twins—they look
just alike and both are very good to gaze upon. When we
were last among those people, one of the twins followed you
everywhere. She wished you to go to the willows with her,
and yet you ignored her. The other twin followed me, but I
did not ignore her. No, I was very friendly toward her. Now
this is what I think...."

"Heron," Klamat frowned, "you are babbling like an old
woman whose teeth are coming loose from chewing upon too

many pieces of deerhide. Is this your way of trying to cheer
me up?"

Heron grinned, almost splitting his face in two.

"It's just that I have been thinking of those twin girls ever
since," he said. "We could lie down with them and then walk
away and they could change places or not, and neither of us
would ever know the difference. I believe this is a game we
should play."

"Go visit the Atsugewis?"

"Of course. It is almost *Kapchelam* and after that it is
Kapcha, and the snows will be deep and it will be too cold to
lie down with any woman outside the lodge, and we will have
to wait for *T-hopo* when we go to harvest the wokas. And on
the way to Pit River we can hunt for deer and elk and
antelope, just as we have always done, ever since we were
young boys."

"So what it really is is this—Heron wishes Klamat to go
hunting with him."

"My friend is coming back to life now," Heron said, laughing. "He is very perceptive when he is alive."

Klamat stood up, turned about, and took his bow and
quiver of arrows down from their pegs.

"The twins?" he asked. "Which one was following me?"

"How could one tell?" Heron asked in return.

Crippled Deer rode with them, but they did not journey
toward the valley of the Pit River. Instead they traveled
north, close by Medicine Mountain and the summer village,
deserted now in the time of leaves-falling. Then they turned
northwestward, along the flat-backed mountains beyond Shasta,
hunting as they went. And by the time they made camp at
Grass Lake, its shallow, reed-filled waters nestled in a swale
atop the range, the pack animals were already laden with
venison and wapiti meat.

Close by the lake's edge the three of them prepared drying
racks and upon these placed thin slabs of meat. Storm clouds
were beginning to move in, and the crown of Shasta, gleaming
a soft violet by sundown, would soon be hidden from sight.
In good weather the making of jerky was best accomplished
in direct sunlight, but when the weather turned toward
winter, the only recourse was a great bed of juniper coals,

with the strips of meat suspended at shoulder's height above
them.

"Warrottetot will be pleased to see us when we return,"
Crippled Deer said. "Soon the snows will come, and the
dried meat will be very good to have."

The heaps of juniper burned down quickly, and the three
young warriors stood about the fire, contemplating their
work.

"We are far more fortunate than Slippery Salmon's people,"
Heron mused aloud. "It is usually easy for us to take game,
for there are many animal people in our lands. But in the
valley where those people live, and along the River of the
Klamats, I have heard that there are many Whitemen digging
for gold. And those men shoot everything that moves, so
there is no game left for our cousins. And they work endlessly
to pour mud into the river, so that the salmon can no longer
find their way up it. Why do you think they do this, Klamat?
Did Nate Miller ever explain that to you?"

"No, he never said. Or at least I could not understand what
he was saying. I do not think the Whitemen themselves know
why they work so hard to dig holes all over. It is a mystery."

The thought of Poonkina among Slippery Salmon's people
leaped into Heron's mind, and he attempted to change the
subject.

"We are very close to the Modoc lands now," he said.
"Have you ever wondered if your mother and father may still
be alive? Perhaps we should go there and try to find them
before we go back to our own village. Would you like to do
that, Klamat?"

"That life is long past," Klamat said simply. "I am an
Achomawi now. I would not wish to go back to being a
Modoc. I was very small when the Klamats stole me. My
mother and father have long since supposed me dead. For
them, I have been dead for fifteen years. It is better that
things remain as they are."

"I think the coals are ready now," Crippled Deer suggested,
poking at the fire pit with a long staff of mahogany wood.

Klamat nodded and chuckled to himself as he began to
place strips of meat onto the curing rack.

"Did you think it was Old Man Coyote who brought us

here?" he asked no one in particular, and then began to whistle absently.

I am one with these people, and yet I am forever an out-sider to them, a man with no family, Modoc or Klamat, it makes no difference. They love me, and yet I am different— and for that reason I cannot be guided by the wishes of their chief. Yet Warrottetot has a great black beard, like one of the Whites, not like an Indian. Did a White trapper, years ago, find his way into the village and father him? No—one of the Spanish who had come up from the Great Valley and took a wife and got a child and then left. . . . Warrottetot is also an outsider, and secretly he knows it. And yet he has become the head chief. He could not have done that by simply accepting his fate as one whose blood was not true. No, he achieved reputation in battle against the Modocs and the Klamats— that is how he became powerful. His mind, his will, is not more powerful than my own. What he achieved, I can achieve also. And I will do it because I am able to do it and because that is the only way Little Grouse can be mine. . . .

"What if she has already married?" he said aloud.

"I do not understand you," Heron answered. "Do you speak of one of the twins who live with the Atsugewis or . . . ?"

"Oh," Klamat said, startled from his reverie, "yes—one of those. We must go there soon, Heron. It is time for both of us to take a wife. We will build huge lodges and have many children."

Crippled Deer let out a whoop, and off across the shallow, reedy waters of Grass Lake, a loon cried out.

But already Klamat knew that he would not return to Warrottetot's village with his two friends—indeed, he had known it all along. And that was why, even if it had not been his conscious purpose, he had led his two friends northward on their hunting expedition.

From where he now stood, it was but a two-day ride due west, across the dry valley with hills on its bottom and over one rim of mountains to the big, flat valley where the small White village of Fort Jones stood. Gold miners were there, as he knew, and a mill where pines were taken from the forest and cut into planks, and a few who built houses and fenced portions of the valley and raised cattle, animals just like the ones Whitmore Charley had been herding along—creatures that were slaughtered and their meat sold to the men who dug holes everywhere.

Beyond Fort Jones, to the north and west, where the river flowed down into its long canyon on its way to join the Klamat River, so he concluded, would be the small villages of Chief Slippery Salmon. And in one of those he would find Poonkina.

Poonkina had taken up life with Slippery Salmon's Nomki-dji Shastas not of her own choosing but because Warrottetot insisted on it. And the reason, she knew well enough, was simply that her father wished to put her as far from Klamat as possible. Among the Nomki-dji, she would be respected as the daughter of a powerful ally; and a man of some wealth and consequence, so the chief reasoned, would soon begin to pay court to her. At some point or another, the strong-willed girl would come to realize her own best interest, and a small delegation would be sent to Warrottetot to negotiate a bride price. And that was the way it would be.

But Poonkina well understood her father's designs, and though she put up no great obvious resistance, she had already made up her mind. Klamat was the one she would have, and the way to get him was to be as patient with her father as possible. If it was necessary for a year or more to pass, then she was willing to wait.

All this she confided to White Dawn during the journey to Scott River. The younger sister listened, was sympathetic, but believed it would do no good.

"You think foolish thoughts," White Dawn had said. "Marry one of the village chiefs, for in that way you will have a good, warm lodge to raise your children in. Now that you are away from him, Klamat will find another to love, for that is the way men are."

"Klamat is not that way," Poonkina had insisted.

Then her father and her sister had gone, returned to their own lands, and she had taken up residence with an aunt and an uncle, Red Fawn and her husband, a man who preferred to be called by the name the Whites in Fort Jones had given him—Tommyrotter. When she had asked her uncle what the name meant, he would tell her only that it indicated the great respect the Whites had for him. Indeed, Poonkina came to believe that it must be so, for her uncle sometimes worked for the Whites at the board mill, and he had acquired Whiteman's clothing, and wore this rather than the usual Nomki-dji costume most of the time.

Among his own people, Tommyrotter was deemed quite wealthy, not because he owned many horses but because he often had Whiteman's money to spend. The man was not good to his own wife, however, and sometimes he would return late from Fort Jones, crazy from drinking whiskey. And at such times he would slap Red Fawn about and tear off her clothing, sometimes ordering Poonkina from the lodge before he coupled with her and sometimes laughing and ordering Poonkina to sit by and watch. It was good for her to learn, he told her.

Once, Tommyrotter, unable to make love to Red Fawn because he had drunk too much, demanded that Poonkina should assist him by means of taking him into her mouth. She refused and cursed at him, using the same Whiteman's words that she had learned from him in the first place. Then he stumbled across the room toward her, and she drew the slim-bladed skinning knife she kept in the hem of her deer-skin dress and held it out in front of her.

Red Fawn began to scream and moan, and Tommyrotter laughed and lunged at Poonkina. She stepped deftly aside, however, and jabbed the blade into the side of his leg.

Tommyrotter fell to the earthen floor of the lodge and acted as though he had received a mortal wound. Red Fawn was at his side immediately, binding the wound while Tommyrotter cursed at Poonkina and insisted there was not a man among the Nomki-dji who would wish to sleep with her after he had made known what had just happened. Then he told her she would have to go live with someone else, daughter to old Warrottetot or not.

"By sunset tomorrow," he raged, "you will be out of my lodge. Go sleep among the boulders by the river, you whorebitch. Perhaps a grizzly or one of the wild men of the forest will come to you and stick his thing into you. You are no good to anyone the way you are now, you pissing-dog-that-squats."

Within a few moments, his leg bandaged but bedaubed by his own blood, Tommyrotter fell soundly asleep.

In the morning he rode off early to work at the mill, and Poonkina and Red Fawn were quiet together inside the lodge. Poonkina resolutely packed her things, but Red Fawn insisted over and over that she must not leave—that Warrottetot had entrusted her safety to her and that she would be dishonored in failing her brother-in-law.

But at noon Slippery Salmon himself appeared at the lodge entryway, his eyes somber and his facial muscles set.

"The man called Tommyrotter has been killed," the chief said. "He was shot by a Whiteman, one of those who works at the mill. I am not certain what happened, but apparently Tommyrotter started a fight, and the other killed him. You must be strong, Red Fawn, for there is nothing we can do about it. I do not wish you to scar yourself with a knife or cut off any fingers. Listen to me now, Red Fawn. You two were not happy together, and it is good that you had no children. Your husband wanted to be a Whiteman, I think. He preferred the Whites to his own people, and now they have killed him. There is nothing that we can do about it. The other men did not like Tommyrotter and are unwilling to go on a revenge-taking against the Whites. It grieves me to tell you these things, Red Fawn. Now I am ordering everyone to leave this village behind. It was a good place for many years, but now we are too close to the Whitemen. Tomorrow morning we will go down the river to look for another site. Perhaps we will go over to the Klamat River, for there are several village sites that have not been used in years. I think game will be more plentiful over there. Poonkina, stay with your aunt. Do not allow her to harm herself."

For a long moment Red Fawn's face remained set, impassive. And she said nothing.

When she spoke at last, she asked simply, "Where is Tommyrotter's body so that I can bury him?"

"His White friends have already buried him," Slippery Salmon answered.

The small band of Nomki-dji Shastas moved away from the Scott River Valley now and down into the canyon. They did not hurry, for the good months of summer and autumn were ahead of them—now camping here, now there, and fishing as they could when the waters of the river were not fouled because of the small-scale dredging operations upstream, in the valley beyond Fort Jones, and taking what game they could, though it was observed that most of the animal people had apparently disappeared.

"The Whitemen shoot too many of them," Red Fawn said. "Then the deer and the elk grow frightened because of the noise of the guns, and our hunters find it difficult to get close enough with their bows and arrows to make a kill. Perhaps it will be better on the Klamat River, Poonkina."

"Klamat is a fine name," Poonkina remarked.

"The name is good," Red Fawn agreed, "but the people for whom it is named are not good. They prefer war to peace, and sometimes they steal children."

"That is true. There is a young man among my father's people who was stolen by the Klamats. Now that is his name."

"Pretty One," Red Fawn said, "I have heard you speak his name in your sleep. But I did not understand he was someone from your own group. Perhaps he came to live among your people after Warrottetot's brother who is dead asked me to be his wife. He was a good man, Poonkina. He was not at all like Tommyrotter. I do not speak his name, out of honor for the dead, but sometimes he is still in my dreams, still trying to look out for me. I do not mind mentioning Tommyrotter's name because I do not think he has gone to the Spirit World at all. I think he is with the dead Whitemen, wherever they go."

Poonkina nodded and was uncertain what to say to her aunt.

"Will you take another husband one day, Red Fawn?" she asked at length.

Red Fawn smiled—the smile of sadness.

"Do you think another man would want to have me? I am not old yet, but I have had no children. I think I must be like a barren doe. See? Already I have begun to grow fat. But maybe by springtime I will be skinny again, like you, Poonkina. Last night I dreamed that the snows were deep and the men could not find food. The salmon had not come up the river, and the deer had all gone away. There are acorns to gather and camas roots and wild cherries and plums and manzanita berries and pine nuts. These things are still here, for the

Whitemen do not touch them. But they will not provide enough for everyone to eat."

"The salmon will have no trouble finding the river, for the water is often brown with mud from the mining."

"The fish people will know where the rivers are, but they will not swim up them, I think. I am afraid of what may happen this winter, Poonkina. It would be better for you to return to your father's people, to lands where there are no Whitemen."

The summer wore on, and for a time the band of Nomki-djis joined their relatives in the large village that stood near the confluence of the Scott River and the Klamath. But with the mining towns of Scott Bar, Hamburg, and Horse Creek all fairly close by, game was even more scarce than it had been farther up the river. Those in the village would say nothing, for Slippery Salmon was considered their head chief as well, and he kept a permanent lodge there for one of his wives and several of his children.

But when the time of acorn gathering was past, the residents of the larger village grew somewhat less enthusiastic and friendly, and Slippery Salmon, realizing the nature of the problem well enough, led the smaller band upriver along the Klamath, establishing a village at one of the old sites, half a day's ride to the east.

Men from the larger village, now suddenly friendly and helpful once more, assisted in the move and helped to construct new lodges over the old dugouts. And so, well before the onset of the cold weather, the dwellings were completed, and life in the new encampment was begun.

Red Fawn and Poonkina now shared a house with two women whose men had died several years before, and with the women were a total of seven children of varying ages.

A young man named Fire-on-the hills, as well as several older men who were far wealthier but who were already married, had taken a shine to Poonkina. He was partially crippled from an accident that had occurred while netting salmon two years earlier, and he walked with a limp. But he was an industrious young man, one who had his own lodge and a herd of more than a dozen ponies as well. As all in the village were aware, Fire-on-the-hills had decided it was time to take a wife.

Often he came to the lodge where the women lived and helped out in whatever way he could. And when he was able to kill a deer or even some rabbits or squirrels, he would bring the best portions to the women's lodge. Red Fawn and the two women with children smiled at one another and were exceptionally pleasant toward Fire-on-the-hills, while Poonkina seemed content to acknowledge his presence and otherwise to ignore him.

And Fire-on-the-hills, for his own part, rarely was able to summon the courage to address Poonkina directly.

On the first morning when hoarfrost formed on the door-ways to the lodges, however, and thin ice appeared on standing puddles of water, the people of the little village observed Fire-on-the-hills and Poonkina walking closely to-gether along the well-worn trail beside the muddy, sluggish Klamath River. Word of the liaison spread quickly, and soon everyone was talking about it. Even Slippery Salmon, who had come to visit his upriver wife, nodded when she told him what she had heard.

"I do not think young Fire-on-the-hills is the husband that Warrottetot was hoping his daughter would find," the chief said.

"Well, many of the other men are interested also. You would be, too, I think, if you didn't already have two wives. Isn't that so, my husband?"

Slippery Salmon pressed his fists together and cracked his knuckles.

"Wife," he said, "many say that Poonkina is a very lovely young woman, but she is also very thin. What would I do with a wife that skinny? We have not been able to catch many salmon this year, and the deer have all been killed already or have run away. It is the same downriver. If bad storms come and everything freezes so that we cannot get up into the mountains to hunt, then everyone will go hungry. And a girl as thin as Poonkina will be the first to starve to death because she has no fat on her bones at all. Taking on another wife would be a terrible responsibility."

"But you would like to lie down with her, wouldn't you?"

Slippery Salmon laughed.

"I am the chief of my people, woman. I do not have time to entertain such thoughts."

Climbing Honeysuckle, the upstream wife, continued to ply her prized steel needle through the leather she was working on—a new pair of moccasins for her husband.

"Well," she said, "I think Fire-on-the-hills is a good young man, even if he does limp badly. He has bought a rifle from the Whites at Scott Bar, so he will have an advantage when it comes to hunting. It would be good if all our men had such weapons, I think. And also he has more horses than even the chief."

Slippery Salmon snorted and then laughed.

"That is true, Honeysuckle. But he won't have so many after he's paid Warrottetot a bride price. The skinny girl will be very expensive, that is what I think."

Storms came and went, and the cold weather intensified. Snow fell, and the smaller streams froze solid.

Men returned empty-handed from their hunting ventures, and before very long the supplies of acorn meal and preserved camas and dried fruits were running dangerously low.

Several married men, without consulting anyone at all, loaded their ponies and, their families with them, disappeared down the river trail, presumably thinking to take refuge at the larger village or to return to their former dwellings in the Scott Valley, where, if necessity demanded it, it might be possible to steal a cow or two from the Whites.

Faces grew gaunt, and the older people ceased eating at all—so that what food remained might be reserved for the needs of the children.

Then dysentery struck, running a rapid course through the entire population, and within the space of a few days, some six of the youngest children were dead. Terrible sadness hung over the little village, and the dead infants were placed in reed baskets and committed to the now rolling brown current of the Klamat River.

None of the children in Red Fawn's lodge died, and the faithful Fire-on-the-hills struggled in whenever he had managed to bag some game, even if it was no more than a single squirrel. But he would take only a few morsels of whatever meal was prepared.

Poonkina saw the pain in his eyes, but even though she encouraged him to eat so that he would have the strength to continue with his hunting, he would only smile and shake his head.

"We will survive," he insisted. "Old Man Who Does Everything will not allow things to continue as they are. We must all be strong, Poonkina. I will go farther back into the mountains tomorrow. I know there are animals somewhere, and I promise I will find them."

He did not return the next night, and all the women feared for his life. But near to sundown the second day he struggled in, hardly able to move, and without game.

"My feet are bad," he said as he unlaced the leggins that Poonkina had made for him. "I think they are frozen."

The toes and ankles were black, and the women applied various kinds of medications, but without success.

At the end of a week Fire-on-the-hills sat up suddenly on the bed the women had made for him and shouted, "My horses! You must butcher one of the horses so that there will be enough for the children to eat. Poonkina, where are you? It is very dark—I cannot see very well. Will it be morning soon?"

The women looked from one to another, for the skies had cleared, and sunlight was pouring in through the aperture in the roof.

"I am here, Fire-on-the-hills," Poonkina answered, rising and going to where he lay.

But he was already dead, his being destroyed by the fever that had run through him.

"He is gone," Poonkina said simply. "He died thinking still of how to find meat for us to cook."

Red Fawn nodded, rose, put her arms around Poonkina, and drew her from the one who lay dead.

"Yes," Red Fawn said softly. "It is good that he never knew that the last of his horses was killed this morning. All have been slaughtered already. The other men will see to it that the meat is shared among all, but some have already begun to kill their dogs. I dreamed this thing—do you remember, Poonkina? And now it is happening just the way I saw it in my vision."

Close by the lodge fire, one of the children was lying,

bundled heavily but still shivering. It was the little girl called Chipmunk, and her eyes were drawn tightly shut, her mouth pursed. Her face was flushed, and she was whimpering wretchedly.

Poonkina sat back down, bit at the index finger of her left hand, and shook her head slowly back and forth. It was time to cry, time to let her grief well out. But she was unable to do so.

SIX

▲

The Men of the Forks

The pines were open on the side of the mountain so that sometimes we could see through the trees to the world without and below. Over against us stood Shasta. Grander, nearer, now he seemed than ever, covered with snow from base to crown.

If you would see any mountain in its glory, you must go up a neighboring mountain, and see it above the forests and lesser heights. You must see a mountain with the clouds below you, and between you and the object of contemplation.

Until you have seen a mountain over the tops and crests of a sea of clouds, you have not seen, and cannot understand, the sublime and majestic scenery of the Pacific.

Never, until on some day of storms in the lower world you have ascended one mountain, looked out above the clouds, and seen the white snowy pyramids piercing here and there the rolling nebulous sea, can you hope to learn the freemasonry of mountain scenery in its grandest, highest, and most supreme degree. Lightning and storms and thunder underneath you; calm and perfect beauty about you....

Bearcat Mountain, Haystack Peak, Deadwood Peak, McKinley Mountain, Indian Creek Baldy, Gunsight Peak. Down from these flowed Humbug Creek, taking on Sucker Creek as a tributary and flowing northeast toward the Klamath River. Shortly before its confluence with the greater current of water, Humbug drew down two lesser streams, which joined the Humbug almost directly opposite each other. It was from this branching of Humbug that the name of the mining camp, The Forks, was drawn.

Nate Miller and The Prince staked out their claim close by, on a long, slanting lateral slope of Badger Mountain, some likely-looking ground away from the water and for that reason neglected by earlier miners, and built their cabin at the low end of their claim, close by the Humbug.

The two men dug, and talked, and planned—and were delighted when their ever-growing hole in the mountainside produced a few colors, despondent when it refused to reveal the treasure they were certain lay buried there. From sunrise to sundown they worked, their picks and shovels growing rapidly shiny with the polish of labor, often too obsessed with what they were doing even to take time off to eat their meals.

Nate envied The Prince's strength and endurance. He felt honor-bound to attempt to keep pace with his older friend, but often he could not. He would lie against the cutbank and hope the weariness would flow out of his limbs so that he might continue, but still The Prince would press on, one obsessed. The man might easily enough, Nate realized, return to his former profession, one at which he clearly excelled and from which he could easily glean a prosperous living. But after that first night at The Forks, the lure of the card table had apparently vanished. The fancy black shirt with the silver-thread designs hung limply from a nail in the corner of their tiny log cabin and collected dust. Finally a spider ran a series of webbings to it, attaching the opposite side of his gossamer flytrap to the wall behind.

Ultimately The Prince took notice.

"Looks like a dead man's shirt, doesn't it, Nate? Who was that guy, anyway?"

There was gold in the alluvial gravels of their claim, but getting the yellow metal out was another matter. They utilized a pedal-driven dry washer, but in the damp weather of winter, the strange-looking contraption did not work well at all. At times Nate and The Prince, having grown exasperated with their appliance, would haul burlap sacks of their best sand, sliding and dragging them, down to the Humbug, where a makeshift sluice and a pan were put to work. At last they built a chute out of salvaged boards and, using a mattock, conveyed considerable amounts of material down to the stream, there to wash it.

Their collection of gold fines began to accumulate, but they could see that time would run dry before they would be able to amass any fortune.

"Hell of a way for two grown men to be making six dollars a day between them," The Prince would say. And at such times Nate knew his friend was thinking of monte and poker, of the clinking of glass tumblers and the sounds of laughter in the Howlin' Wilderness. From notorious gambler to ragtag miner—a terrible descent, a grand reversal of fortune.

And yet The Prince never weakened in his resolve, and the hole on the hillside grew larger and larger.

Indeed, few at The Forks had made rich strikes—not after the first two or three. But the whole face of the surrounding area was punctured—holes everywhere. The streambeds were jumbles of heaped stones, and the water ran a constant red-brown from the washing of gravels, the effluvium emptying into the clear waters of the Klamath and turning the river a thin yellow-brown. Shafts were pushed back into the hillsides and then abandoned, and more shafts were dug. Gravels were excavated down to the gray bedrock. Windlasses, standing like hastily constructed gallows, stood above the pockmarks of vertical shafts, and from these swung the iron buckets with which the miners, by force of wrist and shoulder and back, raised the gold-bearing paydirt to the surface.

Nate looked off across Humbug Canyon and saw small groups of men dotted here and there for the length of the gulch, engaged in one way or another with the same kind of work that he and The Prince were doing.

Ants, he thought. *We're all like ants, crawling about on the mounded earth and digging holes....*

"Swing down the bucket, Nate!" The Prince called out from below.

The cold weather grew ever more intense, and mornings would find the Humbug running sluggishly and ice-lined, broad, thin plates of blue-gray ice, fractured and distorted by the movement of water from beneath. Then one morning, the canyon still in darkness though sunlight glittered from the high, jagged slopes of China Mountain and Craggy Mountain across the way, Nate went down to wash his face and hands— only to find the stream itself frozen solid; there was no gurgle underneath the ice, no motion at all. Only the delicate patternings of frost and ice, like little white fires faintly glowing in the early morning darkness.

Guess we won't be washing gravel today, he thought.

By noon the sky had become completely occluded, and the temperature rose. Birds flew about nervously, and the gray squirrels and ground squirrels seemed to be moving more quickly, their actions characterized by a new kind of intensity.

"Big storm coming on," The Prince said.

Nate nodded without speaking, and the two men set about gathering in a good supply of firewood for the little barrel stove in their small cabin. By late afternoon, nearly half the interior space was filled with pungent-smelling sections of pine and fir, a gray tangle of dead manzanita branches, and some resinous slabs of juniper. There was a stack of pitchy splinters as well, which they had found lying on the duff beneath a lightning-struck sugar pine on the hill above the cabin.

"Do your worst!" Nate called out, shaking his fist at the sky.

"Don't tempt fate," The Prince said, laughing. "We're likely to have troubles enough without asking for special attention. What say, old man? A cup of coffee, and then we'll do some more digging?"

"A hell of an idea." Nate groaned. "Why didn't I think of that?"

"What did your Indian friends do when a storm was coming on?"

"They went into their lodges, built up the fires, and ate dinner. Not a bad idea, when you start thinking about it."

"Not a bad idea at all," The Prince agreed. "Haul up a few buckets of gravel, and that's what we'll do, too."

"You're determined to dig, then?"

"What else have we got to do? Digging's the important thing, Nate. It isn't the gold. It's the digging. What would we do with gold if we had it? The stuff doesn't taste worth a damn, so they say. . . ."

Down they went—back to work, like two automatons, shoveling out, loading up, winching the bucket, dumping the contents onto the big pile.

Nate looked across at his friend, working patiently, somehow managing to remain cheerful through it all. He trusted The Prince, depended on him, leaned on him, believed in him, and loved him—an older brother, a younger father, a favorite uncle—whatever he was. Never before had he known such a man as The Prince, one who seemed to incorporate all those things that Nate himself wished to be. Not even The Prince's past as a gambler, and as a gunfighter as well, for that matter, made him less attractive in Nate's eyes. Rather, what Nate saw were strength, courage, determination, and above all a sense of humor, a sense of the comic futility of their actions and their aspirations, and yet an iron will that somehow, by means of sheer resolve, they would yet accomplish what they had set out to accomplish.

If The Prince had said, "Nate, let's climb to the top of Shasta and warm our hands above the fires of the volcano," Nate would have agreed, with no more than a question or two, and gone with him.

"You lean on that shovel and the handle will break. Come on, you skinny little bastard, let's get this done."

Nate looked up abruptly from his reverie.

The Prince's eyes were sparkling and he was grinning broadly.

Darkness came on early, and the two men retired to their cabin, built up the fire, heated water, and washed. Wind was beginning to drive in from the west as they prepared and ate a simple dinner, a pot of beans with a ham hock thrown in for flavor.

Shortly before they retired, The Prince poured out two tin cups half-full of whiskey, and they drank.

"It's sure a night for it," Nate said, sipping from the cup.

"A little *aguardiente,* and a man can get through just about anything. Put enough whiskey into him, and he'll forget to die when the time comes. You know what we need here, Nate? A woman . . ."

"Two women," Nate corrected, drinking off his whiskey. "Just one woman, and we'd end up shooting each other."

"All right, two women, then. Cook our stew for us, wash the pans and plates, fix the cook fire, launder the clothes, and warm up our sleeping rolls."

"What would we do while they were washing the clothes, Prince?"

"See what you mean. Stand around bare-ass naked, I guess. It's a hell of a business when a man's only got one pair of pants. And I used to have so many clothes I could never decide what to wear. Well, it's worth it. Ain't it?"

"Damn right," Nate agreed. "Look at everything we got here—our own house, half-full of firewood, I might add, an admirable hole in the ground, some pistols, a rifle, a pony, and that mule you bought last week. We're well-nigh royalty."

"An estate worthy of a prince, naturally."

"And the prince in question has a male valet to do all the work," Nate added.

"The humor escapes me," The Prince growled. "Douse the lamp and let's get some sleep. God knows what tomorrow's going to bring."

That night the small cabin shivered with the gustings of wind, and from far off came the heavy drummings of thunder. Then, about midnight, the storm turned quiet—so that Nate actually awoke, sensing the change in the weather. He thought about getting up to take a look out into the darkness, thought better of it, turned over, and fell back into the warm oblivion of sleep.

When the light came, however, he rose, went to the door, and opened it.

A bank of snow had settled in around the doorway, and, below the cabin, Nate saw that the trail itself was obliterated, completely vanished. In the hollow, Humbug Creek was roaring, the ice melted, and the stream foaming with meltwater. The unmarked grave of No-Name Henry, a mound of rocks next to the creek, was not even visible, and the alders and yews along the banks were bent over, straining under a heavy weight of whiteness.

Everywhere the world was white, the snow two feet deep. The thick forest on the side of Craggy Mountain was hardly visible, so completely had the storm covered everything—the trees were but a gray-black blur showing beneath the snow.

Still the flakes drifted down, and the world was hushed, utterly silent. The chirring squirrels of the day before were neither to be heard nor seen, and the scattering of miners' cabins down the creek looked more like tombs than human dwellings.

The butchers would not make their rounds that day, nor for weeks to come, from the look of things. All activity would cease in deference to the snow, and the world of The Forks, California, was at peace, or seemed to be.

A single exclamation point in all that whiteness. A coyote,

far across on China Peak, from the sound of it, wailed mournfully for half a minute. And then it, too, was silent.

Long Dan was even taller than The Prince. Beyond that, he had a great red beard, narrow shoulders, and a disposition that seemed inevitably to draw him into fights—fights that he often settled with his pistol. The Prince had marked Dan as a man to stay friendly with almost immediately upon arriving at The Forks, and his intuition had been well substantiated. For, as the winter wore on, Dan had gunned down three different men, all in fair contests.

On a night when The Prince and Nate had made their way through the snow, now frozen hard, and down to the Howlin' Wilderness, Dan was making his brag about his prowess with a six-shooter. The Prince sat down next to Long Dan, listened for a time, and then said, "Daniel, my friend, there's always someone who's faster or more accurate...."

"Got to be some coon that's absolutely the fastest, don't there? Well, that's me, Prince."

"Nope, it ain't that way at all," The Prince replied. "Besides, Nate over here could nail you from a distance with that Kain-tuck of his damned near anytime he wanted to. A man holds a grudge, he doesn't have to fight it out with pistols."

Dan looked quickly at Nate, perhaps the least-threatening man in the tavern, and then back at The Prince.

He knew The Prince was right.

"Well, I ain't got nothing against Nate, anyhow," Dan said.

"That's not the point, that's not the point at all," The Prince persisted. "Daniel, one of these days you're going to die with your boots on, and that's the truth. You just keep slinging your Colt around the way you do, and we'll all see you go up the flume, slick as a salmon. You'll die with your boots on before the winter's out."

Long Dan tapped his ivory-inlaid pistol butt.

"Bet you cigars it don't happen, Prince. You're a gambling man—used to be, at least, before you went dirt crazy. You up for a cigar bet? I ain't going to change my ways, give you my word on it. And I'll collect them cigars, sure as shit."

"Long Dan," The Prince said, "I figure you're on the

downgrade, then. Just keep shooting at folks, and we'll bury you sure."

"Cigars, Prince?"

"You're on. Cigars it is."

"And I'll smoke one, too," Dan said, his pride up.

"Life's short, Dan. No point in trying to make it even shorter."

It was a week later when Nate and The Prince, just finishing their day's shift, heard the pistol shots from the general direction of the Howlin' Wilderness.

"Long Dan's at it again," Nate said, wiping his face with a dirty towel.

The Prince nodded.

"Likely as not. Him or some other. There's something in the mountain air, I think, that makes the boys want to shoot each other."

Despite the fact that they hadn't eaten supper yet, the sound of pistol shots was too much to resist. So Nate and The Prince walked on down to the tavern.

Numerous miners were gathered about in a knot.

"It's Long Dan!" someone called out as he saw The Prince approaching.

The Prince and Nate made their way through the throng of miners—and the men, aware that The Prince was Long Dan's friend, drew back.

Dan lay on a monte table inside the Howlin' Wilderness, an old military overcoat beneath his head.

Dan looked up, the flicker of a smile on his bearded face.

"Prince," he said, "I been nailed, just like you said. Guess I'm goin' to die, all right. Pull off my boots, will ye? Make me feel a lot more comfortable. This table's hard—a bad way to go."

The Prince obliged.

Dan motioned for The Prince to draw close.

"Prince, ye got a cigar on ye? Damned if I wouldn't like a smoke."

The Prince reached into his coat pocket, withdrew a pack of cigars, opened them, and offered one to Long Dan.

"Light 'er for me, will ye, Prince?"

Again The Prince obliged, and Long Dan took a deep drag, coughed feebly, and looked up.

"I'll take the rest of 'em now, if ye don't mind. I've won the bet, Prince, old fellow, and now I'd like the rest of my cigars."

The Prince shook his head in disbelief, then handed Dan the package.

"Guess you're right, my friend. You've won the bet, no way around it."

"Thank ye," Dan said.

He clutched the cigars in his big hand, closed his eyes, coughed once again, and lay dead on the table.

After the burial of Long Dan, the weather turned cold again, so cold that the Humbug froze once more. It became impossible to continue with the digging. The damp gravel seam froze solid, and frostbitten hands were the result of attempts at excavation.

The cessation of mining, however, was the least of the problems—for Nate and The Prince were nearly out of money, having used what gold dust they'd managed to accumulate on food and tools. And now they were nearly out of food. The Kanaka sugar mat was empty, the slab of bacon that had hung against the wall was gone, and even their flour sack was dangerously limp.

More snow fell, and after the storm was over, the skies came clear and rigid with cold. Grain for the Cayuse pony and the mule was nearly exhausted, and there was no way to get more gold to buy more supplies.

Nate went out on foot, hunting, but the area around The Forks had been virtually depleted of game. In three days on foot over the frozen snow, he managed to kill one squirrel that was unaccountably out and about, and one porcupine.

These were consumed at a single meal.

The Prince considered an expedition to the Howlin' Wilderness, but he was without the money even for the necessary ante.

Their own cabin was warm enough, but the days were tedious.

"Maybe we could light a fire in the shaft," The Prince suggested. "Thaw out the gravel and then . . ."

Nate shrugged.

They both knew it was a wild idea.

One morning there was only bread for breakfast. The

Prince was gloomy as they sat down and did not remain long at the table. He watched Nate consume what little bread there was.

"Natty," he said, "it's getting mighty rocky. The grass is shorter than it ever was with us before. Tell you, my friend, I'm not sure what to do next."

"Starvin' times. That's what my old friend, Mountain Joe, would call them. I'll get my coat on and head out hunting again. Maybe Lady Luck will smile for a change. I haven't been over the crest of Badger Mountain yet, and maybe no one else has either. Deer could be hiding up there."

"Not in the snow, Nate, and we both know it. What deer are left have gone downriver. If we were deer, we would have done the same thing. Got a better idea."

"What's that?"

"Going to sell my pistol. Don't have much use for it anymore in any case. If a man's not playing cards, I guess he doesn't need a' gun. Ain't no one's going to try to rob us, because we haven't got anything much to rob. If I can get twenty dollars for it, then I've got a stake for poker—not much of a stake, but better than nothing. Or we could buy a week's worth of food—not quite, I guess. One thing's sure, and the other's a gamble. But in five, six days we'd be hungry again. We need your rifle—can't let go of that. Could sell the horse and the mule. Dammit, Nate, we've got to do something. We could kill the mule and eat that, but then the weather would turn and we'd be needing him. You figure this claim's worth hanging on to? Even at the best of times, we've just barely fetched the postman."

"I don't know, Prince. Seems like it ought to be. Seems like we'll be getting at the gold—if we can ever dig again and wash our gravel."

"Maybe, maybe you're right, lad. This going straight's a hard thing, a real bitch-kitty. It was a whole lot easier to just go helling my way through life and bluffing on the bad hands. Wait for the other guy's weakness to show through. But there's no way to bluff an empty stomach, is there?"

"I know you gave me your word, but I never asked for it. Whatever you want to do's fine with me," Nate said. "You got us a grubstake when we first came to The Forks, and I know you can do it again. I could sell the rifle—maybe we'd get fifty bucks for it, maybe even more. Anyway, with that and the pistol, you'd have money to play with...."

"You hang on to that rifle," The Prince insisted. "First, your daddy gave it to you. And second, you can bring in game with it—you're the best shot I ever saw in my life."

"Only there's no game around...."

"Leave the rifle here, Nate. Let's go to town."

The miners were well aware that a band of Scott River Shastas had made their winter encampment along the Klamat, at the foot of China Peak, a few miles downstream from The Forks. The Indians seemed indifferent to the gang of miners— indeed, they seemed hardly to take notice of the Whites at all. Sometimes one of the boys would meet with an Indian along the narrow river trail, but as often as not the Nomki-dji would simply avert his eyes and continue silently on his way, gathering his robes about him and concealing his short bow and arrows under the folds of the garment. The men of The Forks could not recall ever receiving so much as a friendly grunt, or even ever seeing one of these Indians laugh. All in all, The Forks believed, it was an intractable and solemn group, close on to starvation now during this winter of unusually heavy snows and terrible cold. The weather itself had apparently driven the Indians down from their usual haunts to the somewhat more temperate climate along the river.

With game already so scarce as to be almost nonexistent, the proximity of the Indians compounded the problem—for what animals the miners did not shoot, no doubt the Indians did.

For a time the talk in the Howlin' Wilderness dealt with the almost certain prospect that the sullen Indians would simply move camp, go somewhere else. But as problems in taking game grew more intense, feelings toward the misera-ble Indians grew ever more angry.

The Indians, unfortunately, were themselves starving. What-ever fish they might have taken during the summer salmon run were few—owing to the perpetual flow of mud discharged into the Klamath River. In normal years the river might well have been so filled with salmon that it was nearly impossible to force a pony across through the shallows. But with the discharges from mining operations, the Indians had been unable to take their usual catch, the fish to be smoked and dried and pounded into a flour, and so stored for the needs of the winter months.

A few of the men in The Forks, it is true, had contacts with the Indian village—men who hung about the lodges at night, giving whiskey to the Indian men in exchange for the sexual favors of their women.

A Whiteman was found dead, and it was immediately assumed by The Forks that he had been killed by the Indians. The band of Shastas, up to this point simply an annoyance and an unnecessary drain on the supply of wild game, were now seen as a threat. All manner of fears was aroused, and stories circulated about Indian massacres elsewhere, about provocations, scalpings, and torturings.

A large group of miners, their rifles and pistols capped and ready, had gathered at the Howlin' Wilderness—and a kind of town meeting was in process when The Prince and Nate arrived.

The hangers-on about town were more enraged than the miners, for it had been one of their number, a man named Dog-eye Dick, whose body had been discovered—upstream from The Forks, admittedly, and a long way from the Indian encampment. But talk was that the body of Dog-eye Dick had been taken there and left, so as to divert suspicion from the Indians.

A big Irishman named Sean and a cardsharp named Jack Spades, the latter a man well known to The Prince, and one whom he disliked intensely, were leading the discussion—and calling for the extermination of the Scott River village.

Sean was holding forth:

"Fellow miners, a man has been kilt by the treacherous savages—kilt in cold blood. Fellow miners! Let us advance upon the enemy. Boys, let us take one more drink and go wipe them Injuns out!"

A great deal of applause followed this speech.

Jack Spades stood up and said:

"Men of The Forks! As you all know, Dog-eye Dick was the best friend I ever had, an' a gentler, more peaceable man there never were! A week ago we was all playin' cards with him an' drinkin' together. Sure, some of you weren't overly fond of him, but that's just because you didn't know him like I did. I tell you, there never was a better man! An' now he's in the frozen ground with a ball of lead in his heart. We going to allow this outrage to go unpunished?"

"Spades!" The Prince called out. "Did Dog-eye ever pay you that money he owed you? I heard you were carrying his IOU."

For a moment the assemblage of miners and hangers-on was silent, looking first at The Prince, then at Jack Spades.

"Paid in full," Spades said after a momentary pause. "Dick was an honest man. If he had a debt, he paid it. And now them Injuns has got a debt. Boys, are we goin' to go out an' collect?"

The men cheered.

"Drinks are on me!" Sean called out. "Rally to the bar, boys, every mother's son of ye, an' at me own expense, too! Then check your prime, an' let's be off an' at what we got to do. . . ."

"It's really going to happen?" Nate asked The Prince.

"The mob's up," The Prince replied. "There'll be no stopping them now. We'll see this through, Nate. We'll watch from the hill above the Indian village. With a little luck, the Indians will be in on it and heeled. If they've got powder and lead, perhaps they'll give this rabble the welcome it deserves. Tell you, I think I know who it was that did in Dog-eye Dick. Spades is covering his tracks."

"Spades?"

"Just a wild guess, but I've seen the man operate often enough. Some card men have a sense of honor—Whiskey John, for instance. Some, like Spades, don't. These are Shastas, Nate. You figure you know any of them?"

"Different band altogether," Nate replied. But his own anger was up now, and he desperately wished he had his pistol with him. The Prince's Colt, brought down for sale, was not loaded—and so was useless to them, whatever it was they might have had in mind.

Nate and The Prince headed out on foot, and were overtaken by the mounted mob shortly before they reached the Shastas' encampment. They drew to the side of the trail to allow the fifty or sixty armed men pass by.

"Come along to see the fun, did ye, Prince?" Jack Spades yelled out.

"Come to see you scalped!" The Prince shouted back.

Then they were in prospect of the village, the cluster of low lodges, smoke issuing from the vent holes of some, on a crescent bench above the river.

Unless the Indians were both armed and ready, Nate realized, they would have only a choice of death at the hands of the enraged Whites or by drowning in the icy, flooding river. There was no other way out.

The cold afternoon sun was dropping westward, hovering above the interlocked and snowbound ridges of the Siskiyous, and a cutting wind was blowing, occasionally causing little dust devils of snow that spun and swirled and died. And the blue smoke from the lodges rose slowly and hung above the Generous River.

Strange, Nate thought. *None of the camp dogs is barking— is it possible these people don't have dogs?*

Then he understood the silence.

During times of real starvation, the dogs are eaten.

SEVEN

▲

Klamat and Paquita

The crowd advanced to within half a pistol shot, and gave a shout as they drew and leveled their arms. Old squaws came out—bang! bang! bang! shot after shot, and they were pierced and fell, or turned to run.

Some men sprung up, wounded, but fell the instant; for the Whites, yelling, howling, screaming, were among the lodges, shooting down at arm's length man, woman, or child. Some attempted the river, I should say, for I afterwards saw streams of blood upon the ice, but not one escaped; nor was a hand raised in defense. It was all done in a little time. Instantly as the shots and shouts began we two advanced, we rushed into the camp, and when we reached the spot only now and then a shot was heard within a lodge, dispatching a wounded man or woman. The few surviving children—for nearly all had been starved to death—had taken refuge under skins and under lodges overthrown, hidden away as little kittens will hide just old enough to spit and hiss, and hide when they first see the face of man. These were now dragged forth and shot.

The babies did not scream or wail, and the men and women of the Shastas, wounded and dying, did not even groan.

The Irishman Sean grasped the emaciated leg of an infant girl, a child he had dragged from beneath a collapsed lodge, held her up for all to see, grinned, and blew her head to pieces with his pistol.

Similar outrages were committed all about.

Sean threw the nearly decapitated body among the other dead and hurried to where two of the men had fetched up a naked, bony, adolescent girl, the marks of starvation grimly

98

upon every feature, her cheeks drawn in, her legs little more than bone and skin, her belly drawn in, her forming breasts withered, as though by old age. Sean caught the woman-child by her long hair and placed his pistol to her head, turning the girl about so that her brains would not be spattered over his cohorts.

The girl did not flinch. It may be that during this long, terrible winter, she had already come to know death as a constant visitor to the village and so was on familiar terms with him.

Nate stared, horror-struck, at the girl's face—the lips thin and fixed and the mouth held rigid.

"Prince!" he screamed, his voice more a wail of animal desperation than a human voice. "It's Poonkina! I know her!"

He rushed forward headlong, not in rage or in fear, not feeling anything that he even vaguely understood, only the horror and the desperate need to do something, anything. His head rammed into Sean's stomach, and his arms grasped wildly at the older man, throwing him to the ground, the pistol that a moment earlier had been held to the Indian girl's head now exploding harmlessly into the cold air and the near-darkness.

Sean grunted, roared with anger, and lurched to his feet. He gasped for breath and spat out the words: "Crazy little bastard! Now I'm goin' to beat your brains into the dirt. . . ."

But The Prince was there, and in a single motion had Sean by the throat, hurled him backward onto the ground, and delivered a terrific kick to the man's side.

Sean let out a scream of pain and clutched at his side.

The Prince reached over, picked up the man's fallen pistol, and threw it far out over the river, into the gaining darkness.

Sean was up again and had pulled a knife.

The Prince drew his unloaded pistol and pointed it.

"Put the knife away, Sean me lad, or I'll blow a hole through your guts."

"What's the matter with you, Prince? Has everyone gone ballywacker? If ye want the leetle scarecrow, take 'er. I'll find me another to play with."

"Get out of here, you Sydney duck, and get out of The Forks. If I ever see you again, I'm going to pay your ticket to hell."

Sean looked about for support among the other men, but no one was prepared to challenge The Prince. Sean backed away, the knife still in his hand but both hands held up, stumbled over a dead Indian, caught his balance, hurled the knife at The Prince, and missed; then he turned and ran for his life.

Nate pulled off his jacket, wrapped it about the half-dead Poonkina, held her in his arms, and touched her hair.

"Nate Miller?" the girl managed. And then in the language of the Shastas: "Where is Klamat? Help me to find Klamat. Is he still alive, Nate?"

Red lights flared in Nate's eyes. The entire world was shredding apart, the filaments torn, bloodied.

"Prince, Prince—my friend Klamat is here somewhere— take Poonkina—I have to find him. God Almighty, how could this happen?"

The Prince lifted the girl in his arms and followed after the hysterical Nate, now running back and forth, calling out wildly, moving this way and that among the piles of corpses.

Streams of blood flowing down the ice. Lodges burning. Still the explosions, diminishing, of pistol and rifle. The odor of burnt flesh heavy in the freezing air. Exclamations, oaths . . .

"Scalp him while he lives! Scalp the little savage! Scalp him and throw him into the river!"

From somewhere among the piles of butchered Indians, a half-naked Indian had risen. Now he stood, staggering, a knotted war club in his hand—now rushed forward, flailing about with the club, striking blindly at the Whites who surrounded him.

At this show of untamed ferocity, the men from The Forks pulled back and formed a circle around him, their weapons poised, ready. Or perhaps it was simple astonishment—a single Indian boy, as if arisen from the dead, making a show of force against their numbers, their weapons.

Someone began to laugh—then all were laughing.

Nate saw from a distance, and came running, screaming.

It was Klamat.

Whether the young Shasta warrior heard his name called or whether it was the merest coincidence that Nate's screams were echoing at that moment, Klamat hurled himself forward, exhausting what strength remained to him, and was felled beneath a barrage of kicks and blows. He slumped to the ground and was fallen upon by the Whites, whose very numbers combined to save his life—for none could shoot or stab without injuring another of the men from The Forks.

Nate plunged forward, broke his way through the knot of men, and moved toward Klamat. For a moment he had the strength of several and pushed the miners aside like so many tenpins, cursing and screaming all the while.

The miners, astounded by the miraculous change in the quiet boy who worked with The Prince, drew back away from him and from the young Shasta as well.

Then just the two of them were at the center of the circle—Klamat on hands and knees, waiting for death, and Nate standing beside him, screaming with animal rage.

Klamat looked up, still unaware of who it was who stood over him. Then recognition dawned.

"Nate?" Klamat gasped, struggling still for breath.

"Klamat, stay down, stay down. . . ."

The Prince strode forward, Poonkina in his arms, and the men parted to allow him to pass. The frenzy of the massacre had vanished now, and some of the men began to look about them at the firelit scene of havoc and death that they had wrought.

Perhaps some of them began to feel a terrible shame. In any case, they drew back, then stood about nervously, uncertain what to do next. They stared as if in wonder at the small group before them—the wild-eyed Nate, the half-starved young Indian boy on hands and knees, The Prince, tall and powerful, a frail Indian girl in his arms, a girl draped in a man's wool-lined coat, the hand that rested under the girl's legs holding a pistol pointed in their direction.

"Orgy's over, boys," The Prince said softly. "You've had your fun—murdered a couple hundred Indians, and no court of law will ever call you to account for it. You're brave men, brave men. You've fought like real heroes. Kit Carson himself would be proud to know you, I'm sure. Hell, boys, they were starving to death anyway—you just did 'em a favor, is all."

The men shifted nervously about. Only Jack Spades was not subdued.

"Goin' to take the little squaw home an' fatten 'er up so's you've got somethin' to fuck, are you, Prince? An' your sidekick gets the Injun boy? We ought to shoot you where you stand, you hypocrite-some-bitch!"

"Spades, for the sake of men who are friends to both of us, I'm going to forget you said that. But I won't be giving a second chance. Don't ever rile me again, or I'll kill you with my bare hands. All of you now, get on back to The Forks. Tomorrow morning I'll be at the Howlin' Wilderness to meet with anyone that wants to help me give these poor devils some kind of a burying. I'm guilty, too. I came to watch. Those of you who feel a need to do some atoning, meet me at the tavern in the morning. . . ."

The men left behind them a scene of burning lodges, skins, wild-rye straw, robes, willow baskets, a scene of dark-skinned bodies lying grotesquely scattered. A confusion of odors, and one the odor of charred flesh.

Nate and The Prince stared about, but their two companions, as if suddenly struck blind, chose to see nothing.

Everywhere lay the emaciated bodies, faces blown away, bodies crumpled into strange and almost comical postures, limbs twisted with limbs in the wrestle of death, a mother embracing her son, drawing the child to her breast, the embrace fixed in death.

As if these wild people could love as well as die . . .

Nate helped Klamat to his feet, the Shasta's blood, running down from a wide gash on his forehead, smearing on Nate's hands and arms.

"Can you walk?" The Prince asked Poonkina, but she did not understand his words.

"I am daughter of Blackbeard," she said, as if hoping this might answer the question she had not understood.

"Nate—ask her if she can walk."

"I will carry her," Klamat said in English, surprising The Prince.

"Tell her that we must walk," Nate said. "We have a cabin above The Forks. You will live with us now, until you are well again. No harm will come to you, Klamat. Once your people saved my life, and now my people have killed your people. I am sorry, I am sorry. . . ."

"I understand, my friend," Klamat said. "But you and this man have now saved our lives. We will go with you. You and this man are not like the others, Nate. If he is your friend, then he will be our friend also."

"Klamat!" Nate protested. "What were you doing here— I..."

"Tall man," Klamat said, turning to The Prince, "I am Klamat of Warrottetot's people. The girl is Poonkina, the chief's daughter. He will give you presents for saving her life."

The Prince reached out and clasped hands with Klamat, holding the jacket about the shuddering girl with his other arm.

"And I am—The Prince, that is what I am called. You and—Pan-kita—will stay with Nate and me. We have very little just now, but what we have we will share with you."

Klamat nodded twice.

"Poonkina," Nate said, then pronounced the word yet again: "Poonkina."

The Prince nodded.

"Poon-kita," he repeated. "Is that how I say it?" he asked the shivering girl.

"Yes, that my name."

Klamat turned to her then, turned to her for the first time, and spoke in his own language:

"My sister, one that I love, we must go with Nate and his friend now. He is the one who was sick and stayed with us. You nursed him sometimes. Do you remember when that time was?"

"I remember, Klamat. You brought him to live with us. I remember that his eyes are blue, darker than the sky. My brother, what can we do? I am very weak. All of our relatives are dead now. Will we be able to find our way back to my father's people?"

"Nate will help us," Klamat said in English.

It was late when they reached The Forks and passed in front of the Howlin' Wilderness, strangely quiet this night, with very little clamor from within. While Nate guided Klamat and Poonkina to the little cabin, The Prince went directly to the trading post and persisted in banging on the plank door until the proprietor, half-dressed and half-asleep, arrived, pistol in hand, to see what the commotion was about.

"I want to sell you a gun, and I want to buy some supplies with the proceeds," The Prince said.

"What in good hell?"

"Open up, dammit. I'm in no mood to be trifled with. This is The Prince talking."

"I see who ye be. Goddammit, go home an' come back tomorning. I open early, an' ye know it, too."

"Open the door or I'll kick it in. . . ."

The door opened, and the lamps were lit.

"Give me what the pistol's worth, your price. I want flour, sugar, bacon, dried apples, beans, coffee—the usual stuff, and as much of it as possible. I've got a couple of Indian kids on my hands, and they're both on the verge of starvation. . . ."

"Heard about that," the storekeeper said. "Heard about it when the boys rode back in. Most of 'em thinks you and your young pal have been chewin' loco weed."

"That what you think, too?"

"Don't guess so. Let me see the fancy Colt, Prince. Always admired that gun. . . ."

The Prince borrowed the storekeeper's mule, loaded the creature with supplies, and hurried up along the Humbug to the cabin.

Nate prepared a quick dinner, and The Prince soon had a roaring fire going in the barrel stove. Klamat and Poonkina ate slowly, not at all used to dealing with forks and spoons. Beyond this, Poonkina was unable to keep her food down and, crouching on the earthen floor, was forced to vomit.

"Rest for a few minutes," Nate said. "Then try to eat some more."

"They were dying of hunger when I arrived," Klamat said. "That was just two days ago. I tried to hunt, my friend, but all the animals have vanished—and so I could help no one."

"The country's hunted out," The Prince said. "The miners went crazy. . . ."

"Blue-eyes," Poonkina managed in English, "eat?"

Nate put another helping of the apple and bacon and flour mixture on the girl's tin plate and said, "Slowly, slowly."

What had happened was past, and there was no need to speak of it further—this, compounded by the Indians' general unwillingness to speak again the names of those who were dead.

They finished eating, and then they slept. When Nate, Klamat, and Poonkina awoke, The Prince had already gone. Nothing was said as to where he had gone, but upon his return, late in the afternoon, Klamat said simply, "Thank you, Prince."

Those first days crept by, and the meager store of supplies dwindled. The Prince and Nate ate but little, preferring that the food should go to Klamat and Poonkina—the girl in particular, for she had nearly reached the point at which the body simply refused any further nourishment, having in its own dark way resolved upon death.

But with Klamat ever at her side, and Nate and The Prince hovering close by, she responded to care and a sufficiency of food and made the difficult trek back from the land of shadows.

When nearly all the supplies were gone, The Prince slipped away early one morning and an hour or two later came singing up the hill, a fifty-pound sack of Self-rising, Warranted Superfine flour over his shoulder. The Prince was grinning as he placed the sack of flour on the bench in the corner, placed it there as carefully as he would have an infant child.

"What did you have to sell?" Nate asked.

"Nothing, as it turned out. We'll have a guest after a bit. The doctor's going to pay us a call."

"Doc Storz?"

"The very man. The Miller and Prince orphanage has found itself a patron. He paid for the flour, and he'll be bringing as much other stuff as two mules can carry, lad."

To say that Nate was surprised would have been a great understatement, for, in truth, Nate had never much cared for the brusque old doctor, a first-generation German, a man too silent and reserved. Doc Storz was indeed well thought of in the community of The Forks, for he had astounding skill in digging out bullets and in treating frostbite, as well as in tending to a host of other maladies. Further, he never dunned any of the miners with regard to bills they owed, and as a simple result of this practice, most of them made a point of paying him as soon as they could. Sometimes payment was in coin, sometimes in dust and nuggets, sometimes even in deermeat, guns, or shovels and pans. Not that the miners loved the man, for the reserved nature of his personality precluded that, and it was not believed that he had any close friends at all. But Doc served his purpose, filled a definite need, and the men of The Forks respected him for it and trusted his judgment. A small, light-haired man, he spoke to no one who did not speak first, and seemingly preferred solitude to company.

Nate did not know how The Prince had made Doc's acquaintance. Perhaps he had gone to the doctor that very morning and appealed to his sense of humanity.

Whatever had happened, Doc Storz arrived after a time, his two mules laden with supplies, just as The Prince had said they would be.

"This is the Whiteman's shaman?" Klamat asked in a low voice after the doctor had entered the little cabin and was speaking with The Prince.

"Yes," Nate said. "You must allow him to care for your wound. It's not healing as it should—that's why your face is so hot sometimes."

"It is *aheki*," Klamat said. "This man cannot help it."

"When I lay sick in Warrottetot's village, your people tended my wound. Now you must let the doctor tend yours."

Doc Storz examined Klamat's forehead, cleansed the wound with peroxide, and placed a bandage over it. All the while Klamat sat rigid, his face an expressionless mask.

"Come here, Paquita," said the doctor, sitting down on the three-legged stool by the fire. He held out his hand to her, and she, suddenly modest, drew the robe up about her bosom. Then, timidly, she approached the doctor.

Doc Storz looked up at The Prince, and The Prince grinned.

"You make big medicine, Doc, and in the meanwhile, I'm going to bake some bread for my babies."

The Prince busied himself with tin pan, water, flour, and baking soda, and the doctor checked Poonkina's pulse and blood pressure. He touched her face, and Nate could see that she wanted to pull away from this man—and yet she did not.

After a time Doc Storz was finished with the examination. He rose from the stool, perfunctorily checked his pocket watch, spoke briefly with The Prince, bade them *Guten Tag*, and set out on his return to The Forks.

The Prince, having put the bread into a cast-iron kettle to

bake, began to whistle and walked outside to split some kindling.

"Poonkina wishes to know what name the medicine man called her," Klamat said.

"Paquita," Nate answered. "Probably he'd misunderstood what The Prince had told him."

"I can understand what this man says, Nate, but he does not say the words as other Whitemen do. Tell me why that is, if you know."

"Once we spoke of lands across the ocean. Do you remember, Klamat?"

"I remember that."

"The doctor came from one of these lands, from Germany. He speaks English, but he speaks it as a German would—since it is not his own language."

"The way you speak the Shasta language?"

Nate laughed.

"Yes, and the way you speak English."

Klamat considered the matter for a time and then said, "I speak English well, do I not?"

"Better than some Whitemen."

Poonkina, standing beside Klamat but looking straight into Nate's eyes, said, "Will you teach Poonkina to speak your language, Nate Miller?"

"Klamat and I will both teach you, if you wish. The Prince can help also."

"Does The Prince know many things?" Poonkina asked.

"He knows much more than I do," Nate answered.

"And he will also help to teach me?"

Klamat stared at Nate, then looked toward the closed door.

"Do you trust this Prince, my friend?" Klamat asked.

"As I would an older brother or a father or an uncle. He has helped me in many ways. He saved Poonkina's life when—"

"I know that," Klamat said quickly. "Poonkina has told me what happened."

Conversation drifted to other matters as odors of baking bread filled the small room.

When The Prince came back in with a great armload of kindling, placing it close by the barrel stove, the girl spoke to him:

"What is *Paquita*?"

The Prince, taken by surprise, glanced first at Nate and then at Klamat.

"Does she know enough English for me to answer her?"

"I do not believe so," Klamat responded.

"Well, you tell her, then. It's a good name, and I'd use it too, if it's all right. Hard to pronounce the other, though I could get used to it. *Paquita*'s Spanish, I guess. What? Suppose it would mean 'Little Bit' or 'Little Package,' 'Little Bundle,' maybe. I don't know all that much Spanish—some Mexican Spanish is all—but I guess that's about it. What's *Poonkina* mean?"

"'Wormwood,'" Klamat said.

"Suppose I like *Paquita* better, then," The Prince said, grinning. "She's sure not very big."

"'Little Woman,' maybe," Nate suggested.

"I like *Paquita*," the girl said.

The Prince laughed, and Nate laughed too. Poonkina, now Paquita, looked pleased with herself, like a child who has said something clever without really knowing what it is.

For a moment Klamat looked dour, but then he, too, smiled.

"Teach English?" Paquita asked, looking first at Nate and then, eyes barely averted, at The Prince.

"Whatever you want, Little Bit," the Prince said. "But right now, I think that bread's about ready."

Weeks and then months passed by, and the lock of winter was broken. A warm wind blew up the Klamath River from the ocean, and the icicles vanished from the cabin eaves. Snow that had long been frozen on the ground and even on the boles of fir and pine also vanished quite suddenly, and Nate, The Prince, and now Klamat were busily working the claim once again. Lady Luck began to smile, and the alluvial gravels yielded a generous, though not overwhelming, quantity of gold dust and small nuggets. The butcher's mules, laden with beef from the Sacramento Valley, came braying up the Humbug trail. The terrible winter and the even more terrible events of that winter were quickly forgotten by the miners, as each day brought news of someone or another's good fortune.

One "family" alone could not forget, would never forget.

The doctor came often, staying for dinner and conversation, and his *guten Abend, der Junge, das Mädchen, die Bergen, und so weiter, Kartøffeln, Ich habe die Katze gern,* and other phrasings became household expressions, a sort of communal property of a linguistic kind. He was not a man whom one could easily love, and yet the kindness and generous humanity with which he had treated them could hardly have gone unappreciated. For his part, Doc Storz seemed to wish nothing further. He had become an elder uncle to the four of them, and he had reason to know that he was welcome at the cabin at any time.

The Prince and Nate attempted to pay Doc Storz fifty dollars out of their first good take that spring, but Doc would have nothing to do with their money, claiming that The Prince was trying to buy his goodwill, and left abruptly.

The Prince shrugged at Nate and said, "The old bastard'll be back—let's not worry about it." The prophecy was accurate, for the following afternoon, just as the men were finishing their day's work, the doctor showed up, in a very good mood, as though no harsh words had been spoken the previous day at all.

He had bought Paquita a new dress, bright red with frilly white lace about the bodice and at the ends of the long sleeves.

"*Sehr shön, nicht wahr?*" he asked. "Is it not pretty? I have it *ge-sent* for from Sacramento last month by mail. The *Lieblich Mädchen* should have such a dress, I think."

Paquita was obviously and thoroughly pleased, and yet she would not try it on for them to see. Instead, she thanked the doctor kindly and promised to wear the garment.

"Her English becomes *gut, nicht wahr,* is it not so? *Die Schülerin* proves adept. That is good. . . ."

That night, after the doctor had left, thunder sounded heavily from far up near the source of the Humbug, up over Gunsight Peak and Indian Creek Baldy. Soon no stars were visible, and the night was hushed with expectancy. Then the rain, a downpour, set in, lasting nearly until morning. When Nate rose, just after the first light, he heard the roaring of the stream. He walked down to the Humbug and found a small river where the creek had been the day before. The water was very high, swirling and muddy, racing on down to the Klamath.

In the light mist that remained after the storm, birds were flitting about, singing as if, Nate thought, they had good sense. A kingfisher came darting up the stream, chattering and cursing as always but now with increased zest, and squirrels were darting back and forth beneath the pines and firs.

All the snow was gone—no trace remained. The world had been transformed, as if by magic, to springtime.

Warm weather came, and the diggings on the hillside were paying off. The stash of gold dust, from time to time nonexistent through the winter, had now grown heavy and large. The Prince was ebullient, and Nate only slightly less so. Klamat, who worked with them happily enough, seemed never quite certain that these two men were not entirely mad. But if this digging for yellow metal made them happy, then he was glad to work as hard as he could. Between the steady regimen of work and the huge meals they now consumed, Klamat had not only regained his former strength but had grown taller and stronger, the muscles in his arms and chest now quite thick.

Soon it would be time for him and Poonkina to make the return to their people. He was a man now, lacking only the long-desired medicine vision. But that would come.

His share of the gold dust, this much he understood, would allow him in this world of Whitemen to buy horses and perhaps even a rifle like the one his friend Nate had. Nor would Warrottetot be able to ignore the fact that he, Klamat, having set out months earlier to find Poonkina, would now be returning with the chief's eldest daughter, whom Warrottetot had without question supposed dead, for certainly some word of the massacre had reached the chief.

He would relate the story exactly as it had happened, neither increasing nor diminishing his own part in it. His medicine had been good in this one way, for that medicine had, at the moment when all seemed lost, brought his friend Nate back to him, Nate and The Prince, and so Poonkina's life had been saved. Warrottetot could not ignore the significance of what had happened.

Perhaps both Nate and The Prince would now wish to

come and live among his people. That would be a good thing. If he had not fully trusted The Prince at first, he did so now. The man was brave, proud, quick-minded, and kind. Such qualities, Klamat realized, were fully admirable in any man, whether Indian or White.

The man's only flaw, as far as Klamat could tell, lay in his encouraging Poonkina to adopt the White-sounding name of Paquita. However, he concluded, she seemed genuinely delighted with the new name, and her other, after all, was not Shastan in any case.

Nate thought much about Paquita also. The girl, from the moment of his dream-vision a year and a half earlier, had never been totally out of his thoughts. If there had been no Klamat, then he, Nate, would without question have fixed his mind upon eventually marrying her. But there was a Klamat, Klamat his fast friend, one to whom perhaps even more than to The Prince he owed his life.

If he could not have her, then certainly he could take pride and pleasure in her, in simply being around her, in speaking with her, in watching her develop into full womanhood.

She had taken to caring for her three "menfolk" with genuine enthusiasm, knowing well that each, in his own way, loved her. Yes, The Prince too, as Nate understood, had come to love the fragile but high-spirited Indian girl. And she knew, of course, how each of her three men felt about her. She could not help knowing.

Three? Nate thought. *Doc Storz, he loves her too. It's not just for The Prince's company that Doc comes to dinner so often.*

For that matter, Paquita had become, in this short space of time, virtually the belle of The Forks.

Even that snake of a Jack Spades has his eye on her....

Spades, Nate had long since concluded, desperately needed to be shot and quietly thrown into the river.

EIGHT

▲

Man for Breakfast

The winter had abandoned even the wall that lay between them and the outer world, and drew off all his forces to Mount Shasta. He retreated above the timber line, but he retreated not an inch beyond. There he sat down with all his strength. He planted his white and snowy tent upon this ever-lasting fortress, and laughed at the world below him. Sometimes he would send a foray down, and even in midsummer, to this day, he plucks an ear of corn, a peach, or an apricot, for a hundred miles around his battlement, whenever he may choose.

Paquita gathered blossoms in the sun, threw her long hair back, and bounded like a fawn along the hills. Klamat took his club and knife, drew his robe only the closer about him in the sun, and went out gloomy and somber in the mountains. Sometimes he would be gone all night.

The girl by now had learned to speak English fairly well and had adjusted quickly in all other ways to her new circumstances. The keeping of the house became her special domain of responsibility, not because anyone had urged her to take it upon herself, but because, rather obviously, she took pleasure in doing so.

Among her own people, Paquita had early gained notice for her artistic abilities, and as she approached womanhood, there was none who surpassed her in either bead and quill work or in working out designs in the woven, cone-shaped tule baskets that she was fond of making—a thing unusual in itself, for the Shastas acquired most of their woven containers in trade with the Karoks. But these Karok vessels Paquita imitated, and soon a number of other girls were following her practice.

112

Now that she had seen the paintings on the walls in the Howlin' Wilderness, she was eager to make some of her own. One day, utilizing the inside of the cabin door for a canvas— thinking perhaps of the slab of pine on which *The Mexican Bull* was painted—and some charcoal for paints, she did a rendering of Mount Shasta, working from memory, for in the depths of Humbug Canyon the huge white mountain was not visible.

Returning from the afternoon's work, Nate and The Prince were astonished. Even Klamat, after protesting for a moment or two on behalf of a slightly different configuration for the upper portion of the peak, admitted that the drawing was very good indeed.

Paquita was delighted with the praise and quickly set about preparing the dinner that she had neglected on behalf of the drawing.

Whatever she did, she wished to do correctly—but on occasion her ignorance of the things of White civilization foiled her efforts, and at such times she was near to despair. One morning, in an attempt to improve the taste of the coffee, she put salt into it.

Now if a little pinch of this white substance adds to the beans, why will it not contribute to the flavor of the coffee?

Nate and Klamat drank their coffee, but The Prince put his down after a sip or two.

An hour later, when Nate returned to the cabin for some wire with which to repair the overhead windlass, he saw that Paquita had actually been crying. He attempted to assure her that The Prince had not been upset by the salt in the coffee, only that he had not been thirsty that morning.

"I did not mean to ruin the coffee, Nate. I will not do that again. . . ."

But another time she put sugar on the meat instead of salt, and, the mistake being realized, all four members of the household broke into hysterical laughter. Paquita, it is true, had not meant to laugh—but the laughter of the others was contagious and caught her as well.

She hated to admit to ignorance, and the mystery of reading books fascinated her. Shortly after she had begun to be proficient at English, she pretended to Klamat that she had also learned how to read—explained to him what was written on the butcher's bill.

"I cannot read," Klamat said, "but I can see that you are holding the paper upside down."

Paquita protested that this was not so—and turned to The Prince for an authoritative word on the matter. When he was forced to side with Klamat, Paquita became distant and would not speak to anyone for an hour or more.

During the first weeks of her residence at the Miller and Prince claim, Paquita had dared to venture no more than a few yards from the cabin itself; but gradually, becoming ever more certain of her safety, she began to walk as far as the Humbug, and finally, with Klamat at her side, consented to a venture with Nate and The Prince to the settlement at The Forks. Once there, and perceiving no hostility toward her person, she grew immediately curious about everything—the trading post in particular, the doctor's house, the butcher shop, and the Howlin' Wilderness.

Only when she chanced to see Jack Spades walking down the street toward them did she pull back and stand behind her three men.

The commissioners of the newly formed county had appointed an alcalde, a rather ordinary sort of man, one newly arrived from the East and desperately in need of some sort of position. To preside as the fountain of judgment at The Forks, California, was perhaps the least important position that might have been found for him—for the rowdy miners operated by their own laws alone.

But the new judge came to town and was eager to make his presence and his authority felt. The man was wearing a boiled shirt and a stovepipe hat made of English silk.

The wearing of the hat, as it turned out, was something of a mistake. The miners of The Forks, if they had had no other reasons, would have been certain to take an instant dislike to the alcalde on the basis of his hat alone.

"Oh, what a hat!"

"Set 'em up!"

"Chuck 'em in the gutter!"

"Saw my leg off!"

The Prince saw the man, a small and anemic-looking

individual, as nothing more than a harmless egotist—but was of the opinion that a man had the right to wear whatever sort of hat he wished.

Six-foot Sandy agreed.

"It's all right, boys," he yelled out from where he stood at the bar in the Howlin' Wilderness. "She's all right, I say. A coon's got the right to have his top piece as tall as old Shasta, if he's of a mind to do 'er. Anyone takes that hat, an' he's got to answer to me an' The Prince here. We got to get civilization down into this God-forsaken hole someways, I say!"

"Old Nate's already sent mail order for a hat just like the judge's," The Prince proclaimed, "and I'm thinking about doing the same."

"That's not true, and you know it!" Nate howled.

"Gentlemen, I speak the truth. Now, if Nate doesn't wish to wear his hat when it comes, then I'll wear it."

"You'll have to stretch 'er, then, so's it's big enough," Jack Spades said. "You an' the judge make a good pair, Prince."

The Prince stared at him, and Nate dropped his hand instinctively to his pistol.

"It'll be my *man-for-breakfast hat*," The Prince said slowly. "I'm just waiting for it to arrive."

Six-foot Sandy burst out laughing, and, the tension broken, the other men laughed as well. Even Spades, though the joke was on him, grinned—then turned away and left the saloon.

"Damned right," Six-foot Sandy declared, "a judge needs a top hat, by gawd!"

But it was Sandy, a great burly man who was half-miner and half–second-rate gambler, who did the judge's hat in. Sandy had not yet had the chance to meet the man, and when, that afternoon, he saw him, the response was immediate:

"That's our judge? Christ, boys, I've seen that nigger before—an' when I did, he was a waiter in a restaurant in Yreka. The man's a fraud on the gull'ble public. I'll go for 'im, I says."

Sandy walked up behind the judge, who was blissfully sitting on a stool and engaged in a hand of poker, raised his huge hands, and brought them down atop the stovepipe hat. The top of the hat burst out, and the stovepipe portion went down over the alcalde's ears.

The judge jumped up, pulled away the remains of his hat, and put up his fists.

"Welcome to The Forks, Judge," Sandy drawled, his face split in a yellow-toothed grin, and then he turned and slowly walked back to the bar.

Six-foot Sandy decided that, since The Forks now had a judge, the official should have something to do. With this thought in mind, he laid before the alcalde the case of the murders of the Indians the preceding winter—and then instituted a prosecution.

"The leaders, at very least, must go to trial," Sandy insisted.

"Irish Sean's long gone," one man said. "Guess he took The Prince at his word an' made tracks."

"Spades is still here," Sandy said. "He's the one's got to go on trial."

Under the circumstances, the judge was forced to call proceedings.

The men of The Forks quickly took sides, the idlers standing behind Jack Spades—but a majority of the miners going the other way. Six-foot Sandy became the prosecuting attorney, while the other men who had participated at the Shasta village attempted to court favor with the alcalde and made quick to intimidate all those who now took sides with the *Injuns*.

In the courthouse (the Howlin' Wilderness), Sandy argued long and hard, in the process calling both The Prince and Nate as witnesses—and then, feeling the sympathies of the audience beginning to go with Spades and against the Indians, even chose to call Klamat to testify. Klamat, who had been listening and watching with intense interest from the rear of the saloon, came forward and slowly, using his best English, related what had happened during the massacre.

During his testimony, three of the jurors got up, strode to the bar, and ordered drinks.

"Don't make no never-mind what a goddamn Injun says," one of the men said loudly enough that everyone heard.

Another called out to Sandy, "What's he say about what happened to old Dog-eye Dick?"

The alcalde ruled the jurors out of order, and Klamat finished his story.

"Prosecution rests, by God," Six-foot Sandy declared.

While the jury deliberated in the back room, Jack Spades sat drinking with the judge.

"I done my best, Prince," Six-foot Sandy said.

"Any court but this one, and you'd have won, too," The Prince said, nodding.

"Ye don't figger the judge is goin' to hang 'im? By the blue Christ, Prince, even a man as ignorant as the judge can't be total deaf, dammit!"

Spades came wandering over, glared at Klamat, made a gesture at the Indian as though he were firing a pistol at him, and said to Sandy and The Prince, "Well, boys, you done your best, but it weren't good enough to catch old Spades. If I ain't out o' this by dark, I'll sun somebody's moccasins, sure."

Spades looked back at the judge, who was slouched in his chair, the stitched-back-together stovepipe hat on the table before him.

"Ye see, Sandy," Spades continued, "you just ain't proved nothin' on me—even if you do talk real good."

Spades's defense had been short and simple. He'd acted as his own attorney and had called two friends to testify that he'd been playing poker with them at the alleged time of the murders of the Indians at the village. As simple as that.

The jury came back in and declared, by majority vote, that old Jack Spades was innocent of killing Injuns, even if he had cheated a few times at cards.

"Hear! Hear! Hear!" someone in the back of the room shouted.

"Snow is snow!" someone else yelled.

The judge pounded on his table with a ball peen hammer that he had borrowed for the purpose.

"You see," he said, clearing his throat as he did so, "things are often not so black as they first appear, particularly if they are only fairly washed. Mr. Spades was not present at the massacre at all. This here court is now adjourned."

"Whitewashed!" Sandy yelled out. "That's what you lame bastards have done. I say Spades needs hangin'!"

But the trial was over. Men were clapping Spades on the back and crowding forward to the bar.

That night the judge was talking with Doc Storz, with whom, somehow, he had managed to acquire an acquaintanceship. When Doc protested the manner in which the court proceedings had been held, to say nothing of the verdict, the judge became extremely abusive in his language. Finally Doc stormed out of the Howlin' Wilderness.

"Wouldn't be surprised if Doc gives the judge some pizzen instead o' aspirin next time he's got the headache."

"Let 'im," said a short, one-eyed fellow who was stirring his whiskey with a spoon.

"We never needed a judge before," the bartender agreed, wiping his white cloth across the wood. "Mebbe Doc'd be doin' us all a favor."

"Well, it don't concern me," the one-eyed man said, and then broke into a song:

> "Fight dog, and fight b'ar,
> Ain't no dog of mine thar. . . ."

Shortly after the verdict had been read, The Prince, Nate, and Klamat had made their way up the canyon to the cabin. Paquita, who had only vaguely understood what was going on at The Forks, now wished to know everything. And Klamat, his dark eyes even darker with excitemnt and anger, quickly launched into the story, while Nate and The Prince supplied details as interjections when Klamat paused for breath.

"I do not understand this Whiteman's law," Paquita said. "It does not seem like law at all. If one of my people kills a Whiteman, the Whites come for him and take him to their village and hang him. But the Whites do not hang their own for killing my people."

"Or else they attack our villages and kill everyone," Klamat said. "That is why they killed everyone at the village, Poon-kina. They had found a Whiteman dead and believed our people had killed him. And yet this man was found far upriver, where none of our people had been. . . ."

"Whiteman's law is better than that," Nate said. "Usually it is. What happened is simple. Spades had either bought off the judge or else he'd promised to have him killed."

"I figure it was money," The Prince agreed. "Look for the alcalde to be sporting new clothes and a gold watch chain before long. Spades's boys just bought him off, and there wasn't anything Six-foot Sandy or anyone else could have done to change it."

"Spades must be given to the Shastas, Spades and also the others who killed our people. Then they will die by Shasta law. This must happen."

"Unfortunately," The Prince said, "the Whites do not recognize the Indian law. They recognize only their own. But what happened wasn't the law at all. That man's no judge. Like Sandy says, he's a fraud on the public. . . ."

"Does such a thing happen if one Whiteman kills another?" Paquita asked.

"Sometimes it does," Nate said. "But Spades will get his, sure as hell. Whiteman or Redman, there's a law over us all. I don't know how it'll happen, but I don't think either Spades or the judge will be living too much longer after today. Likely as not, the men will take it into their own hands."

"Wouldn't be surprised at all," The Prince said, rising and walking to the stove, where the soup pot was simmering away.

"Yes," Klamat said in a half-whisper, "someone must do this thing. The judge is no judge at all. He is an evil man who has been paid to protect other evil men."

Klamat slipped away from the cabin and, his good knife under his belt, made his way down to The Forks.

A full moon hung over the canyons, its silver-white light more than sufficient for one whose eyes were trained for moving and even for hunting at night. But Klamat stayed away from the commonly followed trail, for the business he had set himself upon required no witnesses—not even so much as a single drunken miner, staggering back up the Humbug from the Howlin' Wilderness.

Roars of laughter, shouting, and arguing issued through the swinging half-doors of the big saloon and from the other establishments of entertainment. A number of men were idly wandering back and forth along the main street, some singing and some ambling silently along. Six-foot Sandy was leaning against the door of the general store, smoking a cigar, alone.

Klamat stayed back, hidden in shadows, away from the thin glow of lamplight. He tightened and then loosened his grip on the carved mahogany handle of his knife.

*The judge and Spades—they're both inside the Howlin'
Wilderness. But they'll come out eventually. The man who
takes revenge must learn to be patient. . . .*

Scenes of the massacre once more flared through Klamat's
brain—the wanton murders, the butcherings of his own
kinsmen when they were no longer able to defend themselves and were dying anyway from sickness and starvation
alike. And a terrible hatred for the Whites and all that they
stood for rushed through him. He clenched his teeth together
and then bit his lips.

*I will die fighting these Whitemen. That will be my fate.
But when the time comes, I will die bravely, and Old Man
Coyote will not turn aside from me when I enter the Spirit
World. In the long run, these Whites with their guns and
their craziness for the worthless metal will destroy all of my
people, but I will see to it that they pay a price. I am not
some helpless coward, I am not a dog that grins and wags its
tail when it is beaten. No, I am Klamat, Klamat the warrior.
And tonight I begin my revenge-taking.*

What he had to do now seemed quite clear to him, just as
it was clear to him that the Whites, all the Whites, were his
enemies.

*All of them? What of your friend Nate—and The Prince,
and Doc Storz, who has been kind to you? You must not hate
all Whites—only those who are truly your enemies. Men like
Spades and the judge.*

Klamat examined his own thinking as he stared across from
his hiding place in the shadows to the front of the Howlin'
Wilderness. Yes, he concluded, it would indeed be much
simpler if he were able to hate all the Whites. But Nate was
like a brother to him, and their ties were very close. From
the time of their first meeting at Whitmore Charley's camp,
they had been friends—as though each had recognized immediately a mysterious kind of kinship between them, even
though in some ways they were far apart, so far that only the
friendship itself was able to bridge the gap. Each had saved
the other's life, and Nate's friend, The Prince, though he
understood almost nothing of the Indian way, yet he too had
proved himself a friend. Indeed, without him Nate would
have been helpless to save either Poonkina or himself on the
terrible evening of the massacre. And Doc, good Doctor

Storz, who had brought them food and had, so to speak, saved them all.

Spades and the judge were different. And the men of The Forks in general? Klamat remembered a few of the hateful faces from the time of the killing, but now when he met these men they were often friendly to him. Yet he was never quite certain which of them had been *there*, had butchered and slain and burned. . . .

Were they different from the Modocs, the tribe he had been born into, and who had descended upon Whitmore Charley's camp that other morning and killed the white-haired one and his men and stolen the horses and killed many of the cattle for the simple sport of it?

Klamat tightened his grip on the knife once more. The judge and Doc Storz together had just come out of the saloon and had begun walking side by side down the street. Yes, and they were arguing. Klamat could hear their words clearly, the doctor still berating the judge, cursing at him sometimes in English and sometimes in the other White language he used.

Klamat moved swiftly along the railings and began to follow the two men, keeping always back within the cover of shadows, but allowing no more than a few yards to separate him from those ahead of him.

At one point the doctor and the judge stopped, faced each other, and began to push at each other. Then Doc Storz turned and walked away, the judge still standing there, shouting insults. And when the doctor turned off the main street toward his own dwelling, the judge began to follow, stumbling and running at the same time, his gait unsteady from perhaps two or three hours of drinking.

Halfway down the muddy side street, the doctor turned to face the onrushing judge, and almost immediately the two men began to grapple with each other.

Klamat sprinted forward, his knife in hand. In an instant he had one arm about the judge's neck and had spun him around. The doctor, pulled off his feet, collapsed between them.

"What in gawd's holy name?" the judge cried out. "Ye damned heathen Injun, I'll have ye strung up for that little trick, by the liver-eatin' saints I will. . . ."

"I do not think so," Klamat said, his voice calm and cold.

"But you have tried to harm my friend, and so I am going to kill you. I do not think you will be a false judge anymore."

"Gawddamned savage!" the judge roared, and lunged toward him, but Klamat, as dispassionately as one who guts a dead deer, three times hooked his blade deep into the chest and paunch of the astonished Whiteman. The victim slumped to his knees; and Klamat, grabbing hold of the hair, slit the judge's throat and stepped back as he quivered and died.

Doc Storz was on his feet once more and stood staring down at the corpse.

"*Mein heilige Gott, Herr Klamat, was haf tun Sie?* What have you done? *Schnell, mein Freund,* you must run away! *Du habst* killed the judge, he *ist tot!*"

Klamat leaned over, wiped his blade slowly across the judge's coat, and then slipped the knife back under his belt.

"He was an evil man," Klamat replied. "I do not think he really wished to live any longer. I think he is at peace now."

"*Ruhe? Ja, ja,* but they will come for you if they have any idea. Klamat, Spades and his *freunden* will kill you and Nate and The Prince *und* Paquita also. Even her, *noch mehr.*"

"No, that is not what will happen," Klamat said. "What man has killed this judge? You and I will simply walk away, and no one will ever know. Death often comes to men when they do not expect it, and that is what has happened to the judge. Did you see who killed him? No, we found him here just as he is. It is over, and now both of us will return to where we sleep. In the morning his friends will take care of his body."

With those words Klamat turned and walked quickly away, blending in once more with the shadows.

Doc Storz also turned then and moved rapidly to his house. Once there, he went inside, lit the coal-oil lamp, bolted the door, and fell asleep in his old wooden rocking chair. A pistol lay in his lap.

"Man for breakfast!" the butcher shouted up as he rode by the Miller and Prince claim.

"Who is it?" Nate called down.

"Cain't ye guess, Natty? It's the judge hisself. . . ."

Leaving Klamat with Paquita at the cabin, The Prince and Nate headed for The Forks, where the judge was lying stiff and cold on a monte table in the Howlin' Wilderness. The man had been stabbed three times in the belly and chest, his throat slit. And it was clear to all that there had been a desperate struggle, for one of the judge's hands was clenched around a lock of hair—curly, yellow hair, like that from the sides of Doc Storz's head.

"Doc killed him," Six-foot Sandy said in a way that settled the matter. "Suppose we ought to go ask, but that's what happened, sure as horse dung. I wouldn't call it murder, would ye, Prince? Looks to me like they went face to face. Doc don't carry a knife, so he must of got it away from the judge. Self-defense, I'd call it."

"Was he robbed?" The Prince asked.

"Don't look like," Sandy answered. "Coon had a big pouch of gold dust on 'im, as well as more'n a hundred dollars in coins and bills. Where you figger he got the dust?"

"Spades, more than likely," Nate cut in.

"Could be, but we wouldn't want to be sayin' that, would we?" Sandy asked.

"No, we wouldn't," The Prince said. "No point in bringing the truth into it. If Doc did kill him and didn't rob him, then it wasn't murder. That's what they'd say down in Mexico. No robbery, no motive for murder. Some other reason, then, and they went at it face to face. Doc took the judge's knife away and killed him in self-defense. It's an open-and-closed case."

"Anyway," Sandy suggested, "since there's no alcalde here at The Forks, we cain't arrest nobody. Any of you boys figger we ought to arrest old Doc?"

No one spoke a word.

"As prosecuting attorney, then, I say let's give the judge a good buryin'. After all, he's the only judge us coons ever had, even if he were a mite crooked."

After that Sandy lost interest in the matter and decided instead to go on a spree. Spades was selected as head of the funeral committee and ended up having to dig the grave himself. Only four or five of Spades's friends attended, and with Spades saying the words, the judge was planted alone on the hillside above the Klamath River.

When the funeral was over and the hole was filled in—no time taken to construct a coffin—Jack Spades headed for the

Howlin' Wilderness. When he entered, he was wearing the recently repaired stovepipe hat.

Six-foot Sandy, quite drunk and in a hell of a good mood, saw the hat, let out a bloodcurdling yell, and pitched forward to where Spades stood. Sandy grabbed Jack Spades by the collar and shook him about, like a big dog with a rag doll. The hat spun off and landed on the floor.

"Gimme that hat!" Sandy shouted. "It's our dear departed judge's, an' who ought to know better'n me? This some-bitch has got no respect for the dead! Boys, get 'im out of my sight before I bust his back!"

Spades, needing little encouragement, left the Howlin' Wilderness.

The hat was handed to Sandy, who dusted it off and then proceeded to place it atop the roaring stack of pine logs.

The attitude of the men of The Forks toward Doc Storz changed after that. No longer could the little German be considered harmless, and therefore he could no longer be entirely trusted. They had need of him, however, so they left him alone, Spades and his friends included. But a good half of The Forks had turned against him.

No decision could be made as to what to do with the judge's money and gold dust until finally Six-foot Sandy, as prosecuting attorney, took charge of it and spent it on free drinks for everyone at the Howlin' Wilderness for as long as the money held out. The other bar owners objected, wishing to have a portion of the business as their own, but Sandy ruled that the Howlin' Wilderness had been the judge's courtroom and so the money should be spent there.

The doctor still came to dinner at the Miller and Prince place, for nothing had changed. Neither Nate nor The Prince asked Doc Storz to explain what had happened, and Doc, in turn, offered no information.

The man was a bit more subdued now, but he still laughed at The Prince's stories and called them *gute Medizin*.

Still, the free-floating antagonism of The Forks began to tell on him. He carried a pistol now, and Nate gave him tips on using the weapon—sometimes went out with him to practice shooting, with Klamat and Paquita watching.

After a week, Doc Storz asked permission to move up to

the Miller and Prince cabin, and so, with the assistance of Klamat and the mule, settled into the already tight quarters. The Prince spoke of adding on a room, but the press of mining forever got in the way of turning carpenter, even for the few days that would be needed to complete the project.

Doc Storz wandered about the hillsides, going down to The Forks only when he was needed, and then often with Klamat at his side. There he would be greeted by a barrage of insults from the hangers-on, who were nevertheless not sufficiently brave to offer actual bodily harm. Doc gathered plants, wrote in a journal, and seemed often in such a depressed state of spirits that The Prince grew genuinely concerned about his former benefactor's health.

On one occasion, Doc, having gone to The Forks to attend a miner who had come down with pneumonia, was accosted by Jack Spades.

"So ye got a red nigger for a bodyguard, do ye, Doc? *Pop goes the weasel!* Well, one's as good as any dog, I reckon."

"You have *zu gross getrunken*, you are a drunk man," Doc Storz replied.

Spades lost his temper, grabbed Doc, and shook him about—letting loose his hold only after Klamat had belabored him across the back with his war club.

"You filthy red bastard—you've damn near busted my ribs!"

Spades started to reach for his pistol but stopped when Doc said, "I wouldn't do that, *Herr Spades*."

Doc's pistol was pointed straight at Spades's heart.

That night at dinner, Doc said nothing. Finally Klamat told Nate, The Prince, and Paquita what had happened.

"He needs killing," Nate said.

"Guess I'll have to have another talk with the lad," The Prince agreed.

And after that they finished their meal, with Nate attempting to make pleasant conversation.

The Prince seemed distracted.

Finally he said, "Folks, for a long while I was a gambling man—and a good one, too. You play cards enough, you get so you can *smell it* when your luck's about to run out. I'm beginning to get that smell here."

Two days later Jack Spades cashed in his last hand. He was found dead close by the door of his own cabin, with several stab wounds in the chest and his throat slit. This time the corpse did not have any of Doc Storz's hair in its hand.

The men talked of forming a lynch mob. A number of Spades's compañeros got together at the Howlin' Wilderness as Spades lay there, boots on, with an old blue army jacket covering his face. They talked impassionedly about what they would do to put an end to the murderings, but before long someone produced a pack of cards, and so Jack Spades was not buried until late the next day.

Six-foot Sandy, for his part, drank his gin and peppermint and said, "Well, let 'em rip; it's dog-eat-dog anyhow!"

Doc Storz went about his business as usual, and no one at Miller and Prince questioned him in the matter of Spades's death. But now there were very few calls for the doctor's assistance from the men of The Forks.

This time around, however, Nate and The Prince knew full well that the matter was not simply going to be swept aside. One killing, maybe. But two? Not even the men of The Forks could ignore such a thing. Perhaps there was neither judge nor sheriff in the mining town, but there were both in Yreka, and that town, after all, was only twenty-five miles of crooked trail away.

Klamat, now the owner of both a Sharps .52 percussion breech-loading carbine and a Colt pistol, purchased with his share of the gold dust from the mining operation, accompanied the doctor everywhere—having taken it upon himself to serve as bodyguard for the man who had provided them all with food during the terrible cold of winter.

With the coming of summer, Paquita had blossomed into a beautiful young woman, thin, tall, fine-featured, and high-breasted. So noticeable was the transformation that The Prince decided he and Nate and Klamat would have to put their work aside for a day or two so that they might build an additional room—for Paquita, they all felt, would now have to have her privacy.

The girl was delighted with the room and especially with the rough-hewn bedstead—little more than a raised platform, in truth—that the men constructed for her.

On numerous occasions, as Nate realized, Klamat had attempted to convince Paquita that they two must now, now certainly, make preparations for their return to their own people. But the girl, more than happy with her present situation in life, resisted all thoughts of leaving. This resistance, Nate concluded, was in large measure responsible for Klamat's occasional moods of black depression—and at such times, forgetting both the mine and the safety of the doctor, he would disappear for entire nights, and once for two full days. Another time The Prince had suggested that Klamat take a deer he had slain down to the men at the claim below theirs. Klamat, without expression, agreed—but he had little use for those men, those in particular, for they had been in the habit of taunting him and calling him "Red Devil." He took the freshly killed deer down to their cabin and, finding no one at home, kicked in the door and deposited the deer on one of the sleeping pallets.

The men, knowing as if through intuition who was responsible, complained loudly to The Prince.

That was when Klamat disappeared for two days.

Nate, on the other hand, found himself almost constantly in a state of ebullience. He could see trouble coming with regard to Doc, and he could see the trouble in his friend Klamat's mind, and he could see as well that it might soon be propitious to move on—another mining camp, another claim, perhaps even a more prosperous one.

The cause for his sense of well-being was the girl, Paquita. It was a hopeless love, and he knew it, but without question, he finally admitted to himself, he was in love. And Paquita's mere close presence, the ring of her laughter, the birdlike hum of her voice—these things were sufficient for Nate.

Klamat wished to marry her and had loved her since they had been children together, as Nate realized, and for this reason, whatever else might happen, he would always be obliged to defer on behalf of his friend and to keep his own thoughts clear and in order.

Should anything ever happen, he told himself, he would be there—should she need him ever, in any way at all.

One afternoon as Nate and The Prince worked in the mine, while Klamat was off hunting, The Prince ceased digging, leaned on his pick, and said, "Nate, why is it I have the feeling you're in love with Paquita?"

Nate was startled by the question, and at first he denied

it—explaining what The Prince already knew, that Klamat wished to marry her.

"Nate, we've been together now for the better part of a year, and I guess we know each other like open books. Klamat isn't here just now, it's just you and me. Come on, now, am I right or wrong?"

Nate's face flamed, and he struggled for words.

"Guess I know the answer," The Prince said. "And I don't blame you, lad. My God, she's turned into a beauty, hasn't she? And I don't mean just her face and body, either. I mean, Paquita's beautiful all over, inside and out. Tell you, if I was the sort of man who could ever settle down, I guess I'd be thinking about paying court to that lass myself."

It took a moment for The Prince's words to register fully.

"You love her too?" Nate asked.

The Prince rapped the side of his pick blade against the gravel cutbank, and Nate stared fixedly at the little quartz pebbles that spilled to the floor of the hole, rolled, stopped.

"Yes, Natty, I suppose I do. How could anyone not love her? There's not a Whitewoman alive could compare with her. And that, of course, makes four of us."

"The doc?"

"Doc, too. He's too old for her—he knows that. But age doesn't make a bit of difference to a man's feelings. I've had women, lots of them, mostly ones that I paid for or ones that were hoping to make *their* grubstake out of my tin. And a couple maybe that I left behind when I shouldn't have. But Paquita—ain't she something, Nate? Whatever happens, all four of us will go to our graves still thinking about that girl. I look into crystal balls sometimes, and that's what I see."

"Will she marry Klamat, do you think?" Nate asked.

"I think so. If that old chief of a father of hers will permit it. You'd know about that better than I would."

Nate sat down, his back against the bank. He made a fist of one hand and patted it with the other.

"It's like we're a family, Prince. And Paquita's at the center of it. I'd be happy to have it go on this way forever, I really would."

The Prince whistled a nondescript melody and gazed up at the opening of the shaft.

"You ever had a woman, Nate? Ever made love with a woman?"

Again Nate flushed.

"I . . ."

"It's okay to say no. Hell, man, you're young—and you've had no opportunities. Certainly none here at The Forks. But the need comes over a man, it really does. Ultimately, a man will make love to a knothole in a plank, if there's nothing else around. It's just in us, that's all, and we've got to do it. And I figure it's the same way for a woman, any woman, Paquita included. She's not some kind of sexless fairy princess—look at her that way, and you're not looking at her at all. The need comes for children, I think, maybe for man and woman both. There are times when I think of having a family, and maybe one day I will settle down, too."

"But right now you're in love with Paquita," Nate said.

"And so are you, my partner. I'll never forget that night at the Indian village, Nate, the way you went plunging in there, no weapon or anything, when you saw Paquita's face. Could have gotten yourself killed, and it's a wonder you didn't. But you saved her life, lad. At that moment, even without thinking, you knew that her life was more important than yours. And then, when she was safe, off you went like a madman, screaming for your friend Klamat. A man capable of that kind of loyalty is a powerful friend to have. Best thing that ever happened to me, Nate, is when I met you—that's the God's truth. We've learned a hell of a lot from each other."

"You're the best man I've ever known," Nate said.

Then the silence grew uncomfortable, and both began to dig once more.

It was true about Paquita. No one alive could have recognized her now as the skeletal creature with large eyes that terrible night at the Indian village. Indeed, the massacre had, without doubt, saved her life—for starvation would directly have taken its toll.

Now she was like—what? A rose just coming to bloom, Nate wanted to say, but realized that he had seen the image used in countless books. And besides, the image wasn't right, not for her. What, then? The spotted lilies that grew here and there along the creek—or a butterfly lily, the mariposa. Or a soaring bird—or a doe in the dark forest.

His mind worked over and over again what he had seen that afternoon.

A small lake high up on the mountain, a lake that was surrounded by wild pink roses and salmon berries, and ferns drooping above the water, other ferns in heavy green bunches under the huge firs of the wood. The forest so thick that even the brilliance of afternoon sunlight could only find its way to the damp duff in narrow bars of brilliance.

It wasn't really a lake at all—a lily pond, rather, perhaps half a pistol shot across, that filled the hollow at the base of a waterfall, the cascading water thin, almost gossamer, swept up into mist whenever the wind blew.

Here he had found Paquita, who never suspected his presence. And he watched her for a time, there on the rim, walking back and forth in the sunlight.

At first he had not been certain what she was doing.

She moved forward, then back, then looking across her shoulder—like a princess, Nate thought, preparing for a ball.

She was wearing the bright red dress the doctor had given her, the one with lace at the ends of the sleeves and on the bodice, and she had decorated her apparel further with ribbons of several different colors.

She was studying her own reflection in the still water. She was contemplating herself, as if trying to understand who she was.

She had transformed the little lake into an Eden, Nate thought, her own realm of utter innocence. And he, watching, what was he?

The serpent?

The hunter who had witnessed Artemis bathing, and his own dogs tore him apart?

This scene, he realized, was not his to witness. At the first glimpse he should have turned aside.

And then he had backed carefully away, staying low, into the darkness of the somber black forest, and had retreated downslope until he had reached the Miller and Prince cabin.

NINE

▲

The Goose Hangs High

Restless men in search of gold, silver, copper, whatever riches the earth might provide—the Americans, a young and violent race, though in truth the miners came from all over the world, from the slums of Europe as well as from the estates of the well-to-do, from China, from Mexico, from South America. And the common patois was the language of minerals.

The mining towns were born overnight, and overnight most of them died. A strange race, "the best and worst of men," the miners pursued the phantom of quick cash and the goods and services that a full poke might procure. Small fortunes were gained through endless hours of the most demanding sort of work and frittered away often in the course of but a few hell-roaring nights.

Saloons, hotels, banks, stagecoaches, noise, excitement, and, from time to time, a man for breakfast.

If the placers diminished and news of a new strike came in, a town might be utterly abandoned overnight.

The summer wore on, and Paquita became the pet of The Forks. Numerous miners sent orders south to Shasta City to buy clothing for her, and, when the goods arrived in The Forks, sent them up to the Miller and Prince cabin via the butcher and his mule. Within no time there were many in town who knew what size she wore, dress and shoe and underthing, and which colors she liked the best. Soon Paquita had an extensive wardrobe, the donors of which preferred to remain anonymous.

Paquita loved the presents of clothing but could not understand either why they were being sent or why she was not to know who had sent them.

She dressed tastefully, with advice from Doc Storz as to matters of fashion, and was universally esteemed as sensitive, intelligent, and beautiful. The simple presence of her person began to exercise a distinct civilizing influence on The Forks. To even the casual eye, it was evident that the men who lived near the Miller and Prince claim dressed more neatly than those who lived elsewhere—and when word spread on some particular day that Paquita had accompanied Nate and The Prince to town, ragged men could be observed scuttling to their dwellings to wash up and put on their best shirts. Beards became less shaggy, and shirts were buttoned up at the front.

But, as delighted as she was with the inexplicable attentions of the miners, there were times when a terrible sadness would come over her. For it seemed to her then that she was not living in the world that had been intended for her—it was simply a dream, and like all dreams it would have to end. And she would wake to find that none of it had happened at all.

There was another world, different in almost every way from what she now experienced—and that world lay to the east and south of the great mountain of the Shastas. Many seasons had passed now since she and her father and her sister had made their journey to Slippery Salmon's people, the Nomki-dji, where she had been left in the keeping of Red Fawn and the crazy man, Tommyrotter. Warrottetot had wished her to be away from Klamat and hence to find a better prospective husband, a man with horses and weapons and a good lodge.

Did she resent her father for what he had done?

No—for in moments when she attempted to put herself into Warrottetot's place, she realized that he had only acted out of concern for her. Any woman who allowed love to lure her into a bad marriage and so realized the unfitness of her mate only after it was too late, was as good as trapped, condemned to the raising of that man's children under what were often the worst of conditions. Red Fawn, for instance, slain in the massacre on the Klamath River, had married well, to Warrottetot's younger brother. But when he had died, she had allowed herself to be attracted by a man who had all but disowned his own people and who had often beaten and otherwise abused her.

What could such a woman do? She could, of course, divorce her husband—but divorce was far easier for the husband than for the wife. She would have to leave her lodge, taking her clothing and her children with her, and return to her father's dwelling. And sometimes fathers, realizing what was afoot, would refuse to let their daughters enter. Then the woman would either have to return to her husband or find some other refuge. In any case, divorce meant that the father was obliged to repay the bride price to his former son-in-law.

A woman of normal standing might be bought for twenty full-sized dentalium shells, fifteen strings of disk beads, and thirty woodpecker scalps. The head chief's eldest daughter might cost twice this amount, with half-a-dozen horses and a pistol or rifle thrown in besides.

And how would Klamat ever be able to amass such wealth? Yet somehow, in a way that was quite beyond reason, Paquita was confident that he would be able to do so.

How long? How long will it take? We could run away, just as we once attempted to do. Have we not already run away? And why should we ever return?

But the bonds of home were strong, and she knew it. Warrottetot, White Dawn, Crippled Deer, Heron, even old Mountain Smoke, all the others... And the Spirit Mountain itself, the peak that rose at the center of the world... The forests, the streams, the animals, the birds. Nowhere else was everything arranged in so perfect a fashion, and the memories flooded through her like a great wave of pure music.

Oh, she thought, I am happy enough right here. Do I not have my four men all about me? We have enough to eat now, and Nate Miller and Prince are finding almost enough of the yellow metal to satisfy them, even though they are not satisfied. With their gold they can buy the things we need, and if the mine proves to be a very good one, Klamat will also share in this Whiteman's wealth. He knows that, and he has spoken of it to me. Perhaps with the gold he will be able to purchase some horses like those Fire-on-the-hills had. Then, when we return to our own people, the other warriors will

gladly follow him, maybe even on an expedition against the
Klamat Indians. They are said to have many horses. Yes, that
will happen when we return....

Much had happened to her since her father had taken her
to live among Slippery Salmon's people, and now Red Fawn
was dead and perhaps Slippery Salmon himself as well, she
did not know. The chief of the Nomki-dji had taken his wife
downriver and had promised to return with whatever food
the lower village could spare. Had he been slain by the
Whites as he brought the supplies back up the river trail?

But often those who were supposed dead found a way of
returning to life, she knew that.

When the miners had found as much gold as they wanted,
would they go away and return to whatever places they had
come from? Or, as seemed more likely, would they finally dig
out all the gold and still not be satisfied? Then they would
raise cattle and fence the land and shoot all the animal
people—so that the Indians would no longer be able to hunt.
And perhaps her own people would come to be like
Tommyrotter—wearing Whiteman's clothing and working for
the Whites. Klamat and his friends had worked for a Whiteman,
just as some of the Modocs and Wintuns did. That was what
she had been told. Yes, and that was how Klamat had come to
be friends with Nate.

A momentary vision of Klamat wearing an old gray coat and
a small black tie around his neck, like the doctor, came to
her—and she smiled in spite of herself. Then she could see
Klamat working in the general store in The Forks. She was
buying things, and he was waiting on her, getting items down
off the high shelves for her.

She shook her head.

Klamat would never be willing to do such a thing. Besides,
what if it should become known that he had killed Spades and
the judge? For the time being, the men seemed to have
concluded that Doc Storz had killed the two men, but how
could anyone suppose the doctor would be able to kill such a
person as Spades? In any case, no *Whiteman's justice* had
seen fit to harm the doctor. Klamat had often insisted that
there was no such thing as Whiteman's justice, but possibly
he was wrong. Spades and the judge were both dead, and yet
no revenge had been taken on anyone.

As Paquita considered the matter, that was certainly the way of justice. And a greater justice would be served if all those men who had been with Spades on the evening of the massacre at the village were also to be killed.

Would Klamat stop after having slain just two of the men responsible for what had happened? And why had Nate and The Prince and the others who were their friends not taken revenge on those who had followed Spades?

Well, that terrible time was past, and now most of the men of The Forks seemed to love her—almost as though she were an adopted daughter to all of them. They smiled whenever they saw her, and often the butcher would deliver presents of clothing, and invariably disclaim any knowledge of the identity of the sender. For a time she had supposed that the butcher, a man known to her only as Tom, had been bringing the presents himself, as though he wished to court her. But Nate and The Prince had explained otherwise.

In general, she was happy here on Humbug Creek, even though she realized that the world she lived in could not last and even though she herself did not wish it to last much longer. And often she wished passionately just to be able to look out and see the White Giant, the Spirit Mountain of her people. In the depths of these dark canyons, however, the mountain was forever hidden from view.

She thought once more of the strange dream that had come to her during the time of her *waphi* ceremonies and shuddered, for she had come to suppose its message to be that she would die in a great fire. Often she had wished to relate the dream to Red Fawn, but the admonitions of old Mountain Smoke had dissuaded her. Instead she had inquired about dreams of bad omen, and Red Fawn had told her that in the olden days a young woman who had experienced such a dream was dressed up prettily and then burned alive.

"Did you have such a dream, child?" Red Fawn had asked.

But the daughter of Chief Warrottetot had not answered her aunt.

Indeed, it may have been Paquita's presence that deterred those few who wished to see Doc Storz hung, kept them from enacting their plans.

Nonetheless, the ill feelings toward the doctor had not

blown over—and everyone assumed, Doc included, that a deputy from Yreka would one day ride up and put him under arrest. After that, with good luck, he would survive the ride to Yreka and take up residence in the small jail until such time as a trial might be held. The longer this matter might be postponed, Doc realized, the greater would be his chances of receiving a fair trial and so having a chance to demonstrate his innocence.

"*Heilige Gott!*" he muttered. "*Ich bin der Mann* who saves the lives of these *Menchen,* not one who kills them. *Aber,* whom shall I say has done these things? When the time comes, *Ich will nichts gesagen....*"

Nate and The Prince had in fact discussed at some length the wisdom of abandoning their claim, though it was paying handsomely now, and of moving on. Yet, such a move might well be taken as an admission of guilt on Doc's part—might actually encourage the formation of a posse.

Nate suggested that they might move to the lands of the Shastas, for there, in the heart of the mountains and at the foot of the great peak of Shasta, who would look for them?

"There's nowhere to go that a man can't be tracked down," The Prince said. "Doc would be better off on a ship headed for Boston. As far away from California as possible—but he won't do that...."

"I still think the foot of the mountain would be a good place to go," Nate persisted. "Klamat and Paquita would be back with their people, and we'd be a long way from The Forks."

"Never heard about any gold being found over that way, have you?"

"Never heard any reports," Nate answered. "But gold comes in these gravels and..."

"Exactly, my friend. And that whole country's covered over with lava from Shasta and all the other old fire holes. About a year before we met each other, I rode up Little Shasta River from Yreka, crossed over Hebron, and on to Klamath Falls. I saw a lot of lava and a lot of mud bottoms, but no gravels—though I guess I wasn't really looking at the time."

"No, you're right. There's none over there that I know of. But Klamat and I went hunting once, just south of the mountain. We dropped down over a bluff into a basin with some hot springs, a kind of semicircle of them. And just down from there, along a creek Klamat called the Numken, I remember seeing a big ledge of gravels that looked just like what we're digging."

"South of the mountain—how far south?"

"Few miles. The creek must feed down into the Sacramento or the McCloud, though we didn't follow it. In any case, Klamat knows that country like he had maps in his head. If there are placers anywhere over there, he knows where they are and can lead us to them."

"Would he do that?" The Prince asked.

"What do you think?"

The Prince whistled softly.

"Guess he would at that," he said. "But if we found anything, and word got out, there'd be a new *Forks* sitting there in no time—and the Shastas would be driven out of their hunting grounds, just like the poor devils at the massacre. And we'd be responsible, Nate."

"Who among us would go advertising?"

"No one. But gold's a hell of a secret to keep in. Wind carries the word. Where would we get supplies? From where you're talking about, it must be fifty miles or so to Yreka and a good deal more than that to Shasta City. It's a hell of a long way to go for a drink, lad."

"Pack mules, and we cover our trail. I've been thinking about the thing for a couple of months now. With talk about a deputy coming over from Yreka for Doc Storz, the idea's beginning to sound pretty good. Get Klamat and Paquita back to their people—solve a bunch of problems. And we'd have the entire area to ourselves."

"Which is worth nothing," The Prince said, "if there's no gold in the gravel. . . ."

"That's true, but . . ."

"Let's think on it, Mr. Miller."

September came in, and a haze formed about the sun, a smeared circle. The air was hot, thick, and moisture-laden. Pine lizards and snake lizards slithered over the rocks, and the black crickets became quiet. Swallows were darting about silently.

Paquita came running to the shaft where three of her men were laboring and called for them.

"A great storm is coming!" she cried out. "I have seen this before, and so has Klamat. The wind will break down the trees, and the streams will become huge with water. . . ."

As she stood there, swaying back and forth, the wind in fact began suddenly to gust up Humbug Canyon, and the pines and firs began moving like huge pendulums.

The men climbed up the ladder to emerge into a world that had grown instantly dark, and a few drops of rain began to fall. Before they had reached the cabin, the wind had risen to terrific intensity, roaring like the ocean, causing pine and fir boughs to surge and finally to crack and splinter. Within moments the tops of the trees were being swung about like tall grass, and the patterns of their movements could clearly be seen across Humbug Canyon. Warm drops of rain were striking and stinging against their faces as they began to run the final few yards to the cabin.

Fir and pine struck at each other and a hail of bark and splinters of pitchy wood rained down.

At the door to the cabin they turned to look back. The entire forest seemed to be exploding, trees were going down everywhere, and sheets of lightning were roaring across the blackened sky.

"My God, it's like the end of the world!" The Prince said, turning to Doc Storz, who was lying on his bunk, face down, hiding his eyes with his hands.

"Someone down at The Forks forgot to put his dime in the church collection plate," Nate suggested.

Klamat stared at his friend, puzzled, for the words made no sense at all.

"Maybe because we sort of forgot to build a church," The Prince said, shrugging.

"Could be that's the reason."

"Think we built this roof strong enough, Nate?"

"Not strong enough to make the lightning bounce off. . . ."

Outside, the storm raged on, with periods of relative calm interspersed with renewed thunderings and poundings of wind and deluges of rain.

No one undressed for the night, and Paquita was not at all interested in retiring to her own room. Wind ripped loose some of the shingles, and small rivers of water poured down onto the dirt floor of the cabin. Nate built up the fire, using what little wood was kept in the house during the summer months, and then ventured out into the storm to haul in armfuls of split chunks. As he returned to the cabin on his second venture, a gust of wind hit him and seemed to throw him backward and lift the firewood out of his grasp at the same instant. He got up, fetched more wood, and struggled toward the house.

They kept the fire going and huddled about it all through the long violence of the night. Now and then they were able to sleep, but always a renewed raging of the elements would awaken them.

By morning the storm had calmed but was still not over. In a group they walked outside and looked down toward the Humbug—a swirling, muddy river now, ripping out the alders along its banks, having already washed away several miners' cabins that had stood too close to its course.

Logs, boards, shingles, rockers, toms, sluices, flumes, pans, riffles, aprons went drifting, bobbing, dodging down the angry river like a thousand eager swimmers.

A scene of utter devastation. The Forks was ruined, the buildings blown or swept away or crushed beneath falling pines. The Howlin' Wilderness itself lay in a ragged heap, and the cemetery hillside, where both the judge and Spades, as well as Long Dan and many another, lay buried, had slid away into the huge brown torrent of the Klamath River.

One miner, who had lost both house and partner to the flood of thick brown water that surged down Humbug, was dancing a hokee-pokee and singing over and over, like a man deranged:

> "O, everything is lovely,
> And the goose hangs high!"

Nate and The Prince walked to their mineshaft. The windlass had been swept away, and the pit was filled with water— a newly awakened spring from upslope flowing down into it with a stream nearly as large as that of the Humbug itself during the dry months of summer.

The Cayuse pony and the mule were discovered huddled against the rear of the cabin, behind Paquita's room, and the mule was peacefully engaged in chewing at the wood of a sappy log.

Nate hugged his horse and said, "Cayuse old man, we should have let you fellows come in the house, I guess."

The pony cast down a reproachful eye but said nothing.

Everyone at The Forks was ruined. A dozen men were missing and presumed dead, drowned, and those who were yet alive had seen their small fortunes or whatever they had managed to accumulate vanish. . . . Who could have anticipated such a storm?

The miners shook their heads and clenched their teeth. For most, the disaster meant yet another season in the mines—if indeed they could find new claims. Others would remain, attempt to reopen their holdings. One way or the other, disease, scurvy, and death would be household companions during the months ahead.

"What will you do now, Nate?" The Prince asked.

"What will *we* do?"

"Guess that's what I meant."

"I'd say, head for Shasta lands. Our claim here will dry out after a month or so, but if we stay, we'll be living in a world of death."

"A world of death," The Prince mused. "I guess that's it, all right. Well, folks, let's start packing our worldly possessions. The Bitch Goddess of Luck has nodded and said, *Thou shalt go!*"

For a long while that night, The Prince talked with Paquita and Klamat—gaining from them an assessment of the plan to venture into the lands to the south of the Great Mountain. Paquita claimed there was gold to be had for the picking up, if Warrottetot did not object. Klamat, on the other hand, was not so certain about the wisdom of admitting to what lay hidden in the sands of the Numken. Yes, he admitted, he knew of the place that Nate had spoken of—yes, they had gone there together, to hunt. And there were deposits of gravel, very much like the ones here at The Forks, throughout the welter of ridge and canyon that lay to the south of the mountain. But at the same time, he remembered Warrottetot's warning.

Doc Storz, Nate, Klamat, and Paquita, for various reasons, were all eager to go. The Prince nodded and said, "I'm with you, then."

In the morning, while the others were busy packing what articles were both necessary and capable of being transported across the mountains, The Prince went down to what remained of The Forks and purchased two more mules, a double-barreled shotgun, and four additional pistols, as well as a quantity of gunpowder and shot. The roof of the general store was caved in, with some loss of goods, but the storekeeper had been able to salvage much. He'd extended a new line of credit to all who needed it and could not otherwise pay for goods, knowing full well that he himself was now a bankrupt man, but knowing also that he could not in good conscience do otherwise.

From The Prince, he gratefully received full payment—money that would get him back to Yreka, where he hoped to find employment.

"I've been keeping this thing for you, Prince. Probably we shan't be seeing each other again, so you'd best take 'er."

It was the ivory-handled pistol The Prince had exchanged for food the night of the Indian massacre.

When he returned to the Miller and Prince cabin, with mules and guns, he brought as well some unwelcome news.

Rumor had it that an officer was on his way to arrest Doc Storz.

"With luck," Nate said, "we'll be gone over the mountains when he gets here."

"Luck," The Prince said, nodding.

With everything ready to go, Nate looked about at what remained of their little world. He felt guilty, he realized, guilty to be leaving. But they were leaving a world that, for practical purposes, had already vanished.

All morning Nate had been haunted by the image of a painting of a great grizzly and its hunter, the bones of Long Dan in a pile upon it, bobbing on down the swollen Klamath River, on its way to the distant Pacific.

Bones, boards, dead animals, makeshift furniture, the

bodies of miners, pouches of gold dust, windlasses, toms—all going down to the Pacific.

The Prince, utilizing a round-tipped fines brush and a half-empty can of stove black, painted a sign and nailed it to the door of their cabin:

TO LET

"All aboard!" he called out.

With Klamat leading, his moccasins bound tightly about his feet and reaching up to the legs of his buckskins, his right arm free of the red shirt whose sleeve hung loosely at his side, and with some eagle feathers in his hair and his rifle on his shoulder—the little group of five humans, one horse, and three mules moved upslope, away from the cabin.

They would pass by the lily pond and the waterfall and then cross over the shoulder of Badger Mountain. From there they would angle along the ridge crests toward Gunsight Peak, cross the trail from Yreka to Fort Jones and the Scott Valley, and proceed south, staying to the high country, toward Antelope Mountain and the higher peaks of the Mount Eddy massif, to the springs where the Sacramento River, as Klamat explained, began.

Once across the smaller tributary to the Humbug, Klamat led them up an extremely steep slope, then began a zigzag route that took them to a bench in the mountain. At this point he halted and motioned for Nate and The Prince to look back toward the mining operation.

"See!" Klamat said, pointing downslope.

They watched as three men rode up to the cabin and leaned from their saddles to read the inscription on the door. One man dismounted, kicked in the door, and entered but did not remain inside very long. The man climbed on his mule once again and rode on down toward the next cabin below. They watched as the lead rider cupped his hands, apparently shouting to those within. One came out and engaged in a brief conversation, then pointed toward China Peak, on the opposite side of Humbug Canyon.

"It's the law," The Prince said. "The rumor was true—and our friends down there are about to send the boys on a goose chase. Klamat, there was a reason why I told you to take them the deer. Even with you busting up their door, they've sided against the law. Get right down to it, nobody likes lawmen—even when they're the ones who sent for them."

"Hairy Tom sent for the law?" Nate asked. "I thought . . ."

"No, I guess he didn't. I was getting at a philosophical truth," The Prince said.

"I still do not like those men," Klamat persisted.

Doc Storz and Paquita had by now reached the bench, and the entire family stared down. They saw the lawmen start in the opposite direction, apparently finding no fresh tracks, and come to a halt. The great rains had made the earth extremely soft, at the same time effacing all earlier tracks.

The lawmen talked it over, then finally gazed up the slopes of Badger Mountain. The Prince and his group were standing behind a cover of low growth, and Klamat was pinching The Prince's mule's nose so that the animal could not shriek greetings to the mules far below.

Paquita nervously plucked leaves and grass for the Cayuse and her own pack mule, and Klamat, shrugging, began to do the same. Still holding the mule's nose, he bent over. At this moment, the mule sensed its opportunity, jerked back its head away from Klamat, and brayed long and loud.

His foot tapping in the wooden stirrup, The Prince jingled his Spanish spurs and said nothing.

Below, an arm was lifted and pointed in their general direction.

"The chase is on," Nate said. "Let's get going."

Klamat, on foot, moved off ahead, on up the mountainside.

"We should perhaps wait for *die Menschen*," the doctor said. "They are after me, not all of you. They will take *mir* to Yreka, *und* there I will stand trial. They will not kill me, *nicht wahr?*"

"Doc," Nate said, "you're forgetting one important thing."

"*Ja?*"

"We got no idea who those fellows are. Could be the judge's cousins or Spades's brothers, for all we know. We're in this together, and we'll get out of it together."

They could not keep pace with Klamat, who moved through the forest like a spirit—constantly beckoning and urging them onward.

Their three-mile headstart was significant but certainly no guarantee that they would be able to make their escape—for the men below had the advantage of traveling lightly, without the encumbrance of pack animals. Beyond this, one wrong turn, one wrong estimate of what lay ahead, might well bring them to an abrupt halt before the thick chaparral, manzanita, madrone, wild plum, and white thorn that sometimes rendered the north slopes of hills nearly impassable. It was necessary now to work toward southern slopes, where the forest was more open.

Klamat decided finally to make for the summit and so to keep along the backbone of the mountain. There were numerous trails, these made by game crossing the ridges during their times of migration, the deer and elk that sought summer grass in the mountain meadows but descended with the onset of cold weather to the lower elevations of canyon bottoms and riversides. And spurs shot away from the main crest, often higher than the crest itself, so that sometimes it was necessary for Klamat to take off running in order to reach a high point from which he could clearly see what lay ahead of them.

The men following behind, of course, operated under no such necessity. They had only to follow the trail, and one clearly marked, several sets of hooves distinctly impressing themselves into the soft, wet earth.

From the second bench, Nate looked back. He could observe the men below.

"They've seen us by now for sure," Nate said aloud.

The Prince dismounted, set the saddle well forward, and pulled the cinch as tight as he could. The others did the same, mounted, and followed on after Klamat, clearly visible ahead, both arms now free of the red shirt, the sleeves dangling at his sides.

From the summit, Shasta suddenly and breathtakingly appeared—the huge mountain, shimmering with light, the storms that flooded the Humbug having dropped a uniform whiteness down to the timberline and even below in places, so that the higher reaches of forest glistened gray-green.

"Thirty or forty miles away, and it looks like a man could reach out and touch it," Nate marveled.

"Grand scenery," The Prince agreed, "but no time for it now. Let's keep moving!"

Even at this desperate moment, the utter spectacle was too much to ignore. A warm wind blew across from the Klamat lakes and the lands of the Modocs, and northward rose the perfect, symmetric white cone of Mount Pitt, the high peak in southern Oregon. Below lay the Shasta Valley, irregularly mottled with small cinder cones and lava flows. In the distance, dwarfed at the foot of mighty Shasta, rose Black Butte, so steep and sharply pointed that it looked completely out of place, unreal. And due south, across a welter and tumble of lesser ridges, rose the snow-covered heights of China Mountain and Mount Eddy, beyond the crest of which emerged the springs that were the headwaters of the Sacramento River.

Paquita leaped from the Cayuse and threw out her arms as if to embrace the Snowy God that dwelled in the land of her people. Her face was radiant, and she gazed spellbound at Shasta. Then, unable to restrain further the emotion she felt, she turned abruptly, threw her arms around the horse's neck, and kissed him on the nose.

Even Doc Storz smiled.

Nate's emotions were nearly as volatile—he felt like a child again and clasped and twisted his hands together, remembering vividly that first day he had seen the mountain, a boy on the way to the goldfields, alone, and frightened. Even as the peak had mesmerized him then, so now was its impact exactly the same.

Klamat threw up his hand—one of the lawmen had appeared on the bench below. But the pursuers were falling behind—perhaps a saddle had slipped off during the uphill struggle.

Nate looked toward the sun and wished for the cover of darkness, the world of night.

Klamat beckoned the party onward, the eagle feathers in his black hair rising and falling with the little gusts of mountain wind.

The chase continued, and the hours of daylight dragged on interminably. There was no talking now—only the constant forward motion, and Klamat ahead, searching out the trail, beckoning, urging them onward. They had eaten nothing since sunrise, and neither had they tasted water for some hours. The doctor was unsteady in his saddle, and the mules had taken to braying their complaints at intervals. The tongue of The Prince's mule was hanging out between its teeth, and the ears were flopping back and forth.

When a mule lets his ears flop, Nate thought, *he's lost his ambition....*

Who had told him that? Was it Old Mountain Joe or Whitmore Charley? Nate could not remember.

It was one of the mules The Prince had bought at The Forks—and what kind of care the animal had previously enjoyed, who could say?

The animals the lawmen rode, no doubt, were old companions and so had been treated well. Nate, for the first time, was becoming genuinely concerned—and his confidence that they would be able to outdistance their pursuers waned. It was time to consider the eventuality of an actual showdown—guns against guns. They themselves were well armed with rifle and pistol, and they outnumbered their pursuers. Doc might be of little help in a fight, though he was armed and by this time knew well enough how to handle his weapon, but Paquita could load for them and knew how to use a rifle in any case, for both he and Klamat had instructed her.

Klamat did not seem particularly concerned—more annoyed, perhaps because those he led were sometimes unable to keep up.

The pursuers closed ground, and then, when the lawmen were nearly within hail, a saddle slipped, and the men lost perhaps ten minutes when the mule refused to be recinched until it had been given rest.

Shasta gleamed a thin orange-red in the late sunlight, but no one did more than glance at the display of glinting snow. Their bodies were tired, and their minds grew tired as well.

At one point, Doc Storz nearly fell from his mule, and Nate rushed to his assistance, as did Paquita. At this moment, their hands touched, and their eyes met—a moment of surprise, when neither knew what to say, each hesitant to move the hand that touched the other.

"Doc," Nate managed, "are you all right? Can you stick with it?"

"*Mochte du*—you should leave me behind, Nate. It is me they want. I do not know if I can keep up any longer—*Nach einer glücklichen aber für mich sehr schweren Landreise erreichten wir endlich den Grenze."*

"What are you saying, Doc? Use English, dammit. This is no damned time for language lessons!"

"I cannot go farther, Nate. Leave me behind. That's what *Ich sagte.*"

"Damn you, Doc," The Prince bellowed. "You're not giving up on us, not after we've come this far. Swear to God, I'll tie you to that mule if I have to!"

The Doc's eyes widened, and he sat up in the saddle.

"I am *Kind* that you should talk to me this way? You are nothing but gambler, *nicht ein Fahrer!*"

"I'll *Fahrer* you, you old jackass! Now let's move!"

The Prince's tactic worked, and within moments the little caravan was pushing along, Klamat ahead, gesturing.

Shortly before dark, Klamat suddenly led them away from the crest and onto a spur, but The Prince said nothing. There was no longer time to dispute the route to be taken.

But it was evident that they were being led at a right angle to the previous trail—so that the lawmen, if they knew, might cut across and so apprehend them. At an open point on the spur, Klamat stopped and signaled for the others to approach. When the lawman and his companions came into sight, Klamat raised his arm, as if desiring to catch their attention. Then he nodded, sat down, and said, "It is time to rest for a while now."

The lawmen drew their pistols, revolved the cylinders, tapped the handles on their saddle pommels, thus settling the powder, and spurred their mules down the depression to head the fugitives off.

When the lawmen suddenly vanished among the tangle of brush, Klamat said, "I do not think they have chosen a wise path. They will not be able to cross that ravine. It may be that their mules will break their legs or throw their riders down among the rocks."

And it was true—no one emerged from the ravine. A cottontail rabbit came up, stopped, gazed back down, and then hopped off. A covey of mountain quail flew, but nothing else happened.

"Sometimes the short way is actually the long way," Klamat said.

He was grinning.

Doc Storz had to be assisted back into his saddle, but he now insisted that he was all right and wished to continue. The Prince nodded, and, with Klamat leading, they made their way back toward the crest, along the rim of the spur.

Klamat was walking more slowly now. Even he, for all his immense endurance, was bone-weary.

▲

TEN

Home on the Numken

Some say that a bear has no sense of smell. A mistake. He relies as much on his nose as the deer; perhaps more, for his little black eyes are so small that they surely are not equal to the great liquid eyes of the buck, which are so set in his head that he may see far and wide at once. But the bear carries his nose close to the ground, while that of the deer is lifted, and of course can hardly smell an intruder in his dominions until he comes upon his track. Then it is curious to observe him. He throws himself on his hind legs, stands up tall as a man, thrusts out his nose, lifts it, snuffs the air, turns all around in his tracks, and looks and smells in every direction for his enemy. If he is a cub, however, or even a cowardly grown bear, he wheels about the moment he comes upon the track, will not cross it under any circumstances, and plunges again into the thicket.

A crimson tide of sunset washed over the mountains, with black pools of night rising up from the canyons and valleys below. Blood-red plumes trailed from the summit of Shasta, and the entire mountain glowed a pale scarlet, as though the deeply harbored fires within the great shell of rock and ice would at any moment spew outward, the entire mountain erupting all at once and hurling itself away from its molten core in an explosion of cataclysmic proportion.

But then the light began to fade, and Shasta, revealed now by the amber glow of a new-risen moon, blazed cold and intense white against a thin, blanched blackness punctuated by stars.

The small caravan of humans and animals moved on southward for yet another hour, but weariness had overcome them all. Doc Storz, ill throughout the afternoon, could now barely cling to the mane of his mule, and The Prince, riding beside him, endeavored to keep him in his saddle. At length they stopped and prepared a bed of pine needles for the doctor. When this was finished, Paquita, not complaining whatsoever, went about gathering armfuls of pine needles so that everyone might have something other than the cold, loose sand and pebbles of the mountain crest to lie upon.

Doc became unconscious, whether a sleep of simple exhaustion or something far more serious they did not know. Klamat climbed down a boulder-strewn ravine, found water for the empty canteen, and brought it back—wet the doctor's lips but failed to revive him. Nate tucked the pack blankets about the suffering man, who, though unconscious, continued to shake and shiver.

The Prince suggested a fire, but Klamat warned against it. The Prince nodded and lay down beside the doctor. But as the hours passed, the cold grew ever more intense—dropped to well below freezing. And Doc grew worse. There was no longer a matter of choice, and Paquita gathered pine knots for Nate to place in a nest of dry pine needles. The Prince struck a match, and the fire went up with startling quickness, throwing out an orange glow of light and heat against the mountain cold.

The Prince, Nate, Klamat, and Paquita stared at one another, and then all eyes fell upon the sick man.

"Is he going to die?" Paquita asked, her voice a whisper.

"He's too damned grouchy to take flight this easy," The Prince said, firelight glinting from his teeth as he grinned. "Nate, get the coffeepot out. That's what we all need—good, hot coffee."

Nate moved quickly to the pack mules, found what he was after, and, using the remainder of the water in the canteen, set the coffee to boiling. With the rich odor drifting up into the night air, Doc Storz turned over, shook his head, and sat up.

"*Danke schön*," he said. "You fix coffee for the doctor, *ja*?"

The Prince laughed, a deep, easy laughter of relief.

"Old bastard's been faking it," he said.

"*Was fehlt dir? Ist der Kaffee* ready?"

Klamat may have heard something, but no one else did. He stood up, listened for a moment, picked up both the empty canteen and his Sharps rifle, and, saying nothing, disappeared once more down into the ravine.

Perhaps ten minutes had passed, and Klamat had not returned.

One of the mules snorted, but the sound did not mask the three distinct clicking noises.

"Hands up, boys. Don't move a goddamn inch. You run us a race, Prince, but now it's time to pass in your chips. We want the doc."

Doc Storz hid his face in his hands, and said nothing as the lawmen took his arms, fastened him with manacles, and chained him to a small pine.

Paquita said nothing, but her brown eyes grew very large— as the terrible memories of the massacre on the river must have risen before her. She pushed back her hair, making a show of her calmness, and rested her hands in her lap. She stared at the three men in broad-brimmed hats and expensive boots.

"Ought to take you in, too, Prince. Assisting a fugitive from the law..."

"Do I know you?" The Prince asked.

"Reckon not—but I know you. Make it my business to keep track of card thieves, practicing or retired. Name's John Workman, deputy sheriff from Yreka. Tom," he said to one of his subordinates, "check over them pack animals—just in case The Prince here is carrying stolen goods."

Tom moved off, gave the animals a cursory inspection, and returned to the fire.

Workman drew out his pipe, filled it, and lit up.

"Guess we'll have some of that coffee now. Sure smells good on a cold night like this'n."

The Prince shrugged and said nothing.

"Where's your other pet Injun, Prince?" Workman asked. He glanced toward the saddles, saw there were but four, and returned his gaze to The Prince. "Ye shoot 'im—or leave 'im in camp? This one," he said, staring fixedly at Paquita, "rather a good-lookin' piece, ain't she? I gather you boys share 'er?"

Nate started to rise, but The Prince shook his head.

"Eddie," Workman snorted, "best we relieve them of their weapons. You got a gun, little lady?"

Paquita indicated that she did not.

"Mebbe I better search ye. Stand up an' let me see what's under the cloth."

"Touch her, and I'll kill you," Nate said, suddenly on his feet.

"Sit down, kid—or I'll manacle you, as well."

"The girl's unarmed," The Prince said, his voice like gravel. "What Nate said is right, only I'm saying it now. If you've heard about me, you know I only bluff at cards."

"Resistin' an officer, are ye? We can have a triple hangin' as well as a single."

But Workman had lost interest, for the moment at least, in Paquita.

"Okay," he continued, relighting his pipe. "Guns in this bag, whatever ye've got. Don't figger you boys want to get yourselves hung for the old man there. An' let's get some sleep. Prince, you got extra blankets with ye?"

"Unchain Doc," Nate said. "Chain me up instead. Doc's sick."

"He's the one that stays in iron, kid. Guess he'll last long enough to see the rope. Toss the old man a blanket, then. Few hours an' it'll be light. Then we'll be on our way, an' you boys can be about your business as well. Gather you're headin' to Fort Jones, but this ain't the best route to be gettin' there. Well, it's not my concern, I guess."

It was past midnight when the fire died down. The lawmen took turns sleeping, one keeping guard, the other two at rest. The Prince rose, and the guard, suddenly wide awake, leveled his weapon.

"Going to build up the fire," he said, then turned away from the man and began to gather pitch knots. Paquita also rose, looked questioningly at The Prince, and did the same. With the fire blazing once more, The Prince pulled off the doctor's boots so that the fire might warm his feet.

"*Danke*," Doc Storz mumbled, still half-asleep.

The guard watched every movement, his finger on the trigger of his pistol.

"Go back to sleep, Paquita. You too, Nate. I'll keep the fire going."

The long hours of darkness passed slowly, but at last a silver-gray light appeared in the east, outlining the black shadow of Shasta. The Prince had fallen asleep by the fire, which had burned down to gray ash. Nate awoke, for a moment uncertain where he was. Then, without moving a muscle, he looked carefully about him. Everyone was asleep, the three lawmen included. Doc Storz had pulled his naked feet back under his blanket, his knees drawn up, his back against the tree, his head sagged over to one side like a dead man's—like the head of one who had been hanged.

Nate watched the gray light in the east, a light that seemed for a long while not to increase at all. Then, subtly, the dark form of Shasta began to change color, the high peak beginning to gleam, a radiance tinted with hues of faint redness. And as the sky began to darken to blue-black, the mountain burned once more, as though again contemplating eruption.

Then a brief motion nearby—a shadow, nothing more. But Nate studied the undergrowth and detected another slight movement. Then another, this one startlingly quick.

Klamat stood above the deputies, his Sharps rifle pointed at the head of the man who was supposed to be on guard.

"I will kill you if you move," Klamat said. "Nate! Prince! Get their guns!"

The Prince, apparently already awake, moved also with sudden quickness, and in an instant John Workman and his assistants had been disarmed.

"You fellows just cashed in your chips," The Prince said. "Don't bother to get up, now. Here, Nate . . ."

He tossed him a pistol.

Nate picked it up, cocked it, and pointed it directly at Workman's head.

"Don't point that thing unless you figure to use it, kid," Workman said. "You're in big enough trouble already, all of you."

The Prince shook his head.

"My name's not *kid*," Nate said, thinking how good, how really good it would feel to pull the trigger. "It's Cincinnatus Hiner Miller. I want you to remember that name, Workman, because one day I'm going to kill you."

"Are we not going to kill them?" Klamat asked The Prince. "Are these not some of the men who murdered my people at the village?"

"Guess not," The Prince said. "Tell you what, Workman. I've got no grudge against you—except for chaining up Doc over there. You're my prisoners now, but I'm not going to handcuff you. Do what I say, and you can have your guns back and ride off to Yreka. No blood, nobody shot."

"What are ye talkin' about?" Workman asked, the last vestige of confidence having gone out of his expression.

"Paquita!" The Prince called out. "Unlock Doc. Give me the keys, deputy. And, Paquita, get the fire going and fix us some coffee. Klamat, it took you long enough. Did you remember to fill the canteen?"

"I remembered," Klamat said. "I knew you would wish to have your coffee this morning."

"Good, good!" The Prince laughed. "Well, gents, looks like it's a new hand all around. I mentioned something I wanted you to do for me? One little thing in exchange for your lives. . . ."

"It's your pot, Prince, take it down. You hold the papers, called us on a dead hand. I should have chained you down, too. But I figure the time'll come when I'll see you swinging, you an' your friend here. What is it you want?"

"A man ought to remember the name of the one that's going to kill him," Nate said. "Looks like you've forgotten already."

"I ain't forgot," Workman said. "*Miller*. I'll remember, don't you fret."

"A simple thing," The Prince said, "and better for everyone concerned. I don't figure you want the boys in Yreka laughing at *Big John Workman*, do you? So it's simple. You give me your word not ever to mention this little affair, and we won't be mentioning it either. You just *never caught up with us*, is all. The other way, you're a laughingstock."

Workman glanced at Tom and Eddie.

"You've got a point, Prince. All right, I give you my word, you've got it."

"Are we not going to kill these men?" Klamat repeated, a distinct note of disappointment in his voice.

"We could," The Prince said, scratching behind his ear. "What do you say, *Cincinnatus*?"

"They chained Doc when he couldn't even stand up. . . ."

"They kept their paws off Paquita, though. At least they were half-decent."

"True," Nate said.

When the coffee was ready, The Prince poured a cup of brew for each of the lawmen. Then he unloaded their guns, put the percussion caps in his pocket, and had Nate go through their saddlebags for the ammo stash. After this he returned the empty pistols and said, "Gents, I've enjoyed playing with you. Maybe next time around the bitch-goddess Luck will smile your way. Never can tell about these things. Adieu, my friends. We'll see you in the Great Hereafter."

The caravan moved south once again, this time at a more leisurely pace, choosing the easier trails since they were no longer concerned about being pursued. Doc Storz was on the mend, and all of them were in high spirits. With roaring fires at night and with fresh venison that Nate had brought down with his Kentucky, they approached the huge form of Shasta and on the third night made their camp at the bottom of the gorge below the north face of Mount Eddy, just where the high springs tumbled down from the rocky escarpment above them.

"Head of the river!" Nate laughed. "Klamat, I've seen this river down where it's half a mile wide."

"Now where would that be, lad?" The Prince wanted to know.

"Well, maybe not half a mile. But wide and deep, a dozen times bigger than the Klamat River."

"Far down the valley, where the water is still?" Klamat asked.

"Yep. All along the mountains the rivers come down to join it."

"Actually, it is half a mile wide where it runs out into the San Francisco Bay," The Prince said. "Sacramento and the San Joaquin come together, puddle up into a kind of inland lake, and then run out into the bay through the straits at Carquinez. I guess you could say that's still the river."

But Paquita was not interested in talk of the river.

"Beyond the little buttes on the side of the Great Mountain," she said, "that is where our people live, Klamat. That is where you stayed with us, Nate. I am certain that Warrottetot believes that Poonkina and Klamat are both dead. How surprised everyone will be when we return from the Spirit World. . . ."

A warm wind was blowing from the basin far below, and sparks from their fire swirled up into the moonlit darkness. Screech owls called from down canyon, and even Doc Storz dispensed with knife and fork for eating the hot, greasy venison.

"I will tell you a story," Paquita said. "Do you wish to hear?"

Klamat nodded, and Doc, Nate, and The Prince assured her that they did.

Paquita studied the fire for a time, and then she began.

"Our people say the Great Spirit, or perhaps it was Old Coyote, made Spirit Mountain first of all. First He pushed snow and ice down through the sky. He made a hole in the sky by turning a great stone around and around until He had formed the mountain. Then He stepped out of the clouds and onto the mountaintop and came down until He had walked a long way. Then He began to plant the trees by sticking His finger into the ground. Do you see what I mean? Then the sunlight melted the snow, and Milk Creek and the others ran down from Shasta, also Elk Creek and Beaver Creek and Steaming Water Creek. Next the Old Man used the small end of His staff to make fish for the streams, and He made birds by blowing upon leaves that had fallen from the willows and the aspens. And all the animals—these came from the rest of the Old Man's stick. But He made the grizzly out of the big end, and so the grizzly ruled everybody else. . . ."

"The grizzly was so strong that Old Man Coyote was afraid of him," Klamat added.

"That is true," Paquita said. "The Old Man Who Made Everything had to sleep far up on the mountain so that the grizzly could not kill Him. Because this wasn't like the grizzly we have now. First Bear was much stronger and much more cunning. But Old Man didn't want the grizzly to come up the mountain because He still had other things to make. He had to make the ocean and all the other mountains and the lakes. He had to make Shasta Valley and Scott Valley and all the other places. Once the Klamat River ran through Shasta Valley and down the canyon where the Long River is now, the one you call Sacramento. It begins where we are now, but once it was part of the Klamat River. That was a long time ago, and no one knows when. But something happened, and the Klamat had to go toward the west. Anyway, Old Man wanted to make some more land, and so He turned Mount Shasta into a wigwam and built a fire in the center of it. It was a good home for Him. Afterward His family came down, and they have all lived in the mountain ever since. Before the Whitemen came, we could see the fire coming from the mountain at night and the smoke by day. We could see this anytime we wanted to."

"Is it true," Nate asked, "that the Shastas are afraid to climb to the top of the mountain?"

Klamat shook his head.

"That is not true, my friend. We climb all over the mountain, to hunt, and sometimes to have visions—for that is the best place to go. But we do not climb up to the top. We believe that we should not disturb the Good Spirit who lives there with His family. If you lived there, would you wish the people to come up to look at you all the time?"

"Makes sense," The Prince said, laughing. "What do you think, *Herr Doktor?*"

"Es liegt auf der Hand, it makes sense."

Paquita continued:

"All of this happened long before there were people. The Old Man wandered far to the north, to the valley called *Pooakan Charook,* far beyond *Walums Yaina.* Then He wandered to the south, into the great valley of the Long River, *Noorkan Charook,* and He thought about things. That was in late springtime, many thousands of years ago, when there was a great storm about the summit of Shasta. And the Old Man sent his most beautiful daughter up through the hole in the top and told her to tell the storm to be quiet. She was His favorite daughter, and He didn't want her to stick her head out into the wind, which might catch her hair and blow her away. He told her to stick out her long red arm and make a sign. But the girl was curious about the ocean where the storm came from. So she put out her head to look, and the storm blew her long red hair clear down the mountainside. In fact, the storm blew her down, clear down to where the forest is. In those days the grizzlies still lived in the forest, and they walked on two legs and had clubs to fight with. Well, a grizzly father was on his way home, with an elk in one hand. He saw the Old Man's daughter, saw her red hair beneath a fir tree. Her hair trailed in the snow, and the snow was melting. So the grizzly took the girl to his wife, who kept her and raised her. When the red-haired girl was grown up, she married the oldest son of the grizzlies. And they were married and were very happy and had many children—but the children did not look exactly like either the grizzly or the red-haired girl. That is where we came from, for those children were Shasta Indians."

"But Old Man Coyote missed His daughter and was very sad," Klamat said. "And He mourned for a long time."

"Some say it was Old Man Coyote, but maybe it was just Old Man. Whoever it was, the grizzlies were very proud of the red princess. When the old grizzly mother felt she would soon die, she thought she should tell the Great Spirit what had happened to His daughter. All the grizzlies got together and built a new lodge for the princess, and that is Little Mount Shasta. Then they called to the Old Man. When He heard what had happened, He ran down the mountain, and His steps are the buttes on the side of the mountain. He went so fast the snow melted off in some places, and thousands of grizzlies came out to meet Him, but He protected himself by staying in a cloud. And when He saw his daughter's children, He realized the grizzlies had tricked Him into creating a new race of people, and He killed the old mother grizzly right then. The other grizzlies howled mournfully. He changed the grizzlies then and made them to look as they are now, so they cannot speak anymore. Then Old Man drove all the children out into the world, and He took the red princess back up the mountain with him and closed the doors to His lodge. Now the grizzlies could only stand up when they had to fight, and they could no longer use their clubs. So they grew long teeth and great claws, and they are still stronger than anyone else."

Doc Storz, Nate, and The Prince were amazed—and all three men sat in a contemplative silence.

Klamat said, "The grizzlies are still the kings of the forest. They were the ones we came from. If one of our people is killed by a grizzly, his body is burned at that place. And all who pass will put a stone there, until a great pile is thrown up. Sometimes you will see these piles of stones, but there are not many grizzlies near Mount Shasta anymore."

They followed the canyon down from the mountain, down to where, within the space of a few miles, some six good-sized streams joined to bring together the various headwater creeks of the Sacramento River, just at the southwestern base of Mount Shasta. Here they fell in with a small band of Karok Indians who, frightened at first and then openly hostile, were soon brought around by Klamat's persuasive abilities.

If these people have the daughter of Warrottetot with them, if this is she, then we will be friendly toward them. . . .

Both Doc Storz and The Prince were edgy, but Nate assured them that all was well.

The Indians were fishing for salmon—a few warriors and a number of women, a scattering of curious young boys, and perhaps a dozen young women, some of them round-faced and overly plump, Nate thought, and some of them long-legged, slim, and very pretty. With the arrival of the caravan, the fishing stopped—willow basket traps were left in the water, untended, and spears were driven into the banks. The Karoks shared their midday meal, and a few sipped coffee poured from the pot that Paquita had set to boiling.

Then they began the gradual climb to the bench above the lowest of the buttes marking the south slope of Shasta, the foot tracks Old Man had made when He had come running down from the mountain.

By late afternoon they had entered into the lands still controlled by the Shastas, with Klamat ranging far ahead and Paquita singing happily to herself.

Klamat awaited the others at the saddle.

"Where do you wish to go from here?" he asked Nate.

"Are we where I think we are?"

"How can I know where you think we are, my friend?"

"Out that way, where the canyons begin. Isn't that the Numken?"

"It is."

"Prince." Nate motioned. "Down there's the place I told you about—the gravel deposits."

The Prince held his hand above his eyes and stared southward.

"Looks promising, lad. Do you know this place, Paquita?"

"Yes," she said. "Klamat and I know all this land. Our village cannot be too far away from here."

"Unless they have gone up to the lakes on the other side of the mountain—or over to the Medicine Lake," Klamat explained.

"Well," The Prince said, "let's go down and find that gold."

The doctor said something in German, purposely low so that no one could hear but all would know he had said something, shook his head, and sighed.

"What's that, old-timer?" The Prince laughed. "The riches of Midas are down there—we have Paquita's word for it."

"*Ja, ja, und* you know what happened to *Herr Midas, nicht wahr?*"

"That was in another land, and long ago. Troops forward! Once more we descend to the netherworld!"

Klamat looked at Nate, who simply shrugged.

Early sundown as they reached the edge of some broad meadows, the land inclining toward the south, the grass high and rich—much to the liking of the Cayuse and the mules. The air was balmy, pleasantly warm, an easy wind drifting up canyon from the distant Sacramento Valley. Crickets sang in the grass, and pigeons clattered among the branches of an isolated stand of black oaks, the leaves dull yellow-white in the fading light of day. An elk ventured out from the edge of the forest, thrust his nose forward, and bugled loudly—so that the mules and the pony startled backward in surprise. Then the elk turned about, indignant that his meadows had been invaded, and disappeared into the thick cover of dark woods.

Soon a fire was blazing, and the members of the party sat down to a mountain meal—the last of the deer Nate had shot two days before, beans, dried apples, and coffee.

In the morning, Nate and Klamat hunted, taking several deer. Paquita dressed the venison and set to smoking and drying the meat. The Prince wandered about and was soon of the opinion that there was probably no spot on earth more lonely or isolated. The pony and the mules rolled about in the rich grass or slept in the warm sunlight, their heads drooping and their eyes nearly closed. Even Doc Storz seemed to revive with miraculous speed—perhaps because inside this fortress of utter wilderness, no lawmen would set foot. He wondered if indeed any Whiteman had ever before set foot here. The shoulders of the Great Mountain, visible above the low bluffs at the head of the meadows, provided a mighty wall. Eastward lay lava lands, totally unsettled. And south lay an immense welter of canyon and ridge, so Klamat had said, reaching out to the distant valley of the Sacramento. Only westward, the way they had come, had the Whitemen made inroads, a stray log cabin every ten miles or so along the wagon trail from Shasta City to Yreka, up through the canyon of the tumbling Sacramento River—a road that Doc knew well enough, having traveled the entire thing on several occasions.

"*Ja,*" he said, "*hier bin Ich unter Freuuden*—I am among friends here. . . ."

He looked about, saw a large alder tree, and walked toward it. He withdrew his sheath knife, held it up—then hesitated. He felt like a boy again, and he had been about to do what a boy would do—carve something into the green bark of a tree.

"*Ich habe den Pulver nicht erfunden—Man hat ihn auf frischer Tat ertappt. . . .*"

Doc shook his head and started to put the knife away.

"*Was ist?* What *der hell!*" he said, and set the point of his blade to the bark.

Within a matter of moments he had carved the word: *home.*

ELEVEN

▲

Nobody Could Build a Fire
Like Paquita

Mount Shasta is even now . . . an active volcano. Sometimes only hot steam, bringing up with it a fine powdered sulphur, staining yellow the snow and ice, is thrown off. Then again boiling water, clear at one time and then muddy enough, boils up through the fissures and flows off into a little pool within a hundred feet of the summit. It is very unsettled and uncertain. Sometimes you hear most unearthly noises even a mile from the little crater, as you ascend, and when you approach, a tumult like a thousand engines with whistles of as many keys; then again you find the mountain on its good behavior and sober enough.

Nearby rose the crescent-shaped band of sulphur and soda springs at the foot of the upper rim. The area would remain free of ice through the winter, owing to the outward flow of hot water, and the grass would remain green—a natural attraction for deer and elk.

Here, close by the very source of the Numken, they built their cabin, going to work on it without delay, for winter was approaching. Storms that brought warm rain to the meadows beneath the rim dropped increasing layers of whiteness on the mountain above, covering the entire peak down to the timberline and even beyond.

The cabin itself stood on a hillside a short distance above the meadows, facing the sun and very close to the warm springs, and was not much different from any miner's cabin. The one great structural difference lay in the location of the fireplace, a matter of some importance, since they had no stove. Klamat and Paquita argued for putting the fireplace in the center of the floor, as was the practice within the Shasta lodges.

"If my people come," said Paquita, "then we will all be able to sit facing the fire when we talk."

"If you put a hole in the roof," Klamat said, "the smoke will go right up to it—if you make the fire in the right way."

"Think it'll work?" The Prince asked Nate.

"It works in the lodges—works perfectly."

"Doc?"

"It sounds *gut*."

And so it was built.

THE CASTLE

The words were painted on the door, the latter of broad, hand-hewn planks, with hinges of leather and a sliding wooden bolt fit into place with strips of rawhide. Doc Storz, now full of enthusiasm, actually carved two small wooden cannons and mounted them on a pair of stumps outside the doorway.

Some way below the cabin, just where the Numken dropped into the upper portion of its long canyon, were the gravel beds. With the cabin completed and secure against whatever the winter might bring and a great store of firewood split and stacked behind the building, Nate, The Prince, and Klamat as well went to work on the gravel deposits. Almost immediately they found gold, including a pound or more of nuggets lying in the creek.

"What's the point of digging?" The Prince asked. "Nate, all we have to do is pan the stream. If our luck holds up, we can just pan on down the Numken for the next twenty years— we're going to be rich men, lad."

They panned for a week, but the farther away from the gravel bank they got, the less their labors yielded. And so, after a time, Nate said, "Let's start digging. We get back in under the overburden, at least we've got a place to work when the rain's coming down and the creek's flooding."

"I hear the voice of wisdom," The Prince agreed.

The horizontal shaft was begun, its location chosen almost at random, and, with a sluice set up beside the stream, they began to accumulate a good collection of fines and small nuggets. And when the shaft had been hewn out to a depth of perhaps ten or twelve feet, they came to a slanting seam of white clay. The sands above this ledge proved far richer than anything they had worked with at The Forks, and the three of them, gazing down into the little sluice and seeing the rich accumulations of black sand, gold dust, and pea-sized nuggets behind each of the riffles, pounded one another on the back and laughed until their eyes watered.

"We're going to be rich men!" Nate exulted. "All three of us, and Doc too. We've got gold enough here to keep us going for years!"

"All the chips on the table, and we're holding four aces!" The Prince whistled. "Klamat, isn't that *beautiful?*"

"It is beautiful, but what good is it? The Whitemen make coins out of it, but what else is it used for?"

"What good are dentalium and clam shells?" The Prince asked, squinting one eye.

"Only for money," Klamat answered. "But why not something else, something that is easier to get at—something we don't have to dig big holes for?"

"If it wasn't hard to get," Nate said, "then nobody would want it. For that matter, if everyone had a mine like this, then it wouldn't be worth anything."

"Grizzly skins are hard to get. Why not use those for money?"

"Not enough grizzlies, of course," Nate answered.

"Well, it does not matter. With gold I will be able to buy things from the Whites."

And get together a marriage price for Paquita, Nate thought.

The Prince nodded, but the smile was suddenly gone from his face.

"Well," he said, "let's clean out the riffles, lads."

Warm weather and clear skies returned near the end of the year, and the forest took on an almost springtime air. New grass appeared in places, and the odor of damp leaves and needles on the forest floor was nearly intoxicating.

For perhaps the hundredth time, Nate analyzed his feelings toward Paquita—Paquita the mysterious one, warm and loving toward all of them, showing no apparent favoritism. Indeed, her free nature and good spirits sometimes caused lines to form in Klamat's face, and Nate knew the reason for them. Was the girl consciously attempting to make Klamat jealous? For certainly that's what the young Shasta warrior was feeling at times—resentment of Paquita and jealousy of his friends. And Nate could see that each time it occurred, Klamat was obliged to wrestle with it, to breathe more deeply, to look the other way.

And what of The Prince? Nate could see the desire in his older friend's eyes.

Maybe it's just easier for me, Nate thought. *I've never made—love—with a woman.*

But it wasn't easier, and he knew it. Paquita haunted his dreams. She would come to him, would lie next to him, would put her hands on him until he ached with need of her; but it was dream, just dream, and he would awaken, sweating, and pray to God that he had not spoken out in his sleep.

He went off alone now, pouring his desire into hunting, bringing back such supplies of game that Paquita could not keep up with dressing the skins and smoking and drying the meat.

"Why do you hunt so often, Nate?" she asked him. "There will be deer nearby all winter, and we already have much meat."

"Paquita..." he began.

But Klamat was inside the cabin and might well be able to hear what he had been about to say.

"What is it?" Paquita asked.

"It is—nothing," he replied, and turned and went into The Castle.

He ate, forced himself to joke with the others, drank coffee, and went out to split some more firewood—something else he had been doing quite a bit of lately. But after a time he put down the splitting maul, saddled his pony, and rode off toward the bluffs. He sat down beneath a tree, drove his knife into the damp earth, and considered the possibility of leaving. But if he chose to do that, he would have to explain—explain to all of them. And that he simply could not do.

The Prince was aware.

And, dammit, Paquita knows, too. Likely, they all know—Klamat, Doc Storz. And she's what's holding us all here, just her presence—and we can't any of us leave, and for some reason or another, she can't leave either.

He heard her calling then—her voice from down below.

"Nate Miller—it's me. I will come up, and we will speak to one another!"

He answered her.

Within a few moments she was there beside him, more lovely, more appealing than ever, but her eyes were troubled. And Nate felt suddenly very ashamed of himself.

Whatever he started to say to her, the words that came out were: "Paquita, forgive me, I'm in love with you, I love you. . . ."

She stood very close to him, her dark hair braided and lustrous, her eyes strangely like those of a doe or a fawn, the full mouth, sunlight trickling across nose and brow, one cheekbone shadowed, the other glistening—the delicate, discordant odor of perfume, the little bottles of perfume the doctor had given her, the nipples of her breasts standing out against the bodice of white deerskin she had tanned and cut and sewn herself. . . . *Poonkina! Paquita!* He wanted to embrace her, to hold her, hold desperately to her as he had that terrible night on the river when he had wrapped his coat about her starved and naked little body. But this—was this someone else? A woman now, a year younger than he, and yet he was still a boy, while she was a woman, desirable, complete, certain of herself.

Did he see yearning in her eyes as well?

"Why would you wish me to *forgive* you, Nate?"

He wanted to explain, to explain everything—but he could only manage to utter her name: "Paquita . . ."

"Do you not know that I love you also? You are the one who saved my life. I would have died there, even if Spades and the others had not come. And Klamat would have died also, for there was no food. He would have stayed and died with me. It was a death village. Klamat would not have left me, though, not even to save his own life."

Nate took a step backward.

"Klamat is—my brother. I am wrong, I am wrong to feel as I do, Paquita. I must go away from here, but I will never forget. . . ."

She stepped toward him once again, reached up, and touched her fingers to his face.

"You have blue eyes," she said, the tone of her voice almost one of wonder. "I think we will always be together, as long as

I am alive. The Earth Spirits have done this thing, and their medicine is more powerful than the medicine of humans, even more powerful than the medicine of the shaman, Mountain Smoke. We cannot understand the magic, but we must do as it says."

Nate could barely breathe. Minute bolts of lightning were exploding inside his skull—Klamat, his friend Klamat, and The Prince, the entire uncontrollable swirl of what had happened and was still happening, like the swollen waters of the river after the great storm, tearing trees from its banks, overtopping the banks and washing away cabins, claims, dreams.

"I will marry Klamat," Paquita said, "and perhaps you will marry my sister, White Dawn. Yes, perhaps you will do that. Do you remember her, Nate? All the young men like her. She is prettier than I am, and she knows how to toy with them. She has always been that way. I do not know whom you will marry, but it will be one of my people. And you and I will always be friends, just as we are now. We will be more than friends. I have thought about all of this. I will be the wife to Klamat, your brother, no matter what Blackbeard says. I have known what it is like to live among the Whites now, and I am not the same as I once was. I can speak your language, and I can even write a little bit—yes, I can. I can do it now. I don't know what this means, Nate, but I am no longer a child. I am fully a woman, and I am Shasta—but I have chosen my own husband. I tell you now, but Klamat has known it ever since we were children together. Once we ran away together, and my father caught us."

"Will Warrottetot allow . . . ?"

"My father will not force me to do what I do not wish to do. Klamat will be rich among my people, and he will be a leader. He loves me, and I love him also. I will be his wife. But I love you, too, Nate Miller, just as he does. Soon I will be married, but I am not married yet. I am here with you. . . ."

"Paquita?"

"I wish to lie down with you, Nate. Will you be gentle with me? I am not ignorant, but I have never truly lain with a man before."

"I have never. . . ."

She smiled and shook her head.

"We must both be gentle, then. We must learn how to do this thing."

His face was flushed, and he was trembling.

"Come," she said, "over here. We will lie together in the sunlight; there will not always be sunlight for us."

"No!" he said, "I must not. . . ."

"Yes," she insisted. "It is time now for both of us. Later we will be as brother and sister."

Paquita drew him to the matted pine needles, and he lay down beside her. Her hand was pressing gently between his legs, and for a moment he was forced to close his eyes. Then his hands, as if with a will of their own, as if some force that was different from anything he had ever known were animating his limbs, his entire body, an animal force, male, pure, ancient. . . .

They shed their clothing.

The sunlight warmed them, gleamed on their naked flesh.

And when it was over, Nate clung to Paquita, clung with a desperation, almost a frenzy.

He was crying, and she touched her lips to his eyelids.

Then she was up, dancing about in the nude, hiding behind a tree and laughing delightedly at him.

"Put your clothes on, Nate Miller! Give me my clothes! The sunlight is going, and we must go also!"

They dressed and then walked together, Nate leading his pony, back toward The Castle.

When they had passed out of sight, down the slope through the pine woods, Klamat rose from behind the great fallen fir where he had lain in concealment. He had seen everything that had happened, and he had heard everything that Nate and Poonkina had said to each other.

He felt a terrible sadness, and also a fierce joy.

That night at dinner Paquita announced that she would go in search of Warrottetot's village—for, since the Shastas had not as yet become aware of the existence of The Castle, the village must be off to the north, perhaps at the Medicine Lake.

"I will go with you," Klamat said.

"No, you must stay here with the others. This is something that I must do myself."

Her tone of voice was definite, and after a moment or so Klamat nodded his agreement.

"What if the winter snows begin?" The Prince said. "I think that either Klamat or Nate should go with you."

"I must do this alone," she insisted. "I'll tell you how it will be. I will ride into the village at sundown, alone. The dogs will bark loudly, because I will be wearing my red dress, and I will have ribbons in my hair. They will not recognize me, not after so long. I will go straight to Warrottetot's lodge and sit down by the entrance. The people will pass by and pretend they do not see me, but when they have gone by, they will look back. Then someone will bring me some water. Probably White Dawn, my sister, will do that. If it is White Dawn, I will show her the three little marks on my left wrist, and that way she will know me and lead me into the lodge. Many things will be different than they were. Perhaps White Dawn is already married, I do not know. . . ."

She glanced at Nate, then continued:

"Perhaps my father has taken a new wife, and that would be a good thing, for the chief should not live alone. A chief may have several wives, if he wishes—and yet my father has never married since my mother died. That was five—no, six years ago—and after that he grew very sick, and White Dawn and I wondered if he might also go on into the Spirit World. But I will tell them everything that has happened; I will tell the story just the way it was."

Klamat glanced at Nate, then back at Paquita.

"I will tell Warrottetot that Klamat wishes to marry me. . . ."

She smiled, and little lights seemed to dance in her eyes.

"I will say that if that is what Klamat wishes."

"That is what I wish," Klamat said.

For a moment the log cabin with the fireplace at its center seemed filled with a thick and yet fragile silence.

The Prince set down his tin coffee cup, spilling a bit on the pine slab of the table beside him.

"And I will tell my father that I will marry Klamat and no other. He cannot force me to do anything I do not wish to do. Then he will think for a long time and set the marriage price, but Klamat will soon be rich and able to pay whatever Warrottetot says."

"Congratulations, lad!" The Prince burst out, rising and

clapping the bewildered Klamat on the back. "That's what White niggers say to each other when the cards are dealt face-up. That's wonderful! We'll all pitch in our tin, whatever the marriage price is! Paquita, Paquita! A wise—choice—little one, a wise choice!"

"*Mein Gott!*" the doctor cried out. "What does *ein Mann* wear to a Shasta wedding?"

"Then my people will come back here," Paquita continued. "My father will tell you that you may stay here as long as you wish, for that is what I will say to him. He will believe that I have returned from the Spirit World, and so he will do what I tell him."

The following day she left, her red dress packed carefully into the saddlebag and a pistol tucked beneath the yellow sash around her waist. A good supply of cured meat was stashed on the opposite side, for one could only guess how long the ride might be.

The men, Klamat included, were sick with worry about her traveling alone, but she laughed at them and said, "I am the chief's daughter. Not even a grizzly bear will harm me."

They watched as she rode away, her mule's ears forward, watched as she turned to wave back. Then the mule and rider passed into the forest beyond the meadows and were out of sight.

With Paquita gone, Doc Storz actually accompanied The Prince, Nate, and Klamat to the mine, dug sporadically, and cursed in German. But they spoke little, and the hours dragged by.

Nate concluded that he did not like the place as well now, and for the first time he found himself finding fault with things around him. Across the Numken, the forest brooded, black and gloomy, and a start of fear ran through him.

What if Paquita should somehow encounter the Modocs?

That evening Doc Storz fixed the fire, but the wood refused to burn properly, and The Castle was suddenly filled with smoke. Nate opened the door, and Klamat rearranged the pieces of wood, crouched over, and blew at the embers.

"Why'd we make this place so small?" The Prince complained.

"I have done my best," Klamat said, "but the fire will still not burn right."

"Nobody could build a fire like Paquita," The Prince added as he sliced strips of venison for the stewpot. "Gents, our guardian angel has deserted us."

Neither did the stew taste as good as it had on previous occasions.

The days following Paquita's departure were long ones, and to pass the evenings, The Prince produced an unopened deck of cards, dumped a bottle of gold nuggets on the table, and roughly divided them up four ways.

"These things have to be good for something," he said.

"*Ach!* I do not gamble," Doc Storz protested.

"It's not gambling, Doc. I'll win, of course. When I've got all the nuggets, the game's over. And we'll put them back into their bottle and try it again tomorrow night."

Storz was less than fully convinced, but he sat down at the table. Nate and Klamat did likewise, and The Prince fanned the cards, grinning, and shuffled with one hand. Klamat was greatly impressed with the trick and wished The Prince to show him how it was done.

"Later, lad, later. That's just a little show-off. What I want to do is teach you to play poker. Hell of a lot more interesting than your hand game. What we've got to do is to introduce some culture to the Shasta nation. You'll be chief someday, I predict it, and you've got to know how to play cards."

Klamat, indeed, proved an adept student and soon was, as The Prince put it, "a fair country cardsharp."

Klamat grinned at the praise.

"It is good to know this thing," he said. "One day it may prove useful. Among my people, too, there is much gambling. Nate has seen it. Sometimes the men play the hand game for days at a time. I have seen men lose everything this way."

Two weeks, then three, had passed, and yet Paquita had not returned. Klamat was preparing to go in search of her when the snow began to fall, a heavy, white downpour that lasted several days without cessation. When the sky finally cleared, the meadows at the head of the Numken lay deep beneath a three-foot blanket of snow. The temperature fell immediately, and the snow was frozen hard—hard enough for a man to walk upon without snowshoes and still not break through. Only in the area near the hot springs did the grass show, and there, often, the elk came in to feed.

"The deer move downslope in winter," Klamat said, "but the elk are different people. They come up higher into the mountains and search out the warm springs. They eat the vine-maple shoots, watercress, and swamp berries that grow along the edges of the warm wetlands. Also, they are strong enough to break through the frozen snow. Their hooves are sharp. That is also how they fight off the wolves when they must—with their hooves and not with their antlers. That is a strange thing."

More weeks passed and more snows fell. Still Paquita had not returned.

Doc Storz and The Prince engaged in long discussions as to how the gold in the placers had originally formed—whether it was different from the gold that could, in some areas, be found in veins of quartz. Doc believed that it had formed in the quartz, and that erosion had subsequently deposited it in the gravels—though what had caused the deposits of gravel he couldn't say.

"Gravel only gets rounded in one way, Doc," The Prince said. "And that's by getting rolled down a river. And yet, many of the deposits are way up above the rivers—and sometimes no rivers around at all. Maybe it was Noah's flood that did it—washed it all up and down the mountains and left it."

"*Und* covered it *mit* volcanic dust? *Du hast gut reden, aber der Welt ist* much older than you think, *Herr*. A million years ago, *veilleicht*, the world appeared much different than it does now."

"How can a man hold an intelligent discussion with someone who won't even stick to one language? I think you do it to try to win a point. You think there used to be a lot of quartz with gold in it, and then something wore it down and left it in layers?"

"*Mein* Prince, I do not know how it happened—but I think it had to happen that way."

"Klamat," The Prince said, turning around, "what do your people say about the gold?"

Klamat shrugged.

"It is just something that Old Man Coyote left lying about."

"Best explanation I've heard," Nate said.

And more time passed.

Warm rains then, and the snows began to melt. Catkins appeared on willow and alder, and then the delicate new green of willow leaf. When the snow was fully gone, Nate and Klamat rode out great distances in all directions but found no sign of the Shastas. Elk, bear, deer, geese building their nests along the margin of a lake, among the tules; a wolverine, coyotes, an occasional wolf, quail, blue grouse, hawks and eagles sailing the air, blue herons in the still, shallow water— but no sign of the village.

"They have gone north to the lakes," Klamat said.

"Do you—think—she found them?"

"I think so, Nate. I do not know, but I believe so. Perhaps Warrottetot wishes to protect his daughter from me, now that he has her back from the dead."

Nate's dream startled him fully awake. It was not yet dawn, and the inside of The Castle was still quite dark.

I saw her body. . . . She was torn apart by a grizzly. . . .

It was only a dream, he told himself over and over, and yet the image returned to him for days afterward.

The Prince and Doc Storz went up the canyon in search of gold and at last found a quartz seam running through heavy gray rock that was nearly as hard as granite. Using an iron bar, they managed to wedge loose segments of the quartz, and these they crushed—finding, indeed, definite traces of gold. Since the quartz vein was uphill from the gravel bank, Doc nodded wisely. The Prince said, "You know that doesn't prove a damned thing, Storz."

The rains stopped, and summer was upon them. The four men, Klamat included, had almost ceased to mention Paquita's name—though each, separately, found himself constantly looking up—some movement, perhaps a deer or even a bird on the rise above, at the edge of the forest. Each time, it might have been Paquita returning, but it wasn't.

Doc Storz broke first. He was gone for several days, had left without notice, and when he returned, he said he had been to Shasta City. He spoke of using a different name and of setting up his practice there.

"Doc," The Prince said, "you're older than we are, and

besides that, you're an educated man. I can understand that you're tired of fiddling around with mining, and I don't blame you. But dammit, Shasta City's just not far enough. It wouldn't take any time at all for them to get it figured out, and we wouldn't be around to help."

"I am innocent," Doc said, suddenly exploding. "What right have they to pursue me? Oh well, *er ist mir egal*, it makes no difference to me. Why do we stay here? She was beautiful, that one, *sehr schön*, but she is gone, *tot*...."

"Don't say that," Nate urged.

"Why not? Is it the truth we are afraid of? *Wahrheit?*"

After that there was no keeping him.

The Prince gave him fully half the gold that had thus far been extracted from the placer, at the same time urging him to leave the Northern California mines far behind.

"This will get you started again, old man. But if you stop even for a day in Shasta City, for God's sake don't show anyone your poke. Half the city would be up here in no time."

He placed the buckskin bag into one of Doc's cantinas and buckled them down.

Then Doc was gone, gone from the solitary little world at the head of the Numken.

Klamat was unusually silent throughout the afternoon. Finally, at the evening meal, he said, "I, too, must leave now. I must know what has happened to Poonkina, the one who said she would be my wife. No, Nate, I must go alone. Prince. I must go away by myself, and yet I promise to return. Whatever I may learn, I will share with both of you. You loved her as much as I did, and I know that. She loved you, too. We three should have been just one person, but because there were three, Poonkina had to choose."

"We will go with you," The Prince said.

"No. That cannot be. But I will return, as I have promised."

"I..." Nate began.

"You wish to tell me something, my brother. I know that. And I know what you would tell me, even though it would be very difficult for you to do so. But already I know. Do not speak. I must tell you something, also. The doctor saved my life, for he did not kill Spades and the judge. I killed those men. I killed the judge because he was not just and because he attacked the doctor. He had a knife, and I took it away from him and killed him. And when Spades attacked the doctor later, I knew that I could not allow him to live any longer, for he had helped to murder my people at the village. It was no longer a thing of Shasta law or White law. The doctor brought food when all of us were hungry, and so I protected him. In doing this, I became a law myself. It was my own law and my own medicine. The doctor knew—he was there to see me cut the judge's throat. And I told him what I had done to Spades. He said nothing, even when they came after him. For me there would have been no law. They would have killed me without listening to what I might tell them. The doctor would not let that happen."

"Klamat..." The Prince began.

"Did not either of you guess? It is no matter now, for the doctor is gone."

TWELVE

▲

Shasta Marriage

Marriage was by payment or specified contract to pay, and people's social status depended upon the amounts paid by their fathers for their mothers. A rich man might buy his son a wife of high standing while he was still a young boy. Although the marriage was not consummated for many years, payment was made immediately. Should the betrothal be broken by the death of the girl or for any other reason, full repayment was of course requisite. Young men of medium wealth were assisted by their relatives in accumulating the property necessary to obtain a wife. If the amount thus gathered remained insufficient, the youth often received his wife on promise to make up the amount later. A poor man lived with his father-in-law and hunted and worked for him until considered to have liquidated the debt.

Summer came, and Nate and The Prince continued to work the gravels of the Numken with much success. It was difficult for either to remember, now, the long winter, the back-breaking labor, and the pitiful returns from their previous mine at The Forks. They were well on their way to becoming rich men.

The Prince grew thoughtful. "Nate, this isn't the kind of work a fella would want to do for a lifetime. You go to the goldfields in the hope of getting a stake, a good stake, and quick. Most don't find it and just keep digging away until they've forgotten there's anything else they might do with their time. Come autumn and both of us will be able to put away our picks and shovels—head off to see the world— whatever it is we've got in mind. You hear what I'm saying?"

Nate rose from his stooping position beside the stream, shook his hands to get the blood flowing again, and nodded.

"It's true," he said. "We've accomplished what we set out to accomplish—will have soon now, if the gravel doesn't suddenly run poor."

The Prince tapped his boot on the blade of his pick and whistled.

"Young guy like you, Nate—you've got a good head on your shoulders. Maybe you ought to go back to Oregon—even go to college or something. Study the law. *Be* somebody."

"To tell the truth," Nate said, "I've thought about it. I really have. But what about you?"

The Prince shrugged.

"Always wanted to see South America. Jungles. Monkeys in the trees. Snakes thirty feet long, from what I've heard. Figure some of the boys down that way might want to play cards. . . ."

He grinned.

"Thought you were through with that life, Prince."

"A man shouldn't ever decide he's *through* with anything. He might want to change his mind. It wasn't a bad life, all in all, and, Lord, it's been a long time since—I've had a woman. Love being with you, Natty, but it's not the same. As it is, both of us are candidates for the priesthood. . . ."

They had just returned to The Castle for the evening when Nate reached out suddenly, stopping The Prince in his tracks.

"Something's wrong. I can feel it. . . ."

The Prince drew his pistol, and the two men cautiously entered the cabin. It took their eyes a moment to adjust to the sudden darkness—it took them a moment to see the two people inside.

It was Klamat and Paquita.

"We wondered if you would ever grow tired of digging," Klamat said, his face without expression.

"I'll be goddamned to hell!" The Prince burst out.

And then all four were embracing one another, Paquita squealing with laughter when The Prince grasped her around the waist and lifted her above his head. She pushed the brim of his hat down, and when he had set her once more upon the earthen floor, she fell into his arms and hugged him.

She embraced Nate a bit less energetically but whispered,

"I have never stopped thinking of you....It has been long, my brother."

There was much to talk about now that the little family was once more together. Chief Blackbeard, old Warrottetot, had agreed to the marriage of Klamat and Poonkina—had set the marriage price at seven horses, two rifles, and some blankets.

"I will have enough before too long," Klamat said, grinning.

But Nate and The Prince, speaking almost at once, offered to make up whatever additional funds were needed—and to acquire the goods as well.

"We're running a rich lode right now," The Prince said, "and there's no telling how far it'll go. Even finding the good stuff in Doc's old hardrock mine, though we've had no need to work it much."

"Are you happy, Paquita?" Nate asked, turning to the girl—no, not a girl any longer, a woman, fully a woman, and more lovely, more desirable than ever.

"I am happy," she said. "Perhaps we will marry at the time of the late summer feast."

"Where is the village now?" Nate asked.

"Not far away," Klamat replied quickly. "The village is being assembled in the Naw-aw-wa, where the stream comes down from the Great Mountain, only a few miles. We will go there tomorrow."

Klamat had brought fresh steaks of elkmeat with him, and Paquita quickly built a good fire, its smoke trailing up through the vent hole as if in obedience to her wishes. The bonds of human closeness, far from having been damaged by the period of separation, were stronger than ever.

"Only I wish the doctor were here," Paquita complained. "He was a very good man—he was very good to all of us."

Klamat nodded, and The Prince lifted his coffee cup.

"Here's to Doc Storz, and I hope the old bastard's smiling, wherever he is."

It was late when they finally slept, and when the three men awoke, Paquita had already built a fire and had a pot of coffee boiling. The odor itself was sufficient to draw them out of their slumber.

They rode to Warrottetot's village. The women and children of the village moved out of the way as the riders came in, taking cover behind lodges, then peering out in speculative curiosity.

At the entry to Warrottetot's lodge they were greeted by White Dawn, Paquita's younger sister. Nate took note of the girl—recalled having seen her before on numerous occasions, just a long-legged woman-child then, her body being metamorphosed to womanhood. She was the one who had always been smiling and laughing. He could see in her face the imperfect copy of Paquita's, and he was astounded to consider that he had not earlier noted the resemblance. At the time, however, his vision of Paquita had been hardly more than a sharp-edged hallucination.

Now White Dawn led them into the lodge where the chief sat.

Warrottetot acknowledged first the presence of his daughter, then of Klamat. With that he rose and awkwardly, in Whiteman's fashion, extended his hand.

"I am Warrottetot," he said. "Nate Miller knows me already. You are the one called The Prince?"

The chief was a man of less than average height, the Prince noted, some inches shorter than Klamat, but with huge arms and chest, great, powerful hands, deep eyes, and a striking black beard, giving him almost the appearance of an Old Testament prophet dressed in Indian garb.

Facial hair and the lines of the face, The Prince thought. *White blood somewhere a generation or two back, a story here if one could get at it . . .*

Paquita was dismissed—and she backed out of the lodge to where her sister waited. When the cedar-bark mat was pulled aside, The Prince could see that a throng of young women had assembled outside—and now they began to buzz with curiosity.

He heard the faint sounds of Paquita's voice, speaking to them.

Warrottetot lit his stone pipe filled with native tobacco, tasted the smoke, and passed the pipe to The Prince. The pipe had gone around three times before Warrottetot spoke again.

"You have saved my daughter's life, for my friend Slippery Salmon had sent word of what had happened on the Klamat River. I thought Poonkina had gone to the Spirit World, and I grieved for her a period of two moons. And I had ceased to think about either her or Klamat, the warrior who will now be my son-in-law, perhaps soon. Then Poonkina came riding into the camp, came riding like a ghost, so that the women of the village fled to their lodges. But it was my daughter, and she told me all that had happened to her."

Nate moved about nervously, controlling his breathing.

"So I am grateful to you two Whitemen. Nate, you have lived with us before, so in a way you are one of us. But Warrottetot and his people are grateful, for you have given us back two of our own. It is true that you only rescued them from others of your own kind, and so, perhaps, my gratitude is not so great as if you had saved them from a grizzly bear. But I am still very grateful, and I give you permission to continue to mine for gold in my lands."

"We both thank the chief," The Prince said, nodding.

"Klamat," Warrottetot asked, "are these truly good men?"

"They are men of honor," Klamat replied.

"Do these men think the chief of the Shastas is able to speak well in their language?"

"Of course," Klamat said.

Warrottetot smiled, just a faint smile.

"Now we will smoke some more."

He relit the pipe, puffed a bit, and handed it to Nate.

"Prince?" the chief asked. "Is a prince not a ruler, like a chief? For this is what I have heard."

"That is true," The Prince answered. "But I am not a prince of that sort. It is only my name."

Warrottetot nodded.

"A strange name, then. But many of the Whitemen have odd names. I know the names of many."

"This man is very brave and very strong," Klamat added. "He is a good man to be friends with."

"And are you friends?" the chief asked.

"I have told you," Klamat replied. "He is my brother, just as Nate is my brother."

The Prince took the pipe, blew smoke out, and nodded.

"It is good, then," Warrottetot said. "But there is one thing, and this thing is important. You must let none of the other Whitemen know where you are—for then the Whites would come, and we would have to fight to protect our lands from them. Do you agree with me?"

"We agree completely," said The Prince, passing the pipe to Klamat.

Klamat returned to The Castle with Nate and The Prince, but Paquita remained in the village. Each afternoon she would come to them, however, to be with her husband-to-be and her friends and to prepare their supper. Then, after darkness had fallen, she would return to Warrottetot's lodge.

The second afternoon, White Dawn accompanied her.

"I think my sister is willing to be your wife," she said, her eyes sparkling with mischief.

"Paquita!" Nate whispered.

"Do you not find her very pretty?"

"Yes..."

"Is she as pretty as I am, Nate Miller?"

"No one is."

Paquita laughed.

"You are still like a boy, Nate. You must marry her or one of the other young women and live with us. I do not wish to be apart from you, and neither does Klamat. It is the will of Old Man."

Nate looked about to see where Klamat was. Then he said, "Paquita, it's you I love. How can you expect me to—"

She cut him off.

"You will love White Dawn also. This thing will happen, Nate, you will see. She is my sister, and you are Klamat's brother. It should be this way."

When Paquita and White Dawn had left that evening, Nate went out for a long, solitary walk. The return of Paquita had once again set his mind to swirling. Endlessly he had thought of their afternoon of lovemaking—the sunlight, the bed of pine needles, the feel of her lithe body next to his own, her confused response to his kisses, not a thing the Indians did, and then her accepting, struggling to do it right. Her legs about his hips, himself inside her...

Wrong.

Klamat, his friend, his brother—was that what Klamat had meant? *He knew?* Had Paquita told him before she left?

But now each day White Dawn accompanied Paquita to

The Castle. The girl was quiet, shy, not like Paquita at all. But often she stood near him, her eyes downcast at such moments, and if he walked out to bring in firewood, she would follow him, insisting on helping.

He felt—what? Resentment, anger. Finally, desire?

Then White Dawn came alone, and Nate detected a hint of a gleam in Klamat's eyes, though he went through the form of asking why it was that Paquita had not come along this afternoon.

"She wishes you to come to her this day," White Dawn said in carefully practiced English.

Klamat nodded, masking any surprise he might have felt.

"It appears that the entire Shasta nation is learning English," The Prince said, grinning, as though he too were in on some sort of conspiracy.

"I will go, then," Klamat said.

"Guess I'll go with you," The Prince said. "An old bachelor like me would just be in the way here. . . ."

Trapped, Nate thought.

He gave in, and that night he and White Dawn talked until late. When it was time for her to go, he accompanied her back to Warrottetot's village. At the edge of the encampment, but before they had drawn close enough to cause the camp dogs to start barking, Nate pulled up the reins of his pony.

White Dawn drew her horse beside his.

Until he had actually spoken, he'd had no idea what he would say. His own words sounded strange in his ears.

"Will you—meet me—tomorrow night—here?"

The girl looked away, in the direction of the village, and then turned to him.

"I will meet you," she said—and then she urged her pony forward and disappeared in the direction of the lodges. Nate sat his pony, watching, waiting. When he heard the dogs begin to bark, he turned the Cayuse back toward The Castle.

He had not ridden far when The Prince and Klamat came up behind him. Both of his friends seemed to be in a jovial mood.

Another marriage price was set: five horses, some blankets, and two pistols.

Nate and Klamat left The Prince to work the mine and

traversed down the canyon of the Numken to visit the new
trading post that, the Indians had discovered, had been
established along the wagon road from Shasta City to Yreka,
in the meadows above the Sacramento River, at the foot of
the astounding gray formation the Whitemen called Castle
Crags.

Klamat rode nervously behind as the two men approached
the post, a fairly large structure of unpeeled logs notched
square and jointed at the ends. Some outbuildings and a large
corral and also a small patch of garden planted, with even
rows of corn, climbing beans beginning to tendril their way
up over some stacks of brush, hills of potatoes, and large-
leafed squash plants.

Two upright logs and a cross member formed the gate, this
constructed of peeled logs. And from the cross member hung
the sign: MOUNTAIN JOE'S POST, JOSEPH DEBLONEY, PROP.

Nate stared at the sign in disbelief.

"Mountain Joe DeBloney?" he said aloud. "Klamat, I knew
this man when I was a boy. He's half the reason I came down
from Oregon. . . ."

The reunion was a glad one—and indeed Mountain Joe
was, if anything, even more astonished than Nate had been.

"Gawd an' the divvels," Joe thundered, knocking over a
coat rack on his way to greet Nate at the doorway. "I don't
believe my damn eyes! It's Hiner Miller hisself, an' all
growed up! Kootnis! Damn yore soul, get out here! We got
company!"

Joe clapped Nate long and hard about the shoulders—until
finally Nate had to grasp the man's arms and gently push him
backward.

"Mountain Joe. We came to see the new post, but I didn't
know. . . . How long have you been here?"

"Four months now, ye young nigger! Heard ye was over to
The Forks when the flood washed 'er away—last anyone'd
heard of ye. Hiner, it's good to see ye, damned good!"

Kootnis, an old Indian woman who worked for Joe, came
out—and Joe introduced his "gawdson." Kootnis nodded, and
Nate introduced Klamat.

"By the curly-headed gawd, ye boys is old enough to drink
a mite!" Joe laughed, and in a moment had poured four shot
glasses of whiskey. Joe raised his glass and Kootnis, following

Joe's lead, raised hers. Nate gestured to Klamat, whose expression appeared doubtful. All four drank, but Klamat choked, then swallowed anyway.

"Damn me, son, part of the reason I come down here was to find out what had happened to ye. Yore pa's fine. Ye ought to write old Hulings a letter. You write one afore ye leave, hear? You might be dead an' skulped, for all yore pa knows. Damn, lad, that's sure why he taught ye readin' an' writin'."

Kootnis said nothing, and Nate wondered if the old woman might not be deaf and dumb. She smiled and kept nodding, one front tooth missing and the other teeth uniformly worn.

Joe was further astonished at the amount of gold Nate and Klamat had with them.

"Boys, where'd ye get this stuff?"

Klamat glanced at Nate and shook his head.

"She's a secret, Joe. I can't tell you—you understand. Not that you'd say anything, but . . ."

"Respect that," Joe said. "My job's to get the nuggets an' dust away from ye. What is it ye boys want to buy here at old Joe's emporium?"

Rifles, pistols, blankets, and a dozen horses. These and various supplies, coffee, molasses, salt, bacon, smoked pork, flour, dried apples, beans . . .

"Guns an' horses," Joe said. "Ye be livin' with the Injuns, Nate?"

"Just three of us," Nate replied. "Mining claim."

"Then?"

"Getting married, Joe. The Shastas require a marriage price."

"Hell of a lot for a squaw, ain't it?"

Klamat's eyes narrowed.

"Two squaws," Nate said. "Klamat and I are both getting married."

"Humm?" Joe responded. "Beauties they must be, both o' 'em. She's a steep price, boys. A man's got to be economical about such like. Kootnis, here, she didn't cost me nothin'."

Kootnis smiled and nodded.

"More drink?" she asked—the first words she had spoken.

They examined the weapons and horses, selected the ones they wished to purchase, and paid Mountain Joe, who insisted they stay the night.

Conversation went on long and late, until Joe finally fell asleep in his chair, drunk, and oblivious to the world.

Kootnis poured herself another drink and offered the bottle to Nate and Klamat. The friends declined and found their way to one of the spare bedrooms that Joe kept for travelers. Nate sat down on the bed, bounced on the springs to test them, and said, "Klamat, I haven't slept in a real bed since I left Oregon."

Klamat shook his head, lay down on the floor, and instantly fell asleep. Nate grinned, turned off the oil lantern, and stretched out on the bed.

Morning brought excitement. A small band of Karoks who had been camped below the post, next to the river, was gone—and so were all the horses from Mountain Joe's corral. Joe cursed, got out his double-barreled shotgun, and sent two blasts up into the air.

Within a short time a group of more than a dozen miners from nearby claims had arrived at the post. Joe explained the problem with few words, and the troop set off on foot up toward the high, gray domes of Castle Crags. They followed the big creek, then its northern branch back into a precipitous gorge, the trail climbing steeply.

"Have to rest them horses at Soapstone Lake," Joe said. "Damn fool Karoks! Sure they didn't think I wouldn't foller them...."

Klamat moved swiftly ahead of the others, but before Nate and Mountain Joe had ascended the gorge, he was back.

The Karoks were indeed at Soapstone Lake, about half of them roaring drunk.

"It is possible for two or three of us to get around behind them," Klamat said. "Nate and I will do it. When the Karoks realize they are in a trap, perhaps they will be willing to give back the horses. Then we will not have to fight them."

Joe DeBloney stroked his beard and nodded.

"Yore compañero's got a good noodle on 'is shoulders," Joe said to Nate. "Like the idee. Guess I was figgerin' to fight some Blackfeet or Utes. Man's got to keep up with the times. Yore way's best, Klamat, if we can make 'er work...."

Mountain Joe and his miners approached Soapstone Lake and then waited for Klamat and Nate to scale around the crest so as to cut off the only avenue of escape. When the old mountain man supposed sufficient time had passed, he moved his troop through the high saddle and down toward the little lake.

But before any communication could be made with the Karoks, one of the miners fired his rifle. Within moments a haze of gunsmoke was rising from the thicket of mountain hemlocks beside the lake, and all the miners had opened fire as well.

The Karoks, presuming their way clear to make a run for it down the canyon below the lake, and so on to the south branch of the Sacramento and across the pass to the drainage of the Trinity and safety, left the herd of horses behind and moved away on foot toward where Klamat and Nate had taken position.

"Don't fire!" Nate whispered. "They're leaving the horses—we've got what we came after."

Klamat considered the matter for a moment and lay down his Sharps.

Then two of the fugitive Karoks were standing before them, both armed only with bow and arrow.

Klamat made the gesture of peace, and one of the Karoks backed off. But the other drew his bow and launched an arrow.

The shaft passed through Nate's mouth and lodged in the side of his neck, the tip projecting out.

A flash of intense pain, and Nate rolled to one side, struggling to breathe and clinging to consciousness.

Sporadic rifle fire for a minute or two, and then the Karoks were gone, leaving several dead behind them.

Mountain Joe had also taken an arrow, the shaft cutting his forehead and the blood running down his face so profusely that he was unable to see from one eye.

"Lie still, Nate, lie still!" Klamat commanded.

"Am I done for?" Nate wanted to say, but the shaft was through his mouth and he could not make the words come.

Klamat grasped the arrow and pushed it deeper—so that the obsidian point cut through the flesh and emerged from Nate's neck. Nate's body arched up with the renewed pain, and then a spiral of darkness spun before him, and he realized he was powerless to resist it. It drew him down into unconsciousness. Klamat cut through the bloody shaft, removing the head. Then he grasped the feathers and pulled the arrow back out.

Blood bubbled from Nate's mouth, but then, within moments, the flow lessened.

"It is not yet time," Klamat said to his unconscious friend, then struggled to lift him and drape him about his own shoulders.

Several of Mountain Joe's men were wounded, but none, other than Nate, seriously. With Nate sometimes conscious and other times not, the men drove the horses before them, crossed back through the low spot in the ridge, and worked their way once more into the depths of the gorge.

By late afternoon they were back at Mountain Joe's post. Joe provided free whiskey for everyone, appointed a bartender, and then took up watch over Nate—along with Klamat and Kootnis.

"Too young, too pretty to die," the old woman muttered from time to time.

Night fell, and the three took turns sitting up with their half-dead patient. At one point, Joe thought Nate was gone—and awakened the others.

Kootnis was immediately at the side of the bed. She placed the tips of her fingers at Nate's throat and waited a moment.

"Still alive," she said. "Him not going to die. Too young, too pretty . . ."

It was well into morning before Nate's eyes opened. He looked about the room, the place not familiar, and started to speak—but pain flashed as he attempted to move his mouth.

He turned, and attempted to sit up, but was unable.

"Nate Miller," a voice said.

Where was the voice coming from?

Klamat?

"He is awake now."

Whose voice?

"You were wounded," Klamat said. "Don't try to talk."

"Be all right," Kootnis said.

"Red divvels got ye, Hiner. But yo're goin' to pull through. Klamat here saved yore life."

"Too pretty," Kootnis said, and passed a damp cloth over his forehead.

It was now time for the late summer feast of the Shastas. Nate's wound had healed with amazing rapidity under the care of old Kootnis, who, when Nate was ready to leave, wished only the reward of a single kiss from the one she had insisted was "too pretty" to die. Nate, though his mouth was still sore and somewhat swollen, responded—kissing Kootnis full on the mouth.

Kootnis grinned her ragged smile, turned to Mountain Joe, and said, "This one too young for me, Joe. I stay with you."

Nate and Klamat returned to The Castle, where the horses were allowed to graze freely in the meadows. They found The Prince packing his saddlebags.

"I was coming to find you," he said. "My God, Nate, what's happened?"

The story was quickly told.

The Prince nodded, asked a few questions more, and then related some news of his own. In their absence, he had begun to spend full time at the quartz vein and had hit a rich pocket, a little "glory hole," as such things were sometimes called, a term used also for a vertical shaft into which a man might accidentally step and so break a leg or a neck in his fall. In the present case, as The Prince explained, barely able to control his glee, a couple of hundred pounds of quartz with gold bandings laced through it had yielded in excess of two thousand dollars—perhaps twice that much by the time he had the rock completely crushed down and the gold extracted.

"You strong enough to swing a double-john, Nate? Think we've got half a mountain of the stuff up there!"

But further slabbing-out produced nothing of consequence, as the quartz turned bony white—and the miners returned to work on the gravel bank.

Paquita and White Dawn had been coming daily to The Castle in the hope that their husbands-to-be had returned. Now their patience was rewarded, and the two young men and the two young women drove the dozen horses on to Naw-aw-wa to present them, along with blankets, rifles, and pistols, to Warrottetot. The chief carefully inspected the horses and weapons, his face impassive until he had finished.

"This is much to pay for women," Warrottetot said.

Nate and Klamat said nothing.

"Are you certain you wish to have my daughters for your wives?"

Nate and Klamat assured Warrottetot that this was the case.

"If they are not good wives, I will return all that you have paid me. I accept these bride prices."

And then the day of the feast was at hand. The Prince assisted Nate and Klamat as they dressed for the occasion and then himself donned the apparel from his days as a gambling man—the black Oregon felt hat with new silver dollars affixed to its band, the black shirt embroidered with silver thread in intricate design, the ivory-handled pistol tucked beneath his red waist sash, tight black pants, and high-topped Mexican leather boots. The costume had all been laundered and laid away in anticipation of the occasion, apparently while Nate and Klamat had been off to Mountain Joe's Post—for neither Nate nor Klamat had been aware of The Prince's elaborate preparations.

"A man has to look *right* on the day his family's getting married," The Prince explained.

He was in high spirits as he and Nate and Klamat rode toward Naw-aw-wa, but as they drew near to the village, he became more subdued—a little detached, silent.

For Nate, the ride to the village was dreamlike. Long bands of deer were moving on the worn paths, and a black bear, its coat shining in the sunlight, crossed the trail before them and seemed not to notice them at all.

The village was crowded, for other bands of Shastas had come in the night before. Warrottetot rode out to meet them, several of his warriors at either side, and presented the pipe of welcome. At the center of the village, all the men seated themselves in a circle around a great fire, and once more the pipe was passed from hand to hand.

The young women danced, a number of them nude from the waist up, others in flowing deerskin robes. Their eyes shone with excitement, and their black hair, combed out, swirled about their heads as they moved first this way, then the other.

On this day neither Poonkina nor White Dawn danced.

But wherever Paquita moved, walking from one group to another, talking briefly, walking onward, The Prince's eyes were never off her. Tall, lithe, and graceful, utterly self-assured, confident of her own worth and of her importance within the tribe, yet still he could see the half-starved girl with the great, haunted eyes—still he could see the developing woman-child who had so thoroughly captivated the rough miners at The Forks. She was changed now, and yet she was still the same, would always be the same to him. He looked upon her with devotion, with reverence, with love. Now she would marry, and one man would be blessed; another man would marry also, but to a different woman, to her sister, and so, The Prince believed, would live forever after in unspoken regret and a secret sadness.

And what of the third man?

For he too had loved this child who became a woman, knowing all along that she was not for him—his to watch and love, but never to touch.

This man, too, would forever nurse a secret sadness and would forever contemplate a different world, a different time.

Nate studied The Prince's face, saw whom it was that his partner looked upon—read in The Prince's expression what he imagined his own feelings to be.

If only . . . Nate thought, but then reminded himself that this was to be his marrying day also. Paquita could not be his wife, but she had promised that her life would be joined with his, the joining permanent.

"I think we will always be together, as long as I am alive. The Earth Spirits have done this thing, and their medicine is more powerful than the medicine of humans, even more powerful than the medicine of the shaman, Mountain Smoke. We cannot understand the medicine, but we must do as it says."

Paquita's words.

Paquita stood now before The Prince, and Nate studied the two of them. Once The Prince had taken this girl in his arms, had folded Nate's coat gently about her, had lifted her up as if she had been a mere child. And she had become *everything* to him. Now, though she appeared to be waiting for him to embrace her, he did not do so. Instead, he wished her Godspeed, removed his red sash, and presented it to her. Then he turned quickly and strode away.

Paquita came to Nate.

"Something is wrong with The Prince," she said. "His eyes looked beyond me. . . ."

"He loves you," Nate said. "He loves you, and now you will marry Klamat."

Paquita nodded; she seemed to understand and yet was vexed by what she understood.

"Do you feel this way also, Nate? White Dawn will make you happy, and we shall still be together."

There was almost a note of pleading in her voice.

"I—I will be happy," Nate managed. But the words were hard to speak.

"I am also sad, even though I love Klamat," Paquita said. "I think often of our—sunlight. I. . . ."

Then she too was uncertain what to say, and started to turn from him.

"Paquita?"

She turned back to face him. She was smiling, and yet there were tears at the corners of her eyes.

"Hold me for this moment, Nate. It is proper to do this now, but later we will not be able to. . . ."

The afternoon was devoted to feats of horsemanship, and the Shasta warriors demonstrated amazing tricks of riding. While all were watching the performance, the Prince approached Nate, extended his hand, and said, "Good-bye, my friend. I have to leave now."

The Prince's tone of voice caused vibrations inside Nate's skull—something that had been said without the appropriate words being spoken.

"In two days we'll go back to work," Nate replied, taking The Prince's hand. "But why leave now?"

"No," The Prince said. "I have to leave the mountains, Nate. You're happy here, and you'll stay for a time, perhaps for a long time. But I have to go. In a few years I'll come back—we'll see each other again, I'm certain of it. By that time perhaps I'll have been able to forget her—it—I don't know what I mean. It's just that I've been in the mountains too long, Nate. I've felt this coming for some time. One day I'll come back. You're the best friend I've ever had, and we've shared a world, four of us, five of us. But another world is calling me, and I. . . ."

It was all so unexpected, so sudden, that Nate did not know what to say, could not imagine what words he might utter that would alter things back to what they had been.

The two men embraced, clung to each other, embraced almost as lovers might do. Then they pushed back, held each other at arm's length, and neither could think of anything further to say.

The Prince mounted his horse, a black mare that he had purchased for the price of a rifle—from one of Warrottetot's warriors—a month earlier. He reared the animal, fired his pistol three times into the air, and yelled, "Nate! Check your cantinas!"

Then he urged the mare to a full run and was gone, disappearing into the dark cover of the forest.

The sun was dropping westward now, and beyond the village at Naw-aw-wa hung the huge, phantomlike presence of Shasta, the Spirit Mountain draped with long downward bandings of ice and snow that glistened a deepening hue of silver-violet.

A band of cloud, gray and in appearance much like an extended smoke plume, drifted eastward from the high summit.

The marriage ceremonies in themselves were not impressive, so it seemed to Nate Miller. Celebration fires blazed up with the onset of darkness, and there was a great abundance of food—much laughter, chanting, singing, dancing. Of all those present, only four would not partake, for such was the custom. The feast was not for those who were being joined in marriage.

Two new lodges had been constructed, and inside each, carefully hidden from sight, would be a woven basket filled with food.

Both Klamat and Nate, having no families of their own among the Achomawi Shastas, were escorted to their respective lodges by small groups of warriors. Poonkina and White

Dawn were already within, and now their new husbands were told to sit next to them.

The torches that the warriors had carried were placed together on the fire spot. Man and woman did not speak, though the warriors themselves continued to laugh and joke, chuckling about how Grizzly Bear once managed to copulate with Old Man Coyote, and the like.

Only when the torches had burned up into one fire did the escorting warriors turn and silently depart.

THIRTEEN

▲

Klamat's Vision

The great composite cone of Shasta rises to a summit elevation of 14,162 feet, and the volcano itself has a volume of more than eighty cubic miles. On a clear day, the mountain is visible in all directions for a hundred miles.

Late in its geologic history, the mountain developed a new vent high on its north slope, and this vent, extruding huge masses of lava and cinder, became the satellite peak, Shastina, rising to an elevation of more than twelve thousand feet.

On Shasta's southern margin is a shield volcano which sent fluid basaltic andesite down the Sacramento River Canyon for forty miles.

The most recent eruptions have come from the main summit cone, the explosions hurling out pumice, cinders, lapilli, blocks, and volcanic bombs of hypersthene andesite.

Earthquake swarms are common about the base of the peak.

Autumn came, the lower forests of black oak blazing a rich golden hue, creek maples trembling their large amber leaves in the sunlight, quaking aspens a golden frenzy of motion in any breath of wind, and the endless evergreen forest seeming only to darken.

A large band of Shasta women, Poonkina and White Dawn included, accompanied by a handful of warriors, journeyed south into the oak forests among the tumbled canyons of the various branches of the McCloud River for the purpose of gathering the winter's store of acorns, these to be leached on an elevated platform of sticks covered with pine needles, over which was placed a layer of fine sand. First, however, the membrane overlaying the acorn kernel had to be removed, rubbed off by hand. When the bitterness was gone, the acorns were pounded into meal and a dough was formed, to be dried for storage.

Liveoak acorns were buried in mud until they turned black, and the darkened kernels were then cooked whole or roasted in ashes.

The men, meanwhile, occupied themselves with fishing for salmon and hunting for deer, elk, and black bear, the hides dressed out by a number of older women whose abilities as tanners were esteemed, and as much of the meat as possible was smoked and dried into jerky. Salmon were smoked and dried, either in thin slabs or completely pulverized. Even the crushed bones of salmon and deer were stored, the makings of winter soup.

Klamat and Nate continued their efforts at the mine, but now Warrottetot had begun to worry. He rode alone to The Castle one day, found his sons-in-law at work on the gravel beds, picked a nugget from the riffles, chewed tentatively at it, and tossed it back.

"The yellow metal allows my sons to buy things from the Whites, and this is good," he said. "But is it not true that if others find out there is gold here on the Numken, they will come to dig their own holes?"

"That is true," Klamat said. "The chief has seen that happen in many places."

"Yes," Warrottetot said. "I have been thinking. We always have need for guns and horses, so it is good to mine the gold. The Whites have killed many of the Yanas, and the Whites and the Modocs are always fighting. The Whites have mistreated our brothers, the Achomawis and the Atsugewis near the Pit River. Settlers have come to that valley, and they have begun to fence the land. It may be that we will have to fight these Whitemen soon."

Nate and Klamat studied the chief's face but said nothing. "What will you do then?" Warrottetot asked Nate. "You are my son, and yet you are White. Which side will you fight for?"

"I am Warrottetot's son-in-law," Nate answered. "The Shastas have become my people. I will fight for them."

Warrottetot reflected on the matter, then nodded.

"That is good, but I think it will be difficult for you to fire upon your own people."

"We are not yet at war," Klamat said quickly.

"No, we are not. But it is wise to do what we can to prevent war, is that not so, Klamat?"

"Of course."

"Then I believe something should be done. You both have lodges in the village, for these were built for you by the women. Naw-aw-wa is only a short ride from where you dig. Do you think perhaps we should burn your lodge here and scatter the dead embers?"

Nate and Klamat looked at each other. Blackbeard, of course, was not merely suggesting but ordering that the burning take place.

"The chief is wise," Nate said. "Shall we do it tonight?"

"Wait until it begins to rain again," Warrottetot said. "That way we will not attract attention or burn all the trees."

A week later it was done. When a light rain began to fall, The Castle was set ablaze. Nearly a hundred warriors watched the fire through the night, and when the remains were cold, they carried the larger portions of blackened timbers to various distances and left them. Then the entire area was raked over and pine needles were scattered—until only close examination would reveal that any structure had ever stood there.

Nate stared at the spot—remembered putting up the building, remembered himself and Doc and The Prince and Paquita and Klamat sitting about the fire, eating, talking. The last vestige of what had once been a family, a closed society entire to itself, had been effaced.

But the season was turning now, and soon the snows would begin. White Dawn and Paquita would once more be with their husbands.

As a married man and as one who had fought against both the Whites and the Karoks, Klamat was now esteemed a warrior. A man of great endurance afoot and one with a precise knowledge of the land, a fine memory, and a sharp eye, he was also a skilled rider. Because of his mining, he was now a wealthy man by Shasta standards, and as husband to the chief's eldest daughter, his status within the tribe had risen immensely.

But one thing was missing: he could not claim to having had a medicine vision.

The old shaman, Mountain Smoke, advised him to climb

up onto the mountain, up beyond where the forest ended, to the lodge of Old Man Above—a place avoided by the Shastas.

"It is unusual to do such a thing," the medicine woman said, "but you must do it, Klamat. You have never believed in my power, and that is why you have had no vision. Now you must go up to where Old Man lives. He will either kill you or give you what you desire."

Klamat had some doubts about climbing the mountain, but Nate suggested that, indeed, the high, thin air might well give him visions.

"You believe this, my brother?" Klamat asked.

"I will go with you," Nate said. "The mountain is sacred to me, also, but I will not seek a vision. It's just that I want to see what the world looks like from up there. We will go up the mountain together."

The following morning they set out on their climb, up from Naw-aw-wa, following along beside the foot tracks Old Man had made on the side of the mountain.

By afternoon they had emerged above the timberline. Large portions of the southern face of Shasta were still without snow, for though snow had fallen, the incessant winds about the mountain had swept the crests bare.

They made camp that night far up on the mountain, just at the base of the highest of Old Man's foot tracks. Nate had carried, at great effort, several chunks of pitchy wood to burn for warmth. With some difficulty, a fire was started—and wind drove sparks upward in a swirl, toward the stars.

They slept beneath an overhang of stone, out of the gustings of air, and for a time huddled beneath their robes. Near midnight, however, the direction of the wind abruptly changed, and the temperature rose. Streamers of mist began to form, and within a matter of a few minutes the astounding brilliance of stars against pure darkness grew faint and vanished as Shasta wrapped itself in cloud.

Klamat arose, put the last of the knot wood on the embers of the fire, and watched the pitch begin to melt and ooze and finally take fire.

When Nate came half-awake from his friend's stirring about, Klamat said, "I will be back. Do not worry about me. Perhaps it is time for me to speak with Old Man now."

Nate started to protest, but Klamat was already gone.

Up the mountain in the darkness, strangely warm mist flowing about him as he moved upslope.

When he reached the saddle above the highest of Old Man's foot tracks, he stopped, sucked in air, the high, thin air, difficult to breathe.

Then he moved on, feeling his way, sometimes slipping, stumbling, for a time uncertain whether he was moving toward the mountain's summit or away from it.

He stopped, suddenly afraid—his heart pounding within his chest.

He could hear deep rumblings inside the mountain. At first he believed it to be his imagining, even when he felt the earth tremor beneath his feet. Klamat dropped to his hands and knees, waited, waited.

He could feel it. The earth was actually vibrating.

High above, a ledge of stone broke loose—he couldn't see it, but he knew instinctively what had happened. And nowhere to turn, nowhere to take shelter.

Klamat braced himself, waited.

Then the current of loose rock was hurtling past him, a pale, red glow in places as sparks shot out as the avalanche of rubble hurtled downward through the heavy mists.

A few rocks bouncing after, and below the grinding sound of the rockslide piling up on itself, halting.

He climbed on, the mountain steeper now, the footing more treacherous in the darkness that seemed at times almost a shimmer of white.

Or was the dawn beginning—the faint light of false dawn refracting through the tiny droplets of moisture swirled about by the moving ocean of air?

He crossed snow and ice, sometimes had to go on all fours to keep from sliding backward, and his hands and then his feet ached with the cold.

He stopped, and sucked in his breath.

"Old Man Above, I am climbing up to you!" he shouted. "I am Klamat of the Shastas!"

No echo. His words were muted by the ever-present mist.

And then he laughed at himself. *I, the one who claimed not to believe, I am shouting like a child, like a superstitious old woman. Why have I come here? The mountain has already attempted to kill me, has already told me to go back....*

Almost painful to breathe at times, the air too insubstantial.

He moved on, declining to drop to all fours again. He would climb the mountain like a man, like a warrior of the Shastas, not like an animal. . . .

The mists contained more light now.

He struggled over a crest, moved down over a gentle slope that was still jagged with fractured-off boulders, and could smell heat in the air, could smell sulphur, the odor of boiling springs like those far down on the slopes of the mountain.

Geysers of steam rising irregularly ahead of him, light gaining through the vapors now, the forms of the steam jets like ghosts, like the constantly changing shapes of the dead.

He walked among them, the air rank with their odor, the hot breath of creatures long dead, creatures that had died in a time before the First Grizzlies had vanished, had been transformed.

Boiling, hissing sounds. More thunderings deep within the mountain, far down in the rock.

Klamat laughed.

There was nothing to fear, only the mountain itself. He was standing upon the smoke vent in Old Man's lodge, and the vent flap was closed.

"I am Klamat!" he shouted. "I have come to this place. Can you speak to me, Old Man?"

No answer—only the hissings and gurglings of the springs, only the boiling sulphur water, the jets of steam going up and dispersing in the wind, melting into the greater flow of mists that circled the mountain.

Still the shadowed form of the mountain rose above him, but it was not far now, not far at all. He climbed on through the mist that was luminous with the dawning, and stood finally on the utmost clenched fist of stone. The wind blew about him, a single strong gust nearly hurling him down. Light everywhere—the mists, the clouds were alive with it. Shapes moved through it, bird forms, animal forms, silent, constantly changing.

"I am here, Old Man!" he shouted, his own voice hardly recognizable. "Tell me what I am supposed to know!"

A short, sharp, screeching sound—like the cry of a cougar— like the cry of a warrior shot down in battle.

"I hear your voice, but I do not understand you!"

No further sounds then—only the silent turbulence of vapor streaming past him. The highest rock was not sufficiently large to stand upon, so he stood beside it, his hand upon it, bracing himself against the rough stone. The wind was cold, damp and cold since he was no longer climbing, and his double-lined elkskin shirt could not protect him from it.

The vapors were parting, the mists evaporating about the summit of the mountain, and he could see the sky. A hundred feet below where he stood, the clouds stretched away, a great spiral of gray-white that still clung to the peak, but beyond, far beyond, he could see the black, ragged shadows of the range wall to the west, the jumble of broader, more-rounded mountains to the east, and far away the wide, truncated formation of several small peaks that he knew enclosed the Medicine Lake.

Suddenly the world was on fire, a vast lake of flame, flame spreading everywhere. He heard the cries of his people, he saw them dying, he saw long lines of them climbing up the mountain and passing by him, their faces set, their expressions indicating no moment of recognition. He saw them stepping off the mountain into empty air and continuing their journey. He saw sun, moon, stars explode, bursting outward into spirals of color, sweeping rainbows of light. He saw his people walking among these, moving off into a distance so great that he could not even imagine it.

Then the sun, the white rim of the sun, seemed to melt its way up from the long black mountains to the east.

He was trembling, cold, exhausted.

"What have I seen?" he said aloud, not shouting this time, his voice almost a whisper.

Then Shasta heaved beneath him, and he had to cling to the rocks. A deep, terrible roaring noise, and the summit boulders jerked again, as under impact. Stone split, fell away, the fragments bouncing, hurtling, leaping down to the slope of loose rock below. And an immense, almost blinding flash of lightning burst through the mists, clung wreathlike for an instant, hovering about the slope below, and then vanished in a wave of thunder.

Klamat watched, but his mind was calm. He was hardly surprised at all, he realized—as though at some deep level he had known all along what was going to happen.

"I have seen the end of my people," he said.

Strange. He said the words, heard them, and yet felt no bitterness, only a momentary surge of regret.

He watched the sun continue its ascent of the eastern sky and felt its warmth upon his face. Below him, the mists were vanishing, and the maze of canyon, peak, ridge, and basin was all revealed, almost blue, perhaps blue-black. Far down was the dark pyramid of the cinder butte at the Great Mountain's foot, and off from the summit was the sister mountain, the lodge of Old Man's daughter, the girl with the streaming red hair. And it was beautiful, it was all astoundingly beautiful.

He could even see, far to the south, the big valley where the river went, the Noorkan Charook.

He wondered, as the sun rose higher, if he might be able to see the Great Water to the west—but there were only clouds, a long band of silver-black clouds stretching as far as he could see from south to north.

Someone was climbing up the slope below him.

It was Nate, the Whiteman whose people would destroy his own people, the Whiteman who was his brother.

Klamat waved his arms and called down to his friend.

Nate, the one with the long rifle he called his "Kain-tuck." Which way, Klamat wondered, would that rifle fire? Would he and Nate end up killing each other?

Poonkina, Paquita, who loved the blue-eyes in a way that she did not love her husband.

Klamat grinned and shrugged his shoulders. It made no difference. The man was his brother, and his brother had climbed the Great Mountain to find him.

Klamat recounted his *seeing* to Mountain Smoke, and afterward the medicine woman was quiet for a long while, studying the small flames of her lodge fire. Then she rose and said, "I do not need to speak of this vision. A little time, perhaps a few years, and it is over. I will give you this new name, and you will lead us in a battle we cannot win. This battle will continue even after you are in the Spirit World. I name you *Aheki-Klamat*."

Klamat was stunned. He sat very quietly for a long while,

and neither he nor Mountain Smoke said anything. Finally he rose and started to exit from the lodge.

"What of Poonkina?" he asked, turning about.

"Do you wish to know this thing?"

"Yes, Mountain Smoke, I wish to know."

The shaman nodded and poked at the lodge fire with a stick.

"Warrottetot's daughter will remain true to you and will go with you. She will prepare your lodge, as is proper for a wife."

Klamat, now Aheki-Klamat, studied the old woman's wrinkled face. Her eyes met his and held them.

Then he turned and left the lodge.

The snows fell, blanketing the area about Naw-aw-wa with two feet of whiteness. Then the skies cleared, and the weather turned bitterly cold.

High and distant above the village, and yet so close that it seemed always as if it might fall upon them, Mount Shasta glistened in stunning, uniform white.

An immense herd of elk gathered in about the semicircle of hot springs at the head of the Numken, where the ground remained free of the snow that lay in drifts elsewhere to a depth of more than five feet. The elk could not escape their oasis, and the Shastas, coming in on showshoes, slew hundreds of the big animals as they plunged out into the snowdrifts, broke through the frozen crust, wallowed about, and foundered.

Blood ran thickly over the wind-slick snow as the warriors said brief thanks to Old Man and at the same time asked him to assist the spirits of the elk into the Spirit World so that more young elk might be born to grow and replace those that had been taken for food.

The last remaining few of the elk were driven back to the area about the hot springs, and then the women were able to begin their work of skinning the dead animals and of butchering the meat and preparing it for transport back to Naw-aw-wa village.

It was already late in the day, however, and the work of butchering was no more than half-finished.

"We cannot leave the carcasses here overnight," Poonkina

said to old Mountain Smoke, the latter giving advice and
otherwise overseeing the job. "The meat will freeze, and
then we will have to use axes to cut it. But in that way we will
lose much of our work."

The shaman stared into the eyes of the young woman to
whom she had given the strange name, happily married now
to the man she loved. The eyes were bright, transparent, and
possibly even thoughtless—so Mountain Smoke concluded.
And yet there was something, something strange. Was it a
hint of foreknowledge, some inner awareness of the implica-
tions of the terrible thing she had dreamed long ago? And
now her husband, Aheki-Klamat, had climbed the Spirit
Mountain and had returned speaking of a vision that suggested
the same ultimate things. These two, Poonkina and Aheki-
Klamat—had they been appointed by Old Man Who Does
Everything to oversee the ending of their own people? Were
the Shastas themselves to be entrapped as the elk had been,
helpless victims of a massacre like the one that Poonkina
herself and Aheki-Klamat as well had witnessed and from
which they had miraculously escaped?

"I do not think it will freeze that hard tonight," Mountain
Smoke replied.

"The medicine woman's nose has grown numb, then, because she is older than the pines. Look. The blood is already
frozen on the snow. Is there nothing that can be done?"

"Done?" Mountain Smoke asked, only half-listening to
Poonkina's words. "Oh, done. Yes, Pretty One, there is
something. Go to your father and tell him you wish the men
to build a great fire close to where the elk have died. Once
the fire is going well, have the men lay on many green
boughs of fir and pine. In this way there will be much light
and warmth as well. And the women can continue their work
until all the animals have been properly slaughtered. But
you, Poonkina, daughter of Warrottetot, you are the fire
itself. You must be very careful what you touch."

Poonkina had started to turn away when the last few words
of the medicine woman registered upon her.

"What did you say, Mountain Smoke?"

The medicine woman made a gesture of futility and did not
answer.

"What do you mean to tell me?" Poonkina persisted. "Your words do not make sense to me."

"There is blood on this snow, Pretty One. Many will die, and one of us will live to see it—I do not know which one."

With that she turned away, and Poonkina stood there, puzzled, as she watched Mountain Smoke limp across the snow toward the beaten track that led to Naw-aw-wa.

Crazy old loon. She's been drinking manzanita cider, or else she's been down to visit Nate's friend, Mountain Joe.

At length Poonkina found her father and Aheki-Klamat. The men were apparently disputing some point or another, but their talk ceased as she approached.

"Mountain Smoke says we need a big fire so that we can continue with the butchering and not lose any of the meat, and that is what I think also."

Warrottetot grinned and patted Aheki-Klamat on the back.

"My son," he said, "your wife is right. But I am old, and my muscles grow sore when it is cold. Call the warriors and tell them I said to do whatever it is that Poonkina wishes, for otherwise we will never hear the end of it."

It was late when the last of the laden pack horses and mules came in, and the temperature was dropping rapidly. The Shastas retired to their lodges, built up the fires, banked them, and, after a quick meal of warmed-over food, retired for the night.

The following day, however, the sun blazed down with an almost springlike warmth, causing the snow to settle and to melt out along the edges of the stream. Children were out and about, pelting one another with handfuls of soggy snow, and the older boys and girls undertook the task of trampling down the entire area in the center of the village.

Nate Miller, his arm around White Dawn's waist, watched the initial stages of preparation for the feast and dancing that would follow.

"I must go help now," White Dawn said. "There is much to do. Someday maybe the men will prepare a feast, and then all the women will have to do is stand around and watch."

"Well, we killed the elk, after all," Nate said, laughing.

"Yes, my husband, but anyone could have killed those elk.

Even young children could have done it. The animal people could not get away."

And then she was off, joining in with a band of the younger women who were on their way to gather firewood.

Nate, in turn, joined his friends Aheki-Klamat, Crippled Deer, and Heron.

"Now you are both married men," Heron said, laughing. "Now all you will be able to do at the feast is eat. Crippled Deer and I will take your places, though. We will not allow any of the young women to remain lonely."

Crippled Deer grinned and intimated that most things had been much more satisfactory during Klamat's long period of absence from the village.

"Too much competition is not a good thing," he asserted. "But now you are married, and everything is well again."

"We still have not gone to see those twins among the Atsugewis," Heron reflected.

"No doubt they are married by now also," Aheki-Klamat said. "If a man waits too long, he may have to wait forever."

"It would be a shame, then," Heron said. "Those girls have very pretty faces and very pretty bosoms also. It is wonderful to watch them swimming in the river when they are wearing only their short skirts of woven tules."

"The warm sunlight today makes Heron forget about the snow that is still on the ground," Crippled Deer said, chuckling. "In his imagination it is *Speluish* moon already, and he is diving into the water after those twin girls."

"Who are no doubt already married to wealthy old men who have trained their dogs to bite anyone who looks at their wives," Nate added.

"These Whitemen." Heron sighed. "There is much that they do not understand very well."

"All men become that way after they are married," Crippled Deer said.

"The women are beginning to place baskets of food on the long tables," Aheki-Klamat observed. "My friends, perhaps we should go over to inspect their work."

"He has not seen Poonkina for an hour or so, and already he has grown lonely. Will we be that way after we have married the Atsugewi twins, Crippled Deer?" Heron asked.

Crippled Deer gave Heron a sudden shove, sending him

sprawling into the snow, and then leaped upon him. The two wrestled back and forth, each attempting to shove the other's face into the cold wetness.

Preparations for the celebration moved forward. A great bed of coals was prepared in the central fire pit, and hind-quarters of elk were wrapped in green hides and layers of mud and set to roasting, while other portions were skewered and suspended above the heat. Poonkina and the other young wives at length pressed their husbands into service and sent them off for a fresh supply of firewood, so that there might be sufficient light and heat for the dancing time that would follow the big evening meal.

Heron, Crippled Deer, and a gang of other unattached young men followed along behind and hooted and jeered, staunchly refusing to give assistance in the task of gathering wood.

"Squaw work! Squaw work!" the bachelors called out. "Old Man Coyote sees you and knows you have lost your man-hood. Your wives have taken it from you, and we know where they are keeping it!"

The married men ignored the raillery and moved rapidly and efficiently about their business.

Then the sky flamed crimson to the west, and the massive form of Shasta began to recede into the darkness. The people mingled about the edges of the fire pit, ate from one basket or another, and moved in for portions of roast meat when the sizzling flesh was removed from the coals. Pots of steaming acorn mush seasoned with manzanita berries and dried plum. Baskets of camas and baskets of pemmican balls. Cakes made of salmon flour and crushed wokas seeds.

The moon rose late, a half-moon, and the men and women danced to the beating of skin drums and the clacking of carved mahogany paddles.

Poonkina wore her crimson dress from The Forks, while White Dawn had been entrusted with the yellow one. Be-tween them, the two women were the center of everyone's attention.

Now Heron stood by mournfully, his entire mood changed. Once White Dawn had followed him about, but now she was married to Nate Miller. And compared to Warrottetot's two daughters, he decided, none of the other young Achomawi women seemed attractive at all. Dressed nearly alike, the one in red and the other in yellow, and closely resembling each other, they were almost twins. . . .

Heron thought of the Atsugewis, to the south, on the Pit River. And he thought as well of the twins, Gray Squirrel and Other Squirrel, almost impossible to tell one from the other. He could imagine them, bare-breasted, splashing about in the waters of a pool in the river. He could imagine them, also bare-breasted, just emerging from a sweat lodge.

And he knew that it was time now to go there. Probably he had already waited too long, but he was resolved to wait no longer. If the girls were not married already, no doubt they would have many suitors from among their own people. But he had three horses he could use as part of any bride price, and he had half-a-dozen full strings of dentalia as well. In addition to nearly fifty woodpecker scalps, Heron also owned an extra pistol, one that he had found mysteriously lying in the shallow waters at the edge of the Middle Branch River, the stream the Whites called the McCloud.

The Atsugewi village he had in mind lay nearly two days' journey to the south during good weather. Now, with the snow still quite heavy in places, and with his extra ponies trailing along behind him, the journey would no doubt be quite difficult—four, five, perhaps even six days.

At length he decided to go alone. Crippled Deer was not of a mind to take a wife, and it was certain he had not been able to accumulate a proper bride price in any case. If Crippled Deer took a woman, he would have to do it on credit, enslaving himself to the girl's father for the specified period of time.

In a little over a week, Heron returned to Naw-aw-wa village, all of his ponies still in tow and both Gray Squirrel and Other Squirrel riding with him. He had been required to pay no bride price at all, for both of the twins' parents had been slain by the Whites.

Heron had acquired the responsibility of two wives, but he brought with him extremely bad news.

The Whites had massacred nearly everyone in the Atsugewi village, and the twin girls had saved their own lives only because they had chanced to be away from the village, searching for horehound root, at the time.

"Tell me what has happened!" Warrottetot demanded. "I wish all of my people to hear what you have to tell us, Heron. Did you see this thing, or did you arrive after it had already occurred?"

"No," the subdued Heron replied, "my eyes were not witness to the act, but what they have seen was terrible enough. This is what happened, Warrottetot. The White settlers claimed the Atsugewis had stolen some of their cattle. But the people, learning of the trouble the Whites were having, brought them a number of freshly killed deer and elk. First the Whites accepted the meat and then they opened fire with their pistols and rifles, killing all but two of the young men. These then returned to their village to warn the people. But before the Atsugewis could decide what to do, the Whites attacked the village in force, massacring all who were not able to flee. No prisoners were taken, except for whatever young women they could find after they had finished with their killing. Then the women were raped and shot. The heads of children were crushed with gun butts. I have seen their bodies, and my heart grew sick. The warriors who lay wounded were shot and scalped, and the village was burned."

"And this is what happened?" Warrottetot asked, turning to the twins.

The girls nodded, but their eyes remained fixed on the ground.

"Why would the Whites do such a thing?" Warrottetot asked.

But neither Heron nor the twins could make any answer.

"Who will counsel me?" Warrottetot cried out. "We must not permit such a thing to go unpunished, yet what can we do?"

Aheki-Klamat stepped forward.

"I will go see for myself what has happened," he shouted. "Shastas! Will any among you follow Aheki-Klamat to Pit River Valley?"

A number of voices answered.

"Nate," Aheki-Klamat said, "it is better that you do not go with us. Always we have gone places together, my brother, but now I am setting out to make war. One of us must remain behind with the daughters of Warrottetot. If I should be slain, then you must take Poonkina into your lodge, for that is right. We are as one, my brother, but this time I must go alone."

"Klamat!" the old chief said quickly, his deep bass voice sharp with authority. "I have not given any permission for war. Hear me now, all of you young men! What Heron has told us is terrible, and our common blood cries out for revenge upon those who committed the massacre. But we cannot battle all the Whitemen in the mountains. First we must know what has happened in such a way that there can be no mistake. Heron speaks truth, for he has always spoken truth. And no one could invent so horrible a thing. But we must find out who is responsible, and we must contact Slippery Salmon and Short Antelope and all our other friends. Listen, warriors! I cannot stop my son-in-law from following his medicine, but he is angry now and has not thought long enough about what he wishes to do."

"My medicine vision cries out in my ears," Aheki-Klamat said. "Warrottetot, we have no choice. We must strike back at the Whites this time. I have seen what they do. I was among the Nomki-dji when the miners poured in and killed everyone, even though the village was starving and could not fight back. I was there!"

"To-ka-do!" the warriors shouted. "We will go! We will follow!"

"Young men!" Mountain Smoke cautioned. "Do you think what the other Whites will do if you kill the ones who have murdered our friends, the Atsugewis? Will they not come here, just as you are going there?"

Warrottetot held out his hands for silence.

"Blackbeard has always valued Mountain Smoke's counsel, and I do this time as well. And yet we cannot stop Aheki-Klamat and the others. We cannot order them as if they were still children. At the same time, we who do not go will not be responsible for what the young warriors may do. And if the Whites choose to come here, we will move the village to the Medicine Lake, and there we will be safe. They will not find us. Even if they did, our men could easily defeat them there, for there are many of us and our village would be easy to defend. But I would make this suggestion. Nate Miller, you are my other son-in-law. I will take care of my daughters, as I

always have. You must go with Aheki-Klamat, for he will
listen to you even though he will no longer listen to me.
Perhaps you will find that it is not exactly as Heron has said,
though I trust his words. Even the Whiteman has laws—
perhaps you will find that these men have been taken by the
Whiteman's law. That is not very likely, but it is possible. Or
perhaps you will find these Whitemen who have murdered
our friends—and you will have to fight them. Or maybe the
Atsugewis have already punished the men and have killed
them. If that is so, then you must leave our friends to their
mourning and return to our village. We must protect ourselves first, just as the Atsugewis must defend themselves.
Aheki-Klamat will listen to your counsel, Nate, and that is
why I ask you to go with him."

Nate and Klamat looked into each other's eyes, nodded,
and embraced each other.

"*To-ka-do!*" the young warriors shouted.

Aheki-Klamat led his band eastward from Naw-aw-wa,
along the upper reaches of the McCloud River, through the
high, level forest of pine and fir, nearly to the headwaters of
that stream. Here they crossed a low divide and passed down
a long, winding ravine to the rim of a great lava flow—its
source the huge blue mound of the Medicine Lake crater,
twenty-five miles to the north.

Aheki-Klamat sent two scouts ahead to discover the where-
abouts of the Atsugewi village, for it had been moved in
Heron's absence.

The scouts returned the following day with word that the
Atsugewis were at the little lake near some hot springs at the
base of a low range of mountains.

Aheki-Klamat rode on, grim-faced and silent, his entire
war party equally taciturn and subdued.

They reached the Pit River Indian village just before
sundown and found the people in mourning. Many, both men
and women, had severed their hair and had woven it into
belts, these worn now as a sign of their grief.

Aheki-Klamat spoke with Short Antelope, the village leader, who in turn demanded to know why it was that Aheki-
Klamat had a Whiteman with him.

"Nate Miller is my brother-in-law," Aheki-Klamat replied. "I have come to see if what my friend Heron has told me could possibly be true. It is true—I feel the grief among your people. My brother-in-law rides with me and will help us to drive these White farmers from your lands, the ones who have murdered your people. We will attempt this thing if your own warriors will go with us."

"The Whitemen have many rifles," Short Antelope said, "and we have only three or four. It is winter, and our people are scattered now. There are not enough of us to fight these men."

The language was only slightly different from the tongue of the Shastas, and Nate was able to follow what the village leader was saying.

"How many Whitemen are there?" he asked.

Short Antelope held up his hands three times.

"Thirty?" Aheki-Klamat asked, surprised. "I have more warriors than that. You have many more warriors than that, Short Antelope. Why cannot we drive these men out of your lands?"

"These are only a few of the Whitemen," the village leader replied. "More come all the time. They tend their cattle and fence the land in places. There are others in Big Valley and others in Opahwah. If we killed these men, more would come to fight. They have many weapons, and we do not. And they would kill our brothers and sisters in the other villages."

"If these men have killed your people, Short Antelope, then they are criminals in the Whiteman's law. If we could capture them. . . ."

"There is no Whiteman's law for the Indians," Short Antelope said. "There is only Whiteman's law against the Indians."

"That is the case," Aheki-Klamat said. "I have seen the law of the Whitemen. My friend has seen it also. Once he saved my life when the Whites attacked a village of ours. My brother-in-law does not believe what he has just said."

Nate listened to the angry murmurings about him, and saw the dark eyes filled with anger and despair. He nodded.

"I will follow Aheki-Klamat," he said. "I will fight against these Whitemen."

They moved out into the Pit River Valley, the open grasslands free of snow, the meandering river frozen in places. The thin Spanish cattle moved in groups of thirty or forty, stopped, the bulls with their heads up at the approach of the Shastas and Atsugewis. Aheki-Klamat's force skirted Tule Lake and rode on toward the cluster of log cabins near the center of the valley, making no attempt to hide their presence.

A group of cowboys, loading cut hay into a pair of wagons, saw them coming, fired off a few shots, mounted, and rode for the protection of the cabins.

The Indians continued their advance, neither slowing their pace nor giving pursuit.

Aheki-Klamat called a halt just out of rifle range, then rode forward a few yards alone.

"Whitemen!" he called to them. "I am Aheki-Klamat of the Shastas. Short Antelope of the Atsugewis is with me. Those of you who murdered Short Antelope's people must leave our lands. We will not harm you if you do what we say, but you must leave now. Take your cattle and your horses and go across the mountains! We will give you passage and not harm you, even though you have harmed us! I speak to you in your own language—do you hear what I am saying?"

"Come in closer, Injun!" someone shouted. "We cain't hear you!"

"You hear me," Aheki-Klamat answered. "I will give you until midday to make up your minds."

As Aheki-Klamat turned his pony about, there was a burst of rifle fire, blue-gray gunsmoke blossoming from the windows of the largest of the log structures.

The shots fell short, and Aheki-Klamat ignored them, returned to his warriors.

"The Whitemen do not wish to leave," he said simply.

The Indians fanned out, leaving their horses behind them, and crawled through the half-frozen hay fields toward the cluster of cabins.

Rifle fire, sometimes ripping through wet sod, mud leaping up in long stripes.

The Indians returned fire, crept closer still.

Nate crawled forward alongside Heron, the two of them no more than a few feet apart.

The thud of a rifle ball, followed in a moment by the crack of the explosion, and Heron slumped face forward into the icy mud, his head shattered like an eggshell.

Red fury swept through Nate. He rose to his feet and

screamed, "Bastards! Bastards!" over and over, at the same time emptying both of his pistols.

Aheki-Klamat wrestled him down.

"Nate! Warrottetot sent you along because he believes I am too impetuous—look at you—are you trying to get yourself killed? I will lose other men before this day is over, but I do not wish to lose you."

"These men must be killed," Nate answered, loading his pistols and setting the percussion caps as quickly as he could.

"Yes," Aheki-Klamat said. "We will kill them all unless they surrender to us. They showed no mercy, but we will—if they will let us."

"Klamat," Nate said, "I'm hoping they don't. . . ."

The exchange of gunfire, now intense, now at long intervals, continued for several hours. It was past the appointed time of midday, and Aheki-Klamat, Nate, and Short Antelope had all begun to worry that, somehow, word of what was happening might have been dispatched to the settlement in Big Valley, across the range of hills to the east.

"We have lost five, maybe six warriors," Nate said. "And for all we know, we haven't gotten a one of them."

"The hay piles are dry," Short Antelope said.

"Could we get it to the walls of the building?" Aheki-Klamat wondered.

The three stared at one another.

"I think so," Nate said.

Short Antelope raised an eyebrow.

"This one only *seems* to be White," he said to Aheki-Klamat.

The order was given, and a dozen warriors worked their way to the haystacks. They gathered great armfuls, held them before them, and dashed all at once toward the west wall of the cabin, the direction from which the wind was blowing.

One didn't make it, the hay proving an insufficient cushion against the impact of a rifle ball. He sprawled forward, hurt but not dead.

Two more rifle balls struck the writhing body, and then it lay still.

But flames were rising along the westward wall.

The Shastas and the Atsugewis ceased firing, and waited. It would only be a matter of a very short time.

Fourteen

▲

What Gold Is Good For

The agent of Indian Affairs sent some half-civilized Indians to speak with Warrottetot. These men told Blackbeard that he must surrender and go to the reservation.

"Where is the Man of Blankets?" Warrottetot asked.

"Down in the valley, to the west of Shasta."

"Let him stay there, and I will stay here."

"We must take him an answer, Warrottetot."

"Why should I wish to go to the reservation?"

"You shall have a house, a farm, and horses on land close to the ocean."

"How did the Blanket Man come to own this land he now wishes to give to me? Those lands belong to the Hupas, the Karoks, the Yuroks. Has the Blanket Man driven these people away, stolen their land and camping places? I could have done that myself. No, he does not own the land. Tell your friend the Blanket Man that I do not want that land. I have land of my own, high up here, and nearer to the Old Man Above. I do not want his blankets. I have a deerskin, and we build wood fires when it snows. I will not go away from the Great Mountain. But you may tell the Blanket Man that I will go down by the sea and live on his reservation if he will agree to take the mountain of Ieka down there."

"Nate! Check your cantinas. . . ."

The Prince's parting words had not made sense until several days later, when Nate realized that his friend had left nearly all the gold. At the time, Nate could see little use that he might have for the precious metal, but the passage of these few months had changed much. By participating in the raid against the Pit River Valley cattlemen, he, Cincinnatus Hiner Miller, was conjointly responsible for the deaths of these Whitemen—and, in point of fact, two of the men had fallen to Old Kaintuck.

He had, so to speak, crossed the Rubicon. There would be no turning back now—and when Aheki-Klamat's party had crossed the Pit River, having followed that stream down to the mouth of the McCloud before turning northward, Nate had carved the word *Rubicon* into the bark of a large alder by the water's edge.

Now the gold had a use—that of acquiring sufficient weapons and ammunition and horses for Warrottetot's people in preparation for the struggle that inevitably lay ahead.

With the melting of the snows, the Indian commissioner had sent a delegation of several tame Wintuns to urge Warrottetot to surrender and move his people to a reservation in the Coast Mountains. Blackbeard had dismissed the delegation with a few words of sarcasm.

News came that the United States Army intended to drive the Shastas from their lands and force them onto the reserve, troops under the command of Captain Gideon Whitney.

Warrottetot asked Nate if it would be possible for him, dressed as a Whiteman, to buy the weapons needed, and Nate agreed readily to make the attempt.

I am now an Indian, Nate thought, *I have become wholly an Indian. These people will die attempting to hold their lands, they will be exterminated finally, the last remaining few hunted down like wolves or bears. No matter how many battles we win, there will always be new soldiers to fight. Our numbers will diminish until finally. . . .*

No, there could be no turning back. These were the people he loved, the ones who had saved his life and had accepted him, the ones whom he loved—Klamat, Paquita, White Dawn, old Warrottetot, Mountain Smoke, all the others, even those who still secretly feared him because of the color of his eyes and hair and skin.

Paquita and Klamat, Aheki-Klamat, these two he could never leave; their lives were inextricably bound. And White Dawn, his wife, the quiet younger sister, the one who had taken him as husband though she well knew it was Poonkina that he dreamed of. How similar the two women appeared in most ways—facial features, slimness of body, the way they carried themselves. At any distance, one would be hard pressed to tell the two sisters apart.

And yet how different they were!

But Paquita was married to Aheki-Klamat, and Nate slept with White Dawn, made love to her, and she received him willingly, eagerly, passionately. Should he awaken during the hours of darkness, he would find her curled up at his side, her body fitting the contours of his own.

Her eyes seemed always to say, "I know how you feel, my husband, but I love you—I am a good woman—you will love me soon, just as I love you. It does not matter that you care for my sister just now, for I love her also. But soon you will prefer White Dawn—I will do everything that will make you love me as you now love her. . . ."

She was with child.

Foolishly, unthinking, Nate had never expected this to happen. But it had happened, and as the months wore on, his wife's belly beginning to bulge, his wife's adoring eyes always upon him, Nate was stricken with guilt, remorse—and he finally swore that he would, with a sheer act of will, transfer his intense sense of attachment from Paquita to his own wife. Fate had brought certain things to pass and not others, and only an insane person indeed would continue to dream about something that simply *could not be*.

Aheki-Klamat sensed the change in his friend.

"Nate—you come to our lodge less often now. Are you angry with Poonkina? That is what she thinks. Is it me that you are angry with?"

"No," Nate answered, "it is not that—it is not either of those things."

Nate took a string of pack animals down the Numken, to Mountain Joe DeBloney's trading post, told Joe what he wanted, and presented the old mountain man with a quantity of gold dust.

"Bad times is comin', Hiner. Warrottetot sees it, same as this coon does, an' he's sent ye in to stock up 'is arsenal."

Mountain Joe put the issue quite matter-of-factly and scratched the side of his face.

"Yes," Nate said.

"Talk is that Whitney's gettin' ready to move up the McCloud. . . ."

"Warrottetot will never fight the soldiers. It's a big land, and the Indians know it, every ridge and ravine of it. The bluecoats don't."

"Ye're young, lad, an' I guess ye've got Injun fever. All my old compañeros got it, one time or another. We knew the best of 'er, lad, an' to a man, we married with 'em. After a time, wasn't one of us as would have a Whitewoman, no sir. Myself, I spent three years with the Snakes, got me two sons an' half-a-dozen fillies. Carson, Meek, Gabe, the Sublette boys, Harris, even Prayin' Smith, though don't nobody say so now— they all took Injun women, just like ye have. Kind of blurs a man's distinctions until it starts lookin' like the settlers is the enemy. Fact is, I feel that way myself. But the fat's in the fire, an' the only real answer is *reservation*. Damn it, lad. . . ."

"Joe, I need the horses and guns, the powder and lead. I came to you first because you're my friend."

"What'd old Hulings say if he knowed I sold his boy guns to take to the Injuns?"

"My father has no hatred for the Indians."

"True, true, lad. But I don't guess he wants ye turned outlaw, nuther."

"Damm it, Joe, you going to sell me what I need?"

Mountain Joe poured the last of the whiskey from his bottle and called to Kootnis for a new one. The Indian woman grinned, nodded, and brought what was desired.

"Face all better?" she asked, touching her fingers to Nate's cheek.

"Ye need another Injun wife, Hiner? This one's got a powerful thing for ye."

"Joseph DeBloney, are you going to sell me the guns?"

Joe drank off his whiskey, wiped his mouth, and snorted.

"Of course," he said.

"I'll have a drink, then," Nate said.

"But listen, Hiner. Soon's the first pop gun goes off, ye know I cain't help after that."

"Fair enough," Nate said, emptying his shot glass and rising.

Mountain Smoke counseled removing the village from Naw-aw-wa to the Medicine Lake, and Warrottetot, who had come to the same conclusion, not only gave the order but also sent out messengers to all the smaller Shasta villages as well, urging these people to do likewise. He sent out additional messengers to speak with the remaining Atsugewi villages along the Pit River and Hat Creek, as well as to the villages of the Modocs, a people who spoke a different language and with whom the Shastas and Pit Rivers sometimes came into conflict. But now, with the soldiers being moved into their lands, this not a certainty but a likelihood, Warrottetot believed it was time for all to smoke the pipe together and to speak of those things that might be done to counteract the soldiers.

After a single day, the lodges at Naw-aw-wa stood empty, the people vanished.

Much gold remained, and, as Aheki-Klamat said, there was but one use for it. Nate, Aheki-Klamat, and half-a-dozen of the young men took a string of pack animals and parted from the main body of Shastas at Horse Mountain, perhaps fifteen miles southwest of Medicine Lake. From here they crossed to Frog Lake and Antelope Creek, an easy pass through the mountains, and moved northwest to the headwaters of Little Shasta River, whence the canyon dropped down gradually into Shasta Valley, at the far side of which stood the town of Yreka. They crossed the valley under cover of darkness and moved on toward Gunsight Peak, down whose precipitous north face Klamat had led Nate, The Prince, Doc Storz, and Paquita during the journey away from The Forks.

Nate and Aheki-Klamat rode together, both staring up at the dark, ragged shadow of the mountain.

"It was long ago, and yet it was not long ago," Aheki-Klamat said. "We were both only boys then, Nate, and yet we did not realize it. I wonder where our friend The Prince is now?"

"San Francisco, perhaps—far from here. Sacramento, maybe, or the other mining towns to the south."

"I remember that he spoke of those places," Aheki-Klamat said, "yet I do not know where they are. Do you think he is playing cards, gambling, winning all the gold nuggets as he did at The Castle?"

Nate grinned.

"If he's playing, then he's winning. The last real game he

ever played, there at The Forks, before... Anyway, that's how we got our first grubstake. He was *out of tin*, he said, and I didn't have any money either. So he played cards for a while, and the next day we bought our supplies and staked out the claim. After that he just put the cards away."

"He is a very good friend, but it is better that he left us. He would not have wished to fight against the Whites, I think."

Nate thought about it for a time and added, "A singular man, most unusual. And I guess I never did understand him—too busy admiring him, maybe."

"He is a *good* man," Aheki-Klamat agreed. "Some who are strong are not good. They have strength, but they do not know how to use it as a human being should. The Prince was strong enough to protect those who were weak. We were weak then. I was named for the *Generous River*, but he was the generous one. Often he helped us, but how did we help him?"

Nate had no answer.

The Prince was strong....

Aheki-Klamat had put the thought into the past tense. Over, finished, done with. The Prince could well be dead, for all they knew.

The group circled the ridge, moved up the canyon above Yreka, and made camp at the foot of the jagged mountain called Gunsight.

In the morning Nate dressed in his go-to-meeting clothes, the Whiteman's apparel seeming odd, strange to him now.

Pack mules in tow, he rode down to Yreka.

The town had not changed appreciably since his first visit—two new clapboard buildings now, side by side, and those adjoining slightly scorched. A fire—nothing unusual in that in a frontier town. More unusual, Nate supposed, was the fact that all the structures along the muddy, chuckhole-filled main street had not burned. Perhaps it had been raining at the time....

Bearded now—no one would recognize him. Indeed, there was no reason why they should, he reminded himself.

I know who I am, and they don't. As long as things stay that way, I'm not going to have any trouble.

But it was altogether possible, he knew, that there might

be three men in town who could identify him if he made his presence felt in any way—three who could, and one of these who most probably would, beard or not. And that was the deputy, John Workman—"Big John Workman," The Prince had called him.

Nate entered one of the general stores, picked up a pair of shovels, a kerosene lantern, a hand ax—and, because it caught his eye, a bright red sash, much like the one the Modoc warrior had taken from him that day—indeed, much like the one The Prince himself had worn and had given to Paquita.

"That do you, Jack?" the proprietor asked, glancing at his pocket watch and obviously not interested in him at all.

"Like the looks of those two rifles—Whitney, aren't they?"

"Know guns, do you?"

"Had one like it," Nate said. "Got mud in her and blew the barrel out."

"Mud plays hell with a barrel, all right. You want a new one?"

"Take both of 'em. And a couple of new Colt pistols— those. Might as well take a keg of powder—need caps and lead, as well."

"Don't suppose I got to ask if you got money, young fella."

"Dust—enough for what I'm buying."

The proprietor examined the gold closely, weighed it, and nodded.

"Settin' up a fort, are you?"

"Three of us," Nate explained. "Got a claim over on the Scott."

The proprietor was at work with a stubby pencil and scratch pad, calculating prices.

"How is it you come here instead of Fort Jones?" he asked.

"Riding through—up from Shasta City."

"None of my business, but ain't this a little out of your way?"

"Heading down the Klamat."

"Pronounce 'er that way, folks'll think you're a Goddamn Injun," the man said, laughing at his own joke.

He went from store to store, acquiring pistols, rifles, powder, caps, and lead. After each purchase, he rode out of town to where Klamat and a few of the pack animals were concealed.

"At this rate, it's going to take a month," Nate said.

"There is no quicker way?"

"Not without arousing suspicion. No sign of our friend the deputy, fortunately."

"Perhaps someone shot him," Aheki-Klamat suggested.

"As long as he's not running a trading post, I don't care what's happened to him. Two more stores, then we move on to Cottonwood. . . ."

Nate returned to town, purchased a Sharps and a Jennings 54, as well as a brace of Smith & Wesson lever-action pistols and a good supply of self-contained cartridges to go with these. He stepped out to the hitching post, wrapped the rifles in a blanket and tied them down, and put the pistols and ammunition into his saddlebags.

The last of the trading posts appeared, from the outside, the least likely to have anything of value. The glass window had been broken out and replaced with boards, but an OPEN sign hung on the wooden, cross-braced door.

Nate stepped inside and noted the hand-carved sign on the counter: SAMUEL T. LOCKWOOD, MERCHANT.

Nate selected another hand ax and a pair of leather gloves, then approached the counter.

The balding man with a patch over one eye said, "Looking for guns, I understand."

Nate sized the man up and considered making a hasty retreat.

"Got what may interest you," the one-eyed man said.

"You're Samuel Lockwood?"

"Ain't nobody else in Yreka this ugly, is there?"

Nate squinted down at the man, then grinned.

"Guess you've got a point there," he said.

Lockwood strode to the door, removed the OPEN sign, closed the door, and threw the bolt.

"Now," he said. "I'm busy, and you're busy. Let's talk straight. Word is you're buying guns. That right?"

"That's it, Mr. Lockwood."

"Call me Sam. Now look, I don't care a rat's ass what you're thinking about doin', though there be some what does. I've got two cases of used carbines, sixty rifles, all in good workin' order. An' I've got half-a-dozen kegs of number-two powder, work in anything that pops. You got cash money for somethin' like that?"

"Where'd you get sixty used rifles?" Nate couldn't help asking.

"I ain't pokin' into your business, you stay out of mine. Fact is, I got 'em. If you've got the money, they're yours."

"Gold," Nate said. "What's your price, Lockwood?"

"Sam," the one-eyed man said. "Heard you had gold."

Nate agreed to meet Lockwood at sunrise the following day at Steamboat Mountain, a domelike pile of lava rising from the floor of Shasta Valley, one of numerous such domes of rock. Lockwood was to come alone, bringing the rifles, and Nate was to meet him alone.

Aheki-Klamat didn't like the idea—suspected some sort of trap.

"The others will go back up Little Shasta River," he said, "but I will hide among the lava rocks."

"That will make two of you," Nate said.

"What do you mean?"

"Chances are Lockwood will have someone up there."

"We will investigate those rocks tonight. You and I will stay there. I will remain hidden while you get the guns."

Nate slept next to the mules, in the open, and Aheki-Klamat stood watch above.

At first light a horse-drawn wagon approached, one man on the buckboard. It was Lockwood.

"Brung you a present," he said. "You got one for me?"

Lockwood took a set of scales from a traveling box, and the transaction was quickly completed.

"High-priced guns," Nate said, examining his merchandise. "If they don't work, I'll come looking for you."

"Ain't I got an honest face? Here I haven't even asked your name—what do I do if this gold don't float?"

"It never does," Nate said.

"Point there. Don't suppose you'd be interested in tellin' me what your handle is? I might have some more goods for you in a week or two."

"Joaquin Murieta. I run a whorehouse down in Shasta City."

"That right? Heard they'd cut your head off—guess it was just one of them rumors."

The two men shook hands, and Lockwood rode away, back toward Yreka.

The sun, deep red and nearly egg-shaped, rimmed the volcanic mountains to the east, and Shasta, twenty miles or so to the south, seemed to have blood upon its perpetual snows.

Aheki-Klamat gave a hawk's whistle from the rocks above, and Nate glanced up, nodded, and began bundling the rifles and loading them onto the string of mules. The task required half an hour or so, and he was just finishing when the hawk whistle came again.

Two riders were approaching.

Nate drew his pistol and waited.

It was Samuel T. Lockwood and John Workman, the recently elected sheriff of Yreka, California.

"Best stop where you are," Nate called out.

The two riders drew up, back out of good pistol range.

"You're under arrest!" Workman shouted.

"Who'd I kill?"

"Looks like you're runnin' guns to the red divvels. Put your play toy down—I'm takin' ye in."

"Seems to be stuck in my hand, Workman. Maybe you'd better come over here and help me."

"You know my name, do ye?"

"Did you forget mine?"

Workman studied him, then said something to Lockwood—who now began to ride slowly away, at an angle, still keeping out of pistol range.

"Never forget a name," Workman yelled. "You wouldn't be Hiny Miller, would ye? Got you a beard, I see. Truth is, I heard you were dead, young fellow. Put the gun down. Don't want to kill ye, but I'm takin' ye in. You get a trial, same as any other coon."

Workman began to ride slowly toward Nate, who stood beside his pony and did not move.

Out of the corner of his eye, Nate saw Lockwood pitch over backward and sag from his horse. Only then did he hear the crack of the Sharps rifle.

Workman spurred his horse forward and charged down on Nate, who made a dash to get in among the pack animals.

One of Workman's shots struck a mule in the eye, and the creature thrashed about, braying and screaming in pain before finally collapsing.

As Workman's horse swerved away from the string of bellowing mules, frightened and attempting to throw off their traces, Nate fired.

Workman suddenly sat back in his saddle and threw up his hands in what appeared almost a gesture of prayer, his mouth wide open, his gray felt flopping to one side of his head and bouncing on his shoulder. Then he fell from the saddle, his foot tangled in the stirrup as his horse dragged him several yards before coming to a halt.

Nate walked slowly toward the fallen man, who was now free of his horse and was crawling first one direction, then the other—searching for his lost pistol.

"Don't bother," Nate said, leveling his revolver at Workman.

"Gut-shot, Hiny. Didn't think ye had it in ye. Who'd ye have up on the dome—that same goddamn Injun?"

"No sense changing a method that works."

"Lockwood's dead? Well, no loss there. Dammit, boy, I just got *elected* a month ago—now you've spoiled it all. Might be I'll make it yet if you'll get me some help. . . ."

The muscles in the face relaxed, and the limbs went limp.

The Shastas, the Pit Rivers, and the Modocs met in council at the Shasta stronghold of Medicine Lake. The nature of Warrottetot's appeal, combined with a Wintun report that a force of some three hundred soldiers under Captain Whitney had advanced as far as the forks of the Sacramento and Pit rivers and were encamped there, had been sufficient to bring the Indians together.

"We must not allow these American soldiers to come into our lands," Warrottetot insisted. "But how can we prevent them from doing so? Our land is big, but it is not big enough to hide in forever. Then, when they find us, we will have to fight. I counsel this: allow them to come as far as they wish. Then we will surround them and tell them they must leave— for we have many more warriors now than they believe we have. They will see how strong we are and ask for a treaty of peace. They will go back and leave us alone."

"The soldiers have many guns, while we have only a few,"

the young Modoc leader Kintpuash said. "It is better not to fight the soldiers. If we scatter among the lava beds, they will never be able to find us. They will get tired of looking and go away—then they will offer us food and blankets, and there will be no need for fighting."

"But we do have guns!" Warrottetot said. "My two sons have brought me weapons so that we are able to protect ourselves."

Blackbeard gestured, and the newly acquired rifles and pistols were carried into the lodge and put on display.

"How many guns do you have?" Slippery Salmon asked.

"Eighty-two rifles and pistols together," Warrottetot answered. "Besides these, many of my warriors already have pistols and rifles. Many of the Modocs also have guns, and the same is true of the Pit River people. Now we will share these new weapons with our friends, for the Whites are enemies to all of us."

"The Americans have murdered many of our people already," Short Antelope said. "They have called us in to make treaties and then massacred us. They have destroyed whole villages. They have killed our men and violated our women and then killed them. They have killed our children and filled our rivers with mud so that we cannot catch the salmon, and they hunt for the deer and elk and antelope until there are none left. They kill everything that they see."

"All the Whites are not bad," Kintpuash insisted. "They are willing to trade with my people and allow us to visit their towns. I know many of these men. My people hunt deer for them, and we trade the meat for clothing and even for rifles and powder."

"And they give you new names and laugh at you," Warrottetot said. "That is what I have heard. They call you Captain Jack and him Hooker Jim and him over there Scarfaced Charley and..."

"We do not object to these names," Kintpuash said.

"Perhaps that is true," Warrottetot continued. "But the Whites have also killed your people. They betrayed your people and butchered them."

"It is true, they did that," Hooker Jim agreed.

"It was a long while ago," Kintpuash said. "The Whitemen are better now."

"Is the Modoc chief's memory so short?" Aheki-Klamat demanded. "You know who I am—I led the Shastas to help Short Antelope's people in the Pit River Valley. The Whites had murdered a number of the Atsugewis, and when we tried to force those men to leave, they would not. For that reason we killed them. And I was also in the village on the Klamat River when the Whites killed everyone except me and the woman who is now my wife. My brother, Nate Miller, helped to save our lives. Yes, there are no doubt many good Whitemen, but there are also many bad ones. Let all the Whites live together in their own places, but not in our lands. These are the words that Aheki-Klamat, son-in-law of Chief Warrottetot, says to you!"

Much discussion followed, but when the vote was finally taken, the tally was for war.

Captain Gideon S. Whitney moved his troops northward along the Shasta City–Yreka trail. He encountered no opposition and, indeed, no Indians at all, not so much as a band of friendly Karoks fishing along the fast-running Sacramento.

Willow, alder, and cottonwood near the river now stood in full profusion of new foliage, firs were tipped with yellow-green plumes of new needles, and the only clouds visible hung about the summit of Mount Shasta, the peak white and dreamlike, as if belonging to a totally different order of things.

"This country's too damned beautiful to be fighting an Indian war in," Whitney remarked to his sergeant major, Dan DeVrees, the latter speculatively studying the ragged formation a few hundred feet above them, a likely place to launch an ambush, the old career soldier concluded.

"Be nice if Blackbeard and his boys felt the same way, Cap'. Injuns is funny people. They don't do nothin' with the land, but they'll fight like Moors to hang on to it."

"Or like Yankee farmers during our own Revolutionary War," Whitney added.

"Yep, somethin' like that, too. Well, probably Blackbeard's not interested in us as long as we're down here on the river trail. I figger he's got some of his scouts watchin' us, though."

"Most likely," Whitney agreed. "Turn the situation around, and that's what we'd be doing."

"Five more miles, give or take, to Mountain Joe's old post. We should be there in another hour at most."

"Right, sergeant. Let's move them out. . . ."

The troops camped at the trading post at the foot of Castle Crags, and though the new owner was not especially pleased with the arrangement, he grudgingly agreed to the presence of federal troops upon being assured that the United States government would reimburse him in full for whatever supplies were taken—this at the man's own prices.

Gideon Whitney was somewhat disappointed that Mountain Joe DeBloney had sold out, for on one or two earlier visits to the post, the captain had taken genuine pleasure in listening to the mountain man's perpetual yarns. But now DeBloney was gone, off to Idaho, according to the new owner. Whitney had taken the time to learn a good deal about DeBloney—the man had been a scout for Fremont's California expedition of some years earlier and was reputed to be close friends with such men as Kit Carson and Joe Meek, and a man as well who was experienced in the matter of fighting against the Indians of Northern California, having apparently participated against both the Yanas to the south and the Modocs and Klamats to the north.

DeBloney, of course, had claimed to have been Kit Carson's teacher, the one who had shown Kit how to set his first beaver trap. The mountain men, Whitney realized, were all alike in this one respect, for they all claimed to have gone up the Missouri with General Ashley, and they all claimed to have been present at the time South Pass was discovered. To listen to these men, one would suppose there had been no greenhorns, no apprentices in the mountains—only master trappers. All chiefs and no Indians, so to speak.

Upriver with Ashley is like coming across on the Mayflower. Everybody did it. . . .

A few months earlier, while at the Sacramento garrison, Whitney had met Caleb and John Greenwood, Baptiste Charbonneau, and Jim Beckwith. The three old renegades and young Greenwood had taken a liking to Whitney and had insisted that he accompany them on a venture up to La Porte, a small mining town perched high among the ridges to the northeast of Marysville. Whitney, on leave at the time, had supposed it a good chance to see a hydraulic operation in full swing, but what he had found instead was the entire community half-drunk, the half-dozen local prostitutes doing a banner business, and draw poker the order of the day.

At some point in the early hours of the morning, the mountain men and their "United States Protector," as they dubbed Whitney, had been obliged to make a quick departure from the saloon. Beckwith had managed to relieve the locals of a good deal of their dust, and old Greenwood had been caught with half-a-dozen extra cards tucked under his buffalo-skin vest. Pistols and knives had appeared instantly, and the mountain men, dragging their official protector with them, had managed to shoot out the elaborate hanging lamp, with the net effect of flaming coal oil spilling across the puncheon floor, and had fought their way out the rear door, pistols blazing into the half-darkness, and had managed to get to their horses.

The ride down the mountain had been a wild one, a group of enraged miners in full pursuit. But daylight had found them safely at the little outpost at Brownsville, where Charbonneau had ordered drinks for the house, and the five fugitives from La Porte justice had eaten a hearty breakfast of venison and eggs, the latter items priced at a dollar and a quarter apiece, U.S. coin.

"Could have been the end of my military career, right there," Whitney said to himself, chuckling.

The new proprietor of Mountain Joe's raised one eyebrow and offered the captain another drink.

The men relaxed, groomed their horses, and serviced their gear—while the captain and Sergeant Major DeVrees and the two lieutenants dined with their host and passed the time with conversation and watered-down whiskey.

Whitney's intelligence was that the Shastas were encamped in a village southeast of Mount Shasta, at a place his Wintun scouts called Squaw Valley. These two men, the Wintuns, had actually talked with Blackbeard inside his village and so had been able to give relatively accurate accounts of the encampment, the number of lodges, the number of warriors, an approximate head count of the horses, and a fairly good guess as to the extent of armaments other than bow, arrow, and lance.

After spending two days at the way station, Whitney moved

his men onward, passing out of the canyon and into the lava-belt forest above Shasta Springs. From here he turned eastward, skirting the southern slope of the big mountain, and there divided his troops into their three constituent companies, one to approach the village from the west, one from the south, and one from the east.

No escape possible to the north, Whitney thought. *Just the wall of the mountain itself.*

The troops moved in on the village, but there was neither smoke from the lodges nor the barking of camp dogs. Blackbeard's village was completely deserted except for one significant inhabitant—a monstrous grizzly that had been searching for refuse and tearing apart lodges in frustration when he didn't find what he wanted. At the approach of the troops, the big silver-brown bear reared up, its massive arms waving about, its head rocking back and forth.

The soldiers, without being ordered to do so, opened fire. The wounded bear roared and charged at them, the horses screaming and rearing; and then, thundering in pain, the grizzly fell to its side, its hindquarters in what appeared to be a sexual spasm, and then lay still.

The troops cheered and laughed.

Whitney gave no rebuke for the unauthorized volley and ordered his men to continue their eastward progress.

Wherever that old bastard of a Blackbeard is, I'll track him to earth. Set him and his boys up in board shacks over at Hupa Valley and put them on some sort of a dole. Then they'll get fat and sullen and drink too much whenever they've got the chance. Won't be no trouble to anyone then....

In addition, Whitney mused, a hanging or two would be in order, just to set the matter straight. In general, the Indians responded well to hangings.

At the base of the double-topped peak the Wintun scouts called Black Fox Mountain, Gideon S. Whitney was finally able to engage the Shastas.

The troops were in caravan, double-file, and the men were in good spirits. The initial rain of arrows and sporadic rifle fire took them completely by surprise, and several of the men were hit. Whitney and his subordinate officers quickly drew the troops into a single body, and they took what cover they could.

For more than an hour the enemy's sniper fire held the soldiers in place, pinned down, and several additional casualties were sustained. But at length the captain ordered his third company to move forward on horseback and engage the enemy. The bluecoats mounted and charged out—and were suddenly set upon by mounted Indians from both sides. A haze of powder smoke rose about the scene of conflict, now one of desperate hand-to-hand struggle.

The Shastas turned their horses suddenly and disappeared into the forest, and a strange quiet came over the battlefield, a silence punctuated only by one man's pitiful screaming.

The lieutenant of Company C had somehow been scalped alive.

Captain Whitney checked the casualties, gave words of encouragement to the wounded, and counted the dead. After that he inscribed the appropriate official notation in his register book:

At 1645 hours the hostiles retreated, the victory was ours.

The captain was certain that a number of Indians had been slain, but strangely enough no bodies were recovered for a head count, inasmuch as the Shastas had apparently somehow managed to bear their dead and wounded away.

Whitney had lost nine men and had another twenty-four wounded, one of whom had an arm fractured by a rifle ball, another whose right eye had been lost to a knife wound. Twenty-one others, however, were not wounded seriously and would soon be fit for combat once more. Even Lieutentant Bains, the man who had been scalped, would recover, though in all likelihood his features would never again precisely resemble their previous condition. The captain recalled Baptiste Charbonneau's account of Nathaniel Wyeth, a man who had been scalped and yet had survived, using strips of rawhide to lace back and forth across the bloodied crown of his skull. But, despite this rough precaution, the man's features had thereafter sagged badly.

The personal effects of the dead were bundled, to be shipped to their families, and burial details were formed. Those wounded too seriously for them to maintain themselves on horseback were put onto litters.

The presence of a White renegade had been reported

among the hostiles, whom the Wintun scouts assured Whitney were indeed Shastas of Blackbeard's band.

Everything having been done that could be done, Captain Gideon Whitney ordered his bluecoats back to the trading post at the foot of Castle Crags.

FIFTEEN

▲

The Kingfisher Laughs

The young Whiteman and the old Indian Chief would stop on a hill overlooking the Naw-aw-wa valley, and the old man would dismount and take fragments of lava to build a little monument. He would point out high landmarks below the valley, embracing almost as much land as one could journey around in a day's travel.

"This is yours," he would say. "All this valley is yours. I give it to you with my own hand."

He would go down the hill a little way, take up some of the earth, bring it to the younger man, and sprinkle it upon and before his feet.

"It is all yours," the Indian would say. "You have done all you could do, and deserve it. Besides, I have no one to leave it to now but you."

The Indian would pause, stare fixedly at the white wall of Shasta, and then continue:

"You will go on your way, will win a place in life, and when you return you will have lands, a home, hunting grounds. These you will find here when you return, but you will not find me, nor one of my children, nor one of my tribe...."

"Now that we have defeated the soldiers," Warrottetot said, "we will be able to speak of peace. Now they will be willing to leave us alone in our own lands."

"Whites don't think like Shastas," Nate argued. "For all we know, Captain Whitney thinks he won."

"How could he think that? We lost only one warrior, while many soldiers were killed."

"Whites don't think like human people," Nate said.

Aheki-Klamat laughed.

232

"My brother-in-law's eyes are not so blue as they once were."

But the discussion continued, and though Aheki-Klamat, Mountain Smoke, Nate, and a majority of the warriors, including those of the Modocs who had remained, counseled against trusting the Whites in any way, Warrottetot persisted. Short Antelope and the Pit River Indians tended to agree with the chief of the Shastas, however.

"I have grown old," Warrottetot complained. "My own warriors do not wish to hear my words—only the Atsugewis and the Modocs listen."

At last it was decided, and Warrottetot selected those he wished to have accompany him, including a number of women and children, thereby demonstrating peaceful intentions. The soldiers, they had learned, were at the trading post, and so Nate might be able to call upon his friend Mountain Joe to assist in whatever deliberations were to take place. White Dawn, though she was within a few weeks of giving birth to her child, would come along. Aheki-Klamat and Poonkina, and several of the warriors and their families as well.

But a second party, separate, would go along too—a hundred warriors under the leadership of Short Antelope. These men, Shastas and Pit Rivers and Modocs, would stay back away from the trading post, just in case a further show of force might be needed.

The Indian allies moved down the Numken from Naw-aw-wa, passing by the burned-out remains of the old village, pausing only long enough to build a pyre for the torn and rotting carcass of the grizzly the soldiers had killed and the coyotes, badgers, and vultures had feasted on. The fire was ignited, and the Indians continued their journey.

Near the mouth of the Numken, Short Antelope drew his party up into the canyon of a tributary stream and waited there for whatever news might be dispatched from the trading post.

Warrottetot and his people remained on the east bank of the Sacramento, while Aheki-Klamat and Nate Miller forded the river, a white banner trailing from Aheki-Klamat's lance.

Nate and Aheki-Klamat halted before the gate to the trading post.

"Your friend's sign has been changed," Aheki-Klamat said.

RIVER TRAIL POST, W. BARNABAS, PROP.

"No time to go back now," Nate said, watching the sentry retreat to within the confines of the post.

In a few moments Gideon Whitney and his subordinate officers appeared at the gateway, Lieutenant Bains hatless but with a white skullcap of bandage on the top of his head.

"We come in peace!" Nate called out. "I am with Chief Warrottetot and the Shastas! The chief wishes to conclude a peace treaty with the soldiers."

Whitney stepped forward.

"Does Blackbeard wish to surrender?" he called across the intervening space.

"Warrottetot does not wish to surrender!" Aheki-Klamat answered. "He wishes to speak of peace between the Indian people and the Whitemen."

"Where is Blackbeard?"

"Look across the river," Nate called out. "He is standing there in the midst of men and women and children. We have come to talk of peace and for no other reason."

"Tell the chief he has to surrender," Whitney insisted. "Tell him to leave all weapons behind and to cross the river on foot. After that we will talk peace. But you, Whiteman, you're under arrest!"

Aheki-Klamat glanced at Nate, then shouted at Whitney, "We have nothing to talk about, then. We will return to our own lands. If your soldiers wish to follow us, we will kill more of your men."

With that he held up the scalp, shook it, and drew his pony around.

As a response to this movement, gunfire erupted from behind the post stockade, and Nate was struck in the shoulder and spun from his horse.

Mounted soldiers poured from the stockade gates.

Aheki-Klamat turned on his pony and stood ready to make a futile stand in defense of his fallen friend. But Nate struggled to his feet, threw up his one functional arm in a gesture of surrender, and screamed, "Klamat! Ride! I'll be all right—get the hell out of here before these damn fools start butchering the women and children!"

Aheki-Klamat waited a moment longer.

"I cannot leave you, Nate. . . ."

"Ride, Klamat—get the hell out of here, or we're both going to end up dead. Warrottetot needs you!"

The Shasta warrior spurred his pony and struck for the river, a hail of pistol fire singing through the air about his head. He swung himself to the far side of his mount and plunged the animal into the current of the Sacramento River. Halfway across, the horse foundered, struck in the neck by a pistol ball. And Aheki-Klamat flung himself free of the stricken animal, dived beneath the milk-green current, and finally emerged to the safety of the far shore.

The soldiers attempted pursuit but were driven back by one or two bursts of gunfire from the warriors who had formed a ring around Warrottetot and the woman and children.

Klamat's horse, bleeding and struggling, was wedged against a boulder in mid-current. And Aheki-Klamat, a dry pistol in hand, waded back into the stream, firing as he stumbled through the water. He managed to reach the horse, withdrew his prized Sharps rifle from its sheath, and fired the single remaining charge in his pistol into the by now feebly writhing animal's forehead.

More rifle fire, but this time from the thick timber on the eastern wall of the canyon, high above the river. It was Short Antelope and his warriors, Nate realized as he was being pushed roughly through the stockade gate. Blood dripped from the fingertips of his left hand, and the arm hung limp and completely numb.

The wound, deep but superficial, was tended to and bandaged. Nate was put under guard and confined to one of the guest rooms. He felt weak, tired, beaten—as he listened to the rattle of gunfire that continued, off and on, for perhaps two hours.

Then Whitney sent his scouts across the Sacramento River, and the men returned with word that the Indians had vanished.

Nate was placed under official arrest, Whitney having brought with him a warrant for the renegade White who was known to have aided and abetted the hostile Shastas. He was put in the charge of Lieutenant Bains and four of his men and dispatched southward to the squalid little jail in Shasta City, where he was incarcerated and held without bail, pending charges, for more than two weeks.

At last he was informed that an indictment had been filed against him:

Horse theft, with other charges pending . . .

"The Lord's own luck," the jailkeeper told him. "It's hangin' ye've got comin', but the boys ain't got no firm evidence against ye. Be patient, though, lad. When Whitney an' his boys is finished with them murderin' Injuns, there'll be one or another as will identify ye for certain. Only the sheriff's goin' to try ye for a horse thief, an' so mebbe ye'll be swung already when the captain's finished up north."

Nate pleaded not guilty, declined an examination, and was placed in what amounted to a box, ten feet by ten feet, no more than half the size of his previous cell, the only light that which came through a small window with iron grates, facing east over the top of another building that clung to the hillside below. A half-rotten mattress lay on the floor. He was given no water except with his meals, and there was hardly a breath of air.

With the coming of summer, the temperatures soared to over a hundred during the long afternoons and were not much lower by darkness. The food was cold and stale, presumably the refuse of some local eating house. Sometimes the biscuits he was given were already half-eaten, and the meat was no more than scraps clinging to rinds of cold fat.

During the entirety of this time he was kept isolated, even from the other prisoners, some of whom, as the attendant laughingly explained, stayed only a short time before being hanged. Others, whom he called regular patrons, came in usually on Friday nights, the drunken miners from French Gulch and the dredging operations along the river to the east of town.

"Only reason ye ain't dead already," the jailkeeper said, winking at him, "is because ye're a Gawdamned *federal* prisoner. An' that there qualifies ye for special treatment, I reckon."

As the weeks drew on, several lawyers visited him in the hope that he might somehow obtain sufficient money to employ them, but after a time Nate refused to speak with them at all.

One had said, "They're going to file charges of aiding and

abetting the red devils. And that's a hanging offense, no question about it. No one's got much love for a renegade."

He had received almost no medical attention for his arm, not since he had been taken prisoner at Joe's old post at the foot of Castle Crags, but nevertheless the wound had managed to heal. A small amount of pain when he attempted to raise his hand above his head, but that was all—and he had hope that the limb would eventually become completely sound, depending on when the citizens of Shasta City got around to hanging him.

Finally a young lawyer named Holbrook gained his confidence, and Nate related at least a portion of his story. Holbrook seemed doubtful and suggested a plea of insanity. At this Nate went into a frenzy of oaths, and the lawyer backed away from the cell and did not return.

"He would return to us if he were able," Poonkina said. "Do you think they have killed him, Aheki-Klamat?"

Klamat had been polishing the barrel of his Sharps rifle. Now he looked up, laid the weapon aside, and studied the troubled expression on his wife's face.

"Yes," he nodded, "that is what I think. But our friend's death will not go unavenged, Poonkina. I might have saved him that day, and yet instead I allowed myself to listen to his words. But he insisted that he would be all right. Now the Whiteman's justice has taken him. But I will enact my own justice."

"You cannot do that," Poonkina said. "Klamat, how will you know which Whitemen to kill? The soldiers took him away to the place called Shasta City, where the big river runs out into the valley. That is what we learned from the Wintuns. He was given over to the judge there."

"One like the other judge, perhaps," Aheki-Klamat said, spitting out the words. "If this other judge has killed our friend, then I will find him also, and I will deal with him just as I did with the judge at The Forks."

"Then you will have to go to Shasta City in order to do it," Poonkina said. "That is what White Dawn wishes to do. She has asked me to go with her, my husband. She says that two women will be able to accomplish what even the greatest of warriors cannot do."

"White Dawn cannot go anywhere. She is carrying Nate's child. Such a thing would be extremely foolish, Poonkina. You know that as well as I do."

"But what if he is still alive and needs our help? Many times he has helped us. How can we rest until we know what has happened to him? For a long while I believed Slippery Salmon was dead, was killed that night of the massacre on the river—when Nate and The Prince saved our lives. You are about to tell me that we should no longer speak his name because the Old Ones say we should not utter the names of those who have died. But I do not think he is dead, Klamat. Last night I dreamed that I could hear him calling to us, calling from someplace far away. He wished to come to us, but he was unable to do so. And then his voice changed and began to sound like the cry the kingfisher makes when someone disturbs his fishing. And that is why I am certain that Nate is still alive."

Aheki-Klamat stood up and paced about the lodge, and was silent for a time before speaking.

"There are many dreams," he said. "And I have come to believe that sometimes the spirits do indeed speak to us through them. But there are also other dreams in which we see and hear those things which we merely wish to be true. How do you know your dream is not of that kind, Poonkina?"

"I *know* he is still alive," she answered.

Aheki-Klamat grunted and nodded.

"Then I will go alone," he concluded. "Warrottetot will never agree to have his daughter ride down into the world of the Whitemen, and I would not wish that either."

"I am not governed by my father's wishes," Poonkina said. "If that had been so, then we would not now be here in our own lodge together. I have a right to go with you. He saved my life, and now I must do something to repay that debt. Besides, Klamat, do you think that if you went alone and did not return that I would wish to continue to live without you?"

"You are young and very beautiful. There would be many others who would wish to marry you, Poonkina."

"Does my husband understand nothing at all, then? If there were indeed others, they were not the ones that I chose. I chose you, Klamat. If you ride off without me, then I will follow. I will do that, no matter what you say. If you are killed, then I wish to be killed also."

Aheki-Klamat perceived that it was useless to argue further, for once that peculiar glint of defiance had come into Poonkina's eyes, no amount of reasoning would do any good.

"All right, then," he said. "Once before we ran off into the darkness together, and that time we did not even have our ponies to carry us. This time your father will not catch up to us. Pack up whatever food we have in the lodge, and I will get the horses. If we are going to do this thing, then let us do it now—for if we wait, the morning light will restore our good senses to us."

Within a short time all was ready, and Aheki-Klamat and Poonkina silently led their horses and an extra animal as well out of the village. Only when they were well beyond the place where they could no longer see the faint gleam of firelight reflected from the boughs of pine and fir did they mount and ride away southward.

Night.

Hot darkness, sweat, filth. And from outside came the sound of the *cakea*, at a distance, somewhere up on the hillside above the prison.

Nate listened closely. Was it actually the nightbird, or was it something else?

The sound drew nearer, at each instance repeated three times.

A sudden, irrational wave of hope ran through Nate Miller, and he sprang to the barred window, grasped the sill, and imitated the cry, repeating the notes three times.

He was aware of the jailer in the adjoining room. The man was stirring about.

A long interval of silence followed, and Nate, cursing himself for a fool, slouched back onto the rotten pallet. The long confinement, he concluded, was doing things to his mind—causing him to grasp at straws, to hope wildly for release when only one sort of release was possible, and that would come with a jolt at the end of a rope slung over the limb fork in the big oak he could see by daylight, some two hundred yards upslope from the jail.

But then a soft voice, a whispered voice that came in through the window:

"Nate Miller—it's me, Paquita! Is anyone with you?"

I hear this, but I am not hearing it. Old One Who Does Everything is playing another of his little jokes on me. Beloved, is it truly you? Have you come to watch them hang me? It's too soon, you've arrived too soon. The sons of bitches haven't even brought me to trial yet....

"Paquita?" he managed, his voice hoarse and low, himself stunned with disbelief.

"Aheki-Klamat is here also, Nate. Is anyone inside there with you? The smell is terrible. What have they done to you?"

"No, no, no. Just me. This is my cage, no one else's. My keeper's on the other side of the wall, though. Keep your voice down, Paquita. Klamat—where is Klamat?"

"I am here, my brother," came the voice of his friend.

"We have come to set you free, Nate," Paquita whispered. "The others thought the Whites had killed you, but I did not believe that. White Dawn did not believe it either, and besides, I had a dream. I heard you crying out to me."

"No way, no way out," Nate said, his voice trailing off.

"Of course there is a way, my brother," Klamat said. "How many men keep guard over you? It does not matter. They are only Whitemen, so I will be able to kill them easily."

"Have you been to the Spirit World, then?" Nate asked, laughing softly. "And now you are able to walk through brick walls and steel doors? Not even Aheki-Klamat is able to do that."

"I did not come all this way just to say hello and then to leave you," Klamat answered. "I have a can of gunpowder. I will blast the door down and then..."

"No, no, that won't work. But listen. There's a certain kind of saw—a hack saw. It will cut through these bars. Even a good file would do it."

"Where would we get a *hack saw*?" Paquita asked. "Who would sell us such a thing?"

"Will the gunpowder not blow them out?" Klamat persisted.

"It might, yes. But if you didn't kill me in the process, you'd wake up everybody in Shasta City. There'd be men with guns swarming all over the place, and we'd all end up dead."

"Aheki-Klamat does not fear death. Besides, we have horses, Nate. There is no way they could ever catch us."

"Husband!" Paquita whispered, her voice seething with impatience. "Listen to what Nate is saying to you. He knows about these things, and we do not. Where can we get this *hack saw?*"

"A file," Nate replied. "That will be easier. See if you can find a file and a steel pry bar. There's a Wintun village just north of here, on the big river. Perhaps it is still there—I saw it when the soldiers brought me here. Maybe someone in the village has those things."

"How could we trust the Wintuns?" Klamat demanded. "Some of their men were with the bluecoat soldiers when we fought the battle. Those Indians are only interested in what the Whitemen will pay them. That is what I think."

"Most of the Wintuns do not like the Whites any more than we do," Paquita said. "The Whites have killed their people also. They have destroyed whole villages. We have all heard the stories, Klamat. . . ."

"I don't know, I don't know," Nate mumbled. "Probably it's hopeless. Don't go yet. Are the people still safe? Have Whitney and his troops made any more attempts to find Warrottetot? And White Dawn? Is my wife all right? Is she . . . ?"

"My sister will have something to show you when you return to the village," Poonkina said, laughing. "She demanded to come with us, but she could not do it. By now she has a new young one in her arms, for the birth was only a day or two away when we left Medicine Lake. Perhaps Klamat will give me a child also someday soon. That way the two young ones will be able to grow up together."

"A child. . . ," Nate responded, the wonder of it coming over him. "Is it a boy or. . . ?"

"We don't know that," Aheki-Klamat snorted. "How could we know? My brother must suppose the birds bring us messages from the north. But that is something he will have to find out for himself."

"Yes, yes. Look. The sky is beginning to grow gray. Get away from Shasta City while you can. Klamat. Paquita."

"We will go now," Poonkina answered. "But we will return tomorrow night. The bars of your cage are not as strong as the three of us. Nothing is that strong."

Then they were gone indeed, and for a long while Nate was unable to sleep. But finally exhaustion overtook him, and he awakened only when the jailer brought the morning ration of slop.

"Garbage for the suckling pig!" the attendant cackled. "Suet and parched corn—an' it's more than ye deserve. If ye don't start eatin', Hiny, they ain't goin' to be nothing left to string up."

The man placed the bowl on the floor, along with a can of water, laughed at his own wit, and left Nate to do as he wished.

But this morning Nate no longer resisted eating the food, whatever it was. He could feel his strength returning, as if by magic, even as he was buoyed by the hope, the desperate hope that *somehow* his friends would indeed be able to get him out.

Paquita came alone that night, and much earlier. She had brought with her two knives, their blades notched so as to fashion a kind of saw, and the man and the woman set to work on the inch-thick sections of iron pipe set deeply into the mortar of the brick wall.

"It is working!" Paquita observed, hardly able to restrain herself. "It is very slow, but the knives are cutting the bar!"

The hours passed by, the progress painstakingly, exasperatingly slow. But then the false dawn was upon them, and the girl left—promising to return the following night with a new set of knives.

As soon as she had left, Nate made a mixture of dirt and spittle and pressed it, molded it to the cuts that had been made in the bars.

Once again he ate his meals, and the jailkeeper said, "Thought ye'd give in at last. They all do a week or so before they finally get hung."

"What I heard," Nate responded, "is that they're planning to hang you along with me—for stealing that farmer's milk cow last week. By tonight, my friend, they'll have you right in here with me."

"What cow?" the jailer demanded. "Hiny, ye're as crazy as a shithouse rat—from wallerin' around in yore own dung too long, that's what I'm thinkin'...."

Another night of patient work passed by, and now the bars were cut through and sufficiently loosened to afford escape, and yet Nate waited one more day—for Saturday, when the men of Shasta City, officers and all, would be likely to get drunk and raise hell.

That day the jailkeeper told him the news.

"Yore trial's set for next week, Hiny. Monday ye'll see the judge, an' Tuesday ye'll see the rope. Mebbe ye ought to get in touch with that lawyer again, Holbrook—were that his name? I'll send a message to him, if ye want. Tell ye the truth, I'm startin' to get fond of ye. Won't be the same somehow with the old powder room empty again. You want me to see if I can fotch 'im over here?"

Nate stared at the man and then shook his head.

"Don't need a legal man," he replied. "There's nothing he could do for me that I can't do better myself."

"Truth is," the jailer said, "ye're damned right. Not unless he knows some way of dancin' on air without fallin' down."

With that observation the attendant roared with laughter, fell into a spasm of coughing, spit tobacco juice in through the bars of Nate's cell door, and left the prisoner to his own thoughts.

The day passed, the hours dragging by.

Terrific heat, and hundreds of flies swarmed about in the air of the small, stinking compartment.

Nate sat in the corner, his head bowed, and attempted to get some sleep. He made a point of not going near the barred window, superstitiously wishing to avoid calling the jailer's attention to it in any way. The practice was needless, he realized, for the jailer had never, in all this time, so much as set foot inside the cell—supposing, no doubt, that Nate might make some sort of desperate attempt on his life.

Finally the sky flared red, but even through the long period of summer twilight, the temperature did not abate.

Then darkness came, bringing with it the silver light of a nearly full moon. A soft wind came up from the direction of the river, and stars burned down through the loosened bars of the cell.

She came about midnight, the true and faithful little savage, the heroine, the red star of my dreadful life, crouching on the roof, and laid hold of the bars one by one, and bent them until I could pass my head and shoulders. Then she drew me through, almost carried me in her arms, and in another moment we touched the steep but solid earth.

The words formed in his mind. He could see them before him, and he knew that one day, if he lived, he would write them down. He would write all of this down so that the world, if it was curious, would be able to know at some future time.

Quickly they climbed a hillside to the chaparral thicket where Aheki-Klamat was waiting with three horses.

Nate, almost drunk with his newly restored freedom, clasped bushes in his arms, stripped aromatic bay leaves by the handful, kissed his hands to the moon and stars, and began to dance about like a child.

Poonkina laid her hand upon his mouth and shook him by the arm. He turned, kissed her on the lips, and grasped Aheki-Klamat around the waist and lifted the astonished warrior off his feet.

"Foolish Whiteman," Aheki-Klamat managed to growl, "put me down. We must leave this place—or your friends will have us all in a cage of iron bars."

"If only The Prince were here!" Nate laughed softly. "My God, wouldn't he be pleased with what we've just pulled off? 'Belly up and out of tin, and yet you bluffed the hand through!' That's what he'd say. Play the cards, Prince—wherever you are. By heavens, we learned something from him, didn't we?"

"Yes," Klamat replied. "And he also taught us to run from the hornets' nest after we have thrown stones at it. Come on, Nate Miller."

"Klamat! I have to get my Cayuse—I don't know what they've done with him."

"Your talk is wild," Poonkina said. "Probably they have killed your horse and eaten it. We must go. . . ."

"My rifle. . . ."

"We have weapons—and we have brought you a pistol and a rifle. Do not argue with me, Nate."

Aheki-Klamat's tone of voice concluded the issue with a definite period.

They rode north, taking great care to avoid all possible contact with the wagon trail, along which avenue, they presumed, any likely pursuit would come.

In will come the attendant, with his bucket of slop—and with it perhaps a laconic witticism concerning a rumor that the Second Coming will take place on Tuesday, at the hanging oak. He'll stare into the empty cell a moment and then sound an alarm. The sheriff will curse, rise, and call out his hungover deputies. And the chase will be on. It'll take them a time to decide where to look for me, but eventually they'll get the idea. I have great faith in the rotten sons of bitches....

Oak and pine woods now as the three riders worked their way up through heavy growth toward the red dirt of the ridge crests to the west of the Sacramento River, at length emerging high above the winding green slip of water.

The sun was rising, a vast gray surf that broke over the peaks to the east—Green Mountain, Clover Mountain, Magee's Peak, the long, snowy range capped by Lassen Peak—and off to the north, like an ancient god and rising dreamlike above the welter of dark, hazy mountainous folds, the massive snow crown of Shasta.

After riding along the crests for a few miles, they turned their horses eastward, downslope, and came at full daybreak to the Sacramento, plunging their mounts into the swirling water, dropping their reins and clinging to the animals' mane hair, floating free as the horses swam across, angling down current.

Poonkina began suddenly to laugh as, dripping wet, they urged their ponies up the steep bank and toward the cover of forest and on toward another ridge crest, circling northeastward now.

"I feel as though I were almost home," the girl cried out. "We have ridden a long trail, we three, and now we are heading home. See how our ponies seem to sense it, even though it is still many miles back to Medicine Lake Village?"

"Hush, Poonkina!" Aheki-Klamat hissed. "We must not

grow careless. There are more bluecoats now, Nate, than there were before. We saw some of these men when we were on our way to find you. There will be a great battle very soon, and we must reach Warrottetot before it begins. He is not expecting these additional soldiers who have been sent to help Whitney."

By mid-morning they were close to the Pit River, at a point a few miles up from its confluence with the Sacramento. Aheki-Klamat made a gesture, and the two Indians and the fugitive Whiteman began their descent of a hill that sloped down to a likely spot for crossing the stream.

As the three approached the river, an army officer and a platoon of soldiers emerged from behind a low clump of Douglas firs, the men with rifles to their shoulders, and demanded surrender—an immediate halt and the laying down of weapons.

One chance for escape . . .

"Throw down your weapons and dismount slowly!" the officer called out a second time, "or I'll order my men to fire on you. . . ."

"Jump into the river!" Aheki-Klamat shouted, kicking his own horse forward toward the startled soldiers, knocking them about like so many tenpins, and firing his pistol at almost point-blank range into the lieutenant's eyes, dropping the man on the spot, his face a torn, ragged red mask.

Then the Shasta warrior spun his pony about, firing again as he did so and screaming out, *"Aheki! Aheki!"*

Nate and Paquita leaped their mounts down the steep bank and into the swirling water, with Klamat, howling defiance, plunging after them.

Nate heard the crack of rifle fire even as he hit the water, even as he slipped loose from the saddle and wriggled his way downward through the strong, cold current of the Pit.

The horses emerged, snorting, their heads back and their eyes wild, Nate's animal striking out for the far side of the river.

The three humans went with the flow of the water, surfacing only to gasp for breath and then, rifle balls spearing the surface of the river, submerging once again.

The bluecoats ran along the bank, cast their rifles aside,

and began to pour down a steady tattoo of pistol fire, drawing aim at the shadowy, wriggling forms in the water, at heads and shoulders as they momentarily surfaced.

Nate caught the strong current of mid-stream and felt it lift him. At the same time his mind, the steel force of his will, demanded that the swift water should carry him, carry all of them, downstream, out of range of the deadly stingers of lead.

But Aheki-Klamat and Paquita had been caught in an eddy, and were sucked in beneath the precipitous southern bank of the Pit River. And the soldiers, shouting and swearing above them, drew aim and fired shot after shot.

The flood spun Nate downriver, out of reach, and he crawled exhausted up into shallow water, took cover behind a drift log embedded in the sandy mud of a bar, and sucked for breath. Horrified, he observed the desperate drama being enacted upstream and across the river. He saw the black hair and shiny shoulders appear in the water, saw the soldiers above like so many strange, evil puppets—no, more like a single creature with various selves, intent upon death. He stared in stricken fascination at the little blue puffs of smoke from the pistols and saw the surface of the river snap upward again and again, heard the rhythmic explosions of the weapons.

Two horses struggled to rise from the water, then spasmed as the lead hit them. They slumped forward, twisted about, kicked out, and then floated inertly.

His own horse, whinnying somewhere close in the wooded tangle beyond the river, had apparently made it across and out of pistol range.

Now only one head, one set of shoulders emerged from the water.

Klamat . . .

Nate drew himself up, raced toward where the horse thrashed about in a thicket of willow and alder, reached the animal, tore open the saddlebag, and found what he wanted— the gunpowder Klamat had given him to carry, the substance safe in a watertight container. He grabbed the rifle from its sheath, ejected the wet load, used wadding to dry the bore, poured in fresh powder, and rammed the load home.

The same with his pistol.

Thus armed, he was already racing upstream to a point

opposite the blue cluster of soldiers on the far ledge. He threw himself down, drew careful aim, set the triggers, squeezed, and felt the rifle buck against the wet cloth of his shirt.

One of the soldiers slowly took a step backward, slumped to his knees, and then pitched down head first into the river.

Nate, his mind utterly clear and for this moment utterly detached, carefully emptied his pistol, his shots ringing out across the water and echoing back from the rocky wall of the canyon. He was bruised, battered, and numb with cold. His wounded left shoulder ran a dull trickle of fire down to his wrist—but nothing mattered now, nothing. Working quickly, he reloaded both the rifle and the pistol and set the caps carefully in place.

Gunfire came his way as the soldiers pulled back to the cover of the undergrowth. Nate drew down, fired the rifle, and cursed as he missed the scrambling blue target. He laid the rifle aside and once again emptied his pistol, pulling off shot after shot. One soldier dropped to his hands and knees, called out to his fellows for help, and then very slowly turned to his side and rolled over, like a child preparing to sleep.

In the eddy, two dead horses spun slowly about.

"Paquita? Klamat!"

The human forms, barely visible, were moving with the current, hitting the long sweep of rapids, tossing about like two small logs caught by the blue-green water and then jetting through a long V of white foam.

He could hear confused shoutings from the soldiers, their words not decipherable above the hissing roar of the Pit River.

They're pulling back, Nate thought as he once again loaded the rifle, aimed, and squeezed off his shot.

Then he rose, thrust the empty pistol beneath the wet red sash around his waist, its fabric blotted still with the stains of filth from the long weeks in prison. He picked up the rifle and stash of ammunition and moved quickly downriver.

The Pit swept through a bend in the green riot of its canyon, rounded a jagged overhanging bluff of black slate, and pooled momentarily into a wide expanse of roiling water before continuing its westward progress toward its confluence with the Sacramento. The jumbled, rocky shoulders of earth rose away to either side, and the mixed forest of black oak, pine, and fir dreamed under the orange-red sun of summer. Invisible trickles of heat currents drifted up from exposed masses of diorite near the river, the rocks bare and polished from the continued attrition of eons of winter floodings, and beneath the fringes of willow and young alder, water striders darted over the translucent surface. Trout finned away, their bodies no more than shadows within the water. A kingfisher screamed its annoyance, bluejays shrieked somewhere back within the forest, and overhead a pair of zone-tailed hawks glided, hovered, then glided on through the still, heavy blue heat.

The human episode of a few minutes earlier, upstream in any case and of no significance to the world of still water below the rapids and the bluff of black slate, only a few muffled shouts after all, a few half-heard explosions, was over. But a stumbling noise in the brush along the north bank, the sounds of a human being leading a horse—these sent a blue heron that had been standing one-legged in the shallows oaring its powerful wings upward, the wedge-shaped head forward, and its crackling squawk a punctuation mark that flashed above the sun-dazzled water.

Nate did not hear whatever flute music might have been latent in the drowsy stillness, did not see the raccoon move quickly away from the pool's edge and scurry up the bent alder.

Utter peace, but not inside the skull of the man.

He dropped the horse's reins and plunged through the marshy spot where the willows burned their deep green, the whips of branches unfelt as they clung to his arms and face.

Only the insane screams of the kingfisher as the bird darted down canyon and then, a moment or two later, returned.

Laughing, the bird is laughing.

Two human forms in the water, a diffuse red cloud hovering about one . . .

At first Nate did not even see them—the eyes saw, but the mind refused recognition. Then he lunged forward to the water's edge.

Aheki-Klamat struggled feebly, like a dying fish, his mouth

open and drawing air. Beside him Paquita's face stared up, and one hand reached toward him, hung above the pool's surface, and then fell back. Blood trickled from the mouth, and she could not speak.

"Nate?" Aheki-Klamat managed. "Nate? Help Poonkina, Nate. . . ."

Again the girl reached toward him, and Nate lifted her from the water and drew her to a warm, blue-gray shelf of rock, sat down, and clung to the dying girl. Dark red blood oozed from a dozen gunshot wounds and spread quickly over her wet face and arms until she gleamed a nearly translucent crimson in the intense summer sunlight.

"Paquita?" he cried out. "Paquita! Paquita. . . ."

Aheki-Klamat struggled out of the water and crawled to the shelf of blue-gray, water-polished stone.

The three of them, the arms of the two men about the blood-enveloped girl and about each other as well. They entreated her to speak, called to her, but she was unable to answer, and their voices echoed back from the bluffs beyond the Pit River's slowly churning, spiraling current.

The kingfisher lit in the top of a willow, the bough moving back and forth like a pendulum, and chattered at them, the dull bluish bird with its insane white neck band, its topknot vibrating with the urgency of its cries. The dark, amber eye glinted with sunlight.

Then it was gone, chattering hysterically, upriver. . . .

Paquita lay dead in the arms of her two lovers. Blood was on their hands, their arms, smeared over their water-soaked clothing. And little pools of crimson formed in the smooth, pebble-worn hollows of warm stone upon which they huddled together.

For a long time Nate and Aheki-Klamat neither moved nor spoke a word. Then the Shasta warrior rose, his deep chest heaving with suppressed sobs.

"She said that if I died, she would not wish to live," he cried out. "Now she has gone, and I am still here. What fate is this that has left me alive without her?"

▲

SIXTEEN

Nate's Red Sash

The lonely July night was soft and sultry.

The Speluish moon, the time after harvesting the wokas on the various lakes and marshes to the east of Medicine Mountain. The white orb of nighttime rose up and rolled along the heavens, sifting through boughs that hung above the river and reached out from the cliff face.

The thin, silver light fell in lines and spangles across the face and form of the dead girl.

Paquita, Little Packy, Little Bit, child of the mountains and beloved of the rough miners at The Forks.

And loved passionately by two men, married to one of them.

Poonkina, the one who dreamed the bad dream at the waphi time. The one called Wormwood.

Moonlight trickling across the dead face, puddling at the eyes.

The two men did not speak as they gathered fallen branches, sections of punk wood, and armfuls of dry reeds for the pyre. When all was ready, they placed her upon it, gently, as though she were a sleeping child. They washed her face, combed out her long hair, and placed her hands across her breasts.

When all was finished, and the full moon was high and incredibly white above the dark shadows of the mountain wall to the east, they struck fire from flint and steel, and the reeds began to burn, slowly at first, and then the flames gathered momentum as tinder and pitchy knots began to glow and burn.

A cone of flame and smoke rose about the sleeping girl.

"We must make the pyre larger," Aheki-Klamat said.

He gathered more reeds, twisted them into two torches, and then he and Nate ignited dry grass, leaves, whatever would burn quickly.

Steady, dry, up-canyon movements of air perceived the flames and went to them, and within no more than a few minutes the entire northern slope of the canyon was afire. Deer crashed away through the brush, birds cried out, and raccoons laughed fear and indignation. A bear, huge and silver in the moonlight, came galloping and snorting downslope, rose to full height as it shouldered its way through a sheet of flaming willows, and splashed heavily into the water, swam powerfully to the south bank, and emerged, rubbing at its nose and eyes. Then, bellowing twice, the animal disappeared into the dark forest.

Flame coiled through the rank undergrowth, licked about young pines and firs, and leaped suddenly upward, consuming, consuming, until a massive wall of fire wavered its intense red-orange light against the darkness.

The entire south face of the canyon was now burning, long meteor tails of flame and sparks hurled upward.

The high tangle of cedar and fir above Paquita's flaming grave was the last to go—and then these trees, already withered by the cone of fire beneath them, ignited instantaneously and flared up in an intense rush of yellow and red and blue-white. The air along the water's edge grew thin, difficult to breathe, the oxygen burned out of it. Nate and Aheki-Klamat stared fixedly at what they had wrought, their features clearly illumined by the bursting and wavering light of the flames around and above them.

"She is in the Spirit World now, my brother," Aheki-Klamat said. "We must not speak her name again. She is one with the winds and the snows and the stars. She has climbed the Spirit Mountain, just as we did. But now she has stepped from the summit and is walking among the Sky People."

Uti Poonkina?

The forest fire continued to spread rapidly, cresting the Pit River Canyon, leaping from wall to wall and devouring everything in its way, then working more slowly along the ridge crests to north and south. And when the heat of midsummer morning came to it, the amber sun strangely huge and distorted through the pallor of smoke, the light everywhere a dull yellow, dry and intense, the fire regained momentum and swirled rapidly onward, whole stands of pine and fir exploding into walls of solid flame, the fierce heat withering and then consuming.

For miles the forest was awave with fire, while in the sky above, huge domes of gray-black smoke plumed, as if in imitation of thunderheads over the mountains.

Nate and Aheki-Klamat followed in the wake of the fire, leading their one remaining horse, working their way northward to rejoin Warrottetot's people.

On the second day they discovered Captain Gideon Whitney's troops, these also heading northward. The fire lay behind now, a long, gray wall of smoke above the ranges—whether dying back upon itself or merely gathering new strength they did not know.

"We must reach Warrottetot," Nate said.

"There is nothing we need to do," Aheki-Klamat said. "I think his medicine has already told him. The chief has seen the clouds of smoke—they are visible for many miles. Warrottetot will not know what has happened, but he will know. His scouts have kept track of where Whitney's soldiers are."

Moving due north now, along the McCloud River, the two men came to the mouth of Naw-aw-wa Creek and followed this stream up toward the abandoned encampment at the base of Mount Shasta. They were now separated from Whitney's force by the big bare-topped ridge that rose between the McCloud and the Naw-aw-wa.

"Will Warrottetot choose to fight these soldiers?" Nate asked. "Whitney has twice as many troops as last time."

"Yes," Aheki-Klamat answered, "I think that is what will happen. The chief will wish to drive the soldiers back toward the fire."

Nate envisioned the lay of the land—the tortuous canyon up which Whitney was attempting to lead his men. The walls of rock were steep and heavily forested, with only a narrow trail close by the tumbling river. In places the men would have to pass single-file.

"We could cross back over the ridge at a low spot," Nate

suggested, "and come down behind the soldiers after they
have passed."

"More fire?" Aheki-Klamat asked.

Already he could see what Nate was thinking, and the idea
appealed to him. He accepted the thought, instantly weighed
it, and saw in it the means whereby a full revenge might be
exacted for the death of his wife.

"Yes," Nate answered. "More fire . . ."

Their purpose was clear before them now as they worked
their way up a lateral branch of the Naw-aw-wa. They angled
back through a saddle between high points on the mountain.
When they reached a bench, they could see the antlike blue
line of troops far below, the soldiers moving upstream along
the narrow river. To the south rose a long gray wall of smoke,
in appearance almost that of the heavy bandings of winter fog,
and to the north stood the impassive white rampart of Shasta.
The sky behind the mountain was intense and blue, marred
only by a diffuse drift of cloud that trailed from the peak.

They waited until the soldiers had passed well upstream,
and then Nate and Aheki-Klamat descended from the ridge,
coming down perhaps a mile behind the cavalry. Working
quickly, they made torches, lit them, and began to ignite the
summer-dry brush, creating long burning crescents at either
side of the river.

Aheki-Klamat burst out laughing and then began to yip and
howl like a coyote.

*Has her death pushed his mind out into the Dark Place,
beyond human things? Do not flee from me, my brother. We
must stay together through this terrible time. Do you believe
my pain is not as great as yours? She became your wife,
Klamat, but I loved her also—I loved her from the time I first
saw her—I was sick, and she brought food to me—I was sick,
and she sat beside me and caused me to dream of her in such
a way that I could never be whole without her, I had to be
near to her, and now you expect me to live in the human
realm when you, too, have left and wandered out into a place
I cannot reach?*

Aheki-Klamat hurled his flaming torch into the river and
then turned to face his friend.

"I can see your thoughts now, Nate. I know what you are
thinking. Suddenly I can do that. I know. We both have loved

her, and now she is gone. How could we know it was going to happen that way? Coyote Man must have wanted it the way it was—unless he was napping someplace and did not notice. But it was right that we were with her, both of us. We alone built her pyre and placed her upon it, a last marriage bed and both of her lovers presiding. Do not be frightened of me, Nate. We still have one or two things that we must do.

"She-who-is-gone became one with the fire we gave her, and now I am one with that fire also. We brought the flames down from the top of the Spirit Mountain, you and I, and I think there must be a purpose for it. I do not really think Coyote Man was napping at all. No, I think this is the way he planned it. Are you ready, my brother? We must follow the flames we have set to burning. I do not think the soldiers will like these flames very much."

Within the hour Gideon Whitney found himself caught between the combined forces of Shastas, Pit River people, and Modocs—these on the one side, and a raging inferno on the other. And to left and right stood the precipitous walls of the canyon.

A rain of rifle fire and arrows came down upon the soldiers, for the Indians had massed along either rim of the steepest part of the gorge, a place where the walls were so jagged that no trees could grow there. The soldiers took whatever cover they could, but, as Whitney saw quickly enough, the situation was all but hopeless. There would be no victory recorded in the register log this day. The captain signaled a retreat, down canyon, back toward the fire that was now eating its way through brush and timber alike. Whatever dangers the forest fire presented, the Indians would not easily be able to follow.

The bluecoats gathered their dead, sustaining further casualties in the process, and turned downriver on foot, their horses following behind them.

Nate Miller and Aheki-Klamat had taken position on a spur of rock overlooking the only possible avenue of escape. Below them as well the fire hissed and popped, flared, and then leaped onward. At the same time, a brisk wind drove clouds of smoke along the rough walls of the canyon, at times nearly engulfing the two men.

Troops began to pass beneath the cliff now, their herd of horses screaming with fright, bolting, trampling one another as they became ever more terrified of the fire. The Whiteman and the Shasta warrior crouched behind a rocky spur and took aim, squeezed off their shots, and began to reload immediately. Then they fired again and again reloaded.

Three soldiers were down, and an answering volley of gunfire began to spit up from the narrow defile along the river—but the shots were fired at an invisible target. It was not even possible to take cover against the threat of this new ambush, as the bluecoats realized. They had no choice but to keep moving, to help those who were wounded in the process, and to leave behind those who were dead.

Nate and Klamat continued to fire, fire and reload, fire again—until a litter of bodies lay along the narrow trail and until the two men had no more lead.

Additional gunfire was coming from upstream, for a small number of Warrottetot's warriors had scaled down the canyon wall and were pursuing the soldiers. Arrow and rifle ball took their toll upon the unattended horses. The animals began to bolt forward along the defile, trampling upon and maiming the retreating soldiers.

Aheki-Klamat stood up.

"Now I have truly become my name," he announced. "And it is time for me to follow Poonkina, my wife. We will wait for you, my brother."

He handed his pistol to Nate, who took the weapon without at first realizing why it was being given to him. And by the time his friend's words had made their full impact, it was too late.

Aheki-Klamat, armed only with his war club, had begun a wild descent toward the final cluster of soldiers, the men scrambling out of the path of the maddened horses—cursing, screaming, and leaping into the river.

"No! No! No!" Nate cried out, wailing into the wildly drifting bands of smoke.

But Aheki-Klamat was leaping downward, gliding from boulder to boulder like one who was somehow, magically, no longer human at all—one upon whom gravity and the humanly possible were no longer relevant in the slightest.

The cavalry soldiers saw him coming and began to fire.

Aheki-Klamat was hit, but still he kept moving—as Nate, stunned with this sudden new horror, watched helplessly.

Klamat was at the edge of the river now, was wading into the water, his arm raised, the war club poised. Half-a-dozen gunshots, but still Aheki-Klamat moved forward. The war club arched downward, crushing a skull. Bullets riddled him, but again the war club descended, and a second soldier fell face forward into the current, his blood spurting out into the water. More gunfire, and Aheki-Klamat, his weapon raised for yet another strike, bent backward at the knees, sat down slowly in the rushing stream, and disappeared beneath the surface.

All about the area where the final conflict had occurred the water was red, the foam of the moving water red, and the bodies of two United States soldiers and one Shasta Indian moved, spun southward beneath the pall of smoke and between the twin walls of bursting flames.

The Modocs dispersed northward to the region of lakes, and the Pit River Indians moved eastward and southward, to Tule Mountain and to the high valley at the base of the Warner Range—or to the valley of the small river the Whitemen called Hat Creek, a stream that flows northward from the volcanic tumble near the base of Mount Lassen, the snow peak that rises from the ancient ruins of a great mountain called Tehama, a mountain, so the legend said, that had blown up and nearly destroyed the world.

That thing had happened long, long ago, so the shamans said, at the time when Old Man Above had come to live at Shasta. And some even believed that Tehama had been a greater peak than Shasta itself.

Warrottetot and his warriors returned to the Medicine Lake.

The soldiers had been defeated, nearly wiped out. But by now even Warrottetot and Mountain Smoke realized, *knew,* that more soldiers would come. A few more years, perhaps, and their world would be finished—the sun would die out of their skies. Each year the Whites would come, and at last no one would even remember where Naw-aw-wa had been. Finally not even the fortress mountain at the center of which the Medicine Lake lay would be sufficient to protect them.

When that happened, there would be but two choices—to fight to the last warrior or to do as the Blanket Man wished, to accept the offer of land and house in a valley to the west, out of sight of the Spirit Mountain.

Warrottetot had defeated the soldiers, but there were always additional soldiers to replace those who had been killed. Already, the chief knew, Captain Whitney had been sent further troops and was once again preparing to move into the lands of the Shastas.

Where would the Indians find more weapons, more ammunition? And now the Shastas, Modocs, and Pit River people—who had come together for this one battle—had gone their separate ways. It was nearly time, Warrottetot concluded, to climb the Great Mountain and to step off into the band of stars. Perhaps the hour would come soon.

Cincinnatus Hiner Miller remained with his adopted people for another two months. Along with many others, he had cut his long hair for the time of mourning—a time that was for him one of almost total numbness.

But White Dawn had given birth to their daughter while Nate had been in the prison at Shasta City, a baby girl whom the medicine woman Mountain Smoke had named Cali-Shasta, the Lily of the Mountain, the Lily of Shasta. The child had the brown eyes of her mother, and her hair was black like her mother's. But the little girl's skin was pale.

The first and last of her race, Nate thought. *If she is able to grow to womanhood, she will have no world of her own. She will be trapped between a time that has vanished and a time that has not yet come to be. How will I be able to help her?*

White Dawn knew that her husband would have to leave, for Warrottetot had told her this—even as he had told Nate Miller as well. The presence of the renegade Whiteman was by now well known, and Nate's capture meant certain death at the hands of the Whiteman's law. There would be no Klamat and Paquita to rescue him a second time. His only chance lay in returning to the land from which he had come, to the Willamette Valley in Oregon, where, with luck, his various exploits would not be known.

Already the soldiers were moving toward the destroyed

village of Naw-aw-wa, and the season was turning toward winter. Soon the *Tat-helam* moon would shine, and the leaves would be falling. The end-of-summer festival had been cele-brated in a small way, and the men went about their business of hunting, the women about their business of gathering various roots and berries and of smoking and drying the meat. But it had not been possible to go down into the oak forests along the McCloud and Pit rivers to gather acorns, since that was where the soldiers were encamped.

Aspens and willows flamed yellow, and the bush maples flared their scarlet across the mountainsides.

"You must go now, my husband," White Dawn said. "Per-haps one day you will be able to return to me and to our daughter. We will be patient and wait for that time."

The child in a woven basket on her back, White Dawn walked beside Nate as he rode from the encampment. But then, at the rim, she stopped and cast her eyes down.

Miller rode on a few feet farther and then halted. He turned his horse about and approached White Dawn once more, unwound his red sash, and handed it to her.

Then he was gone, over the crest, moving downslope toward the long, narrow valley that lay between the Dome Mountain and the Mahagony Mountains to the northwest.

When he reached the tablelands, he turned, changed direction, and crossed the Mahagonies at their low point, traversed a wide valley, and proceeded toward the Klamath River.

Wouldn't it be strange, he thought, *if The Prince was there....*

But he carefully avoided all settlements, making detours of ten miles or more if necessary.

By late afternoon of the second day he had forded the Klamath and was high on the southern slope of Slide Moun-tain, once more back into Oregon country. At the rim he drew his horse about and looked away southward, toward Mount Shasta.

The Spirit Mountain was completely enveloped in a mass of circularly moving clouds, and for a moment Nate was certain that the old volcano had gone into eruption. But as he watched, he was able to determine that the mists were forming and dissolving, the result of warm, moist air spinning about the great snowy pyramid.

So it must have been that night when he and Aheki-Klamat had climbed together through the darkness and had heard the mountain speak.

ABOUT THE AUTHOR

BILL HOTCHKISS is a poet, critic, and novelist whose most recent books include *Spirit Mountain, Ammahabas, Soldier Wolf, Crow Warriors*, and *The Medicine Calf*. Born in New London, Connecticut, in 1936, Hotchkiss grew up in California's Mother Lode country and was educated at the University of California, San Francisco State University, and the University of Oregon. He's the holder of several graduate degrees, including a Ph.D. The author and his wife, Judith Shears, live in Woodpecker Ravine, near Grass Valley, California. His next historical novel, *Mountain Lamb*, will be published by Bantam Books in the fall of 1984.

THE MAGNIFICENT NOVELS OF
A. B. GUTHRIE

In his epic adventure novels of America's vast frontier, Pulitzer Prize-winning storyteller A. B. Guthrie celebrates the glory, the bigness, the wildness, the freedom, and the undying dream of the West. His readers savor his vivid re-creation of the vast frontier, what *Time* described as Guthrie's "authentic sense of place," and the unforgettable men and women he brings to life.

☐ FAIR LAND, FAIR LAND (23423 * $3.50)

☐ THE BIG SKY (24142 * $3.50)

☐ THE WAY WEST (22708 * $3.50)

☐ THESE THOUSAND HILLS (20928 * $3.25)

☐ ARFIVE (22756 * $2.95)

☐ THE LAST VALLEY (23114 * $2.95)

Prices and availability subject to change without notice.

Buy A. B. Guthrie's novels wherever Bantam paperbacks are sold or use the handy coupon below for ordering: